For those who believe
no explanation is necessary
for those who do not believe
no explanation is possible

Published by JPP Publishing 2000

An Invitation to Love Jesus
Sacred Heart House of Prayer
46 James Street
Cookstown
Co. Tyrone
Northern Ireland
BT80 8LT

Tel: 028 867 66377
Fax: 028 867 62247

Acknowledgements

"Surrender is a sweet song,
Only to be sung
By those who have done it"
Message 506 Messages of Love Book 2

For our Lord and our God, Jesus, His Mother, Mary, and His foster father, Joseph. Thank You for using us to witness to Your Love. May it be fruitful.

To all of you who helped in any way to bring this work of Jesus to fruition this "Song of the Carpenter" is sung for you.

+++++

Please note that the meanings of the words in italics are in the Glossary of Jewish words at the back of this book.

Israel in Jesus time

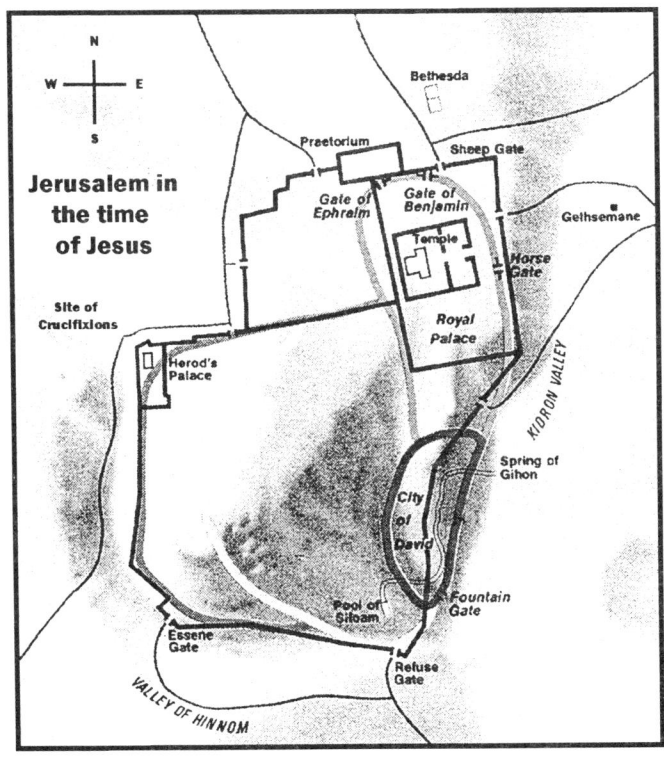

Plan of the Temple in Jesus time

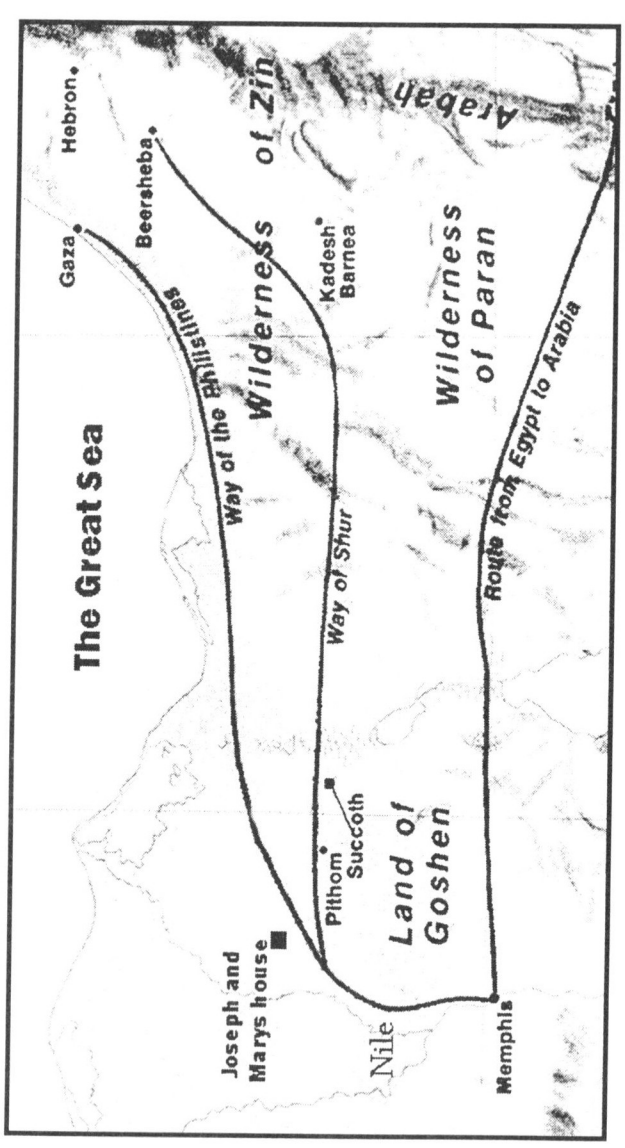

Egypt, showing Succoth and the Land of Goshen

The
Song
of
the
Carpenter

Prologue

The man shivered as he walked between the great pillars and onto the wide-open plane. The birds that circled in the sky above him were vultures he told himself, reminding himself of the power that had once been in his hands. He did not look at the woman but held an even distance between them. He knew, without looking, that her face was cold and unyielding, a mask of innocence that did not, would not, betray guilt or blame. He shivered, not because it was cold, for the heat of the sun that lived in the vault above bore down on him like the burden that he carried, but because he realized too late that he was out of favour and, more to the point, what that meant.

As they walked - the man and the woman - they did not speak for there was nothing to say but both were aware that time had begun. Time was born.

After a time, they came to a hole that burrowed into the rock. It was dark and cool inside and to the right side, a tiny trickle of water glistened its way downward to a rock, which it plummeted into and splashing, created myriads of itself. The myriads formed little pools and these, continuing to be filled, would, in time, form a larger pool.

The man said: "We will stay here."

The woman went to the water and placed her hands together to form a cup so that she could collect it to bring it to her mouth. Her tongue was as dry as the earth beneath her feet and she wet it with the water. She gulped and coughed. The man joined her. He knelt.

When they had drunk from the water, the woman went into the cave and felt its coolness; she wiped her face and drew her hand through her long hair.

"Man..." she said, "Come and feel the coolness, it has been given to us for our comfort." Then they lay down and slept, for they had walked a long way.

When the darkness had come and went away again the man and the woman awoke from sleep and they were hungry.

The man said to the woman: "I am accursed because I have offended the One who created me. My belly is empty where once it was full. Many shall come after me and they will err the way that I have erred and they shall be my seed and be accursed as even I am. They will turn away from the One that created them, even as I have turned away. But the seed that I shall give to you will bear more seed until one shall come, one who shall restore what I have lost and a son of this man, Adam, this first man, shall give the life that I have lost."

And the man wept bitterly.

Herod drained the pewter goblet and flung it at the servant who offered him more from the jug he was carrying. The servant fell to the floor as the cup caught him on the left side of the forehead. Blood spurted. A knife of silence sliced the room.

"You son of a dog," he roared, throwing back the chair that he sat upon in a flurry of robes. "Take him out and flog him, he will not serve me slops again."

His guests were frozen and all eyes in the room focused on him.

Herod surveyed them as though he were surveying the crowds who gathered in the market place each day. "This is a celebration. Drink, my pretty friends. Have you not seen a master teach his dogs to obey him?" He slurred. "He's a slave. Bought at market a few weeks ago. Shipped from Gaul, I believe."

Servants moved around Herod to get at the injured man, fearing to move, yet fearing to disobey. A man laughed nervously. Its echo broke the torturous silence that clawed the very walls.

"Ishmael, my old friend, make merry. Show these guests of mine how to enjoy a celebration." The man laughed again; a forced laugh, forced like the acceptance of the invitation to this gathering. Slowly, painfully, others joined him so that the room filled with laughter. The musicians struck up the music again and the girls danced. The whole room uncoiled once more as though it were a snake, frightened by a sudden movement.

Herod sat in his chair. He looked about him. His guests were now continuing their conversations, no doubt about him. The madness had almost come to the fore once more but he had controlled it. 'Damn this madness,' he thought, 'I will overcome it.'

The wine that he had been drinking all evening to cool him finally caught up with him. He fell asleep.

The priest stood before the Holy Place. He intoned the prayers that echoed through the chamber that he stood in. He had entered this place alone leaving Shobek and Simon, the assistant priests, outside. The short walk to the curtain had seemed a long one, wrapped in honour, as it was.

"Oh, Sovereign Lord," He called upon his God, and centuries of priests from Aaron called with him, coalescing to make this sweetest of offerings to the abiding presence that dwelt here. "I call to you; come quickly to me. Hear my voice when I call to you. May my prayer be set before you like incense; may the lifting up of my hands be like the evening sacrifice..."

The prayers returned to him as they bounced off the thick, marble walls that were the Temple of the Most High God. The perfume of the incense clung to the great Temple curtain that separated God's Sanctuary from the world of men. Its smoke billowed forth upwards as it burned within the brass bowls that held the burning coals, to mingle with the prayers and be carried to Heaven by the Angels who stood to keep guard over God's Holy Place, where He dwelled among men. Its pungent aroma wafted around him and lodged itself in his nostrils. This was the most beautiful and expensive offering to the Most High and its fragrance was pleasing to Him.

The Golden Altar, at which the priest stood, facing the great veil of the temple, was shrouded with age and holiness like a clouded summit. Many before him had stood here since Moses had brought the word from the Most High on Sinai.

A torch near him spluttered and went out leaving him in partial darkness. He heard the footsteps echo behind him as a priest went to replenish it with oil and relight it. He did not flinch from the incantation of prayers. He continued to address his God with the words that were used for this Sacred Ritual, for he, at that moment was the mediator between God and His people.

Zechariah was a holy man and had been a priest for many years. He served in the Abijah section of the priesthood. Out of twenty-four sections of the priesthood it was the turn of the Abijah to take its fortnight in the Temple in Jerusalem, performing the rites that the Most High required. Each priest was given responsibilities. It was the privilege and the turn of the Abijah to serve before the Lord. Their privilege was to enter the Lord's Sanctuary, a place where no man could enter unless he were of the priestly line, to burn the incense and no woman could ever enter. The priest was before God, an honour that befell him only once in his life. He thought about those who had died and had never stood here where he was at: the very dwelling place of God on the earth. He had been chosen. He felt sacred, blessed to be standing here. It would never happen again.

Before the incense hour, many people had gathered into the outer sanctuary. As the time moved closer, the Jewish men had moved into the inner sanctuary to become the congregation that he could now hear behind him, praying. The women had to remain in the outer sanctuary and any uncircumcised male for this was the custom laid down in the Law of Moses. He, and the other priests had to see that it was strictly observed and that no profanities occurred. No *goy* could enter.

As he bowed fervently to the Holy of Holies, his thoughts turned to his wife, Elizabeth. 'I must not forget to bring the pomegranates for supper when I get back home,' he thought, 'I forgot them last week and Elizabeth was not pleased. I keep telling her that I'm an old man now and my memory does not serve me so well anymore.'

He had loved her from the first moment he saw her and he loved her still. She had loved him and both had pledged to serve the Lord with their lives; he, as a priest and she as his wife to serve God's people. They looked forward to many happy years of marriage and would bring up their children to serve the Lord. The money that a priest received was a pittance but they had survived. Alas, God did not send the little ones with the laughter that would fill their home.

He could see in Elizabeth's face that she was heartbroken at being childless each time she saw a mother with children. He knew that she grieved inside for the children she could not have but she did not tell him. Any chance she got to look after another's child she took it. But not all mothers trusted her with their children for they felt that if God had not given her children then they would not trust her either. She was a strong woman, nonetheless and she was a daughter of the tribe of Aaron. Her barrenness did not weigh easily on her but she accepted it. She was showing her years.

It was evening now and the shadows of day's end would soon draw the day to a close. He could imagine the sun as it burned its way down to its setting place leaving a blazing trail behind it. He had heard that the people of the land of Egypt fancied that it was their god's fiery chariot charging across the sky and chased by its brother the moon. These unbelievers! They knew nothing of the One, True God. They knew little and probably refused to believe that Yahweh was the creator of the universe.

'Lord,' he prayed within his heart, 'give me the strength to serve you now in the autumn of my life as I have served. Grant that all would come to you and accept your Law. You have not seen fit to bestow the gift of children on me but it is all the better to serve you if that is what you wish.' He bowed once to the Altar and began the preparations for the ending of the ceremony.

In his peripheral vision, he saw someone standing and concluded that it was another priest come to help him with the end of the ritual. He turned to the right of the Altar to face the priest.

But it was not a priest, it was an Angel of the Lord.

The woman held the dead bird in her arm and plucked its feathers in fistfuls. The small down feathers underneath were more difficult to hold onto than the larger, outer ones. A small flurry of wind caught the feather bundle where she had thrown them beside her and played with it, swirling feathers around the hem of her robe and her dusty feet.

The sun was slightly cooling its heat and the evening was set to come. The preparation of the evening meal was something that she liked to do herself for her husband and, as usual, she had dismissed two of her three servants. She had not wanted a servant but her husband had insisted. He had told her that she was old now and needed the help. It was the first time in their long marriage that she had really got angry with him.

"...Do you think me so old I cannot keep house for my husband?" she had said, indignant, when he mentioned a servant. "Is the food not cooked properly?"

"Elizabeth, my pet, I think no such thing! I have always enjoyed the food that you cook. Your age..."

"My age is under control, old man! I'm not so old anyway. It does not stop me from keeping house."

"I know, my pet, but...."

"I will not have a servant in my house, Zechariah, and that's an end to it."

She smiled to herself. She had won that round but as the years passed she had to admit that she needed help. She needed someone to help her carry the baskets of food that she brought to the widows and the orphans as the Lord commands. The hills seemed to grow steeper as she grew

17

older and more difficult to walk up.

With a small knife, Elizabeth took the head off the chicken in a swift movement and threw it to the dogs that lazed in the shadow of the wall. They sprung to life with the sudden movement and fought over the remnant. Expertly, she slid the knife from the neck of the bird to its lowest point, opening it and exposing its contents to the world. Taking both sides of the skin she opened the carcass so that she could place her hand inside. Deftly, she found the intestine and slid her hand to follow its curves until she could bring it out as a whole. She took it out this way so that there would be no smell. She placed it at her feet to be thrown away later and began to take out the offal.

The aroma of bread baking wafted into her nostrils and she felt a pang of hunger grip her belly. Tamar was cooking the next day's bread.

Tamar was the servant that Zechariah had found for her. She was a good woman and she too was childless, not because she was barren, like she, but because of the disfigurement in her face. She would never marry. Elizabeth had first accepted her because she felt sorry for her but then as the years passed she could see her loyalty and began to trust her with more and more. But the evening meal was her job and she would not relinquish it. Her husband knew better than to argue with her.

He had been in Jerusalem for sixteen days now, performing his priestly duty of High Priest and she expected him home soon. It was such a joy to know that he was there, arbitrating for the House of Israel. Yahweh would hear his prayer she was certain. She knew that he would ask earnestly for his people that they might be patient in the face of this enemy that occupied their given land. 'Was it a punishment for the Jewish people?' she wondered. She could feel the unrest within the hearts of her people, even here in the mountains. She often heard the men speak of it as she passed groups of them in the market. They spoke of how the Lord had won battles for them in the past and his mighty arm had fought against armies that were many times greater in strength and number than they. She could smell insurrection as it wafted its way around like a rat that slunk through the sewage that ran in the street.

Her husband was a man of peace and he would pray for it. She hoped that they were feeding him.

Zechariah jolted and held up his hands as though to ward the Angel off, dropping the incense bowl to clang loudly upon the marble floor. The contents spewed upon the floor and, rekindled, puffed small geysers of incense into the air. Fear gripped him in its talons and overcame him. Adrenalin raced through his body as his mind tried to process through the fear as to whether this was his imagination or whether it was real. But it was real. His fear turned slowly into terror. Was the Angel here to destroy him? Had he committed some sin against God that he had not atoned for with a spotless animal?

As his mind raced for possible reasons for this strange event, he looked at the Angel. He was like a man but greater in height. Zechariah guessed about eight feet. He stood clad in a white robe that seemed caught about his middle and which extended to his feet. His feet did not touch the ground but hovered a few inches off it. For the first time in his long ministry, Zechariah was afraid.

The Angel spoke to him in the tones of one who carries a message of grave importance. His manner seemed friendly but like that of one who was on a mission. Obedience hung thickly with the incense in the stagnant air of the chamber.

"Fear not Zechariah, for thy prayer is heard; and thy wife Elizabeth shall bear thee a son and thou shalt call his name John."

The Angel's eyes seemed to blaze with the authority of

Heaven and in them burned a fire that no earthly fire could compare to. It was not the reflection of the torches but the reflection of the One who had sent him. Zechariah's fear increased.

"And thou shalt have joy and gladness and many shall rejoice at his birth."

Zechariah began to recover slightly from the initial shock of the Angel and felt that his words were too good to be true and began to doubt his intentions. 'Surely Elizabeth is in her sixtieth year and will never conceive a child? Her barrenness will die with her. Is this some trickery? Some evil spirit, come to taunt me in my misery?'

"For he shall be great in the sight of the Lord and shall drink neither wine nor strong drink; and he shall be filled with the Holy Ghost even from his mother's womb. And many of the children of Israel will he turn to the Lord their God.

And he shall go before Him in the spirit of Elias, to turn the hearts of the father's to the children, and the disobedient to the wisdom of the just; to make ready a people prepared for the Lord."

The Angel waited.

She had lived her whole life in this big rambling house. Her parents had left it to her. Originally, it had been built with children in mind. She had two sisters and two brothers and was the youngest. They were all gone now and it had become hers. Her own children had not come and she and her husband had used it as a place to bring those who were less privileged than they. Ragged families that had nothing walked in, penniless and despondent; children carried in mother's arms, faces wet with tears and bellies bloated with hunger. "This house is open" Zechariah used to say, "Open like the Hand of the Lord." She had found them on the streets or they had come to the gate seeking sustenance and she could not refuse them. They were given the lower portion of the house and many of her nights were spent comforting crying children in her own bed or walking the floors to give the mother a night's rest. She had not minded the sleepless nights or the crying children for they were like her own. What she had minded was them leaving to go to their own lodgings, found, usually by her. She missed them for the house had come alive and so had she. She had watched many of them grow, from under-nourished infants who cried constantly to healthy, contented children. She had no children of her own but she had raised many. The neighbouring women had always frowned on her and kept their children away. It made her sad to think that they had rejected her.

She stood now on the balcony looking into the valley and the hills beyond it. The chicken she had prepared earlier was bubbling its way into the evening meal that would be ready for Zechariah when he came.

"Zechariah," she said to herself. His name spoken, always brought a flurry into her heart. He had been a handsome young man and she had begun to love him from the moment she had met him. He was a young priest and she had not seen much of him because of his training.

"Mistress?" came a soft voice behind her.

"Yes, Tamar" she said and kept her gaze on the hills before her.

"I heard you speak, mistress, did you want something?"

"No, Tamar," she looked around at the woman and smiled. "No, I was just remembering." On impulse, she said, "Sit with me, Tamar. Let us talk." She took Tamar by the hand over to the bench behind them.

"Do you remember the family of Leah who came here one time? It must have been about ten years ago. Little Samuel was crippled. And the other children used to take turns to carry him up and down the hill."

"Ah, yes how could I forget?" Tamar smiled, "Samuel had

those others wrapped around his little finger. They would have done anything for that child. I remember he had the most beautiful eyes, striking they were, even from a distance."

"I just heard that Samuel is now a tailor. A merchant that I know told me at the market yesterday. Apparently he makes the finest clothes and many are flocking to him. And I hear that he's still got every one waiting on him hand and foot."

The two women laughed and, as though caused by the laughter, a breeze sprang up and ruffled their hair. The shadow of the house was already stretching to herald late evening. The birdsong quietened and that stillness that comes with evening became audible in the air around them. It was something that they could not quite touch or hold but both felt it. It was not in time but out of time, as though the world had stopped to listen to their conversation. It was as though someone were standing near them, waiting, reflecting. They both felt it and quieted to be a part of it. It was a time to reflect and remember, a time to listen, to feel, a time beginning.

King Herod strolled down the long stone colonnade with his hands behind his back. The gold chains around his neck clanked together gently as he walked. It had been a long morning. The priests of the Temple had been clucking around him like hens, each watching his territory and his place in the pecking order. He sniffed the air. He could smell the roses as they climbed heavenward and across the top of the arches that made up the portico. The colonnade had taken three years to build and he had watched it with delight. It would be his and his alone. It was his to come to and relax and, except for a few servants, no one knew of its existence.

He relaxed now. The priests, in their fine robes, had been

complaining to him that the Temple taxes were too high and they were too poor to pay them. If only he could just persuade the Caesar to lessen them a little.

Herod had looked at them.

"If you are too poor to pay then I am a leper." He had said to them. "Your riches are beyond mine, my fine priests. Look at you! You parade around in the finest robes. No patched robes for you. No, your tailors are promised prayers for less money, which you can well afford, and they and their wives and children go hungry. Prayers will not feed them but just one of your robes would keep a family in food for a whole year! How many priestly offices have you sold today, my holy friends?"

They had looked at him horrified. That look was frozen in his mind. He held it and looked at it and laughed again as he had done that morning. In a flurry of robes and tempers they had left the room, the steam almost visibly shooting out of their ears.

The Romans had appointed him king but it was rightfully his. King? He was no more than a puppet, dangling on the strings of the Roman Empire. He knew it. He could play king to the priests and the people of Israel but he was a slave of the Romans. Nearly six hundred years were between him and Israel's previous king. But he had been able to rule, he was a king. The people should have looked to him for their spiritual guidance but they did not. They hated him. They knew that he was a tool of the Romans. Could they not see that they were better off with him as king? Did they forget the Persians and the Babylonians? Alexander? They were no more than slaves. At least they could walk the streets now.

They complained to him of the immorality that the Romans had brought. "What harm a little immorality?" he used to say to the priests to infuriate them, "You should try a little yourselves."

What did he care for their spirituality?

He had rebuilt the Temple, even if it was to curry the favour of the Jews. Did it not rival even Solomon's Temple? No, it was not finished yet, but he had opened it so that they could have their worship. The stone was cream and did it not blind those who looked at it in its beauty? No Roman building could compare with it.

He stopped for a moment to consider its green marble columns that made up the Court of Women. The cedar that had to be shipped here was the finest in Lebanon; and the gold, Israel had never seen so much gold. It covered everything in the Holy of Holies. He liked to think that, because of his Temple, Jerusalem had become the religious centre of the world, no matter what the Romans thought.

He knew the Romans would like to get their hands on it. But he knew how to sweet-talk the Romans for his own gains. He had built their temples in Jerusalem and defied the people of Israel by placing statues of the Roman gods in the streets. Sacrilege had become his familiar.

As long as they did not find out about the madness. He had fought through it for this long, not letting the Romans see it. To them, he presented himself as a man worthy to be called king. He had probably picked it up from some serving wench or whore that he had taken a shine to. He remembered the great ugly oozing boils that erupted all over him. He shuddered. They left and the madness came.

He had sent his sons to Rome for their education and paid expensive fees under the tutelage of many great scholars and teachers. He had embraced the Roman way of life and gave it to Jerusalem so that he could be king. The Romans had free rein through him; for their money and their customs had flooded the streets like the sewage, without control. The Jews did not like Gentile coin, especially when the head of their oppressor was stamped on it.

'They will benefit from it in time, these stupid people' he thought to himself. 'If only they could see that.' But the economic crisis that stalked him like a quarry would not go away.

He stopped for a moment to look at a rose that had almost opened. He closed his eyes and drew in the scent to his nostrils. Its aroma filled him for a moment and he drew strength from it. It seemed to touch the raw nerve-endings and soothe them, and give them back to him healed and restored. Herod plucked the rose and continued to smell it as he walked.

Herod did not see his people. He did not see the darkness that he had created. He refused to see that, by his stubbornness, his people were weary and wanted change.

Somewhere at the back of his mind, something was troubling him.

Zechariah had to struggle to find his voice. His thoughts seemed to tumble over one another fighting to be the one that would be given voice. His mind boiled over with fear and doubt and disbelief. Confusion ate his thoughts as a lion devours a deer.

His voice was unsteady and felt like another had overtaken it: "How can I believe this that you tell me? Surely you can see that I am old and hardly capable of fathering a child. As for my wife, she is barren and well into old age. How can this be? I cannot believe this. It is too incredible."

Answering, the Angel of God seemed to rise up to his full height as though pronouncing sentence and Zechariah began to feel the fear rise within his throat, like bile that the stomach had rejected, it moved quickly and unbidden over his body: "I am Gabriel," he said, *"That stand in the presence of God and am sent to shew thee these glad tidings."*

The priest shivered.

"...And, behold, thou shalt be dumb, and not able to speak, until the day that these things shall be performed, because thou believest not my words, which shall be fulfilled in their

season."

And he was gone.

The Angel Gabriel had said the words he had come to say and left. Zechariah opened his mouth to speak words to the empty air and he found that his tongue would not form the words that he wanted to say. He was dumb, as the Angel had said. Fear again raced through his body. 'What shall I do?' he thought, 'How will I tell them of this marvellous thing that has happened to me? This is my punishment for not believing. But I do believe! Look at me!'

The priest threw himself down before the Holy of Holies, tears of regret and shame blinded him. 'My God, I have sinned against you. You have turned your face away from me. How can I now tell Elizabeth all that has been said to me? My Lord, my Lord...'

The men in the outer sanctuary grew uneasy. They had heard mumbled shouting come from the place where Zechariah was. Whispers began buzzing like flies finding carrion. Where once there were prayers there was now concerned voices and questions. Zechariah had not come out of the inner sanctuary. All had finished the prayers and had expected him to appear from behind the curtain to dismiss them as part of his priestly duty but he had not come. The whispers became a tangible hum. The assistant priest for that time was Shobek and, concerned himself about Zechariah's absence, got up from his seat and began to make his way towards the Temple curtain. As he did so he held up his hands to feebly indicate to the congregation that everything was all right.

There was a fumbling at the curtain as he approached it and Zechariah half fell, half ran through it. Shobek grasped Zechariah and stumbled backwards as he did so.

"Zechariah, my brother, what is it? What has happened to you? You are stricken." Shobek gasped out the words. He lowered Zechariah to the ground and supported his head with his arm. As he looked at the older priest, his face went white in alarm; Zechariah could not speak. He was waving his arms frantically and pointing to his mouth and then at the Sanctuary. 'What has happened to this man? Surely God must have spoken to him?' Shobek wondered.

The whispers of the congregation had now turned into shouts of alarm and prayers, calling on the mercy of God to descend. Some stood, gaping at the spectacle. And all wondered what this could mean.

"Have you seen something, Zechariah?" Shobek said in a low voice to the elderly priest as the younger ones tried to clear the sanctuary fearing profanities. He helped him unto his feet. "Have you had a vision, my father?" The old man was weeping as though what he had seen was troubling him. He pointed to the Holy Place and nodded.

Shobek wondered. He was concerned for this old man who had taught him all he knew about the priesthood and how to look after the Temple. He had taught him how to wash his hands and arms, up to the elbow in the cleansing ritual before beginning his duty. For the few years that he had been a priest, Shobek knew Zechariah's friendship and fatherly care. 'I'll bring him home to Elizabeth and bring the doctor to him. Maybe a sleeping solution might help him.'

Shobek looked at the house. The sun was singing a swan-song on the horizon in myriads of hues of orange and red. Its song was an echo of the day that was dying. The white-ness of the house was framed against the sky and it looked as though its edges were on fire. 'Elizabeth will be worried,' he thought, as he helped Zechariah up the hill. 'Better to break it gently to her.'

The journey home from Jerusalem had been uneventful and Zechariah had remained quiet and into himself. He seemed relieved now as they pulled up at the gate.

Shobek shouted in greeting and to announce himself, "Hail, good people of this house." He paused for a moment to let the greeting have the desired effect. "It is Shobek. I have come with the master."

He heard footsteps make dull thuds on the dusty courtyard floor as someone made their way towards the gate. It was Tamar.

"Ah, good woman, help me to support your master."

Tamar looked shocked at her master's appearance and took his arm and between them they brought him into the courtyard and towards the house. Elizabeth was looking puzzled in the half-light.

"What is the matter with him? Is he drunk, Shobek?"

"Let us get him inside, Elizabeth."

Shobek and Tamar half carried, half trailed the old man into the bottom floor of the house where oil lamps had been lit to dispel the evening's gloom and to try in vain to imitate the daylight.

After they had lain Zechariah down on a couch, he seemed to settle quickly and they left him to sleep. Shobek and Elizabeth walked out into the courtyard so that they could talk. The darkness had crept in rapidly and now the long shadows were replacing the daylight. The sky seemed to be higher than usual.

"Tell me what has happened this man, Shobek. He seems quite distressed."

"I cannot tell you, Elizabeth, for I do not know. I was outside the Sanctuary and I heard him speaking loudly. I walked towards it to see what was happening for the men were beginning to wonder what was going on. Zechariah ran out from behind the curtain and fell into my arms. He began to point towards the Sanctuary and at his mouth. He could not speak.

Elizabeth, I believe that he has had a vision. The Lord has spoken to him and has bid him not to tell it. I could see it in his eyes. He had seen something. A man that is shouting one moment cannot suddenly be dumb as though he had been like that all his life unless God intervened."

Elizabeth did not speak. She stared into the approaching night, as if some unseen hand in the sky would suddenly write the answer. But it did not.

Shobek talked on, "Your husband has been like a father to me, he has shown me many things about this ministry. I believe that the Lord has spoken to him and at the appointed time it will be revealed."

"But what would the Lord, our God, say to him that needed to be kept secret like this?" Elizabeth asked. She was bewildered at the thought of God speaking to Zechariah. It was true that he had been a priest for many years and had served Him well. Her husband was a good man but to be struck dumb after... after what?

"Did the Lord not say to the prophet Joel: '*And it shall come to pass afterward, that I will pour out my spirit upon all flesh; and your sons and your daughters shall prophesy, your old men shall dream dreams, your young men shall see visions.*' We do not always know, Elizabeth, what the Lord is doing but His ways are not ours and it would seem that Zechariah has been chosen for some task or other for our Lord."

Elizabeth called Tamar and asked her to bring their guest some wine to take the dust from his throat after the journey, chiding herself for leaving it so long. "You must eat with us, Shobek."

Tamar brought the wine and poured it into the earthenware goblet and gave it to him. They were seated on a stone bench just outside the door. Tamar left them alone once more to continue their talk. The serving woman was of slight build and her dark hair and dark eyes seemed to softly penetrate the observer more than the scar on her face. She had become a friend.

As he drank the wine, Shobek tried to reassure her.

"The Lord would not do this if He had no good reason to do it. He is with His people through His prophets and it may well be that Zechariah has had some prophesy given to him and the Lord struck him dumb so that it would not be revealed before its time."

"Yes," said Elizabeth with a sigh, "I believe that God can do all things and I will wait for the fullness of time so that He can make His Word known to me. But I'm prattling on here when I should be feeding you. Come into the house so that we can eat and I will look at Zechariah to see if he is all right. You must tell me about little Jonathan and Susannah and your good wife Sarah."

Elizabeth pressed the dampened cloth to Zechariah's head. He slept fitfully. "You are suffering, my husband, and I cannot help you. You must have had quite a shock." She spoke to the candlelit, shadowed room. "Know that I am with you and that my love for you is as great as it ever was." She leaned over to kiss his forehead. She pressed her lips against the cold, clammy skin and wondered at the ways of God.

–2–

It was the month of *Adar* and the sun had risen hot and fiery and spat the promise of another blistering day at the parched and arid earth. A small breeze flitted in and around the mud brick houses and, like a playful spirit, teased those who were already up and working and were feeling the heat of the day. It was a usual day in the village of Nazareth and it held no promises or surprises. No strangers entered the village, either travellers or important men. There was no one to feed, save the families who needed something in their bellies to give the sustenance required to work and bring home the money for the next days food.

As the day plodded on in its crushing heat, a young girl of about twelve or thirteen paused in her work of sweeping to catch up the apron she was wearing to wipe her sweated brow. The sun caught her hair at that moment and seemed to lighten it in a golden hue and she placed a hand over her eyes to look above the houses and off into the distant hills where her cousin, Elizabeth, lived. Her eyes moved steadily over the hills as did her thoughts. It was quite a time since she had seen her and Elizabeth was old now, and could be doing with her help. 'I'll go to her when the moon is full again', the girl thought, and wondered why she had not thought of it before. Her mother would give her permission she was sure, for she too was concerned about Elizabeth's ailments. The hilly town in Judah where she lived was sore on an older person and a younger one could make life easier.

"Mary...Mary..." came a shrill cry from the inner darkness of a small house. Mary turned and cried out, "I am here, mother, I will come to you".

As Mary passed from the bright, white sunlight into the dark interior of the house she caught the bustle of Nazareth behind her, the distant sounds of work being done and the cries of those who were selling and those buying. She could almost see the colours of the ribbons that would be brightened by the glare of the sun hanging on makeshift stalls in the market place. The women would be bartering over the price of clothes and foodstuffs, playing the game of buying and selling. The noise would be deafening in the town centre and a small space would have to be battled for and won. She imagined the vendors swatting the flies from the fruit and the goat's meat.

As her eyes adjusted to the dim room, that was little more than a small space enclosed by thick walls, whose purpose it was to hold out the sun and provide a cool, restful place during the day and a warm place at night, she saw her mother bending over a rickety, wooden loom and pulling at loose threads that had come undone.

"Ah, Mary, my child, help me. Hold these while I go

31

around the other side..."

Mary took the threads from her and held them. She looked at her mother's gnarled fingers and saw the tired lines that had gathered in her face. The black shawl that she wore structured her thin face and lent grace to her frame. Time was catching up with her.

"I think you need a new one, mother," Mary laughed gently. "Perhaps Joseph will make you a new one after the wedding ceremony."

"Joseph has his hands full already; a good carpenter is always busy. It is good too, for his wife; she has nothing to worry about. Her hands will always be able to make bread for her family when she has money to mill the flour."

The woman spoke gently and easily to her only child as she tugged on the wayward threads to find the offender.

As Mary stood holding the threads and listening to her mother, she began to think about her life and how it had changed in the last few months. She had grown up quickly since her time had come and, overnight, she had become a woman. The *Bat Mitzvah* celebration by the women had begun then and for a few days she had felt strange to be the centre of attraction. She did not really feel like a woman for she had not the experience of running a household and tending to a family. Then her betrothal to Joseph, the carpenter, was announced and she was overwhelmed, as though she had stepped into a different world; a world that seemed ready for her, although she did not feel ready for it. Not long ago, she was playing with the other children and now her mother was speaking about her husband. It was the way things were done. It was the way her life was to be. She would marry Joseph, have a family, she would try to be a good mother and teach her children all she could about her God. He was the One who had given her life and provided her with food. Did she not hear the men in the Synagogue saying these words from behind the partition that segregated the women? Her God was providing the air that she breathed and was she not a descendant of the House of King David, to whose tribe the Messiah would be sent?

Mary's heart leaped inside her breast at the thought of the Messiah. She had heard the ancient prophecies of a great King who would come to be the Saviour of her people. She hoped that He would come in her day and that she could be the handmaid of the one who would bear Him into the world. To serve this woman, who had been prophesied for so long in the Sacred Scriptures, would be her greatest joy *and* to be near the Messiah.

Her reverie was broken by her mother, "It's done, Mary, I've found the broken thread and I've mended it. Go now, child, and finish the sweeping and fill the lamps with oil, my old eyes can't see in this gloom."

As the day became evening and promised night, the cold of the desert crept slowly in to overtake the heat of the day. Mary watched the tiny flames of the fire she had lit fight for survival in the kindling. Feeding upon it, the flames grew in size and momentum and she began to place the larger branches on it. The gloom of the house was suddenly banished by the light the fire gave.

'The Messiah will light up the darkness of this world, just like that,' she thought as she rose to get more wood. 'He will save us from all the wrongness and we will live in peace.' Her mother had told her to light the fire before she left for Miriam's. Miriam's time had come and little Isaac had run across the street wailing loudly that his mother had a snake in her belly and it was trying to get out. It was her fourth child, Mary's mother had said, and she had difficulty each time a baby came. Pulling on her shawl, her Mother had run out calling to Mary to light a small fire.

She thought that she had heard the cry of a newborn infant a few times but the din of the Nazareth streets were not yet in the quiet that evening brings. That time when all eat their meal and prepare for bed; when the Father comes home after the long day at work to see his children in the short hours before bedtime. "A father sees little of his children," Mary said aloud, as she placed the wood on the hearth that she had taken from the supply in the anteroom adjoining the house, "But he loves them and is always providing for them, and sometimes the children don't see it."

"Mary..." A soft voice had spoken behind her.

"Mother, have you returned? Let me finish what I'm doing and I'll fetch a drink for you. You must be tired."

"Mary..." came the voice again.

The carpenter placed the long uprights lengthways on the table that served as a bench. He walked a few paces to an awning behind him to shelves where different lengths of wood were stacked. He stopped at the third shelf and picked up a piece that was about fourteen inches long. The wood felt smooth under his hands.

He loved wood. He loved the feel of it as he caressed the shapes within it that he could see there. He loved to see the innards of the tree as he carved for each was one and never the same. God had created it unique and perfect and fulfilling. Everything that man needed was given by God and the trees held many of his needs. But you had to treat the tree and its pith with respect. The pith was the lifeblood of the tree and it was it that held the chair, the ladder, even the table. His was the gift to find the shape and bring it out, tease it out into the world to take its place.

He picked up several more pieces and carried them back to the table. He placed them in a bundle and picked one of them up. He touched the wood, feeling its length and smoothness. He could feel the shape of the rung beneath his fingertips. He began to mark it in order to cut the joint.

His wedding ceremony to Mary pleased him. She was a beautiful girl. Her dark hair was like ebony and always had a bright sheen. He had watched her grow into a woman and waited patiently for the day when the betrothal would take place. It was to last for a year. The time was given to help the man find a home for his wife to live in and to find work to support her. He did not need a year for he was well established as a carpenter and he had his parent's home for Mary to live in. Both were gone now and Mary would be the mistress of her own home. The betrothal was more binding than the wedding ceremony for it was the contract drawn up between a man and a woman. He had given the money that bound the contract. According to the *Mishnah* a copper coin was enough. But he had given all of his savings; Mary was worth more to him than a *perutah*. The law said that she was already his wife but they had to wait.

Each length of wood was caressed under his hands before it was marked and the bundle changed sides of the bench, lessening on one side and growing on the other as each was jointed and left ready to be the template for the mortise.

It would be good having his wife with him. Having her near him. He felt that Mary would make a good wife for him. In the close-knit area that he lived, Mary's deeds had gone before her. Even before the marriage contract was sealed, he had often heard people speak about Mary's honesty and her integrity.

He remembered her smile. She'd looked at him as the Rabbi and Anne were working through the contract. She'd smiled at him. It was a steady smile and showed her even, white teeth. He'd returned the smile and felt warmed inside. It struck him then that Mary had qualities about her that were rarely seen in one so young. She possessed wisdom in her eyes and he felt that they could be equals within this contract instead of just husband and wife.

Joseph smiled to himself. 'I think that smile was the moment that I knew I loved her,' he thought and picked up another rung. He recalled the words of Solomon as he spoke of his love: *'Behold, thou art fair, my love; behold, thou art fair; thou hast doves' eyes within thy locks: thy hair is as a flock of goats that appear from Mount Gilead. Thy teeth are like a flock of sheep that are even shorn, which came up from the washing; whereof every one bears twins, and none is barren among them.'*

Joseph's heart was glad and he began to sing to himself as he worked.

She felt the room grow still, as if the world had been removed. She felt the stillness penetrate deep into her heart and plant seeds of a longing within it, growing and pulsating within her, finding roots in her and with her and through her. Like a tree it grew, this longing, and with it came a joy that flowed within her blood, caressing and touching, that sprouted wings to carry her to a place beyond her dreams; a Heavenly place, a place that seemed like home and the feeling of love caught her up and danced within the joy that was now a part of her. The world around her and the leaping flames of the fire seemed as one and strange as she tried to bring her mind, her soul, back to reality. But they would not see reality; this was reality. The realness of this moment was stark and strange and beautiful. Mary knew that it was of God, she was not told; she knew.

She turned, not knowing what she would see, with the joy and the love tangible and dancing still. The echo of words upon her lips ebbed away as her eyes took in the full glare of what seemed the sun. But it was not the sun. Of this she was sure, it was many, many times brighter than the sun. The light did not hurt her eyes but she could see into the centre of this sun; this fire that seemed to embody all and penetrate all. A man, a beautiful man, stood before her, yet he did not stand for his feet did not touch the ground. Wings, that only a moment ago she had felt within her, now rose from somewhere behind this man and rose higher than the roof that was no longer there, yet was there. He was not in the room and he filled it and invaded it with his presence.

The voice that had spoken now broke the stillness and the silence that pervaded the room and her soul. It was like clear, running water that tumbled majestically from his mouth and Mary understood that this man was an Angel, a messenger of the Most High God. The Angel spoke:

"Hail, thou that art highly favoured, the Lord is with thee: blessed art thou among women. I am Gabriel, an Angel of the Most High God."

Mary looked at him. These words that he spoke troubled her. They reverberated through her. '*The Lord*', '*highly favoured*', '*blessed*'; what could they mean? Her mind understood the words but they would not penetrate. A greeting! Yes, a greeting. He had said, "Hail!" He had saluted her in this regal manner as though she were someone of importance. She felt as though she should be a person of importance, but she wasn't. She was Mary, only child of Anne and Joachim. And this was Gabriel, the messenger from God. What could it mean? The Angel's manner disturbed her.

He spoke again, as if to reassure her: *"Fear not, Mary, for thou hast found favour with God."*

His words seemed to cut her heart like a knife and yet she felt humbled and penetrated by the Angel's words. Her heart beat wildly and yet she was calm. She believed his words but they would not stay within her heart. They would not stay still.

"And, behold, thou shalt conceive in thy womb, and bring forth a son, and shalt call his name Jesus."

Mary looked at him. She saw his mouth move and she heard the words that he spoke. The whole silent, still world that she was in now, seemed to be swallowed up in them. These words seemed to burst forth from his mouth as though they had waited for an eternity to be said. It was as though creation were beginning again in these words, beginning anew and promising accomplishment.

*"He shall be called great and shall be called the Son of the
Highest: and the Lord God shall give unto Him the throne
of his Father David..."*

The words had become dancing creatures now: dancing
with the sheer joy of their release, their creation. They
danced within Mary's heart like the waterfall that was the
Angel's voice, penetrating her with a most sublime and holy
fear. Her body remained calm and she wondered why it
did not dance the dance that filled her being.

*"And he shall reign over the house of Jacob forever and of
his Kingdom there shall be no end."*

"But...but how can this be? I have never known a man; I
am a virgin." Mary was surprised that her voice still remained calm and the words did not betray her soul.

Gabriel's body seemed to bow and his face softened with
unassuming humility and he began to speak once more:

*"The Holy Spirit shall come upon thee and the power of
the Highest shall overshadow thee: therefore also that holy
offspring of thine shall be known for the Son of God."*

The heart that danced within her breast now stopped suddenly. '*Son of God*'? The words hit home as the black-
smith might hit his anvil or a piece of cold metal. She felt
the ringing within her heart echo and reverberate and
pierce. Mary felt her body grow still, its life stopped within
her, suspended, animated. For only a moment she felt enclosed and protected from all around her. From the stars
and the moon and the universe she felt herself removed
and separated. The whole of creation seemed teemed into
that moment. And that moment became grace. She felt it
touch her, penetrate, imbibe, incarnate. There was nothing
in that grace, in that moment, but her. And the knowledge
penetrated with it. She knew what the Angel spoke of. She
knew. She was chosen to be the Mother of God.

And still the waterfall fell from Gabriel's mouth. *"See,
moreover, how it fares with thy cousin, Elizabeth; she is
old, yet she too has conceived a son; she who was re-*

proached with barrenness is now in her sixth month, to prove that nothing can be impossible with God."

Mary felt her mouth open and the resigned, accepted words flow from her: "Behold I am the handmaid of the Lord; let it be done to me as you have spoken it."

Then Gabriel was gone. Like the wisp of smoke that is seen rising from the fire, unbidden, curling upward and then suddenly disappearing, so he went. Mary was alone and the fire sputtered, calling to be fed.

Looking around her, dazed, Mary saw once again the room that was her home as it flickered in the lamplight. Her hand went instinctively to her belly and as she touched it she said aloud: "I must go to Elizabeth now, she needs me now."

"Why, child, what ails you?" Her mother's voice seemed to scatter the shadows that danced within the room and the lamp and fire stopped flickering for a moment. She put her arms around Mary and brought her close to her breast. "I saw you standing there and your face was white. Did you see something, child?"

Mary pressed close to her mother and smelled the cooking smells mingled with the smell of the outdoors and knew its freshness.

"Mother..." Mary began. She told her everything that had happened.

It seemed to the carpenter that time had surely stopped. In all his thirty years he had never found time to be so sluggish; he could always find something to fill it with. When the *Mishnah Kiddushin* had been signed and sealed, a year had not seemed so long and he was willing to accept the wait but from then the days seemed to drag along and he felt as though he were a snail that carried his house on his back.

The house began to feel empty without Mary even though she had never been here; he knew that it was not the house but he who wanted her here. The house was ready for her. He had repaired its flat roof so that when she came she could dry her grapes and flax. He had removed the old branches and mud and replaced them, taking special care that it was smooth to walk on so that Mary would not hurt her feet. At *Succot* she could build the canopy on it to thank the Lord for protecting them and for the good harvests.

He wanted things to be right for her.

In the light of the morning sun, Joseph could see the hills that surrounded Nazareth. The houses were beginning to climb lazily up the hill as the town grew in size. Each, a rough square, or two, or three; perched like fat chickens on a tree competing for the best view. Between each, it appeared, there were the squat olive trees and these showed green and contrasted with the parchment coloured bricks of the houses. The sky was a deep blue and slightly streaked with clouds that might just come together to bring rain. Rain was always needed and would cool the air for a while.

He pushed the stone against the blade of the axe once more to hone its edge. The grating sound broke the silence of the morning around him and joined the other background sounds of the town, stretching and waking to greet the new day. He used his arm to wipe the sweat from his brow.

Joseph's mind began to wander back into memories that he thought had been laid to rest with the passing of the years. He remembered his mother and knew instantly that she would have liked Mary and welcomed her into her home. Zibiah would have taken to Mary as a mother to her daughter. His mother had been a tall woman and her hair had reached down her back so that she could sit on it. She always laughed and everyone caught its infection and laughed too.

Joseph remembered that, as a small child, when her hair was down, he would stroke it so that it shone, and she would catch him in her arms and tickle him until he had to beg her to stop. He loved her and he remembered that love. He had always felt secure in her love; it had always been there until the day she fell.

They had been on the roof and his father, Jacob, was working. They were building the booth for *Succot.* The booth building had gone well and was completed. Blankets were placed over a rickety frame to make up the hut. Joseph sat inside and his mother had stood back to admire their handiwork. The tent had fallen in around Joseph and he could still hear her laughter as it echoed down the corridors of his memory. He had fought to get out from under the blankets. His mother was still laughing and was weak from its effect; she was stumbling about the roof. As he pulled the blanket off his head he could just see her disappearing over the edge of the roof and her laughter turned into a scream then stopped abruptly.

Shock and horror had filled him and, in its wake, he got up and ran to the edge. He saw his mother lying on the ground, blood oozing from her mouth, stark against the sandy earth. He had run down the steps at the side of the house, panic working his body like a puppet master. When he reached her, the blood was a dark scarlet and bubbling as the last of her breath escaped through it.

Joseph ground the stone harder against the blade and closed his eyes against the tears.

The next few days were hectic as Mary prepared to journey up to the hill country. She had packed up her few belongings and rolled them in sacking to serve as a suitcase. She packed also some bread and the goat's cheese that had been maturing for some time as food for the journey. Nazareth seemed small and quiet to Mary now and the bustle was not hers anymore.

Her mother kissed her head and fought back the tears that seemed ready to burst forth as the camel that would be her means of travel went protesting unto its knees so that Mary could climb on. "Take care, my child, and God's blessings be upon you. Tell Elizabeth that I will get to see her soon. Don't forget to give her the shawl."

The camel began to rise awkwardly and Mary held on to keep from falling. Her own tears as she looked at her mother from the camel's height began to spill over and fall freely down her face. "Yes, mama, I love you."

The women of the village stood to watch the spectacle of the caravan as it began to wend its way through the narrow streets. The camels and the donkeys strained under the burden that they carried. Were the bundles on the beasts to break open then a hundred colours would burst forth gaily unto the sand coloured earth. The silks and cloths were bound for the hill country and beyond. Mary watched the village pass before her as she travelled onward. The houses were like boxes piled one atop the other and they seemed to vie for the little space that there was. People gathered in groups to gossip or barter or to greet one another and there was many slapping of hands when the bargains were struck. All the while the sun beat down relentlessly. Mary wondered about the child in her womb and the child in Elizabeth's.

Joseph continued to hone the axe. The muscles in his arms rippled at the exertion with each stroke of the stone against the blade. The tears had run freely down his face, unbidden, and the pain of his mother's death, still vivid, clawed at the walls of his heart. He had grown up without her and the pain was telling that again. He had missed her love since he was seven years old. He remembered the days of crying after she was gone; long days of wanting her, long days of pain and long nights of dreams that tortured him. The dreams would materialize her in his mind and then snap her, cruelly away from him, only for her to reappear, just beyond his reach, always beyond, a fingers breadth away, so tantalizingly close.

He had awakened, screaming his fear out into the darkness, real and hurting, and he sweated confusion. His father would come to him and hold him and he had tried to find her in him. He had clung close to him, his face pressed tight against his chest; he tried to find her smell off him; her, lingering on his father but there was nothing, she was gone and he was without her.

His love for her became a hard knot of pain that refused to be broken. His father was always there for him and nursed him through the broken and dreamlike days and nights that followed the fall. Like a gentle caress, his father's love patiently softened the hard knot until its contents began to trickle out into the healing balm of the love. His father took her place but the pain remained. He would never forget her.

The camels were puffing noisily as they reached the top of a long steep hill that served as the thoroughfare into the town where Elizabeth lived, the saliva foaming at their maws as they gasped for air; the great pads that were their feet gripping the uneven earth. The village appeared before them, stark against the backdrop of the cloudless blue sky. Elizabeth's house was on the outskirts and was a sprawled collection of grey white boxes that rose upward two storeys. A faded, wooden balcony seemed to hold the whole structure together and precariously at that. It was a country house and a wall surrounded it. Mary stood at the gate and called out loudly: "Elizabeth...Elizabeth... I've come to see you!"

"Mary..." came the reply and it sounded as though the

voice were in pain or at least needed help; the servants that were in the courtyard turned their heads to look upward towards the balcony as they too caught the distress in the voice. Then she saw Elizabeth emerge from one of the upper rooms and make her way toward the staircase that enjoined the ground floor and the upper.

Mary noticed that Elizabeth was pregnant and she placed a hand on the lower part of her back for support as she descended the stairs. As she descended, Mary could see in her face that something had happened to her. That same strange, stark and beautiful moment, that had come with the Angel, permeated the air around the courtyard. It was grace and Elizabeth was filled with it and it caused her to cry out in a loud voice: "Mary, you are so blessed, blessed more than any other woman."

Elizabeth reached Mary and grasped her outstretched hands. She fell on her knees before Mary.

"When you cried out, this child leapt for joy in my womb to hear your greeting. I was overwhelmed. But why am I so honoured and favoured by a visit from the Mother of my God? And you are highly blessed because you believed that the promise made by God to you would be fulfilled."

Mary knelt in front of Elizabeth still holding her hands. It was true. All of it was true. The tears rolled out of her eyes to accompany those of Elizabeth's.

Mary closed her eyes, there in the earth with the blue skies above her and around her, not to stem the flow of tears but to feel at one with her soul. She felt it filled and invaded by the Spirit of God, He, who was the Father of the child within her womb, that temple, set aside for all eternity for this moment; He, who had penetrated her soul. She wanted to touch this God whose Love she felt within her, this God who had chosen her and overwhelmed her and now gave her proof of His Love. *Her* God.

Mary opened her mouth to speak and it seemed as though a song were being sung; a song of her love that did not

come from her mouth but from generations and generations of those who had awaited this moment; it was her
song and their song, gifted and delivered to her for this moment. It sprang from her lips like a clear, gentle river from
the heart of her son growing within her womb.

*"My soul doth magnify the Lord, and my spirit hath re-
joiced in God, my Saviour. For he hath regarded the low
estate of his handmaiden: for, behold, from henceforth all
generations shall call me blessed. For he that is mighty
hath done to me great things; and holy is his name.*

*And his mercy is on them that fear him from generation to
generation. He hath shewed strength with his arm; he hath
scattered the proud in the imagination of their hearts. He
hath put down the mighty from their seats, and exalted
them of low degree. He hath filled the hungry with good
things; and the rich he hath sent empty away. He hath
helped his servant Israel, in remembrance of his mercy; as
he spake to our fathers, to Abraham, and to his seed for
ever."*

The two women embraced. Both knew and understood
that the God of Heaven gave this moment to them and his
Spirit remained in them.

Anne's forehead was a ruled page of lines. She paused in
her baking to swat a fly away from the bread. Her thoughts
were on Mary, her daughter. 'Was I mad letting her go all
that way on her own?' she asked herself. 'The roads up
into the hill country can be quite treacherous. And what if
it rains? Those passes are far from safe. If the bandits happen to...' "You silly old woman!" she said aloud to herself,
chidingly. "Mary is a woman now. And if God's promise
to her is true...then you are a silly old woman for not believing." She pounded the dough she was kneading into the
table and it creaked. 'Joseph will have to be told...and the
Rabbi. What if Joseph wants to divorce her? What will I

do then?' This time she did not chide herself for these were real concerns. These were problems and not just silly notions. She felt dread threaten to grip her stomach at the thought of telling what seemed such a fantastical story. She believed Mary. Mary had always been a truthful girl. And besides, she herself had seen Mary standing there staring into what seemed a faraway space. She had spoken and she herself had heard some of the words. The girl was shaken and had said things that recalled the Scriptures, Scriptures that she could not have learned at her age. 'Tomorrow, I'll see Rabbi Ben Harim. And I pray God that he will believe.' Anne placed the unleavened bread onto the tray and brought it to the fire and began to stoke it.

Ben Harim was just about to close the door of the Synagogue when he saw the tall thin woman cross the narrow street, avoiding the animal traffic that had not yet learned road sense. She pulled her black veil tighter around her arms as though it was windy and he could see her bony frame through its light material.

"Shalom, Anne, what brings you this way? Come into the vestibule."

The woman greeted him: "Shalom, Rabbi." He noticed the strain in her face.

The Vestibule was a small rectangle that served as a passageway into the hall of the Synagogue where the men went to worship and read from the Torah. To the right was the door for the women, the segregation room. Along each side of the rectangle were stone benches, they both sat opposite each other.

"Rabbi, I hope I am not taking your time. Were you going somewhere?"

"And where would an old man like me be going?" A smile danced on his lips and somehow spilled unto his long, yellowed beard. "It is only old ladies that invite me to eat with them these days. They see me as some kind of eligible bachelor." He touched the side of his nose with his forefinger and winked, "Little do they know that I intend to stay one, but I enjoy the food." He chuckled.

The woman only smiled politely.

"Anne, you have a heavy burden. Would you like to tell me about it? That's why you came, isn't it?"

"Yes, that is why I came. Rabbi, I am not one for wasting time, so I'll not waste yours. I'll tell you the way I saw it then you can judge for yourself."

The woman began to speak and as she did she nervously pulled at her veil.

The old man listened, nodding now and again to indicate that he understood what she was saying. He noticed the worry lines in her face. He had known Anne from childhood and they had always been friends. He had come to her home after Mary was born to welcome the child into the world. He had watched her grow into a fine young woman and was witness to her kindness and her wisdom. He had listened to Joseph when he came to him to ask if he would speak to Anne about a wedding contract. Now what he heard seemed like a fantastical story. It was hard to believe. Knowing Mary as he did he was sure that she was not given to an overactive imagination. She had always been sensible and could be relied on. Had she lain with Joseph? Had Joseph forced himself upon her? No, he could not believe that either. Mary was a girl who showed that she believed in her God and Joseph was a man of honour. Would Mary fabricate a story like this to gain attention? No, Mary was a popular girl and did not need attention and she was not given to lies. The people who knew her remarked that she always spoke the truth. Then where could it have come from, this incredible story?

"Rabbi..." Anne was saying, "I do not expect you to believe what I am saying but I believe it. I was standing there watching my own daughter speak to the empty air. I saw nothing but I heard her say: 'I have never known a man; I am a virgin.' And before it ended she said: 'I am the hand-maid of the Lord; do it unto me the way you told it.'

Rabbi, she said yes to this Angel who called himself Gabriel...and I heard her. What am I to do?"

"As you spoke, the prophet Isaiah's words rang in my ears: *'therefore the Lord himself shall give you a sign; behold, a virgin shall conceive, and bear a son, and shall call his name Immanuel.'* I have heard of no other words that are so fully fulfilled and they ring in my ears. My old heart is glad to hear them.

Mary is a virgin, of that I am sure. This is indeed a joy to behold. If the Angel were Gabriel, then he surely must be the same one who opened the mind of the prophet Daniel so that he could understand, *'And I heard a man's voice between the banks of Ulai, which called and said Gabriel, make this man to understand the vision. So he came near where I stood: and when he came, I was afraid, and fell upon my face: but he said unto me, Understand, O son of man: for at the time of the end shall be the vision.'* "

Anne looked at the man, "You believe then?"

"Yes, I can believe because I know that Mary would not lie to you. But let us wait and see. Mary would not know about being with child. If it is some fantasy then we will see the result of it. She cannot bear a child if she is not preg-nant. That is a different matter. For now we must believe what she says is true. If you wish I will tell Joseph. He is a good man and he believes in the Lord. Worry no more and I will see to it. The marriage ceremony must be brought forward. Joseph has everything prepared."

The city squatted disdainfully on the side of the hill. Her ramparts were guarded, her gates open and the merchants, buyers, sellers, animals moving through her was the ebb and flow of her lifeblood, keeping her alive with their constant presence. Narrow streets like veins carried them all to the various parts of her that needed replenishing and ensured a beating in her heart.

The smell of burning animal flesh hung in the still air reminding all who came here that God was at the very heart of this city; his home upon the earth; his Covenant with the people of Israel; the cap of the Ark, resplendent in its gold was his footstool. Inside was the Law, that which had been given to Moses on Sinai, now preserved and revered. The Ark of the Covenant sat safe in Herod's Temple behind the curtain now, but once it had travelled the land with the Israelites.

The city of Jerusalem was steeped in Sacred History. The Lord God had led his chosen people into her, triumphant and glad. The Jebusites had refused to give the city into David's hands but through David, God took it and gave it to his chosen people. The 'wandering Jew' had found a home.

Thousands had gathered for the removal of the Ark from the house of Obededom the Gittite where it had been placed after Jerusalem had been taken. Vivaciously they had collected to follow this king of theirs who had been chosen by Yahweh. With harp and timbrel they had made music unto the Lord as they walked. They danced the dance of joy for the Covenant of their God would be placed beside their king and the blessings given to him would fall surely upon them. David had led them through the narrow streets in his kingly robes; a handsome young man and one dearly loved by this people. They had walked only six paces when they felt they should sacrifice an ox and a fatted calf to praise Yahweh for his victory in battle. Then and there they had offered a sacrifice, such was the triumph of this occasion. In his joy and celebration, their king had taken off his kingly robes and stood in a linen ephod. He lifted up his hands to the Almighty and began to dance and a strange, stark and beautiful moment descended as the

Spirit of the Lord entered his heart. The music stopped and all eyes were on him. The people watched open mouthed for a little while but as David pivoted and whirled, the music struck up and fell into his time. In his heart, it was a joy that made him dance. The Lord had won the battles and had given him Jerusalem; the people were with him and the Ark to be near him in his house. Jerusalem was bathed in joy that day; freedom from enemies was like wine flowing freely in the streets and all partook and sated them in its potency. Not so now.

Her streets reeked of dissent and Jews passed statues of Jupiter and Diana and turned their heads away. She had become drunk in these days with the wine of idols and it was not the Spirit of the Lord that flowed in her veins but the mucus of idolatry. Like the whore of old, she sat on her haunches, selling herself to all who would come. Yahweh's favourite daughter had debauched herself to her Roman lovers.

Three days later outside the Synagogue, Joseph placed his striped prayer shawl on his head and adjusted it as best as he could without the aid of a mirror. His phylacteries were in place on his head and on his left arm close to his heart. These were small boxes of black leather with long straps, which held them in place. The parchment within them held the passages from the *Torah*, the *Pentateuch*, to Joseph these were the outward signs that the Word of God was controlling his thoughts and feelings. It was his faith and that which his heart was steeped in. Like a sponge his heart and soul soaked up the goodness from the Scripture and it influenced his very movements. In his heart he believed in his God; the Lord was as established as the chambers of his heart. God was a part of him; He was Joseph's very heartbeat and the blood that flowed in his body was the love that he felt for this God of his fathers. Joseph was ready for prayer, ready to worship his God.

As he walked up the steps and through the door to the place of prayer the knots in the tassels of his shawl bounced against him to remind him of the Commandments of God. There were other men going to pray also and he greeted them.

As he entered the room, Rabbi Ben Harim was looking at him. He waved a hand in the air to attract Joseph. He went to him.

"Ah, Joseph," he said, "I would wish to speak with you."

"Yes, Rabbi, do you wish to speak now or after worship?" Joseph answered.

"I think we will go to my rooms, now, if you don't mind."

Puzzled, Joseph followed the Rabbi back outside the Synagogue and down the steps. At the bottom they turned left down the narrow street called, *'Street of Alms'*. As they walked, Joseph noticed the beggars as they gathered to wait for the end of the worship for they knew that many would attend. They waited for a generous handout from some priest or worshipper whose piety had been touched by the Words of Scripture that he had heard inside the Synagogue. Many waited in vain.

They passed a shop that sold fish. The aroma of the sea assaulted their sense of smell and they could tell by it that it was not a popular fish shop; it was past noon and there were still many fish to be sold. They used the hems of their prayer shawls to cover their noses.

Joseph pulled at his purse, which he wore around his neck and took from it a few coins and gave them to a child who had no legs and who ambled along on his buttocks. He wished that he could pick the child up and carry him to his destination. They moved on down the street.

About a hundred yards down the street, the Rabbi stopped at a two-storied house that had steps running up the side. The walls of the house were in need of repair and Joseph could see the long cracks in the wall running in every direction. The paint was peeling like skin that was not covered up in the sun. Ben Harim went up the steps.

At the top they landed on a small square with a few stools and a table scattered around and was reminiscent of a child's toys, left for someone else to pick up.

They both kissed the *mezuzah* on the right hand side of the door. Its pewter was cold on their lips. They both knew that inside was a little parchment of Scripture: *'And thou shalt write them upon the door posts of thine house, and upon thy gates: that your days may be multiplied, and the days of your children, in the land which the Lord sware unto your fathers to give them, as the days of heaven upon the earth'.* Fixed vertically onto the door lintel it faced the room, which they were entering. Written lovingly by the *sofer,* it protected the house from all harm.

From the bright sunlight outside to the inside of the room, Joseph was temporarily blinded by the sudden darkness and he stood a few moments to regain his sight. 'The eyes are wonderful creations,' he thought as he waited.

"Come in, Joseph, to my humble home" the Rabbi called from the darkness, "be welcome in the Lord's name."

Joseph entered the room. A small square of sunlight penetrated through the window and stole the coolness of the room. The square of the window accentuated the shape of the room.

"Sit down, my son. Would you care for a drink? Water?"

"No, no Rabbi, thank you."

In the centre of the room there were two couches facing one another and these were filled with cushions made by well meaning women for the Rabbi over the years. His wife was dead now and the Rabbi was unsure some of the time just how well meaning the ladies were. The rest of the room was occupied by chests and tall cupboards that seemed to have always been there, cemented into place by years of dust and dark cobwebs; timeworn papers and scrolls, their writing curled and yellowed and ready to crack with any movement, the contents not now needed to be read but absorbed into Ben Harim's intelligence and were part of the teacher that he was. Muted colours that had been faded by the years were strewn here and there, shapeless bundles of material that the imagination could not make into anything. Joseph sat down on a couch that faced the window. The Rabbi sat opposite him. Joseph sat forward to listen.

"Joseph," he began, "I have known your family for many years and I have always found them to be worthy in the sight of the Holy One. I have some things to tell you that are not easy in the telling. I have told many people many things over the years that were not easy to tell.

You are a good man, Joseph, and your betrothal to Mary has pleased many in this community. Mary will make you a fine and good wife and I am sure that your family will be like a vine that will bring you much fruit."

"Yes, I too am pleased that Mary is my wife and I find no fault with her. It is easy to love Mary."

"Joseph, you know that the Lord our God has spoken to our people over many years and it is through his prophets that he speaks to us?" He waited for Joseph's ascent.

The younger man nodded, "Yes, I know all these things. I have learned them from I was a child. But what has..."

"Joseph, hear me. The Lord, our God, speaks to us in many mysterious ways. His ways are not our ways. He is the lamp for our feet in the darkness of this world. What I must tell you may be difficult for you to believe but I want you to know that I believe."

"Rabbi, your words do not make any sense to me. Please get to the point. Has something happened to Mary? Has she been injured?" The younger man's mind was suddenly full of implications. He looked at the older man for some meaning to them.

"Hear me, my son. Mary was in good health when I saw her last. Don't let your mind run off with you. Anne came to me three days ago and she told me about how Mary has been touched by God."

"Touched by God? How?"

"She has been touched by the Spirit of the Lord, our God..."

"In what way, Rabbi?"

"Joseph, Mary is with child, by the Holy Spirit. She..."

"What?" Joseph's face turned suddenly into a melting pot of pain and disbelief. His heart found a sharp stake plunging into it and twisting. "Are you telling me that Mary, my wife is pregnant?"

"Yes, Joseph, by the Holy Spirit." The Rabbi emphasised the last two words.

The younger man could not feel. His heart was crumbling inside him and the life that was once before him was now like a crumpled piece of papyrus. His mind began to race with the shock.

"I have not lain with her, by the horns of the Altar, I have not lain with her." He stood up as if to emphasise his statement.

The Rabbi stood to try to calm Joseph.

"My son, I know you have not lain with her. I know that you are an honest man..."

In the midst of his mind, somewhere deeper than the other thoughts, Joseph began to realise the answer. It invaded and overtook all other thoughts that tried to make their way forward. With the speed of a javelin in the Roman arena it forced itself out of his mouth.

"I must divorce her." His heart split and fell away. Anger and love fought a battle within him now. "I will do it quietly away from the gossips and the loose-tongued ones, whose fortune would be made with news like this. I will not disgrace her nor will I hand her over to be stoned. This way I can protect her...I love her."

The Rabbi felt himself grow cold and a spider walked up and down his spine.

"Joseph, listen to what happened first before you..."

"Rabbi, I will not listen to more. Have a writ of divorce drawn up and I will honour it." He began walking towards the door. He wanted to continue walking forever. He wanted to run, to run away from the pain in his heart. He wanted to die.

Joseph walked back down the *Street of Alms* and did not see the beggars that clamoured towards him. He could not see anything. The only thing that he seemed capable of doing was walking. His mind had almost closed down after hearing the news about Mary. His heart had a web of pain encircling it as though a great spider had spun it and was eating it. He wanted the pain to go but it did not. A cacophony of emotions disintegrated and rebuilt themselves within him; they did not take time to put cement between them but built and fell, built and fell.

At the end of the street he lurched forward into a run. The *Street of Merchants* was almost empty now that worship was in progress and he could run in freedom. He ran from the thing that taunted him, that had him in its grip.

The pain that seemed to have made its home in him was like the pain of losing his mother. It had no mercy on him. His mind and heart battled to stay out of the darkness that threatened to engulf him. His soul was raw from the battles he fought within himself. He had not slept and he did not feel like working. He tried to eat but all he could do was drink water. He sat now in the awning where the prepared wood was kept and with a small knife he whittled a piece of wood into a point. It was like the spear that his thoughts drove deeper into his heart. He had never felt like this. The Rabbi's words still rung in his ears and no matter how he tried to make it stop he could not make it go away.

A question kept forming and growing a seed at the back of

his mind, tucked away out of sight in a dark corner. He knew what it was but he destroyed it before it had a chance to grow. He did not want to ask himself that question; he did not want it to destroy the love within him. He would live the rest of his life without a wife, he could never love any woman the way he loved her.

He felt that he was the prey of some predator that had begun to stalk him. He felt the threat that permeated from this pain and it taunted him and threatened to destroy him. It was, to him, like he had built a fine house of cedar within his heart, beautifully crafted with his own hand. He had placed his life within it and waited for the one whom he loved, to come and live within it. For her, he had decorated it with so many flowers, that were tokens of his love, so that their smell would fragrance the house. Within it were many furnishings that would please her. When the Rabbi had spoken, the words erupted through him as an earthquake might split the land, its strength and its tremors cutting through the house that he had built for his love. He could see the cedars splinter and crack under the force of it. It tore the furnishings; ripped them so that no further use could be found for them. The house was torn from its roots and flung to the four winds.

He saw his heart. It was the house; his love placed there, carefully piled as one would pile the altar with good things as an offering to the Almighty, now flowed like blood, wasted to the ground. He had not realized that he had loved Mary so much. He still loved her but now they could not be together. The splinters of cedar crackled and split in the fire of pain that burned in his heart.

* * * * *

Joseph reached the olive grove that grew on the upper side of Nazareth. He hoped that no one was here for tears had begun to sting his eyes. His mind still raced with yesterday's news of Mary's pregnancy; still the spear twisted in his heart. He fought a battle within himself. The love that he felt for Mary had to be stifled now for nothing would come of it. He would have to put her out of his mind, not think about her; try not to love her. Divorce was the only answer. It would save her. But he did not want to divorce her, he wanted to marry her.

He had not slept the night before. He had tossed and turned as though he were being assailed by demons. He had got up and walked outside into the clear, cool night. The stars had twinkled at him and he could find no answer in their vastness. He had walked and walked in the darkness to the lower end of the village and listened to the sound of the night inhabitants, animals, as they went about their tasks. No answer; no one to help him piece back the shattered fragments of his life. He had looked back at the sky once more and called upon Yahweh, his God: "Eternal God," he said aloud and with gentle conviction, "I do not know how to ask for your mercy. Why has this been done to me? Look upon me with favour, once again." He had watched the sky; its depths clear in the cold air. The stars in their brightness were the mystery of God and the home of him who created them. He had stood for an hour and they did not reveal their secrets to him. Nor did they give him an answer.

What had happened? All was going so well. He had prepared everything for the day of the wedding ceremony. A few more months and he could bring her home. He had put his whole life into the waiting.

The man could feel the great rends in his heart now as though an earthquake had surged through it and broken it and his love for Mary would not go away; it would not leave him be. It tore at him. Why could he not just stop these feelings inside him? There was a battle within and as each furore presented itself it cut through him.

Walking through the shade of the olive trees, he felt the

coolness and a small breeze sprang up as though to dry his cheeks as the tears fell copiously down his face. He wiped them away quickly. 'Look at me,' he thought, 'I am weeping like a woman. A man does not cry. What must be done must be done. I cannot stop it, this thing that has befallen me is like a nightmare.'

Then the pain tore at him again. Twisting and turning, it bore him down; like a dog that chased and ravaged a rabbit. Inside, he was running, running away from the pain in his heart and the questions that he did not want to ask. His love for Mary was like a whip that flailed him, without mercy.

How can a man love a woman so much? How can love be so torturous? Has Mary lain with another man? No, no he screamed in his heart at the question. It was impossible. He wondered if he was trying to save himself from more pain by not allowing the question to be looked at? No! He was sure that this was not the case. That surety came from deep inside him now, from that place within him that was sure that God had created the world; from that place that was his faith. He *knew* that Mary had not done this.

But how could she be with child? Ben Harim had said something about the Holy Spirit. What was it? He searched his mind for the words the Rabbi had spoken to him yesterday. "...She is with child, by the Holy Spirit..." He stopped walking, realising the words in his mind, understanding: knowledge becoming understanding. But how? Why? He could not comprehend this. He had, the night before; gone over it a million times in his mind, but this, this was too much. He came to the same conclusion that he had come to a thousand times.

Whatever was the reason for the child in her womb, he must still divorce her for her own sake. He would go home and work. His work would take his mind off it. He would work from morning to night and praise God with every piece that he made. Working with wood always made him feel better. He turned and walked back the way he had come.

Turning the corner the two women were assaulted by the din of the market in front of them. Like a forest that is thick with trees, people with little room milled through one another, turning sideways, bending, stopping, deftly side-stepping as branches do when they are forced to. Mary and Elizabeth joined the throng of those who hunted for what they needed and gathered a lot of what they did not.

The market was a square when not filled with people and housed rickety stalls that were only attractive by the goods displayed on them: dead fish lay on the ground with open mouths that once sucked water to glean oxygen; goats that were unruly were suddenly caught and mannered by the rope that tethered them to various poles in the ground; cloths that sported gaily their colours and sold themselves to the passer-by; various spices that lay piled together on cotton sheets spread out on the ground, strange bedfellows that created pungent aromas to arouse the interest of the nostrils. A combination of succulent fruits fought valiantly for space on every corner, like weeds that fought for life on a small verge of land. Live chickens squawked and, to the observer, people, goats, chickens all seemed to speak the same language.

They entered the square with a little trepidation. People seemed to sense an importance in the two women and parted a little for them to pass through.

When they had bargained their way through the afternoon, they returned to where they had left Tamar standing with the donkey and burdened it with the wares that they had purchased. They began to make their way home. Coming had been easy but now the way back was uphill. Mary hooked her arm into Elizabeth's so that the older woman could lean on her.

"Ah, Mary, child, I do not know what I shall do without you when you return home. You have been a blessing to these weary old bones. But you too must be careful of the child that you carry. Let others take the burden for you."

"I know, Elizabeth. This child inside me seems no burden at all. I cannot feel him yet."

"You will soon feel him. You will soon know him. The child that you carry is the promise of the Holy One to the House of Israel. Your son is the One who is to come. You will feel his life in you and you will be blessed a thousand times."

Mary put her head on Elizabeth's shoulder as they walked. She pondered the words in her heart. They seemed strange to her, alien and all she could do was think about them in her heart. She had no answers to the strange events that had taken place within her. They were happening to her but they seemed to be happening to someone else. Talking to Elizabeth had helped and she could tell her things that she could tell no one else, little things that only someone who had experienced them could know and understand. She had put her hand on her cousin's belly and felt the child within it kick and move. He seemed so vibrant and full of life; he appeared anxious to get out.

She thought of Zechariah, his dumbness and wondered again what it could mean. He greeted her each morning in his dumbness with a smile and a wave of his hand. He had become strong again and seemed happy when Elizabeth told him that she was with child but his eyes were always far away as if he were thinking of something else.

A woman screamed somewhere near them. Mary lifted her head quickly and looked about, panic rising in her. She looked back down the hill and as she did so her ears were filled with the thunderous sound of hooves. In the risen, disturbed dust of the road, three Roman horsemen were galloping up the hill. They flailed their horses with lengths of leather to make them climb the hill more quickly. The horse's eyes, she noticed, were wildly dancing with fear.

"Move back, Elizabeth," she shouted. They both pinned themselves against the rocks that made up the side of the road and watched the horsemen pass in a cloud of dust and fine gravel that flew up around them.

Breathing heavily, Elizabeth put her hand on her belly and indicated to the younger woman that she wanted to sit down. Breathless and a little shaken herself, Mary helped the woman to a rock that she could sit on. She began wiping Elizabeth's forehead with her own veil and whispered words of comfort to her.

When she was settled again, Elizabeth said to Mary: "Go down and see if everything is all right down there." She pointed over Mary's shoulder.

"Will you be alright?"

"Yes, yes, go."

As Mary walked back down the hill she could see that a small crowd was gathering about a hundred yards in front of her. Some of the women had their hands over their mouths in an attitude of shock. She remembered the woman's scream. She reached the scene and could see the woman lying on the road. She was pallid and still.

As she looked at the woman, her face covered in blood that oozed slowly from a wound on the top of her head, Mary felt within her heart that she was dying. Her bundles of supplies were strewn across the road.

A deep, deep sadness rose within the girl and a tear formed in her eye and fell silently down her face. In her heart a prayer was born; like a briar it grew and twisted around her heart; it grew into the flesh and pierced deep. As the thorns penetrated and drew blood, roses formed and bloomed; she felt the woman's pain, she felt her life as its last embers faded and died.

She wiped away the tear and returned to Elizabeth.

The road was long and dark. It was dark because of the trees that grew thickly on each side. They seemed to reach long, woody fingers out to grasp at the man who walked fearfully on the road. He was cold and seemed to be searching for the sun but in this land of darkness there was no sun, there was no light. It was so cold that the man wrapped his arms about himself in an effort to keep warm. He looked down at himself. He wore only a loincloth. He walked on and on until he saw a light in the distance, a small, yellow light. It seemed almost smothered in the darkness.

At first he thought it was a star. He looked up quickly but all he saw was the black vault. The light seemed to grow nearer as he walked. He began to run towards it and it grew in size the nearer he got.

Then there were many lights, all glowing in the darkness; they were not just yellow but many colours. He could now see a huge building that was many times taller than him. The source of the light was within this building. The building had a dome and was rounded. Other square buildings surrounded it but these had no light. He walked up to the door. It was not made of wood as he expected but it looked like burnished copper, it rose up in front of him. As he neared it, it opened of its own accord and light poured out into the darkness. He realised that no one but him could open this door; he was the key. He knew it and felt comforted by it. He knew that he must enter and go into the light.

The light itself had become a white light and it warmed him, his body and his bones. He felt its rays penetrate into his soul. He felt lifted and reassured. He walked confidently through the door.

The building was one great hall and he could see that it was made of stone hewn, it seemed, from many mountains and it was empty of furniture. In the centre of the round building was what looked like a large box made of gold for it shone and glistened in the light. Beside it stood a man, a winged man. An Angel. He was dressed in a white robe. He looked at the man who had entered. And Joseph's confidence waned. He fell on his knees at the gaze of the Angel.

The Angel spoke and his voice was like thunder as it reverberated around the granite walls and the empty room.

"Joseph," he said.

"I am Joseph," said the man, not lifting his head.

"I am Gabriel, who stands before God, the Holy One, and I have been sent to you in this way. Joseph, why are you afraid to take Mary as your wife?"

"I am not afraid. I wish to save her the disgrace of being with child before the wedding ceremony. If I divorce her then..."

"The child in her womb is given her by the Holy Spirit. She remains a virgin and will remain a virgin. You are given the honour of protecting this highly favoured maid. The fruit of her womb shall be the salvation of mankind. His name will be Jesus and he will save the world from its sin."

The man just knelt and nodded his head as the Angel continued.

"Take her for your wife and bring up the child. From his mouth shall come the word of God the Most High and he shall be a light to the nations."

The man suddenly felt joy rise in his heart. The answer that he had searched for was here all the time. He did not have to look in that dark, cold world outside any more. He bowed his head in gratefulness to the Angel and when he lifted it the Angel was gone. All he could see was a semi dark room and he lay on a couch.

Joseph looked around him and realized that he had been dreaming. He could hear the birds begin their dawn chorus. The light coming through the small window behind him still had the grey tinge that came before the sun came up.

To Joseph it seemed that a bird was fluttering within his heart, his soul. He felt a strange, stark and beautiful feeling arise within the depths of him. A seed had been planted within him and it was growing even as it was planted. It grew into a seedling and pushed forth, delicate monocotyledons, juicy succulent leaves that seemed to reproduce and build and grow into a sapling that shot upwards towards the sky. Its trunk grew thicker and thicker; roots dug deeper and solidified themselves into the ground of his heart, his soul. Upwards and upwards it grew, spreading outward branches to catch the light in its leaves to turn it into food in order to grow more, to catch more light, to make more food, to grow, to become whole again.

Joseph realized that the bird that had been fluttering about him was a dove and had been waiting for the tree to grow, had now settled in the tree and began to make a nest there.

He stood up and began to pull on his robe, his sandals. He ran out the door not caring whether it was closed Outside the gate he turned left up the gentle slope that was the hill of Nazareth. He ran as he had done three days before down the *Street of Merchants*. Blindly he ran, the joy pumping in his heart into the *Street of Alms*. No beggars lined the streets to catch the passers-by. He could not, would not have stopped even if the sun was up and they lined the streets with begging bowls outstretched.

At the Rabbi's house he took the steps two at a time, the joy within him almost bursting out and he shouted into the grey, dawning morning, "Rabbi...Rabbi." He reached the door and began to pound on the worn surface. He shouted again.

Inside the house, Ben Harim was rising. The deafening thumps at his door had frightened him awake and he rose to see if his house was on fire and someone had come to warn him. He lit a lamp from the dying embers of the fire. As he reached the door he recognised Joseph's voice. He opened the door and Joseph fell in through it. The Rabbi cried out in fright.

"Rabbi! Rabbi!" said Joseph, breathlessly picking himself off the floor, "Destroy the writ of divorce. I am going to go ahead with the contract. I will take Mary home."

—3—

Elizabeth was outside in the sun feeding the animals when she felt the first pain. Its intensity caught her breath and she had to grab hold of the rickety fence to keep her balance. The goats did not give her any sympathy but continued to eat the straw that she was feeding them.

It gripped her belly like a hand grasping for life and it was not like the other dull ones that she had been having over the last few days. It was sharp and seemed to last for longer than the others had. It seemed to affect her balance. For about a week she had been feeling uncomfortable. Had anyone asked, she could not have described it as a pain but more of a discomfort, a pressure. She had not wanted to sit nor stand and it was not comfortable for her to lie. She seemed to want to wander but not put roots anywhere. This pain was sore. This one was real.

She put her hand on the small of her back and began to waddle towards the house. Her belly had tightened with the contraction and was now easing to its supple state once more. She did not realise that there were beads of sweat on her forehead until she went to push back her veil. It was just past noon and the midday sun glared at the earth as though to burn it.

The woman began to feel a fear; a panic began to grow inside her as she reached the shade of the balcony. She controlled it. There were more things to worry about than fear. Was this the birth of her child? Were these the pangs of childbirth that she'd heard spoken of but never experienced? Or was something terribly wrong with the child in her womb? She did not know.

She sat down on the bench and held the seat with one hand as though to keep herself from falling off and the other she placed on her belly. That pain had frightened her though she would not admit it even to herself. If this was the birth of her baby she wanted to be strong and brave. She felt that it was the wrong time. She did not feel ready, nor did she feel prepared. If she had known beforehand on what day this would happen she would have been more prepared...

The hand on her belly felt the tightening and the pain began in her back like the twist of a knife and began spreading around her sides until it became a sheet of pain. The pain had a life of its own and it contracted her womb into a state of solidity that seemed alien to it and to her. The pain seemed to lift her womb and her body had no choice but to go with it. The pressure below her belly intensified and the pain curved downwards with it. Elizabeth gave a stifled cry to the day around her.

This was it. Her baby would be born soon, she was sure. Her mind began a race of emotions. Each seemed to charge forward as the pain intensified. A fear began that panicked her into wondering would this child be all right. And quickly on its heels came joy, which charged tears to well up in her eyes. Zechariah? Where was he when she needed him? The midwife? Esther. Tamar would have to run for her.

"Tamar...Tamar...come quickly."

Tamar was inside the house mending clothes. Her thoughts were far away. She was thinking about her mother. They had never bonded close since the dog had attacked her and left the furrows of scars on the left side of her face. She was ten years old. The dog had attacked her

66

for no reason that she could fathom; it just came from nowhere. She had often thought about this and could not find a reason as to why. Maybe it was the way she was playing that had made the dog think she was a threat to it. She did not know. She remembered the pain for it had taken years to leave her emotionally.

She remembered that after she first felt the dog's teeth, and the tearing flesh, everything had gone black. When she woke she was on her couch in her own home. On waking, the pain had met her and it seemed to throb through her body; it was not just in her face but the pain was living in her. It gained life from her. On waking, she had screamed. Her mother and brothers had held her down on the couch, hands over her mouth, to stop those piercing screams. She had struggled and felt strength within her rise, tormented behind her eyes. She could not move and fear assailed her and overtook her body to grip it and steal her consciousness. From that day she had not loved her mother.

Her thoughts broke and scattered as she heard her name being called.

"Tamar...get Esther!" She heard the words as she ran to her mistress.

"Is the baby coming?" she said as she was coming through the door.

Her mistress was holding her belly as though helping the pain to grip her. Tamar screamed and bolted towards the gate.

Elizabeth was aware of Tamar's scream but could do little about it. The pains were coming quicker now and left little time to catch breath. It had invaded her, rapidly. Its gnawing at her body stole her strength and she wondered if she could stand another one.

As the pain snaked from the small of her back around her sides, across the mound of a belly that seemed to have been

67

hers forever, and downwards with growing intensity, she felt a sudden gush of water. It was warm on her legs and it wet her through. She brought her knees together to try to stop the flow but it came, regardless. Her body sweated and felt weak.

The intensity of the pain had left her weak and she just wanted it all to go away. Her mind would not think the way she wanted it to.

'I'm too old for this, have mercy on me, my Lord,' she thought. Then she heard it.

It started as a small seed inside her heart. She felt it grow, little by little, and it seemed like the vine that grew on the fence. It grew and twisted, holding and gripping her heart. She felt safe as it grew and, as it grew, she believed. It wrapped itself around her heart and its roots pumped strength into her.

Then it began to bud and with its flowering came the voice: "I am with you..."

The flower, or the voice intensified and gripped the pain and she felt it lessen. She felt the strength that those words had come to give her, overtake her and embody her. The pain was still with her but she could cope. She heard someone speak her name.

"Elizabeth..." It was Esther. She had come.

"Let us get you inside, Elizabeth," Esther said, "can you walk?"

The lamplight muted the interior of the house and it seemed to echo Elizabeth's calmness in the face of the imminent birth of her baby. Many lamps, lit to give maximum light to the procedure, were subdued by the gloom created by the thick walls. Her face was resolute and Esther noticed the sweat as it bubbled on her forehead. Between pains, her lips moved in fervent prayer to the Most High. 'She seems ready,' Esther thought, 'for the task that is before her.' The only sound in the room was Elizabeth's breathing as it laboured with the work. The twigs on the fire crackled as the flames bit into them to gather the energy it needed to boil the pot that hung over it.

Elizabeth felt the sixty years of her body as the pains tore through it like a storm, cutting away at the landscape in its path. She did not seem to have a choice and somewhere in the back of her mind she recalled the words of sacred Scripture, *'...Unto the woman...I will greatly multiply thy sorrow and thy conception; in sorrow thou shalt bring forth children...'*

Her breathing was now coming in pants between the pains and non-existent when they were there, as her mind concentrated upon getting the good out of them as Esther had told her. Her womb, with each contraction, was opening like a flower from bud to bloom. Each one determined the size of the infant's head and opened further to accommodate it and her pelvic bones had moved backward to house it on its journey. The birth was at hand.

She squatted on her haunches in an effort to find a small comfort and to aid the process of childbirth but no comfort was to be had in this onslaught.

Esther said, "If you try to get up onto the couch we can see better to help you, Elizabeth."

Tamar and Esther helped the woman onto the couch between pains and did their best to make her comfortable but it seemed in vain for giving birth was a lonely vigil and none could do the work but her.

Esther felt the woman's belly as another pain showed clearly in her face. The contraction was firm and solid and she ascertained that it lasted several minutes. It subsided once more. Elizabeth's knees were bent and her legs apart as she felt the pressure bear down on her with every pain. She groaned loudly as another pain overtook her. She prayed harder now and her prayers were not for herself but for the child that would be born soon. The force within her belly invaded once again and she gritted her teeth to help her bear it. All she could do was wait for it to subside, wait for it to be over.

Esther went to the small table near the fire. The copper basin on it was filled with water and she began washing her hands. She got a feeling, as she always did since she began the work of birthing, that it was time. All seemed well with Elizabeth and no complications were showing up. The water was cool to the touch for it had been freshly drawn this morning from the well and carried up the hill in small jars by the servants. These were then poured into larger jars that were housed in the anteroom in an effort to keep it cool and fresh and away from the sun.

As she bathed her hands, Esther thought of the woman who lay on the couch behind her. Never before in all her years of birthing children had she seen a woman of this age give birth. She was long past the childbearing age and should not be having one except by a miracle of the Lord. Elizabeth was barren and the village knew it. They knew that her time was past. A white haired woman of her age did not give birth; it was impossible.

The village was a close compacted community and she had heard the talk that Elizabeth was going mad in her old age. She was fantasizing that she was carrying a child. The talk was cruel and it was the women who gossiped who made it worse. But this woman surely had been through that change that comes to all women. She did not seem capable of giving birth but here she was in the throes of labour. They - the gossipmongers - had not been prepared for the growth of her belly. Yes, the tasty morsel of tantalising gossip that the tittle-tattles had found was about to be taken away from them and a miracle, proved and real, about to be put in its place.

Then there was Zechariah; he had returned from Jerusalem and could not speak. They said that something had happened to him in the Holy of Holies. The gossips had put it down to punishment for some grave sin or other; some said that he had entered the Sanctuary and an Angel of God was there, waiting to call him to task for being unclean. Yet others spoke of demons in the Holy Place. Esther shivered at the thought.

She herself had never been one for listening to gossip but it was believable that this woman was pretending or was in some madness in her old age. But now, she who was a laughing stock was about to give birth to a baby. A miracle? Esther did not know but what was happening was not pretence, it was real.

'Well,' she thought, as she dried her hands on a rag, 'it's my job to help this miracle into the world.'

The woman behind her cried out as another pain took its course through the lower part of her body. Tamar wiped the brow of her mistress and her dark eyes stared at her in fear. She smoothed her hair in comfort and felt its sweaty wetness with the palm of her hand. Tamar was afraid.

It kept running through her mind that Elizabeth was the mother that she had never known since the dog had ravaged her face. She feared because Elizabeth was in so much pain and she did not like to see those she loved in pain.

Another fear had snaked into her mind and had constricted the others and each time it came, she stiffened as though to hold it away, stop it from coming true. She had heard that older women often lost their lives in birthing, those who had not been strong enough to push the child out. All these things played with her emotions now. Her mistress had been in this pain since early morning and it must have passed midnight now.

Elizabeth stiffened as the next pain prepared itself to come. She was weary now. This body of hers seemed to have always been in this pain, for a lifetime had passed within her since it had begun. She was tired and breathless and her strength had been consumed, spent and she did not have the energy to take another one. Yet, when it came she dealt with it.

The pain now ran from her back into her belly but it was not a pain, it was pressure and was somehow less intense as the others. As it grew and bore down, she felt the pressure heighten and a new sensation overtook her; she wanted to push downwards. So much she wanted to push down, to push out this pain and it felt as though she had a great mass between her legs. She cried out in agony as she felt it. She pushed and went with the sensation. She could feel the mass move as she pushed. Then the pain subsided once again. She cried out for the push did not relieve her.

Again, it came with a life of its own, making her push. She had now lifted herself up on her elbows to put all her strength into that push. Her mind could not think; it could only push. Gritting her teeth, she heaved with the sensation. The pain went again and she lay back panting to gather what little strength she had left.

"Elizabeth," said Esther with excitement in her voice, "I can see the child's head. It is soon over."

Elizabeth heard her but was already beginning to push.

The child, as it slithered in its amniotic fluid into the world, opened his mouth and cried. His voice was a joy to the three women.

The child's father, when he saw him, cried silent, joyful tears.

The news of the child's birth was carried far and wide on the tongues of those who had once carried the lies. The gossips changed direction and were the first to speak of the good man that Zechariah was and that the Lord had shown him this great kindness because of his holiness. Elizabeth too, was talked about. Wasn't the Lord to be praised for giving her this child after so many years of barrenness? All the lies and gossip were forgotten now and many came from all over the hill country to see this 'miracle child', given to her who was barren. The Lord had shown his mercy. As the people came, they praised the Holy One for his goodness and kindness and all who saw the child felt blessed for it. Barren women felt hope.

The child was strong and healthy and had a fine head of raven hair.

And when it came to the eighth day, they brought him to the Synagogue to be circumcised to fulfil the Law of Moses, as is written: '*He who is eight days old among you shall be circumcised, every male child in your generations, he who is born in your house...*' They would fulfil the Covenant with God.

When they had gathered into the Synagogue the number was about twenty. After the rite had been performed and the child had been settled, the Rabbi asked Elizabeth what the child was to be called for her husband was afflicted with lack of speech, she said, "He is to be called John." She was standing back in the segregated women's area, her face pressed against the wooden bars.

"But Elizabeth, no one of your family is called that name, would you not call him after his father? I'm sure he would be proud to have his firstborn called after him. The man cannot speak for himself."

"But I know he is to be called John. From the first I knew that I was carrying him, I felt his name was John."

"Let us make signs to Zechariah and try to see what he wants the name to be."

Zechariah had remained quiet but now he mimicked with his hands as though he were writing.

"He wants a writing tablet. Beriah, would you get him one, please."

Zechariah took the papyrus page and the reed pen and

scratched words on it. He handed it to the Rabbi who looked puzzled by what he read.

"He has written, 'Let his name be called John'." The people who gathered there gasped with surprise.

"Yes," said Zechariah clearly, "His name is John."

It was a miracle! Zechariah had not spoken since his time in Jerusalem. Whatever had afflicted him had affected him so badly his assistant priest, Shobek had to practically carry him home and here he was speaking normally again. They marvelled with gasps and shouts of incredulity. In their midst the Lord was truly merciful. Some of them held up their hands and began praising God.

But Zechariah was not finished yet. He felt a strange sensation in his tongue. It started like pins and needles but it became a taste; honey seemed to flow around his mouth and, as though lubricating it, he felt his tongue loosen and words formed in his mind and they burst forth into the air as would a fire, sprung to life. He tried to stop them but they had a life of their own and seemed not willing to be halted. All eyes turned to him.

With his face flushed with joy, a strange, stark and beautiful atmosphere permeated the Synagogue, he spoke and prophesied with his eyes and his hands raised to heaven: " *'Blessed be the Lord God of Israel; for he hath visited and redeemed his people and hath raised up a horn of salvation for us in the house of his servant David; as he spake by the mouth of his holy prophets, which have been since the world began: that we should be saved from our enemies and from the hand of all that hate us; to perform the mercy promised to our fathers, and to remember his holy covenant; the oath which he sware to our father Abraham, that he would grant unto us, that we being delivered out of the hand of our enemies might serve him without fear, in holiness and righteousness before him, all the days of our life.'"* Zechariah then went to the child, saying, " *'And thou, child, shalt be called the prophet of the Highest: for thou shalt go*

*before the face of the Lord to prepare his ways; to give
knowledge of salvation unto his people by the remission of
their sins, through the tender mercy of our God; whereby
the dayspring from on high hath visited us, to give light to
them that sit in darkness and in the shadow of death, to
guide our feet into the way of peace.' "*

There were shouts of praise to the Holy One as he finished. The Rabbi looked at Beriah, "What kind of child
will this be when the Lord our God has spoken so highly of
him?"

Elizabeth watched these things from behind the wooden
bars. Her heart was a dancing thing and danced to the music of joy. The Lord had truly heard her prayers. Her
child had been given to him and accepted; her husband
had been restored to her. Those who had put her down
and believed she was mad had been put to shame, by the
hand of the God of Israel. She closed her eyes and whispered, "Thank you, my God." As she did so, she remembered Mary. 'Soon shall come her joy.'

Word of the strange events passed from tongue to tongue
like bread in a famine from hand to mouth. Travelling
swiftly through the mountain country, those in backward
places heard it sooner than they normally would for it was
good news. Children spoke of it. Men spoke of it as they
toiled in the fields; women baked it into their bread, and all
marvelled and praised God.

* * * * *

Mary had been home for two days when the Rabbi came.
In the morning her mother had sent her to the family of
Jonathan and Sarah. They had a family of eight children
ranging in age from newborn to ten years. She loved going
there to help with the little ones. She played games with

them and washed them and dressed them. She had missed the children when she was at Elizabeth's. Jonathan had met with an accident in the fields while he was ploughing; the ox had kicked out at him as he tried to adjust the harness, which had come loose. The hoof had caught him on the right leg and shattered the femur. He had lain in his couch for about eight months and could only hobble on a home-made crutch and his wife had to support him when he needed to relieve himself or to bring him out into the cool of the evening. He could not work and Anne had helped them out by sending food when she could. The little ones loved to see her coming. She brought food that she and her mother had prepared.

Sarah was a tired woman. The black around her eyes told Mary that she had been up most of the night trying to feed the sick child. Mary had taken the baby from her and told her to rest for a little while, that she would care for the children.

When Sarah had risen again Mary had taken the older children on a walk with some of the food that she had brought with her. In the shade of an olive grove she had watched the children climb the trees and then enjoy the food. They ate ravenously because they were hungry.

She had thought of Elizabeth. Her baby must be born now. She knew that all would be well with Elizabeth for she felt that the Spirit of the Lord was with her.

She heard the Rabbi before she saw him. He called out in a voice that seemed to trill with the birds that sung all around her.

"Anne...Mary, shalom to you. Are you at home?"

Mary walked to the gate, lifted its latch and opened it.

"Come in, Rabbi, and welcome."

The old man looked at the young girl and could hardly conceal his high regard for her. In the intervening days since Anne had visited him he had spent his spare time going over the Sacred Scriptures searching for the Messianic teachings of the prophets. It all seemed to fit. He hardly dare think that she was carrying the Messiah in her womb. He stopped himself quickly from bowing to her.

"Mother is in the house, she is resting. I will tell her that you are here."

"Thank you, Mary, that would be good. I must speak with her."

Mary walked across the yard with the Rabbi behind her. It was a small garden with an old olive tree providing the shade. She led him to a few benches that sat under it and helped him to sit down. When he was comfortable, the girl went to fetch her mother.

In the doorway, Mary looked at her mother. She was sleeping soundly and she did not wish to disturb her but if the Rabbi had come then it must be important. Mary touched her mother's shoulder and Anne jumped awake.

"What is it, Mary? Are you alright?"

"Mother, the Rabbi has come to see you. I will fetch him a cup of wine. I'm sure he is thirsty."

Anne rubbed the sleep from her eyes and walked out the door to greet the teacher.

"Anne," said Ben Harim rising from the seat to greet the woman with respect.

"Rabbi, shalom, God's peace upon you. You are welcome here as always." The two embraced.

Ben Harim sat down again and Anne joined him.

"Have you news of Joseph? I have been a little anxious these last days."

"Yes, yes. I have good news of Joseph but I wish to speak with Mary too. She is a woman now and must join in the adult things. Ah, here you are, Mary. Thank you. An old man's throat is always in need of quenching. Sit with us."

Mary sat down beside her mother who faced the Rabbi.

"I will be truthful to you both and tell you what has happened since I last spoke to you, Anne. No doubt, Mary, your mother has told you that she informed me of the events that have taken place in the last few months?"

Mary nodded. "Yes, she told me that she had spoken to you and told you about the visitation of the Angel. She said that you would tell Joseph."

"I have spoken with Joseph and he wishes the wedding to be brought forward. I must confess that I do not understand the ways of the Lord. When I first told him of the news of the child, he left my home very quickly. He would not listen. He wanted a writ of divorce. I did not see him for three days. I searched for him but I could not find him anywhere in Nazareth. I asked many people who came to the Synagogue for worship but they had not seen him either. Three nights ago he came to my door and the way he banged on it, I thought the end of the world had come." He chuckled to himself remembering. "When I opened the door, Joseph fell in through it in great excitement and joy. He told me that he had a dream in which the Angel Gabriel spoke to him and reassured him of his fears about the child that has been conceived in your womb, Mary. He would like to plan the ceremony a week from today. He has told me that he will do the Lord's will in anything that is asked of him. He will bring up the child as his own. Mary, Joseph is deeply in love with you."

He looked at Mary. There were tears in her eyes. She did not speak but let the tears roll down her cheeks. She was happy. In her heart all was fulfilled now. Anne put her arms around her daughter, "What is it, Mary? Do you not wish this to be done?"

Mary looked into her mother's eyes and both women could feel the tender love of that moment touch them. Anne understood the look in her daughter's eyes.

"I love Joseph. He is my husband. He has accepted the will of the God of Israel as I have. I will do whatever he asks of me for I am his wife. I will go with him to live in his house and God's will only, will be our will."

Mary pulled the cotton dress over her head. She smoothed it out as best as she could. It was white and its square neck was coloured bands of thread. Anne had carefully woven her raven black hair into plaits and they reached down to her waist. Its sheen was like a mirror and caught the oil lamp that had been lit in the interior of the house. She pushed her feet into the new sandals. On her head, she placed her cotton veil. It had two borders running its length, intricately designed and sewn for a bride. Over this she put the blue woollen shawl with its fringes of red. She was ready. She had asked her mother not to give her any trinkets or jewels to put on; she wanted no adornment. Mary turned to face her mother.

Anne looked at her only daughter. She was beautiful. Mary did not need adornment. Her face was radiant and a little flushed with the joy that leaked out from her heart. Her only child had become a woman and was about to walk away from her to be a wife. The tears stung the woman's eyes and she put her arms out to her daughter. The two women embraced. Anne held her daughter and her emotion overflowed.

"Now you are truly a woman, my daughter. You have a good husband and you will always have his love." Anne held up her hands to Heaven, palms upwards. "I praise the God of our fathers for this joyful day. God is good to this old woman." Anne found herself quoting the Sacred Scripture, "*'My dove, my undefiled is but one; she is the only one of her mother; she is the choice one of her that bare her. The daughters saw her, and blessed her; yea, the queens and the concubines, and they praised her. Who is she that looketh forth as the morning, fair as the moon, clear as the sun, and terrible as an army with banners?' "*

She looked at Mary, "I love you, my daughter, and never more beautiful have I seen you as on this day. You are a delight to my eyes."

"Oh, mother, I love you too", said Mary and a single tear rolled down her face.

"You will be happy with Joseph, he is a good man and he has God in his heart and the child within your womb will make you happy also. Do not be afraid, Mary, your life is before you now, like a great road stretching out. You are not alone on this road and you will be happy."

"This child within my womb is my happiness and my joy. I have accepted responsibility for this Man within me and my life must be his. Whatever is before me, I know that, like a child, he will hold me in the palm of his hand. I am but a handmaid to do his will. Mother, I love Joseph deeply and I know that he will take care of the child and me. I am happy for it has been revealed to me and given to me. I believe that God has adorned me with this jewel in my womb and he will be my joy and my sorrow." Mary embraced her mother.

Anne wondered at her daughter's wisdom. She said, "I am glad for you. I will miss you when you go to live with Joseph. But, we have guests, I must see to them. We must share the good things that God has given to us." She kissed her daughter on the forehead.

When she had gone, Mary thought about her father, Joachim. He had died four years before. She remembered as a child he had taught her songs that King David had sung. His raspy voice caught the melody of the psalm and they sung it together. *'With the merciful thou wilt shew thyself merciful; with an upright man thou wilt shew thyself upright; with the pure thou wilt shew thyself pure; and with the forward thou wilt shew thyself forward. For thou wilt save the afflicted people but wilt bring down high looks. For thou wilt light my candle: the Lord my God will enlighten my darkness. For by thee I have run through a troop; and by my God have I leaped over a wall. As for God, his way is perfect: the word of the Lord is tried: he is a buckler to all those that trust in him. For who is God save the Lord? Or who is a rock save our God? It is God that girdeth me with strength, and maketh my way perfect. He maketh my feet like hinds' feet, and setteth me upon my high places.'*

She loved her father and he had called her his little 'Queen of Israel'. When she was little and he came in through the door, she would run to him only to be caught up in his arms. There, she felt if the world crumbled and fell away, he would still hold her safe. He would not let her go. She remembered the greyness of his beard and hair.

Sometimes when she thought of him it was as if he were standing beside her. She felt him now as she stood waiting for the wedding ceremony with Joseph to begin.

The pain detonated inside Herod the Greats head. It was here again. It would not leave him alone. He screamed and threw himself on the cold marble floor. The madness would begin again. Days and days of endless wanderings that left him weak like a child, nightmares that walked with him in the light of day, demons chasing him. The screams would hurt his throat. Then there was the strength. It would come in a fit of rage that empowered him to throw ten men off him. He had tried wine, he had tried the fruit of the mandrake; large doses of anything that would make it go away. But it did not. Like a shadow it haunted him, terrorised him. Its great fingers reached out for him. For a while he could keep it at bay but it always came back.

He screamed again. It was night and the servants surrounded him. He knew that they would tie him to the couch. He knew that he would fight with the strength of ten men but eventually they would overpower him and gag him. He had told them, ordered them, to do it. He did not want the Romans to know; to think that he was weak; that he was not fit to be king.

Joseph looked down at his bride. She was his wife now. They had their whole married life ahead of them. He remembered the words of God to Adam: *'and the Lord God said, it is not good that the man should be alone; I will make a helpmate for him. And the rib, which the Lord God had taken from man, made he a woman, and brought her unto the man. And Adam said, this is now bone of my bones, and flesh of my flesh: she shall be called Woman, because she was taken out of Man.'* He felt now as they walked the short distance to his home, and her home, that he would be happy. God had given him this woman that was his wife. He knew that now. He knew that he must look after Mary with his life for her body was the Tabernacle of the Most High God.

After the dream he had accepted all of it easily. His faith in his God had helped him and once he accepted what was happening in his life then it was easy. He wanted to be beside Mary, to look after her. Yes, it was true, she would never be truly his, but she belonged to God and that was what mattered. The Rabbi had shown him the words spoken by the prophets and it seemed strange to him to be a part of that sacred history; that someone had spoken of this time, hundreds of years ago. He did not pretend to understand it all, he would simply trust in his God as he had done from a child and let life take its course. He and Mary would have no close, intimate relations, but wasn't that her right according to the *Mishnah Kiddushin* that they had both agreed to. She had the right to remain a virgin. In his dream - Ben Harim had called it a vision - the Angel Gabriel had said that she would remain a virgin and if Heaven had decreed it, who was he to change it. It would not be easy and he hoped that God would give him the grace to overcome.

As far as the outside world knew, the child was his and no one would know until the time came for it to be revealed. He felt now, looking at her, that his love for Mary would sustain him, that, and what the Angel had said. He was like a new man. He felt new and the tree that had grown inside him, after the dream, was blooming now, with flowers and would soon bear its fruit. Only God knew his plans, he was just a small part of them.

He greeted a farmer who was coming back in the late evening from the fields. The farmer stood to look at them with a smile on his face. Weddings made people happy. They were a new beginning for a man and a woman. If they were willing to work through their differences and remain faithful to one another, then God would bless their efforts and the marriage would last a lifetime. The farmer grinned a toothless grin at them and watched them as they walked further down the narrow street to begin their lives together. Women gathered along the way to clap them and praise God for them. They called out happiness and joy to them. Some danced to share it with them.

Joseph and Mary looked at each other. They both laughed for the joy that they were receiving and it seemed that two vines had met and intertwined; twisting and turning around one another to become one; to become whole. They were a perfect sacrifice to God, without blemish.

The preparations that Joseph had made for Mary were all waiting for her to begin her life in the house. There was a sprinkling of new straw on the floor and it gave the room a golden hue in the soft firelight. She looked at the newness of some things and she could see strength still in those that were old. The wooden furniture within the house had all been replaced. She could see the grain of the wood that showed its lifetime. The rings within the wood were a testament to the summers and winters of growth. The first faint glimmers of the rings of her married life were beginning this day.

The new wood smelled fresh and added a fragrance to the room. The stools and benches had not the worn look of many years of use, they were beautifully crafted by Joseph's hand and she could see the master craftsman at work. They were not ornate although she knew that he could carve beautiful things but for everyday use these were strong and would last for many years. She knew that he had made these for her and her heart swelled. The inside of the house had been painted white and it brightened the room and the smell of it mingled with the new wood. She could feel his deep love for her in that aroma; it was the smell of wanting to make things right, of wanting to give of oneself for another. She smelled it deeply and hoped that she could please Joseph in her life with him.

It was a larger house than her mother's with its two floors and balcony. It would be strange to live in a house with floors and all that space. She hoped to begin a little garden soon for it was nearly *Tammuz* and the growing season was beginning. Her mother had taught her how to get the best out of the soil in her garden. It had to be treated right with plenty of water. If given the right ingredients, even barren soil could be made to grow something. She noticed the new loom in the corner beside the fireplace where a small fire burned and she thought of her mother's rickety one. She would ask Joseph about that.

Her belongings had been brought here by one of Joseph's relatives this morning and they were on the floor beside the table waiting for her to unpack them. She had little to bring with her. The two small bundles wrapped up in squares of linen were verification of the poor life that she had led.

On the table were a small bunch of red anemones and next to them was a small ornate trinket box. The lid of the box had been carved with a gazelle among the grasses, ever watchful. Beside the gazelle was its hind, watching too, as their offspring munched the grass. Mary's mouth fell open as she looked at it and a little cry of delight escaped. She could see the story unfold in the delicate cuts in the wood, its grain used to form the depth in the picture. It was real to her and she treasured it to her heart.

Joseph had been outside seeing to the goats, which had not been fed since sun up. He stood now in the doorway and watched his bride as she looked at the trinket box. Standing there in her wedding clothes and framed by the light of the fire, she took his breath away. God had chosen his mother well.

"Do you like it, Mary?" he asked into the room. He moved from the doorway.

"Oh, Joseph," she said, "it's beautiful! It must have taken you a long time."

"It did," he said, "but it was worth it." She looked at him. She could see his love for her in his eyes. It was like a great banner shouting and declaring it to her. She went to him and put her arms around his neck. At first he was afraid, for this woman was God's possession and God had chosen her and he did not want to spoil her.

Pulling back gently from him she said, "Joseph, please do not be afraid of me. Yes, I am carrying the Son of God within my womb and he has given us to each other. We cannot be close but we need one another for love and affection and support. That is why we are together. Our companionship will be what praises him. Our love and oneness is what he wants. It is all right to show love by embracing."

He held her then and kissed her on the forehead and she felt the prickles of his beard.

"Joseph, as the Law states you are my father, my brother and my husband. I am subject to your will in all things. I love you. God has given us a way to live, let us live that way."

As she looked up at him, he held her face in his hands, "Mary, I wish only God's will. Our love will carry us through wherever this path takes us. I do not pretend that it will be easy but I know that we can, with God's help, get through it. My work is to protect this child and with all my heart I will do it. It is your work to be his mother and I accept that. I am telling you that I will accept whatever God sends. I just hope that I can do all that he expects of me."

Mary looked at him. She could feel the roughness of his hands on her face. All the years of working with the wood had toughened and hardened them. "Then we will do this thing that the Lord asks of us. Let us prepare ourselves for what is to come."

He embraced her again with tenderness. Both hearts were swelled with love.

The couples life together began that day. Joseph showed Mary around her new home so that she could familiarize herself with all its nooks and crannies, telling her that she could change it all to suit herself. Mary did not change much but kept it as much as possible the way that Joseph had kept it.

When Joseph returned from the workshop that evening, Mary had prepared him a stew for his evening meal and afterwards they sat outside in the cool of the evening.

"The evenings are beautiful," said Mary, "it is my favourite time of the day. I love the colours of the sky when the sun begins to set. I think sometimes that the Lord, our God, has written his name in the sky to let us know that he has created the day for us."

"Yes, it is a beautiful time. I like it when the work is done and there is that quiet when the whole world seems to go still. I like to sit here in the silence and watch the foxes come out of their hiding places to begin to sniff around for food. If you are quiet enough, they will not notice you until they are quite close to you."

"I would like to see that, Joseph. God is so good to us to provide all these things for our benefit. I notice that sometimes people are so busy doing work that they do not notice these things. I think that the passing of the day is a good time to pray and be in touch with God. These moments are precious times to be spent with him."

Joseph looked around him. The birds in the olive tree above where they sat were making their roosting sounds as they prepared to sleep in the hours of darkness. A silence that was created only for evening invaded him and he felt the hand of the Lord brush his heart through the creation that was before him. He spoke aloud the words of Scripture that whispered softly in his soul; " '*They also that dwell in the uttermost parts are afraid at thy tokens: thou makest the outgoings of the morning and evening to rejoice. Thou visitest the earth, and waterest it: thou greatly enrichest it with the river of God, which is full of water: thou preparest them corn, when thou hast so provided for it. Thou waterest the ridges thereof abundantly: thou settlest the furrows thereof: thou makest it soft with showers: thou blessest the springing thereof.*' "

"That is beautiful, Joseph. It reminds me of a Psalm of David that my father used to sing." Mary began to sing and her sweet voice echoed into the quiet of the evening;

" '*Man goeth forth unto his work and to his labour until the evening. O Lord, how manifold are thy works! In wisdom hast thou made them all: the earth is full of thy riches. So is this great and wide sea, wherein are things creeping innumerable, both small and great beasts. There go the ships: there is that leviathan, whom thou hast made to play therein. These wait all upon thee; that thou mayest give them their meat in due season. That thou givest them they gather: thou openest thine hand, they are filled with good. Thou hidest thy face, they are troubled: thou takest away their breath, they die, and return to their dust. Thou sendest forth thy spirit, they are created: and thou renewest the face of the earth. The glory of the Lord shall endure for ever: the Lord shall rejoice in his works. He looketh on the earth, and it trembleth: he toucheth the hills, and they smoke. I will sing unto the Lord as long as I live: I will sing praise to my God while I have my being. My meditation of him shall be sweet: I will be glad in the Lord.' "*

"I am glad that you are here, Mary. It is a beautiful Psalm of the evening." Joseph said.

"I am glad to be here too, Joseph."

* * * * *

"Mother...Mother", called Mary in a squeal of delight, "the child kicked me." Her mother looked up from her mending and smiled.

"He will kick you a lot more by the time he is born. Enjoy it while you can, my daughter, for when a child is born there is little time for a woman. Her time is taken with its needs. She must see to its needs before her own. She must try to see herself as two people and not one."

"Yes, mother. I wish he were born so that I could see him. It seems so strange that he is growing inside me. Sometimes it feels as though he is not there but yet he is. It seems so long to wait."

"You'll see him soon enough. Meanwhile he must grow inside you and take from you what he needs to grow into a healthy child. If you do not eat then he will have nothing to eat."

"Oh, yes", said Mary with a grimace, "Sometimes I do not feel like eating. I just feel ill."

"Your body is adjusting all the time to accommodate the little one. It is how God designed it to be."

Anne folded up the clothes she was mending and walked over to the fire to stir the pot that hung there. The vegetables were hissing at her and she knew they were cooking nicely. The aroma caught her sense of smell as she lifted the lid to prod and stir them. She picked up a small bundle of twigs from the supply at the side of the fire and began breaking them. The fire crackled and sparked as she placed them on it.

Mary sat with her hand on her belly feeling for any movement that might be the child. She was about four and a half months pregnant and the changes in her body were becoming apparent. Her breasts had begun to prepare themselves for the milk that would suckle the child and give it life. Her face was fuller and had taken on that glow that belongs only to a woman who carries a child. The roundness of her belly was becoming more pronounced as the days passed. When she was with Elizabeth, she had wondered if her belly would ever begin to grow. Now she could see and feel the changes. Her body felt different; it felt like a flower that was about to bloom. Mary pondered within her heart these things and wondered at them.

Rome cooked slowly in the noonday sun. All plant life and animal life gasped for air and water. There was no coolness in the shade of the poplar trees that populated most of the city. All human life that could afford to sleep slept through the agony of the day's humidity. Those who could not afford it worked and served their masters, preparing the baths and clothes that would be demanded when their lords and ladies awoke in the cooler afternoon. The whiteness of the stone buildings almost blinded the observer when the sun shone like this. The pillars and statues that dotted the city seemed to sag in the blistering heat. In the evening, the city would burst into life and the bustle would begin again, and like termites all forms of life would scuttle through the city, and the hum would begin that would last into the night.

The man who observed this stood overlooking Rome in his purple toga, his laurel wreath on his head and a goblet of wine in his hand. Augustus drank deeply from the goblet. The wine had been taken from the cellars deep under his palace and it was cool in his mouth. It was a good wine from the vineyards of Gaul. He did not like the Gaulish tongue but their wine was excellent. They had sent him their best as a tribute to him. The great walls of stone were many feet thick and they, too kept him cool. "I wonder how many people there are in this empire that I have. If I knew that then I could make it better." he said aloud. "I could use the information with regard to the trouble spots still left. It would not be so easy for the rebels to hide then." He laughed to himself and raised the goblet to his lips. The idea was germinating in his mind and he let it grow. All countries in the empire would be subject to a census, whether they liked or not, and each would present himself to the town where he was born for his name, occupation and status to be taken. Augustus laughed again. This was getting better. If he knew the status of each one then he could gain higher taxes and no one could hide their money from him or the empire. The idea seemed better and better. It would be the ultimate grasp that he needed to fulfil his plans. It would show them that he was worthy to take his place among the gods. He would have full control over the empire and no one would oppose him. Julius always said he had a brilliant mind.

He would speak to the Senate about it, no, he would tell them to do it. It seemed to him that the Senate, although most of them liked his ideas and leadership for he had given them peace on almost all fronts, were always gaggling about something. They needed something to disagree with and they picked on everything that was brought to them.

He looked out again over Rome. He saw the changes in its seven hills since he had come to power. Clay had now become stone. Architecture had become a fad under his reign. He had shown them how to build buildings and shown them that they need not be content with clay. If you would build, then build in stone. Use marble to make it beautiful. He had done just that

He loved Rome and since he had come to power through being the favourite of Julius, he had purged it of its enemies. Rome was a safer place to live in. Julius had bequeathed the throne to him although it was only after he had died that he learned that he was his favourite, adopted son. He never had a chance to thank him. He had loved Julius who had been a father to him. He had seen his political potential and he was paying it off.

Augustus Octavius Caesar had vowed at a tender age that no one would ever take again what was rightfully his, the way his guardians had taken his inheritance left him by his father. He drained the cool wine and walked out of the chamber to gather the Senate for an emergency meeting. They would be angry but politics was politics.

When the news of the census reached the corners of the countries occupied by the Roman world, it met with a tirade of insults from an already trodden people. The Romans had taken their lands, their sons, their daughters and squeezed the best of their produce out of them to be shipped to Rome and sold to fat Romans whose only work it was to pamper themselves. Each time there was a bloody murder, or a wine spiced with a fatal toxin or figs whose only sweetness was the nectar of poison; it was they who had to pay for it. New statues had to be built for these human gods to be worshipped and new temples to their favourite gods; whims of a people who paraded a decadency cloaked as decency. Amphitheatres of death dotted the world and had become a fearful image of Roman authority. They had spliced their lives and customs and tastes into half the world. Many lands had been crushed between Roman fingers and the juice ingested into Roman mouths.

No one had a good word to say about the census.

In Nazareth they spoke of it with disparagement. Many cursed Augustus, whether under their breath or aloud. In the market square young men spoke of rebellion as loudly as they dared and not within earshot of the Roman soldiers who patrolled the streets looking for any signs of insurrection. Out of all in the Empire they did not trust or like the Jews. The old men cautioned them in their thinking for the Romans were a might to be reckoned with. They had crushed them once and would again; they had half the world that they could call on to help them fight their battles. And they would show no mercy. No, it would have to be obeyed. Caesar was an astute man and this would tighten their chains. Only God could save them now. Yahweh Sabaoth would save them. Surely he would hear their prayers.

Joseph told Mary that they would have to go to Bethlehem for the census. It was the home of his fathers and his tribe. It was the City of David and according to the decree of the Roman Emperor all the tribes of Israel must gather in their territory. The census would take place in a few weeks time at the end of this month of *Heshvan.*
"But Joseph, the baby is due then. Can I travel all that way with my belly the size it is?" She indicated the swollen mound of her belly.
"There is nothing that I can do, my love. The Romans are threatening death for anyone who does not comply. This comes from Augustus himself. I have heard that extra cohorts are being shipped from Rome to 'help' the situation. I have heard the talk in the market place of revolt against the tyranny of the Romans. The people are seeing it as more cruelty."
"There is not much we can do only prepare to go then. How long will it take us to travel there?"

"I would think that it might take us more than a week, considering your condition and the crowds that will be going from Nazareth and other places. Those who claim David as their father runs into many hundreds, perhaps thousands."

"I must begin to pack supplies for the journey right away then." Mary waddled across the floor holding the small of her back. Her belly was at full capacity in its growth and it made her walk the way she did. Her face was full and rounded with her condition but she looked like a flower in full bloom, Joseph thought as he watched her.

Mary suddenly realised what she looked like and laughed at herself, "Look at me." she giggled, "I can hardly walk around my own house, never mind set out on a journey to Bethlehem. Maybe the Romans would provide me with one of their carts."

Joseph walked to her and put his arms around her in an embrace, he laughed with her.

"If they don't then I will provide you with a donkey and we will go to Bethlehem with all the grace of a king and queen." They both laughed. They were happy but inside Joseph was worried about his wife.

Mary stopped suddenly and held her belly, "Do you realise what this means, Joseph?"

Joseph looked puzzled, "What does what mean?"

"It says in Scripture that the Messiah shall come out of the city of David. Is David's city not Bethlehem? If we must go there now then it is the Lord God who has decreed it and not Augustus. This child will be born in the city of David in accordance to Scripture. Oh Joseph, God is like a Father to us. He is leading us to where we must go." They both rejoiced in God at this revelation.

The evening of the next day brought greyness to the usually blue skies over the city of Jerusalem; there reigned a calm and all things simmered in the sultry heat. The buildings waited expectantly for the rain that was long overdue. The city seemed to pause in the dreamlike calm. Dogs sniffed the air as though searching for a reason. At the northern gate three camels entered, each with a small caravan in tow. A roll of thunder broke the skies.

The donkey was ready with its panniers strapped to its body filled with all that they thought they would need for the journey to Bethlehem. They did not know how long they would be there and the more they took with them then the less they needed to buy or trade for. Mary sat on the donkey and looked awkward because of her state of pregnancy. Neighbours told Joseph that it was not right that Mary should go at this time. Perhaps if he explained her condition to the priests in the Temple they in turn could speak to Herod. Joseph told them that they must go because the threat from the Romans was too great. Was Nazareth not full of Roman soldiers, even now?

So now they were ready. It was early morning and the sun was not long past the horizon, ready to scorch the land. Joseph took the rope that was the halter and led the donkey on the beginning of their journey.

It was possible, Joseph thought, that they were going too early but because of Mary's late stage of maturation he was not taking any chances of her giving birth along the road. He wanted her to be safely in Bethlehem before she gave birth to the child. He was worried about her but she reassured him that she was all right. She did not seem worried but she felt tired all the time. Sometimes she fell asleep while they were talking in the evening, as the sun was going down and it was cool. She loved that time of day and he had teased her about being like the evening star, the first to appear in the heavens. His love for her grew as he watched her sleep on those evenings and then he would gently wake her so that she could bed down for the night. She was always surprised that she had fallen asleep.

Now she smiled at him as they went down the gentle slope that was the road that led out of Nazareth and would bring them to Jerusalem and Bethlehem. He could see her holding on tightly.

There were many people about, even at this early hour. Some were going about their morning business of going to the fields or to bring in the days supplies. He could see the women on the flat roofs of their houses doing various chores in the cooler morning. The birds sung bright cheerful songs to greet the day and it seemed that they were trying to share their joy with the humans that passed by. Joseph could see the brightly coloured rugs and blankets hung over the balconies of the larger houses and smelled the bread that wafted on the morning air. They had stopped a few times to let shepherds drive their sheep along the road. It was good to be alive to see all this activity and in his heart a song was singing that rang through his body and his mind and it gave him a spring in his step. He looked back at Mary; she was bobbing along with the movements of the donkey, relaxed and looking around at the day as it progressed. He would stop later and let her rest in a cool place. He prayed the sun would not be too hot this day.

The room that they were in was the room that King Herod used to entertain the Romans when they came to see him. It was cool and airy. It was rectangular in shape and measured thirty feet by twenty feet. Thin graceful pillars ran down the long sides of the rectangle, which were corridors that led to various parts of the palace. Murals decorated the walls and portrayed Herod himself building the Temple or the Roman temples and statues of their gods. He looked benevolent in them and they flattered him with the slimness of his body. It had been years since he was so muscular and taut. He was not a particularly religious man and saw the help of the gods as only being advantageous when he needed them for his own gain. One short side of the rectangle opened out into a large balcony from which could be seen the Roman amphitheatre. This had pleased the Romans.

Herod looked thoughtfully at the three men across the table. They were eating a midday meal and the choice cuts of lamb had been eaten with relish for they had fasted for three days; or so they told him. They sat now eating figs in their coloured robes. One was a swarthy, thin man who looked to be from the Orient. His bearded face had the look of many hours spent in prayer and his hair was sleeked with perfumed oils and it hung rigid down his back. He seemed to favour purple. The second was a squat, square man who munched greedily on the figs and had already had too many helpings. His bald head and face looked cool although he sweated profusely. He wore a simple white ephod. He was a priest. The third was a large, thick man who wore a large hooped earring. His hair was long and a bronze band across his forehead seemed to disappear into it. The garment that he wore was down to his feet and made of red silk and looked cool in the heat of the afternoon. 'Is he a prince?' thought Herod as he watched them.

The king thought them travellers at first when they had requested an audience with him. It was announced that they wished to see the new king. Herod had winced when he heard it and he had them brought into his presence immediately.

They told the story of how each of them in his separate land had followed the astronomical charts for many years and had all come to the same conclusion: a new king would be born or is born in the land of David. He would be a mighty king and would come to the aid of many. They went into marvellous details of how the sun entered Venus and how Mars aligned with the sun, words that he could not understand but from it he gathered that these were learned and wise men.

But they did not seem to realise that *he* was the only king and he would not allow a usurper to ply him off his throne. He decided to play along with these distinguished men for a little while until he could get his own astronomers together. The swarthy one was speaking of the star.

"When a man of grave importance is to be born, his star is placed in the heavens and this means that he will do great things. From what we have ascertained, this will be a king of such importance and significance that he will rule forever. You see, your Majesty, a star is not given by the gods for nothing. A star cannot appear in the sky of its own contravention. No, the hand of the god which that king is subject to, places it there to show us lesser beings their way of things. It is a sign that greater things are to come."

The bald man spoke, his accent heavy and thick, "The conclusion that we have all come to since our first meeting near Mount Tabor in Galilee, is that the God of the Jews has placed this star in the sky for this purpose. We have discussed this with other learned minds but they do not have faith on their side, unfortunately. What they do not realise is that the stars are not gods in themselves, no; on the contrary, they are simply heavenly beings that do God's bidding. God can place a star in the sky to announce a powerful event and then remove it again, if he so wishes."

The other man then spoke. His voice was deep and resonant: "Yes, my king, if you believe in your God then he will speak to you through the things that he has created. Minds of today have decided that the science of things is more important than the God who made them. This leads to all kinds of errors. The star that we speak of has the most unusual qualities; it has a life of its own. It moves when we move. If we go in the wrong direction then it stops to wait for us. It is truly the work of a powerful God. We were led here from our different countries each following the same star and yet coming in a different direction! It brought us together under the shadow of Tabor. We thought at that point we had found the place but we found each other. We discovered, when each spoke of his mission, that we sought the same end. The star stopped for a time and when we had agreed it moved again. We felt that it would be a tribute to you to visit you and inform you of these events. Do you have any idea of the exact whereabouts of this powerful one for we would very much like to pay him homage?" He looked at Herod. The others were looking at him too and Herod felt hot under the collar of his garment.

"Ah, even I do not know where the exact location is, if I did, I, too should like to pay him homage. After all, it is an event that should be celebrated with gifts. A king of such magnitude should be given tribute. But come, gentlemen, you are guests in my humble home. I will call the slaves and they will lead you to my own private baths so that you may be refreshed. The sun here can burn a man to a cinder." Herod clapped his hands to a servant who stood by. "Show these fine men to my private baths and make sure that they have everything they need." He had no worries about the servant telling their conversation abroad for he had had his tongue cut out for the purpose of having a servant nearby who could not pass on information. He trusted no one. He watched the men leave each one bowing to him in respect. He wondered at their story.

"But where is this king!" Herod shouted at the men before him. "Why have you not told me of this before? You sit in this fine palace of mine and you take my money and my food. You use my dancing girls when you take the fancy and you do not tell me that a king is to be born who will rule forever? I will hand you over to the Romans to be crucified. They would very much like to hear of your negligence in this! Find out where he is to be born and let me know immediately."

The men stood in a frightened little knot with hunched shoulders afraid to speak as Herod glared at them, his eyes demanding an answer.

A thin, frail man in a pale robe opened his mouth nervously. It twitched a few times and then closed again, fear overtaking him.

"Well!" demanded Herod at the top of his voice, "Have you something to say?"

The man shook as he spoke. He kept his head down, afraid to look into the eyes of the king. "If you would beg pardon, as far as we can tell, Sire, according to our charts and configurations and the alignment of the moon..."

"Don't give me that drivel about moons and stars, tell me where he is."

"We think it is Bethlehem, your Sire...I mean, your majesty. It is written in Scripture: *'But thou, Bethlehem Ephratah, though thou be little among the thousands of Judah, yet out of thee shall he come forth unto me he that is to be ruler in Israel; whose goings forth have been from of old, from everlasting.'*"

"You think? You think? I am paying you to know. Get out of here all of you. Imbeciles surround me; they take my money from me. They take my kindness and they can't even tell me a simple thing like this. Get out before I hand you over to the lions in the amphitheatre. Get out!"

The men tripped over one another as they tried to get out of the room as quickly as possible.

Herod seethed. 'I cannot depend on anyone but myself,' he thought, 'but I know what I shall do. I will let these wise men find this promised one, since they are so intelligent. I will tell them to come back here with the news where I will be anxiously waiting with my own tribute...a sword to cut his throat.'

* * * * *

In Herod's private baths, the steam rose around the three men as they soaked. When their bodies had been steamed long enough, they would plunge into the cold water, after which a slave would scrape the impurities from their bodies. They did not feel relaxed. The bald man voiced the thoughts of the other two. "I do not trust this Herod. My instincts tell me that he is a dangerous man."

The other two nodded. "It is my belief, gentlemen, that we should be on our way as soon as possible, otherwise we are likely to end up with our throats cut."

Elizabeth held her baby to her breast so that he could suckle. The child could smell the milk and moved his head from side to side in an effort to find the source. When he found it he sucked hungrily. Elizabeth looked at him. "My son, you are beautiful and you are the joy of my life and your father's life. You have brought a peace to my life in the shadows of my years and yes, light too. In your coming, many have rejoiced. Your coming is before the Lord." She began to sing a little song.

Tamar entered the house. She had been to the market place for vegetables. She placed what she had bought on the table and sat down to rest after her walk up the long hill. Her breath was coming in short gasps. "Look at me. I am an old woman. I have no breath in me."

Elizabeth laughed and said, "Wait until you get to my age and you will know what old is!"

The two women laughed. Tamar looked at John as he lay in the crook of Elizabeth's arm, "And how is the man-child today?" she said with a smile and in exaggerated tones for the benefit of the baby. "He is growing more like his father each day. Do you think he will be a priest just like the master?"

"Yes, Tamar, I think he will be a priest. But according to

the prophecy given through Zechariah on the day of his presentation, I think he will be a special kind of priest. In those prophetic words it was said that he would go before the Lord, to prepare the people for him. He will be a prophet to announce the coming of the Lord. He will need the Lord's strength and I certainly think he has it now." The child came off the breast and yawned.

After the first few hours walking, Joseph stopped the donkey to give Mary some water. Although her white veil and robes did not attract the sun, he could see that she was tired and hot. He lifted her from the animal in his powerful arms. As he set her on her feet she stumbled a little as she found her legs.

"Can you walk to the shade of these trees, my love, for they will relieve the heat a little for you? I will give you some water."

Mary looked up at Joseph, her face red in the heat, and smiled at him. "That would be good, thank you, Joseph. But, please, do not worry about me. I am good. Just a little uncomfortable as you can see."

They reached the olive grove and felt its coolness. The terrain that they had travelled through was almost desert land, with a few pockets of arable land. They could probably reach Samaria before nightfall and Mary could rest in comfort.

They had met with others who were travelling to Bethlehem and other towns for the census; donkey laden groups of families who had left their houses in the care of neighbours and who were staying in Nazareth for that was their place of origin; children had danced and played around them as they walked on until they became bored. They tried singing, but as children do, they became bored with this too. Women caught up with them and talked with Mary about her condition and sympathised with her, their sun beaten faces twisting into pitying looks and then a smile to encourage. Old men and women sat atop donkeys or camels, their age and white hair giving them precedence over those who were younger.

The men too, had talked with Joseph. They talked of the Roman tyranny and what would the Romans come up with next? They spoke of their own towns and how the census had affected them. Joseph heard news that he did not normally hear in their conversations and it helped them to pass the time on the journey. Along the way, one donkey stopped and refused to move. They beat it with sticks, they cajoled it with food; they even tried to push it. The spectacle attracted the children who enjoyed it thoroughly. They fetched sticks and poked it but to no avail. The donkey was staying there, whatever its stubbornness was about, and it was not moving. A carnival atmosphere pervaded.

On the road the dust had risen at times when others joined them and they had to cover their mouths and noses with shawls, veils or hands; anything that was handy.

As the couple sat now in the shade of the olive tree, intermittent breezes sprung up to cool them. They drank water and ate a little and watched the crowd on the road begin as a trickle and ripen into a thick stream. They were on their way to take part in Augustus' census, to take part in the Roman tyranny or die if they did not.

The men from the East knew that they were being watched. They tried to leave on a few occasions when the opportunity arose but Herod would not hear of it. He began long discussions with them in the throne room of the palace; his own lawyers, astronomers, scribes, all powerful men in their own right, discussing and arguing with them about the whereabouts of this king to be born. They felt that they were being sucked dry of the knowledge that they had gleaned for years and sucked into a powerful intrigue that was hatching in Herod's mind.

After the sixth day of travelling, Mary felt herself get uncomfortable and sometimes that discomfort niggled at her abdomen. She could feel it tightening at times. Then she would feel all right again. They had reached Bethany and they would be in Bethlehem tomorrow evening. Joseph had paced the journey for her so that she could bear it easily. He was a good man and she could feel his protection. He had brought her water to drink often, during the day; to be sure she did not dehydrate. He stopped walking before the noontime sun had reached its powerful time and only began again in the late afternoon when she had rested. The nights were spent in inns that they found along the way. He always insisted on sleeping on the floor of her room in case she needed anything in the night or the baby started to come. She thanked God for him. She thanked God that her time was near and she could begin her duty of mother to this child of God.

Her mother had been right; she had felt the kicks of the child within her and knew that he was strong and healthy. She was glad of that. Sometimes she felt an unseen hand help her through difficulties and she was not afraid. She was not afraid of the birth of this child because she knew for certain that all would be well. At other times she felt that, although the Angel Gabriel had left her visual sight, he was still with her, like a wisp of smoke; she felt him near her and she felt his gentleness. At odd moments she could feel what seemed a hand brush her face and she knew it was he. With such power, she felt him hold her on this journey as though she were a child being carried by her father. It was good to know that he was with her, especially now when this child, Jesus, was about to be born.

Augustus Octavius was pleased with himself as he listened to the news of the messengers coming with tidings of how his census fared in his empire. A few skirmishes to the North had been quelled quickly by his soldiers stationed there. It was going according to plan. He felt good in his status of god. His statues were going up everywhere including the Circus Maximus; they had placed it beside Julius. When he saw it, he had cried for the thought of how proud Julius would have been of him. When he went there now his applause almost went on longer than the games. Even when he had sat down and called for the games to begin, they had continued to applaud. 'Such tribute, such admiration', he thought proudly, 'and I deserve it!'

All the messengers that came with news were each given a gold coin with his head on it, so pleased and benevolent did he feel.

Bethlehem Ephratah, City of David and the least, stretched before them. The area was a basin and the city was crawling up one side. They looked across the valley and saw the town cling to the gentle hill. They could see the lush and fertile fields that surrounded it; they were cut and divided into neat squares; portions of land for the families who owned and tilled them. Mary looked with eyes a little misty to see the land of her fathers. She held herself as another pain overtook her. The evening sky was beginning to burnish the pale azure with gold and it seemed like a welcome; it seemed like a signature being written in the sky.

"It is beautiful," said Mary, "but, Joseph, let us not look too long. This child is on its way. We must get settled somewhere for the night."

"Let us move on then", said Joseph.

As they moved down the hill, they saw the crowds entering the town; many hundreds had answered Caesar's call and Bethlehem surely could not hold all of them. Many had camped along the side of the hill and they could see fires beginning to twinkle all around them as the shadows lengthened. They could see the shepherds on the hillside begin to settle for the night and the smell of sheep caught their nostrils. The first stars were being sprinkled across the sky and glimmered faintly in the dying light; with them came the coolness of the night. Mary's labour had begun and with it a new hope sprang as a wellspring into the world. Its waters would suckle the world and give it life as the Nile floods the land to replenish its growing capacity.

—5—

As Joseph led the donkey into the town, he walked at its side, aware that Mary might fall off as she grappled with each new pain. The throng began to mill around them, each scurrying to find a place for the night; with these crowds it would not be easy. Had one floated above the scene, then one would have seen people, like mice, over populated, overcrowded, who walked or ran with animated movements; greeting one another, walking silently or gossiping in little knots; some stopped to angrily shout at those who carelessly stepped on a child or knocked food out of an eater's hand. They bumped and touched without meaning to; stopping to look now and then at the vendors, causing jams and interrupting the flow, as people joined queues to buy supper. They pulled their light cloaks and shawls around them as cool became cold. The smell of food made Joseph remember that he had a stomach and it needed to be fuelled now and again. He whispered words of comfort to Mary and told her that they would eat as soon as he found a place for them to stay. She looked at him and smiled and said that the pains were getting stronger. He could see her pain and he prayed under his breath that they would find a place soon. He saw an inn a little way ahead and made towards it as best as he could in the dense thicket of people.

He said to Mary, "Will you be alright, my love, while I go in to see if I can get a room?"

She smiled at him again, that sweet, beautiful smile even in the midst of her pain and said to him reassuringly, "I will be safe. I am being looked after. Go, Joseph." He had come to love that smile for it told him that she loved him; it told him that she was not complaining but understanding that this was the way things were and she would do what she could to help in the situation. All that she could do, and all that he wanted from her was that she be safe and keep well for her baby. He returned the smile to reassure her.

He kissed her forehead, "I will be back soon." He tethered the donkey to a thin pillar that was one of four that held up the roof of the inn and went up to the door. The din of many people met his ears and the smell of wine consumed and wine about to be consumed was heady in his nose. The door was closed and he knocked loudly and stood waiting. After a moment, he knocked again. The door opened abruptly and a woman with unkempt hair and the smell of wine on her breath stood silhouetted in the bright lamplight that fell into the darkened street.

"What do you want?" She fired the question at him like a dart.

"I am Joseph. I need lodging for the night," he returned politely, to counteract her rudeness. "My wife, Mary, is having her child. It is on the way," he indicated to Mary on the donkey a little distance away.

The woman looked into the semi light and saw Mary. Her face and attitude softened a little.

"I'm sorry, sir. I gave the last room away an hour ago. The cellars are full too, and the attic. Why, every place in Bethlehem is full to capacity tonight. Not even gold could buy a room in this town. There's not a lot that I can do for you, I'm afraid." Joseph's heart fell, disappointment clawing it. The woman seemed to study something in her mind for a moment then she spoke again.

"If you follow this street down until you pass two streets to the left, then turn down the next one and about halfway down it you'll see an inn called *Merchants Rest*. Knock at the door and ask for Eli and tell him that Ruth sent you. If he has any room to spare he'll give it to you. It might be a cellar or an attic, or even an outhouse but it would give the lady a bit of privacy."

"Thank you," said Joseph. "And God's blessings be upon you, Ruth." The woman just stared after him with pity in her eyes.

When he returned to Mary, he saw her weary face. Already she was tired out and needed a place soon. She bent her head in pain. He could feel panic rise in him.

"We will find somewhere soon, Mary."

Eli could not help but directed them to another inn that, in turn sent them to another. For an hour Joseph led the donkey around Bethlehem receiving the same answer: 'there is no room here.' He prayed silently in his heart, 'God of my fathers, help this poor man. I am at a loss. Let the next place have a room. If I am to protect your daughter and her unborn son, then you must find a room where I can take her.'

People still milled about them, although the crowds were considerably less; there was less of a crush. Drunken men and women tottered past them trying to find their way home. Joseph was just walking now. He felt helpless. He could not find a place for Mary to have the baby. He had been chosen to help her and protect her and here she was having her child and he could find nowhere to give her a little privacy and comfort. He felt crestfallen.

A voice behind him called out sharply, "Joseph...Joseph." He turned around. 'Surely its not me' he thought, 'there must be a hundred Josephs in Bethlehem tonight.'

He saw the bulk of a woman running towards him and he recognised Ruth from the first inn that they had tried. She came up to him breathless.

"Ruth! What is it?" said Joseph. He saw Mary turn her head to look at the woman.

It took her a moment to catch her breath and she bent over and held her breastbone as she waited.

"You are a hard man to find, Joseph. As I was looking for you, a tall man stopped me and told me that you were on this street. He was a stranger to me but he seemed to know you" she said as she found her breath. She shrugged her shoulders. "Are you alright?" she asked Mary, peering into her face. "Are the pains bad?" When Mary nodded, Ruth turned to Joseph, "You see this street here?" She pointed to where two streets forked and went their separate ways.

"Yes," said Joseph.

"The one that goes down the hill; follow that street until it ends. After about a hundred yards it begins to go uphill again. Follow it up the hill for about half a mile. There are some caves there. You will find one with a gate on it to keep animals in. That is my husband's. It is the only one there with a gate. Go there and give this girl a place to have her baby."

Joseph felt his heart leap in praise to God. "Ruth, how can I thank you?"

"Don't thank me. Just go." She put her hands on her hips and raised her eyes to the heavens. "Men!" she said.

As they walked towards the street Ruth had indicated, they heard her shout, "It will be all right now, Mary. It is a comfortable place. I'll come up tomorrow if I can. God be with you."

Joseph waved at her in thanks and began the journey to the cave. It was midnight.

The stars overhead twinkled and winked in the black sky and the cold clearness of it showed the vastness of the heavens. The depth of the vault that Yahweh had created seemed infinite on this night. There were no clouds to block the view, not even the wispy trails of smoky clouds that were latecomers and had missed the day. The earth appeared not part of the vastness but separate, somehow cut off and exiled. The earth craned towards the vastness and craved reconciliation. The millions of stars that inhabited the vault seemed pluckable and close as they continued to wink at the world. In seeming unison, the cooking fires on the hillside winked back at their counterparts in the sky. The hillside was dotted with sheep all trying to settle for the night, munching their last bit of cold cud. They lazily watched the fires on the other hillsides, wondering at the human activity.

Above them on the hillside, the hill flattened out as though resting before it continued to the top. The flat area was roughly about twenty feet square. A small fire burned in the centre of the square and four young men sat huddled around it for the cold night air was biting. They faced down the hill so that they could see the sheep. They had on shepherd's coats made of sheepskin or woven from camel's hair to bite back at the cold. They were talking excitedly of the day to come and the activity of the crowds that had invaded their town like an army. The increased Roman soldiers in their town did not perturb them for there were too many exciting and wonderful things to see than to worry about Roman soldiers. They ranged in age from about thirteen to about twenty.

"And we'll be stuck up here, again," said the youngest. He had his knees pulled up to his chin and his arms around them.

"We can sleep less tomorrow, Jacob, and see some of the activity on the way here."

The younger boy's eyes brightened. A strand of his dark straight hair escaped from the woollen shawl wrapped about his head. He did not bother to put it back. "I heard there was a man with a dancing bear from Persia." He stared into what seemed a far off place in his mind. He thought about all the places in the world he wanted to go and the wonders he wanted to see. When the older boy nudged him he jumped back into reality and wiped his nose on his sleeve and sniffed. "Its alright for you, Daniel", he said, "You will be allowed to go and see all you want to see. I never get anywhere and I see nothing, I'm too young." He spat at the ground in disgust.

"Ah, Jacob, I'll take you to see the dancing bear, stop whining. I'll speak to your parents about it." The other two laughed into the night and the laughter echoed and eddied around the hill finding, and lodging, in the ears of those not yet gone to sleep.

"What about you, Abner, and you, Ephraim, did you see anything spectacular on the way here?" Daniel said. He was a dark haired youth and the blemish of teenage acne still haunted his tanned skin. The dark hair on his face was patchy now but it would grow into a thick beard. It would help to keep him warm on the cold nights on the hillside. He shifted his position to get comfortable.

"I saw men performing acrobats," said Ephraim, wiping away the droplet of mucus that formed at the end of his nose. At sixteen, he was a quiet, shy youth and said little to his companions, preferring to only speak when asked a question.

"And you, Abner? What did you see?"

The boy yawned and said, "I didn't see anything. I slept too late and had to run to catch up."

The other three exploded into laughter for Abner was always asleep. It seemed that his fourteen years had been spent sleeping. He slept at every opportunity. He took some twigs from the bundle behind him and placed them on the fire. The fire spat tiny sparks up into the air, as though complaining at the disturbance.

Daniel, as well as being the eldest of the four, was the natural leader. He spoke now into the night, "When we go home in the morning, try and get a few hours sleep. If we awake early and if you, Abner, can stay awake long enough..." the other two chuckled, "we'll meet up at the bottom of the hill and spend all day in the town. And when it is beginning to get dark come back and let the others go home. We can take turns at sleeping in the night. What about that?"

The others nodded agreement.

As they nodded, they became aware of a strange, stark and beautiful feeling within them and around them. It touched them and made them want to dance for joy and sing and shout and not care; all the things they did when they were happy; it was like as if they had found a Roman gold coin and it was theirs to keep, to do with whatever they wanted. It felt as though they could walk on the air and the stars would be like steps and they could walk on them and lift them like stones and skid them across a lake. The strangeness held them and they were suddenly looking at the sky above them but the sky was not there. There were what looked like men, dressed in white robes and all were dancing, no; flying around in the sky. In great leaps and bounds they flew or danced and were framed in a large smoky cloud and the youths smiled and then were afraid and then were happy. Tears fell from their eyes as they watched this spectacle. They did not know why they were crying but it seemed right to do so. The starkness of the night sky was gone and Heaven was touching the earth in a dance that cut through time, and over it and around it and rendered it useless. Time was not needed any more.

The young men realized that they were looking at Angels. And their awe and wonder caught them in a different dance. This dance was reality. All the spectacles that they had dreamed of seeing on the morrow were wisps of smoke, disappearing in the breeze of Heaven. They were tricks and glitter that men had made to try to imitate the miracles of the One who created them. They had blinded themselves from their God and sought with their cheap

111

tricks to imitate Him, who was real now in the lives of these poor and innocent shepherds. He was lifting up the humble and the poor and seating them on the thrones of Heaven and all because they believed in what they saw and did not change it. Yes, this was God's reality. *It* was real.

The Angels began singing then; singing a song in time to the dance that they danced. It was a song of reconciliation and love and peace and joy. It was a song that could be sung forever and beyond the vastness of this night, beyond time and eternity if men would only learn to sing it: *"Glory to God in the highest, and on earth peace, good will towards men."* They sung it over and over again and with it the night seemed to warm.

From the multitude of Angels that danced, one of them separated himself and came down and stood in front of the youths. They began now to be afraid and they went on their knees in fright. For all their fear, they could not take their eyes off this beautiful vision that stood before them.

And the Angel spoke with a voice that was soft and gentle and soothing and they were reminded of clear, gushing water: *"Fear not:"* he seemed to speak into their hearts for they heard it within them, *"...for, behold, I bring you good tidings of great joy, which shall be to all people. For unto you is born this day in the city of David a Saviour, which is Christ the Lord. And this shall be a sign unto you; ye shall find the babe wrapped in swaddling clothes, lying in a manger."*

When the Angel finished, the sound of gushing water stopped and was once more replaced with the marvellous singing of the song of Heaven. The shepherd boys had not noticed whether it had stopped, or that the Angel who spoke to them had spoken louder, because it was the way of things on that Bethlehem hill that night; things just happened in a moment that was now; there was no yesterday or tomorrow; all that was tangible was the *now.* A now that was not of this world but had come on the wings of the An-

gels that now frolicked in the joy that was God. Heaven -
the home of this present moment - opened and was pouring itself onto the earth; an event not seen since Eden was
sealed up and closed. God was touching the earth with a
newness and a joy and his word was spoken this night.
Somewhere near, his word was swaddled and safe and had
been spoken into the world of men.

Then it was gone; the vision folded itself up and packed
itself away and was gone. For a few moments afterwards,
the boys continued to laugh and weep and feel joy until realisation declared it over. They saw again the bright stars
sprinkled across the black, inky sky winking at them and
they seemed to know the secret; they seemed to know what
had happened.

The dawning that it was over first hit the shepherds when
they felt the coldness of their wet faces. They were on their
knees still and they felt the crisp cold grass beneath them.
Jacob was the first to speak, "That was Angels! That was
God!" He paused then as though it were a solemn moment
and that any voice or sound would shatter it. He spoke
again with a question: "What is a Saviour, Daniel?"

"It's a...a..." it took him a moment to find his voice, still lost
in the vision, "I think it's somebody who saves you. Like
the Messiah, when he comes he will save us from the Romans and all the other people that don't like us." There
was silence again as the boys fought the stunned feeling that
had come with returning to the world's reality. The night
hushed and waited with them.

"The Angel told us we would find a newborn baby and he
would be Christ the Lord and that he was a Saviour and he
would be wrapped in swaddling clothes." It was Ephraim
who spoke. "I don't know what happened here but my
heart is filled with happiness and I feel that it's going to
burst. I can feel that God is truly, truly inside me. I want to
see him for if he is a Saviour, as they said, then what we're
doing here doesn't matter anymore, nothing matters any-

more." He got up and began to walk, and then he began to run down the hillside. He scattered the sheep and they ran in all directions but he did not care. The vision was driving him.

The others looked at each other. They realised that Ephraim had spoken, more than they had ever heard him saying and he was right. Pockets of the vision that they had been given came to life again. They followed Ephraim.

He did not know where to go to find the child who had been born but Ephraim *knew* deep in his heart because the joy that was there was telling him. He approached the cave now and he could see a faint light behind the gate. It still showed through the various colours of rugs and blankets that were draped across it. It was no more than a hole in the rock, like a mouth that was wide open. The entrance to it was about seven feet high and about five wide; the gate covered almost all of the entrance except for the arched part at the top, which was ragged and uneven. He approached cautiously remembering his manners. When his own mother had his little brothers and sisters, being the eldest, it had been his job to play with the other children and keep them out of the way; his reward was to be the first to see the newborn infant. His mother had always been tired after the birth and this woman would be no different.

The others had caught up with him and were behind him. He did not look around but cautioned them to be quiet with his hand. They walked quietly up behind him until he could feel their breath on his neck.

Ephraim stood looking at the gate with the others in a tight little knot behind him. He had become the leader now and was giving the orders. He knew instinctively that they would obey him. It was the vision that had done it. It had made him feel new and wonderful and loved; it was like someone had hugged him and was still hugging him, even now. He put out his hand, made it into a fist and knocked the gate quietly, fearing a little to disturb the woman inside.

The strange and beautiful feeling that he had felt on the hillside, before the vision came, was here. It clung everywhere like the perfume that a woman wears; it is still there even after she has gone. This was the source of it.

The gate opened and a tall man stood there. His face and head was covered with dark hair that curled a little where it fell on his shoulders. He had muscular shoulders and arms. He had a puzzled look on his face as if he had not been expecting company. 'Well,' Ephraim thought, 'I could not fault him for that. It must be almost daybreak.'

"Hail, young men!" the man said, stepping out through the gate and closing it behind him, "what brings you here, so early?"

"We have come to see the child that was born this night. We were on the hillside and many Angels came to us in a vision and they said that a saviour had been born in the City of David and that the child wrapped in swaddling clothes would be a sign for us and that he was Christ, the Lord. No one told me where he was, I just knew. Would it be alright to see him, if the lady does not mind?" Ephraim wondered where all the words had come from and why he had not stammered as he often did when he had to speak to strangers. But this man did not seem like a stranger.

The man looked shocked and said, "When did this occur?"

"About one hour ago," Ephraim answered. "We do not know how long the vision took but it seemed like forever."

A woman's voice sounded from behind the gate. "Joseph, let them come in and look at the child. They have been sent."

The man, Joseph, smiled at them and said, "You are welcome, young men." He pushed open the gate and walked inside waiting behind it for them to walk in.

Ephraim went in and the others followed him.

They entered a lamp lit room; the straw on the floor and

115

that piled up in the corner, coupled with the light, gave it a golden hue. The woman lay on the pile of straw with a blanket under her and over her and crooked in her arm was a baby. The child was the golden light that permeated the room. The woman seemed to be clothed in the child; and he was like the sun. The strange and stark and beautiful feeling was coming from the child and it touched him like the vision had but in a new and different way. It seemed to Ephraim that tendrils of love came out of the child and touched him. That's what the feeling was; it was love. This child was love. He had never felt it before with any of his younger brothers and sisters when they had been born. He knew that this saviour would save with love. He was overcome and fell to his knees in front of the child and his mother. He could hear the others rustling in the straw as they too, knelt. Ephraim pulled the shawl that had kept him warm in the cold night from his head in respect.

Ephraim heard himself speak and it did not seem out of place to do so for the woman had the same love in her eyes that the baby had. "What is his name?"

The woman answered him. Her voice was soft and beautiful. It reminded him of the gentle lapping of a lake in the evening time; that quiet time when the day was dying and all things seemed to rest and you were caught up in it because it was an ancient feeling, given by God to Adam and the echoes of it were still deep within.

"His name is Jesus," the woman said.

'Jesus'; the name echoed and cadenced itself within him and it found his soul and stayed there. He had heard the name before but never in this way.

"Joseph," the woman said, "will you put Jesus in the manger so that our guests may see him better?"

"Yes, Mary."

He took the child and placed it in the manger, which was to the side of the cave; he was swaddled, as the Angels had said, and he was in the manger.

Ephraim moved closer to the child and remained on his knees for it seemed right to worship him in this way. Ephraim spoke to the child: "Little child, I do not know you but I feel that I have known you all of my life. I know that you are the Christ, the One who is to come. I am not good with words but these are flowing from my heart. I want you to save me, since you are the Saviour of the world. Gather me among your people and bring me to where you live. You must be from Heaven because the Angels came and told us that you were born. Little child, I believe in you.

The boy stood up and bowed to the child in the manger. He turned to the woman. "Thank you, Mary, for allowing me to speak with the fruit of your womb." He turned then and left. The other shepherds mumbled words of thanks and followed him.

Joseph looked at Mary after the shepherds had gone. "More and more each day there are signs that God is doing just what he said he would do."

"I know, Joseph. God is truly wonderful. I must sleep now, for the child is asleep, so that I am ready for him when he wakes. I do not think that it is the end of our visitors."

Ruth came in the late afternoon and was overjoyed to see the child. "I'm so glad that it is all over for you, Mary, and what a sweet child he is. There is something about him that I've never seen in a child. The blessings of God on him! By the way, that man that I told you about last night; the one who showed me where you were, he came to the inn this morning to tell me that you had a son. He said his name was Gabriel. He made me feel very strange."

Mary and Joseph looked at one another.

The men from the East had sat day after day in Herod's

throne room and discussed the movement of the heavenly beings in the universe. Herod had sat with them and watched them as an eagle watches his prey; ready to swoop and grasp at the first weak moment. He plied them with questions to find out if they knew where this new king would be born. They were under polite house arrest.

Finally, he let them go with reluctance telling them that he would be waiting for news of the new king. They knew that homage was not in his mind.

They left by the Essene Gate in the dead of night and noticed that the star was waiting for them. They headed south to Bethlehem at the stars guidance. The star was not a comet; it did not have a trail behind it.

When they arrived in Bethlehem the star indicated that the place was not in the town but on the outskirts. The star hung low in the sky and just above the horizon and they discovered the cave easily.

The people of Bethlehem were thrilled with the exhibition and watched the three foreigners on their camels, gyrating with the animal's ungainly strides. Some whispered that royalty had come to the town and yet others called it an omen. A small group, who had nothing better to do, followed the strangers outside the town, disappointed that they had not stayed. They were bored waiting for the Romans to begin the census. The booths had been set up but they were waiting on more troops from Jerusalem for they had not expected the crowds.

They stopped about a hundred yards in front of the cave and dismounted, camels complaining about having to go on their knees. Each man searched in his supplies for the gift that he had brought. It was heading into evening and the long shadows were beginning to draw. The crowd who had followed them stood now some distance away enjoying the antics of the strangers; they were hoping that they would do something different, unusual and that was customary to their own land so that they could be in awe.

Mary was preparing a little food for herself and Joseph when they heard the voices outside. Joseph looked at Mary and went to see who it was that had spoken. He opened the gate and saw the three men before him, each held something in his hand.

The three stood now before the gate and marvelled at the humility of this king. The bald man walked up to the gate and spoke, "We come in peace to give homage to the new-born king. We have brought gifts of tribute."

Joseph was not surprised when he saw them but led them into the cave. They greeted Mary with graceful bows and words of compliment to her beauty. Jesus was in the manger and was awake. They peered at him and mumbled words in a foreign tongue. Then they knelt in front of the manger. It was like an altar and they were worshipping before it.

The bald man spoke: "My gift to this king is gold for it is the most precious metal that I can offer to my king. This king is also a God and I embellish him with gold in keeping with his status. With this gold I worship him." He placed the gift at arms length away from him and then he bowed low until his forehead touched the ground. He remained there for several minutes.

When the bald man had finished, the swarthy one began to speak: "Before this God, I kneel. We have seen his star given by the God of Israel to announce his coming. I give frankincense, the most fragrant of incense. In my country it is burned before the gods to give honour of the highest degree. I too followed the bright star in the sky and have believed in his coming." Placing the gift in the straw, he bowed low as the other had done.

The other wise man took his gift and held it in his fingers: "This Myrrh that I hold within my hands is my gift to this king. In my land it is sought after for its perfume. It is the fragrance of kings. I place it before you to do you honour, your Majesty." He bowed low as the others had done.

Mary spoke to them, "We thank you for your generosity in these truly beautiful gifts. You are welcome to eat with us. It is not the fare of kings but a little wine to refresh you and bread to welcome you."

"We accept your invitation to eat with you, my lady, a little wine to quench the thirst that travelling on the road brings is welcome." The swarthy man said. "The fare of kings such as Herod is somewhat more dangerous than appetizing."

The men sat for some hours cross-legged in the straw on the cave floor speaking with Joseph and Mary of the star and of Herod. Night had placed a cloak around the world when finally they rose to be on their way.

On the eighth day they brought the child to the Synagogue in Bethlehem to be circumcised to fulfil the Law of the *Torah*. They named him Jesus, which means 'Yahweh saves' as the Angel Gabriel had told Joseph in the dream.

Joseph found it hard to sleep. The days bled into one another and the Romans were taking their time about the census. They had set up their booths in the market place in Bethlehem but they were painfully slow and the crowds who had come for this purpose were becoming restless. The Romans could see it and had ordered extra foot soldiers for they feared a riot. New contingents had arrived and taken up their places in Bethlehem, watching with their eagle eyes for any signs of dissention. It was difficult to enter Bethlehem now, even for what little supplies they needed. An air of fear and tension had settled over the town; a great eagle whose wings created an ominous shadow over a colony of mice; each waiting for the other to move.

Joseph turned over in the straw. He wanted it all to go

away, or at least come to his turn so that he could take Mary and Jesus back to Nazareth and get settled into their way of life once more.

He had been thrilled when the child was born. It was a joy to his ears to hear the healthy, strong cry of the infant, and such a beautiful child. He was not Joseph's son, by blood, but he claimed him for his own and that made him his adoptive son and an heir of David. He felt the thrill of a father on the birth of his firstborn, that feeling of responsibility and change of lifestyle to accommodate and incorporate another life into his own. He would teach the child the Scriptures and the ways of God as laid down by Moses. He had watched Mary feeding the child and felt one with them. At this time it was easy to pledge a promise to God of fidelity, for the child's birth and the events surrounding it were a tangible force in his life and he could see the hand of the Almighty within it. He wanted nothing else but what he had now.

The men from the East had spoken of Herod and that it was their belief that he wanted to do the child harm. They had told him of the gruelling week that they had spent in Herod's palace. But Joseph felt safe in the arms of God. He trusted that whatever dangers were afoot that God would protect them. Was Gabriel not making his presence felt? Joseph wondered at the Angel. He came as a messenger and he was still here. It was comforting to know that he, the protector, was being protected.

The shepherd boy, Ephraim, had come to see the child again. His eyes were full of love. Whatever had happened the night that Jesus was born was still within the heart of the boy. He wanted to help Mary and Joseph in whatever way he could. He was a polite, well-mannered boy and they enjoyed his company.

The man could feel his eyelids grow heavy in the darkness of the cave and was glad that sleep had found him. He liked to be up before Mary awoke to prepare some food for her. He was not good with food but a little bread and goat's cheese was easy to prepare.

Joseph fell into the folds of sleep and it was like arms soothing and lulling him.

Joseph walked through the lush growth. Palms spread their umbrellas over the hot land to give shade and coolness. He felt the sunshine give life to the teeming plants that grew on either side of the road that he walked on. He could feel the plants absorb the light into their cells and create food in abundance. He felt it pummelling along the veins as a river in flood to carry the nutrients to the new leaves that were springing and bursting into the sun's light to prepare for the fruits that would carry the next generations. He could smell the growth; he could smell the greenness and it was heady with a richness that only spring could bring. He was happy and felt his soul reach up and praise the God who made him. As he walked the lushness came to an end abruptly and it was gone. Gabriel stood before him, resplendent in his white robes and he was like the sun. His wings glinting the light, he did not move and his face seemed unyielding. He stood tall and obedient like a soldier on a mission.

They were standing on a great open plain and Joseph could see the mountains and the hills in the distance. There was a light all around them and it seemed to be coming from behind the Angel's head. He could feel the earth beneath his feet and the stones dug into the soles of his feet. Joseph knew it was the Plain of Moab.

"Son of Jacob, you have been brought here for a purpose. King Herod wishes the child of God harm. He will kill the Holy One. You must take Mary and the child into Egypt. You will leave this night and go by way of Beersheba. From there you must travel on the Way of Shur, keeping yourselves with caravans. From there you will enter Egypt and go into the Land of Goshen that was once the land of your fathers when they were exiled and settle there until you are

122

told to return. Herod's days are numbered. Do not fear, Joseph, for you will be safe. Follow these instructions. You have done well in your mission, continue to do so."

"You wish me to do this now?"

"Time is not on your side, Joseph, you must go this night and do not delay."

"It will be done according to your wishes."

He woke with a start. It was Gabriel. He was here again. Joseph stood up. He must rouse Mary. He lit the lamp. As he walked over to her she looked so contented and blissfully unaware of the danger to her child. His heart overflowed with good things and reminded him of the lush fields he had walked through in the dream.

Was it only a dream? He began to doubt and it flawed his faith. No! He would believe that the dream was a vision and he would go there. He must live now on blind faith. He did not need to see; he would not ask to see. Is that not what he had promised God? He shook Mary gently before he could change his mind.

"Mary, Mary, you must wake up now." He watched her come back into reality and stretch. He looked at her again in the lamplight. The red blanket that she lay on framed her face and her hair looked blacker, like ebony. Her face was still a little pallid and swollen from the exhaustion of the birth. He waited until she sat up.

"Has Jesus awakened?"

"No, Mary, he still sleeps. I had another visitation from Gabriel."

"Oh!" Mary said. "Did he speak to you?"

"Yes. As the Eastern men spoke to us of Herod, so Gabriel spoke. He echoed what they had said. Mary, this child is in danger and it seems that Herod will do him harm. He sees Jesus as a threat to his reign but he told me that Herod's days are numbered. He was before me in a great light and he spoke. He told me to take you and the child into Egypt and live there for a while until it is safe to return. He said that Herod would die soon. He even told me what route to take into Egypt."

"Then we must go. We cannot place Jesus in danger. When did he say we were to go?"

"What he said was that we were to go now, tonight. That is why I woke you. I am sorry that it must be this way."

"Do not be sorry, Joseph, we must waste no time, we must flee."

They were ready to leave within the hour. They left what they could in thanks to any who would come and would wonder at their sudden departure.

Herod realised that he had been tricked. The men from the East had not returned to him. His anger spilled over and he spoke with the Roman guard. His orders were clear.

Two days later as the sun broke over the horizon a legion of Roman soldiers left the garrison in Jerusalem. The day was quiet and uneventful and they galloped towards Bethlehem. The sun caught the metal of their shields and reflected itself, blinding anyone who might be looking, giving the soldiers a formidable look. People along the road covered their eyes and wondered what fuss the Romans were making now, probably riots somewhere. The legion rode on regardless of what people thought. Lucius, the centurion who headed the command of the legion behind him, was in two minds about the orders that he had been given. He was an ordinary centurion and had been in the army for five years. Promoted to the rank of non-commissioned officer only two years ago had raised his pay a little and he had felt proud of his achievement. One hundred men under his command and he had done his job well always hoping for more promotion. In the army, if they thought you had potential they would recognise it. If you were smart you could stay alive.

His muscular body was taut as he held the reins. He had been given command of these hundreds of men who rode behind him. It was not that he did not want the promotion, no; his father would be proud of him were he to see him today. It was his orders that bothered him. He gritted his teeth and pushed down the bile of fear that had lodged itself in his throat.

The five hundred horsemen galloped down the hill towards Bethlehem leaving a thick, foggy trail of dust behind them. They slowed as they approached the gate. They pushed through the crowds that had gathered there and made their way to the market square.

There they dismounted and divided themselves into centuries and stood waiting for Lucius to give the order. He gave it.

The people who were there in the market place could taste the fear that these Romans permeated into them. It penetrated with spikes and tore at their very hearts. They could smell death as an animal can, as it is ready to be slaughtered. The cold realisation of what was happening now gripped them and a wave of panic caught them as it catches a herd of cattle when it smells a wolf. Panic was the driving force that made them run for homes or tents or lodgings to get out of the way of whatever was coming.

The soldiers pulled well-sharpened, short swords from their scabbards and each century fanned out and made its way to its destination. Lucius headed his own century. He knew his own men.

They walked down a narrow street – *Street of Lights* - exuding might and force; and soldiers broke rank and entered houses along the streets length. Lucius kicked in the fragile wooden door of a house and entered, telling himself that this was the enemy; they would kill him if he did not kill them.

There were five people cowering in that house, a mother,

father and three children. The mother recoiled against the wall; the side of her face was pressed into it as if she could get through it. Lucius saw the abject terror in her eyes and she reminded him of an animal just before slaughter. She was holding a male child; her arms tight around it and his face squashed against her breast. The damp smell of the house caught his nostrils.

"How old is this male child, woman?" He shouted into her face.

The father who was beside her spoke in a fearful voice, "He is one year old, my lord. He..."

The man got no further for Lucius had whipped the child from its mother and was holding it by the arm. The child screamed inconsolably, the mucus running from its nose.

The noise within the house was deafening as the mother screamed and the other children screamed. Lucius did not dare look at the child but gripped his sword. He placed the convulsive body of the child with its back across his knee and ran the cold edge of the blade across its neck. Its cries stopped suddenly and a gurgling, bubbling sound replaced it.

The blood from the child's neck spurted out like a fountain and the mother screamed a new scream. It was different from before; this was not fear of a Roman soldier, this was shock; this was unbelief. The shock made her stand, animated and, still screaming, she went to him, her wild eyes dancing in her head and grasped the child. He let go. Still screaming the woman made for him, her face and hands covered in blood as his was; she was like a lioness ready for the kill. She held the dead and lifeless child in one arm and with the other hand she scratched her nails down the side of his face. The nails dug deep for they were long and they were dirty. And still she screamed and stared at him. He felt the pain in his face and winced.

The woman began to hit him, one fist flailing about his head and chest. The father was now on his feet and was ready to defend himself. Lucius' ears were deafened by the screams of the children. He felt like a caged animal and panic rose in him like a volcano and threatened to overcome him. He grabbed the woman by the face and pushed her away from him. She fell against the wall that she had pressed against only moments ago. He heard the crack and blood stained the wall.

Now the father screamed but Lucius did not wait. He was out the door and into the sunshine once more. But there was no relief. He was covered in blood, the child's blood; scarlet blood. 'It should not be on me,' a fleeting thought told him; it had escaped the mask he had put over his mind. This would wash clean in the baths but the memory of this day was stained on his soul forever.

He was aware now that all around him the same carnage was desecrating the town. Soldiers with swords dripping blood chasing women to kill their children; the blood lust had a life of its own driving at them; needing sated, needing sacrifice. Newborn infants, toddlers, even women, men, lay dead and dying on the streets. Screams: high-pitched wailings, rang in his ears. They rang in his body and penetrated his soul. The smell of human blood was everywhere. Panic and fear stalked these streets and preyed upon civilians and soldiers alike. Soldiers had become butchers, slaying innocent babes in their mother's arms.

A scream began in the pit of Lucius' stomach and worked its way up into his throat. He screamed at the world; he screamed at the gods; he screamed at the people for not fighting hard enough for their children. He screamed at himself for he could feel hell grasp his heels. He could feel it hold his soul in its icy grip.

Despair caught the centurion deep in his chest. The Romans, his people, his blood, had conquered the world. Their roads stretched far and wide across the empire; gods that once remained within the walls of Rome now decorated every city and town that they had burned and murdered, killing the culture of each that was blooming like a flower within its own soil; Rome had become the briar that had encircled itself, unbidden, uninvited around the very heart of each nation and impaled it upon its thorns of death. Rome, the city that all roads lead to was a whore that was drunk with goblets of blood and sitting astride the beast of death.

The blood of innocent children and people now stained the narrow streets of this royal town. It was another thorn in the side of the whore: the slow beginning of the end of an empire. The whore was aged and blotched under the cosmetic camouflage of her beneficence. Rome would die.

Lucius looked about him. The fight was gone out of the people of Bethlehem; it was gone from the soldiers that had perpetrated it and now all stood or lay weeping in blood. Little bodies lay limp and lifeless; bodies that had once been full of expectant life; faces that once brought delight, lay now unmoving. Stunned grief was like a snake that slithered through each heart, each soul; coiling its way into the soil that it found there. It gave birth to its young and quickly they reproduced.

There was wailing where once had been the air; it filled the space between the firmament below and the firmament above; a high keening; a thick lament that reached Heaven.

A man was speaking through his tears, quoting the Hebrew Scripture, his thick brogue harsh on the Romans ears: " *'In Rama was there a voice heard, lamentation, and weeping, and great mourning, Rachel weeping for her children, and would not be comforted, because they are not.'* "

Nothing was growing on the road of hard pressed sand that they walked on for they had long left the areas of lush growth and arable land and were now in a harsh terrain. The road had been beaten solid by the many traders who needed to travel into Egypt and Arabia bringing trade goods and slaves, bartered for cheaply in one land and brought here to be sold at a greater price; camels and donkeys and elephants that carried the wares of merchants had all walked it since the days when Jacob and his people had travelled on it to escape the famine in the Land of Canaan. They had seen verdant fields that were producing crops of gold and green and dotted with oranges and pomegranates, disappear into sand and dusty, dead rock. Millet seemed to have colonized most of the fields to be either made into bread or eaten raw, its multi seed heads making it popular among the poor. The wall of heat shimmered just above the sand and burned the inhabitants of the caravan of about seventy people that travelled south in this formidable wilderness. The sun was the undisputed ruler of this redoubtable landscape. Like a drunken snake, the caravan slithered its way along the road, its body coloured by the clothes of those who were paying to be led to Egypt. A weariness had settled over the travellers and all longed for it to be evening. The animals consisted of camels and donkeys and a few horses. All carried the trades, roped and strapped to their backs. The exuding smell of human and animal sweat far outweighed the perfumes that were deliberately dabbed and shaken to counteract it.

Darb El Shur had been the wilderness that Moses had taken his people in the days of their freedom from captivity. With the Egyptians who had followed them into the

Red Sea, safely drowned and dead, the wilderness became a safe place for them; they were safe from their enemies. Mary wiped the sweat from her brow and gasped in the airless day that seemed to penetrate even into her body. The heat of the sun had no mercy and in this wilderness; the sand and rocks cowered against it. Although it was harsh, Mary felt the safety of it. This road took them further away from the enemies that wanted to kill the child. In the dead of night they had travelled and had hidden as best as they could during the day. Now in this wilderness they could mingle with the other anonymous travellers that were making their slow way into Egypt. It was approaching noon and Mary knew from the three days previous, that they would stop just before noon and set up temporary booths and tents to guard against the hottest part of the day when the sun reached its *zenith*. She was glad. Although she carried a damp piece of cloth to wet the child's face and lips, it kept drying and had to be constantly replenished from the goatskin water bag. She needed to rest and to be cool and feed her baby.

Joseph was leading the donkey, which was burdened with their supplies, bought at the various stops along the way. The sweat poured from his face and she could see it glistening in his hair and beard. He looked tired and he smiled at her and wiped the sweat from his brow. She loved this man who was her husband now and she thought about all that had happened to them in the last weeks. Joseph had been a tower of strength to her and she had leaned heavily upon him. Sometimes she could see the look of puzzlement on his face but he had never contradicted any of it. He believed in it. He knew that God was leading them, even if he did not understand it.

Mary looked around her. In the far distance she could see the mountains and hills of some other land and wondered about the people of Israel. They had spent forty years as nomads in this land. The Lord God had fed and watered them; he had given the Commandments to Moses on Sinai and showed them the way he wished them to follow him. From there they had travelled onwards and into the Promised Land. They took the land from the Canaanites and parcelled it off to the twelve tribes.

A woman close by her screamed and she was abruptly brought out of her reverie. The caravan came to a halt fearing it was an attack of bandits. The woman had her hand over her mouth and was pointing to a spot several yards in front of her. A cobra had crossed paths with the caravan, its black scaly body erect, its hood displayed, it hissed at the woman who screamed, its forked tongue smelling the air. A child picked up a rock and threw it at the snake, catching it on the head. The snake became enraged and turned its body in the direction of the attack, lashing out at the boy who was at a safe distance. Then a rain of rocks pelted the serpent and although it fought bravely for a short while, it soon retreated, still hailed by the missiles. It slunk off into the desert on the side of the road, enraged and licking its wounds.

Children laughed and began to boast about how many times they had hit the snake; women went to comfort the woman who had first seen it. Mary breathed a sigh of relief.

It was decided then that the caravan would halt and rest until the afternoon when the sun had cooled slightly. The whole caravan heaved a sigh of relief.

The night came down cold and hard on the caravan and the fires were lit to counteract it. The light clothes that were too heavy during the day were now added to with woollen shawls and coats to build a wall against the bitter wind. The animals were tethered and fed for the night, the precious water given sparingly. The night sounds of a group of people settling down for the night broke the silence now and again; laughter enjoined stories that were being told of the day's events and the hours stole away. Many dreamed of Egypt and its delights in the oblivion of sleep. Others going further into Arabia thought about the miles they still had to go. Children dreamed of the different land they were entering and the adventures that were in store.

Mary and Joseph lay together with the child between them to ward off the cold of the night. They covered themselves in blankets for warmth. The stars above them shone brightly against the freezing of the black sky. They were safe and a web of well-being cocooned them and they relaxed and they fell asleep quickly, listening to the sound of a camel bellowing in the darkness.

A week later and tired of the road, they arrived in Succoth in the Land of Goshen and felt again the coolness of buildings. The town itself was flat and the day that they arrived was market day. In the blistering heat, the people of Egypt came out of their houses to trade for their food and anything that had broken since the last market. Animals swelled its centre, which was a square surrounded by two storied buildings with streets running off in every direction, and the noise that they made was easier for Joseph and Mary to understand than the people of the land that they were exiled to. Stray dogs barked at everything that moved. They watched, fascinated, as potters turned lumps of clay into pots with an ease of hand, leaving them to dry in the sun with the bricks that they had made earlier and were now dried and ready for sale. Cloth merchants called out the attributes of the material that they were selling, their colours vibrant and fresh to the eye that had, for a while, only seen desert. They stopped to look and were accosted by the merchants in the hope that they might buy. The reds, greens, yellows and blues, contrasting in stripes and patterns that caught the eye, even from afar. They tasted the freshness and coolness of watermelons and appeased their thirst.

They got their supplies of food and water and left the town to itself. Here they felt that they were to part from the caravan and travel deeper into the Land of Goshen.

Zechariah felt the pain in his chest. It seemed as though a spear had struck him in his breastbone. It was Morning Prayer. He fell quickly to his knees. Shobek, who was standing behind him, went forward to catch the old man.

The morning sun had risen hot and the day was sweltering, even this early; it was the third hour. Zechariah clutched his chest for it seemed that there was a great gaping hole in it. He felt Shobek's arms around him and he heard him speak but he could not answer for his breath was coming in great gasps and he felt as though he had been running.

"Are you alright, Zechariah?" Shobek's voice had panic in it and it was conveyed to the other man. Shobek called to the priests who milled about them, apparently unconcerned. "Help me, help me get this man to the outside to give him air."

A flurry of robes was at his side in seconds, hands grasping the older man. They lifted him easily and walked the length of the Inner Court and out through the great pillared doors with Shobek telling them to go slowly and to be careful. The great portico was dark with lack of light but when they reached the doors light flooded in and blinded them. Zechariah was still holding his chest and gasping.

As the priests placed him gently on the ground, Shobek took the old man's head in his arms and cradled it gently; his face pallid and drained.

"Do not try to speak, my father, but rest here where you can breathe. Do not worry about the *Schacharit*, one of the other priests will do it.

They were just outside the great doors that led to the Inner Court and Shobek could see the Altar of Sacrifice to his left. It was a stone structure of about eight feet high and about twelve feet long with steps leading up to the top. The smell of burning animal flesh was thick and pungent to their noses as the flames curled and licked around the dead body of the animal on the Altar and the *Kohein* stood near the altar watching it. This sacrifice of a ram he would be allowed to eat with his family. He had cut the ram's throat earlier, and prepared it for the sacrifice. It was a sin offering. The smell permeated the Inner Court. To the right was the *Laver* for the washing ritual, where priests washed their hands and feet before offering the sacrifices. He could see two priests now, washing vigorously in the morning heat, preparing for more sacrifices. The shadow of the porch shaded them from the sun.

"My father," Shobek said, "What can I do for you?" He could see the old man fading into unconsciousness. "Father?"

The old man's throat gurgled as he tried to breathe and then it stopped; he gasped fighting for breath. Shobek realised that the man was *goses*. Shobek saw the line of colour begin at Zechariah's forehead and slowly creep across his face and down into his neck. Zechariah was dead. His spirit, was now gone from this world and into the bosom of Father Abraham. It happened very quickly.

Shobek's cry was one of love. The love that he had known from this man was the love of a father. He looked up to the sky and tears filled his eyes and they rolled unashamedly down his face. Shobek cried out loud until the sobs overtook him and he heaved convulsively. He put his head on the now lifeless Zechariah's chest and wept like a child. The priests who had carried him out now looked crestfallen and grief was evident on their faces. Some cried in sympathy and more priests gathered. They had all known and respected this High Priest and a vast mine of information on the Law was closed, never to be reopened.

When the sobs subsided and he was able to speak again, Shobek said to the inert Zechariah that he held within his arms, "I love you, my father." He kissed the dead man's forehead. Zechariah was seventy-two years old.

The priests washed and prepared the body for burial. They wrapped it in a burial sheet, which was made of linen; in its folds they placed aloes and myrrh; a square of the same material was wrapped about the head. They buried him the same day for the heat would not allow the body to be kept any longer. He was buried in Jerusalem.

When Elizabeth heard it she was inconsolable. Forty-six years they had been together and they had loved each other for all of them. She wept and keened for her dead husband, holding her son John against her breast, until relatives had to come and remove the child for her grief was excruciating to watch. Tamar held her mistress to comfort her but it was in vain. People came from all around the hill country to give sympathy to this woman who, only a few short months ago, had given birth to a baby in her barrenness. She would never see her husband again and the pain that she felt was grief; a deep sorrow that could never be comforted. A part of Elizabeth was gone, dead with her husband.
The child John was a healthy baby and was growing strong.

King Herod smiled. It was done, now he could be content once more. He watched the dark skinned girl dance in front of him, her body clad only in wisps of silk. She had been brought here from Africa on the slave trades of the Romans. He slurped the wine from the cup, spilling it as he did so; the red liquid causing rivulets and drips in his beard. He laughed; it was a laugh of deep contentment.
"Drink up, my friends." he said, raising his goblet, "I am a king, a real king. There is no one to dispute it." He laughed long and loud. Few joined him.

* * * * *

Mary was worried. It was nearing time for her purification, the purification that had been laid down in the Torah. She remembered the words for she had been taught them lest she would forget: '*And when the days of her purifying are fulfilled, for a son, or for a daughter, she shall bring a lamb of the first year for a burnt offering, and a young pigeon, or a turtledove, for a sin offering, unto the door of the tabernacle of the congregation, unto the priest, who shall offer it before the Lord, and make an atonement for her; and she shall be cleansed from the issue of her blood. This is the law for her that hath born a male or a female. And if she be not able to bring a lamb, then she shall bring two turtles, or two young pigeons; the one for the burnt offering, and the other for a sin offering: and the priest shall make atonement for her, and she shall be clean.*'

They were living in a tent in the Land of Goshen and Jerusalem was a journey of a week or more away. They had been living in the tent while Joseph was building a small dwelling house for them to live. The Law of Moses must be fulfilled but how could she fulfil it under the circumstances? Mary pondered this for a few days and then spoke to Joseph.

"Yes, Mary, there is no doubt that the Law has to be fulfilled. But how to do it, that is a problem. There is only one Temple where resides the Holy of Holies and the place that we are bound to be purified. Let us pray and ask God to give us the answer."

That night Gabriel came in a dream to Mary. She was standing in the Temple in a part of it that she had never seen before. She looked about her wondering where she was. The great walls of stone were lit by many lamps and to her right she could see a large stone structure and on it was a sacrifice, burning and spitting in the sacred fire; she smelled its pungency. Behind her she could see the great doors, which were closed, and the vast room was empty.

136

Mary could feel the coldness of the stone floor on her bare feet. She was standing in the centre of the room; she turned and faced the front. Before her she saw a raised area with steps up to it; on the top was a platform of about six feet square. There was a doorway that was covered by a very thick heavy curtain. Then it struck her: 'this is the Holy of Holies; I should not be in here.' She was turning to go towards the doors when she heard a voice call her name, "Mary".

She spun around recognising Gabriel's voice. He was standing on the platform at the top of the steps, dressed in his white robes.

"I do not know how I am here. I would like to leave for I am not supposed to be here." Mary said to Gabriel.

"I brought you here, Mary", said Gabriel. "The Lord, our God, bade me to bring you here. There are things that you must know. It is right that you should fulfil the Law of Moses because the Most High has laid it down. But, Mary, you were chosen by He-who-is because you are sinless. If you are sinless then you do not need a sin offering. It is not required: your womb is already purified by the one that you have carried within it. But so that Scripture might be fulfilled and until the New Covenant is established you must fulfil the Law.

Go to Jerusalem with Joseph and the Holy One to fulfil the Law of Yahweh. You will be kept safe. I will go before you to prepare the way. Mary, because you are sinless you may enter the Holy of Holies." Then he was gone.

Mary woke up and wondered at the dream. She woke Joseph and told him.

The journey back to Jerusalem was uneventful and very hot as it had been before. When they arrived, they purchased two turtle doves from the animal sellers that lined the outside of the Temple steps in order that the purification requirements could be met. At the same time they would present and consecrate their firstborn to the Lord.

When the purification rite was performed and the child was presented, Joseph and Mary were walking out of the Temple and began to proceed down the steps; Mary could feel that strange, stark and beautiful feeling all around her. She stopped to look around. An old man approached them, his hair was long and unkempt and he had a staff to aid him up the steps. "May I speak with you?" he said.

"Yes", said Joseph.

"My name is Simeon. An hour ago, I was in my home going about my usual business; when I felt the Lord, our God, prompt me to go to the Temple. At first I did not wish to go but the prompting continued and it became quite strong. I was told that my prayer would be answered when I came. Let me explain that my prayer has been for many years to be able to see the Messiah before I die. I am eighty-five years old and I make the journey from my home to the temple every day. I know that the child that you have in your arms, is the Messiah, the One who is to come. I have waited a long time. Would you give the honour to an old man to hold your child, my lady?" He looked into Mary's eyes.

"Yes, sir, it would be an honour for myself and my husband if you were to hold him." Mary handed him the child on the steps of the Temple. Many people milled about them; their daily business to attend to, they had people to meet or sacrifices to be sacrificed for the atonement of their sins. No one noticed the little group on the steps of the great Temple of the Lord.

Simeon took the child Jesus gently in his arms. His face was a lamp lit up when he looked into the child's face.

"Might I be permitted to kiss the child, my good lady?"

"Please, Simeon, do as you wish."

The old man kissed Jesus on the forehead. Mary could feel the tangibility of the Spirit of the Lord grip them. She could feel it exude from the Holy of Holies and from the heart of her own son. The two were one now and the old man's reverence and piety was drawing it out. Simeon said, *"Lord, now lettest thou thy servant depart in peace, according to thy word for mine eyes have seen thy salvation which thou hast prepared before the face of all people; a light to lighten the Gentiles, and the glory of thy people Israel."* He handed Jesus back to his mother.

Simeon then lifted up his hands, palms upward and blessed them. He looked deeply at Mary and said, *"Behold, this child is set for the fall and rising again of many in Israel; and for a sign which shall be spoken against; yea, a sword shall pierce through thy own soul also, that the thoughts of many hearts may be revealed."*

The woman caught his words like a sparrow is caught in a net. She felt the prophesy in the words and she felt their truth. She felt her soul prepare itself for the truth to come.

Simeon continued to praise God with his hands raised. Some people heard him and stopped to see what the fuss was about. Mary could feel the stark feeling grow stronger.

They stood for some moments praying and were about to leave when a woman began praising God loudly, "May the God of Heaven and earth be praised this day for he has bared his mighty arm for his people Israel. This day we stand in the presence of the One who is to come; he is here among us. This child will carry the word of the Most High within his soul. All you who look forward to the deliverance of Jerusalem, see this day what the Lord has wrought for us." She went up to Mary and Joseph and said, "I am Hannah. I am the daughter of Phanuel. I have lived eighty four years on this earth and for sixty three years I have been a widow, spending my time serving the Lord day and night in the Temple. I have fasted and prayed. And now the Lord has rewarded me with the sight of this child."

*****

Mary and Joseph built a one storied house on a piece of land rented from another Jew who had settled in Goshen. His name was Absalom. He had been a merchant and had travelled into Egypt for many years trading silks. He had brought his family up in the tradition of the Jews and the Egyptians took little notice of the little Jewish community that was forming in their midst. After years of being a trader, Absalom, could speak the language well and he knew how to treat these people; they had wanted to trade and he traded with them. He told Joseph and Mary that he loved this rich, fertile land of the Nile Delta. Notwithstanding that the people of Israel had escaped from this area many hundreds of years, it mattered little to Absalom; this Land of Goshen was his home now. His merchant friends, who were still young enough to be in the business, came to stay with him while they were in Egypt. He had become a wealthy man.

The land that he rented to Joseph and Mary was to the north of his own land, which was situated some thirty miles from Succoth in the Land of Goshen. It was a small plot, one hundred yards by one hundred yards and it allowed Joseph to build the small temporary house, awaiting Heaven's command to return home. It was flat and fertile and was just big enough to grow what they needed to keep themselves alive. They felt compelled to trade the gifts that they had received from the men from the East to purchase what they needed to begin their new home. It allowed them to buy seed, bricks and a few carpenters' tools for Joseph to take up his trade once more. Once he got started making furniture and began to sell it he soon built up a healthy clientele who came to him for all their needs. Absalom too, saw the fine workmanship of the carpenter and employed him on various projects within his own house.

After a year of careful planning and austerity, the small unit of land was soon green with millet, onion, mint and spelt.

A few goats eked out an existence on the wild grasses that grew sparsely in the surrounding area. Joseph built a lattice extending out from the front door of the house to grow grapes to be made into wine. It was not the most palatable of wines but the land gave what nutriments it had.

Mary looked after the plot of land, tending it and watering it while Joseph worked with the wood. On the flat roof of the house she dried her fruits and grains in the sun. The baby, Jesus, grew and thrived. Joseph and Mary lived a poor but comfortable life.

The desert shimmered in the heat and the untrained eye would have been forgiven for thinking it was steam rising from the sand. Apart from the mountains that framed the area, the only high ground was a few dunes here and there that were forever changing their position, building here then pulling themselves down only to reappear somewhere else. In this Wilderness of Zin nothing moved or wanted to move in the intense heat. A very few animals moved about on their daily forages for what little food there was. A snake might find a hapless mouse to fill its belly for a day or two; a desert rat might find a tasty morsel in a beetle but little was to be had on this day. An enigmatic stillness hung like a portrait and nothing moved save the iridescent heat. The sand itself rippled now and again as a rare breeze tripped lightly over it.

It began as little holes, appearing suddenly in the sand. The holes were no bigger than that a twig might make if pushed into it and pulled out again. First there were a few little cave ins, here and there; then a few more and then it grew into hundreds and then into thousands. The desert seemed to break into holes as if someone had given a signal for it to begin and the floor of the desert became like a sponge.

The first locust crawled out; it was hungry. A second, then

a third, then a forth, all crawling, walking seemingly synchronised and programmed to go the same direction. Within minutes an army of the creatures were blackening the sand with their presence and they were all hungry, ravenous and the silence evaporated into the noise. A few stopped here and there to try the odd opportunist grasses that clung to the sand trying to colonise it. The grasses disappeared as though they had never existed. They crawled, walked and hopped in a westerly direction as though some instinct were driving them, their bony bodies well equipped for the task. They were heading towards the Nile Delta.

It was the month of *Kislev* and all in the Nile Delta were preparing for a bumper harvest. It had been a good year. The inundation had begun in *Nisan* and the waters had flooded high. The triangle or D that gave this region its name was deep in water from *Nisan* to *Sivan*. In *Tammuz,* the water rose again. *Tishri, Heshvan* and *Kislev* saw the fields drying and the earth was soft and fertilized. The inhabitants of the Delta would live another year. The Egyptian god Hapi was pleased with the people and had given them his blessing with the high water.

The people of the Nile depended on Hapi's beneficence for their very lives and much worship was given to this god. Only a few years before he had refused to yield the waters to cover the plains or banks of the Nile and famine had hit hard. From its two sources in Ethiopia and the great Lake Victoria, the Nile Delta was inundated with water each year. The waters begin to rise about the month of *Adar. Nisan* sees the rapid rise of the waters that burst the banks to provide the land with a new layer of topsoil, as well as nutrients, that it has carried with it on its long journey of some three thousand five hundred miles. Without the annual floods, Egypt would not exist for the desert on both sides of the Nile would rapidly overtake this fertile region and it was always lapping against it like the waters of a lake.

The Delta with its floods produced the papyrus that is so essential to the life of the Nile peoples. From it is made the mats for the floors of the houses, baskets, sails for their boats in order to fish the river, and the paper that they wrote their hieroglyphics upon. Hapi was good to them.

The millet was turning golden in Ra's light, shone from the sky as his fiery chariot passed across the vault each day. There were no clouds to block it on this day. People greeted one another as they worked in the fields or passed along the sandy roads. Cheeriness hung in readiness for the rich months that lay ahead. They were a glad people.

Mary was in her plot of land weeding and breaking up the soil around the base of the plants. They were ripening well and she was pleased that their efforts were materialising in these plants that would keep them alive for another year. She marvelled at the growth and praised God. Jesus was with Joseph in the workshop, while she tended to the plot. He enjoyed the child who was in the process of cutting teeth. She wiped the sweat from her brow and straightened her back. It was good to work; it was good to be alive to see this growth that was so abundant. As she stood looking out over the plain, she could make out in the distance Absalom's crops, as green and lush as her own.

As she stood resting and admiring the growth around her with her hand shading her eyes, she realized that the sun had gone behind a cloud. She looked up and saw the cloud moving rapidly across the sky. 'It is moving very quickly,' she thought, 'is it going to rain?' As she watched it, the full realisation of what it was gripped her mind. "Locusts!" she said aloud. Then she shouted it. "Locusts! Joseph, a swarm of locusts, there are millions of them. Joseph!"

By the time she reached the house, they were falling on her, hundreds of the insects falling out of the sky. Like rain they fell, landing on everything that was available; that was green. She could feel their bony bodies cling to her skin.

Millions of whirring wings made a noise like many, many stones falling on a metal surface and was almost deafening. Mary had to shout at Joseph through the din, "Where is Jesus?"

"He is safe I have covered him and closed the door. They will not get near him," Joseph said and she was satisfied. She lifted a threshing fork and began to beat the insects that had invaded them like unwelcome guests. Joseph took the broom and joined her.

They beat and flailed the locusts to kill them, to stop them devouring their precious crop; a crop that they had worked hard for, that they needed to survive until the following year. This was a fight against starvation; their own or the locust's. They fought for their livelihood and they prayed that something might be left for the locust always won.

As Mary flailed, the awareness began to dawn. She stopped. The insects continued to buzz and whirr around her but they did not eat her crops. They were *not* eating them.

"Joseph, Joseph, look!"

The man stopped and he, too realised that the insects were not eating, devouring their precious plants. They were simply resting.

"Mary, this is God. He is protecting us. Come; let us go to the child. Let God do his work, he does not need us to help him for he has tamed even the wild beast."

They fought their way through the throng of insects and entered their home.

The people of the Delta did not fare so well. Their god, Hapi, did not save them. The terror from the sky devoured everything that was edible and moved on to find more. The people of the Delta wept and mourned and wondered what they had done to deserve such devastation.

Absalom and his wife Shelomith were looking at the damage all around them. His wife was weeping. The once beautiful fields that had boasted their greenness to the sky were no more. The myrtle tree that had shaded them from the sun was bare. All was naked and Absalom felt the shame. It was good for him that he was so wealthy, others that were not so well off would be feeling the devastation. He thought of Joseph and Mary and their little plot of land. They would be in dire straits for their lives had just begun and they would have nowhere to turn to. This disaster would mean starvation for them. He liked the couple. They were honest and hardworking. They had approached him with sincerity in asking for a small piece of land and he had given it to them. He would have let them have more but they had insisted that they only rent out what they could afford. Their dreams would be dashed now. He would go to them now. He called his servant and asked him to make ready the Arabian horse. He bid his servants to follow him on the slower donkeys that would be laden with food. He galloped away from his home towards the flat plain.

Approaching the rented land of the couple, Absalom suddenly tugged on the reins to brake the horse. The animal had to turn sideways to stop under the force.

The man could not believe his eyes. There, in the midst of the devastation and carnage left in the wake of the locusts, was an oasis, growing happily in the sun. Its fertility struck him like a slap and he slowly walked the horse towards the house. He could see the vines covering the doorway in abundance, the lattice straining under the weight of the produce and the fields behind the house. Golden millet stirred in the small plot gracefully in a stray breeze. He could see the green of the onion leaves. It was like a dream.

"Joseph" he called. "Come out, my friend and tell me what has happened here."

Joseph appeared through the vine leaves that were threatening to take over the whole doorway. He had to bend his head to get under it, its verdant life starkly contrasting the bare land all around.

"What has happened here, Joseph?" Absalom said, his hands outstretched and eyes wide with disbelief.

Joseph shrugged his shoulders, "Nothing has happened here, Absalom."

"I can see that, Joseph. Why has nothing happened here?"

"We prayed while the locusts were here and they did not eat the crops. They seemed to rest on them for a while but they ate nothing. Then they rose into the air and were gone save the ones that we killed before we realised what was happening."

"It's a miracle, Joseph and Mary". Mary had come out onto the porch and was now standing beside her husband, holding her son. The boy was smiling. "Every home in the Delta has been wiped out by the locusts and yours...yours is a haven of green. I came over to feed you. Even now, my servants are on their way with food." The older man began to laugh. When he had stopped he said, "Why is God so good to you?"

—7—

After the locusts, life went on for Joseph and Mary as it had done before. They were settled into their way of life in Egypt. Every morning Joseph would put on his prayer shawl and pray; at evening, he would do the same. They fell into a routine of waking, working and sleeping. They were left alone by the Egyptians and did not seek contact with them only in trading and for Joseph to sell or mend furniture, for friendship with Absalom and Shelomith and the other Jews who lived there was enough for them. They visited each other and remained friends.

The carpenter plied his trade among the people and was

able to live comfortably with his wife and child. Joseph did not become rich for he could not charge the full amount that his work deserved but simply charged what they could afford. He became very popular among the poorer citizens of the area. Joseph was soon able to build on a small work-shop to the right of the house and it eased the burden of working in and around the house. He soon learned some of the language with everyday use and was able to commu-nicate. Joseph was an honest man and many came to re-spect him.

Mary tended her crops and fruits and soon discovered new plants and how to grow them. She too, learned the lan-guage and was able to barter and trade with the best of the women. Her life revolved around her son and her hus-band.

The desert fascinated Mary. Its stillness reminded her of God. God was the stillness that penetrated her and she could feel sometimes his presence with her. At these times, she stopped what she was doing and felt, just felt. It was a deep stillness that penetrated and could take your breath away in its stark clarity. Sometimes Joseph would find her like this and at first had asked her if she was all right. Now he knew and left her to these moments. It seemed that the Living God simply wanted her to experience that presence for her to touch it with her life, with her soul. His love for her was a real thing; a reality that came now and again and it seemed to fill her with knowledge of him. At these times her heart would be on fire as though he had set it alight and from it came the sparks of his love. It was tangible, defini-tive.

She looked east out over the desert and it seemed delicate, yet harsh. The shimmering heat distorted the view and something about it seemed ethereal. She could see an iri-descence that looked like water in the distance as though a spiritual thing hovered over it. She knew it was a mirage but it was still beautiful. She thought about Scripture and was reminded of Abraham when the three men walked towards him. She felt that they walked out of such as this. They were Angels of the Lord and they had told Abraham that Sarah would have a child even though she was past childbearing age. It reminded her of her own visitation from on high. When she looked back now, the events seemed strange and unreal but she had lived through the reality of it all. She was living in Egypt because of it. The child was growing rapidly and at eighteen months was walking. The first steps that he had taken had been a joy to her heart and she and Joseph had laughed with the child when he fell, only to pick himself up and try again. He was a quiet child who learned quickly. He was often in the workshop with his father and was quiet and watchful of everything that Joseph was doing.

Mary looked at Jesus. His hair was growing and would be like hers; dark eyes that shone like the sun and could penetrate; could hold you softly in their gaze. He was playing in the shade of a young Myrtle tree; its glossy leaves caught the sunlight and its white flowers wafted fragrance into the air. She could feel her heart swell with love for the child. Simeon had said that a sword would pierce her heart. She knew that he had meant suffering. Was it because of Jesus she would suffer? She did not feel any suffering now. She was happy. She went over to the child, picked him up and kissed him.

The sun seemed hotter in Egypt than it had been in Israel and every day seemed to run into the other and their lives were blessed with good crops and good friends. They had helped in any way they could after the locusts had destroyed the crops of everyone. All had marvelled and had spoken of the miracle. They longed to return to their homeland. Mary had not been able to inform Anne, her mother, of this journey and she would wonder what had happened to them. She longed for her mother too. Mary wanted her mother to see the child.

* * * * *

In the hill country of Judea, Elizabeth was slowly coming to terms with the gap that Zechariah had left in her life with his death. She still mourned his love. She remembered the life that they had built together over the years, the heartache of relatives dying and the joy of the marriages of the younger ones. His life as a priest that took him away from her and up to Jerusalem; she had accepted the life that God had provided for them and had never complained at his absence. If the Lord wanted her husband to do his work, then she would not, could not, stand in his way.

Their life without children had been difficult but this little one on her knee had made up for the difficulty. They had accepted fully that Elizabeth would never carry a child and this, too, was offered to the Living God.

At times she could feel Zechariah standing beside her and had turned, saying something to him but soon realised that he was not there physically but perhaps spiritually. She had wept at these times for grief was a spirit that seemed to attack her when she least expected it to, when she thought she was strong again. She sometimes dreamed of Zechariah. When she dreamed of him they were young again; young and free of the burdens of life and they were in love. She had wanted no other man and he had wanted no other woman. She felt again the rare love that they had together and could feel it with her like a friend, always there. She did not want to share these reminiscences with anyone, not even Tamar, for they brought her close to her husband once more and Elizabeth wanted that more than anything. She needed to remember the life she had had with Zechariah; she needed the memories to take his place for a little while for they eased the burden of his death. She needed to hold on to what she once had for the grief threatened to take all away. She did not want to lose herself in it.

Tamar had proved herself to be a good friend. When Zechariah's death had been announced to her she had collapsed in grief and Tamar had taken over the whole running of the house and saw to the welfare of John while she was incapacitated. She had often spoken to Elizabeth when all had left her to her grief; they had homes to run and families to raise and when grief is not your own it's best to leave you with it. Tamar had not left her but did practical things and was always there when she needed her.

Elizabeth felt that death had taken the very best of her and she held onto what she had left.

The City of David was slowly picking herself up, after all this time. Rachel still wept for her infants, the innocents that she had lost. No decree or notice had come from Jerusalem as to why the slaughter was necessary and no apologies. Neither Rome, nor Jerusalem thought it of much worth to keep a record of.

Anne raised herself up stiffly from the fire. Her back ached. Years of bending and stretching and being a wife were taking its toll. It was easy enough to cook for one but she did not always want to eat the food. It was always better to eat in company, someone else's talking and laughing made you hungry somehow. It made you want to eat. She moved across the room to the table and sat down. She took a handful of the millet and began to eat it.

Where had her daughter gone? Why was there no word from her? Was she dead? These thoughts crossed the woman's mind again as they had done for over a year. She had watched Mary and Joseph leave for the census. Mary had waved happily and shouted, "You will see your grandson soon, mother." She had watched them from the end of the street waving and she had shed a few tears. Then nothing. That was coming two years ago. What had happened? No travellers from Jerusalem had brought any news of them. She had sought and asked all who had been to Bethlehem and the surrounding areas for news but to no avail. She had heard about the massacre in Bethlehem but she could not quite bring herself to believe that her daughter and her husband and the child were dead. She was sure that if Mary were dead then she would feel it within her heart. The child that she carried was the precious one and no harm would come to him. If all was well with the child and his parents, he would be nearly two years old now.

She picked a grape from the small bunch in front of her. She would not give up hope. She had spoken to the Rabbi on several occasions and he had tried to reassure her that all was well. If this child were the Messiah then all would be well.

But it had been all this time, surely Mary would have found some way of contacting her. Anne sighed, "I pray that the Lord is looking after them all."

The last bout of madness had bothered Herod. He lay now on his couch, free again from the bonds and the gag. He felt weak. His personal physician, Simon, had told him that the disease had advanced and that no medicine on earth could help him. They had shipped rare herbs from all over the world to make medicines that only eased the disease; it did not cure it. There was no cure.

He had to begin to make plans to divide his kingdom among his three sons, Archelaus, Antipas and Phillip. That would not be easy. He was afraid that the Hasmonaean's would try to claim the throne again. The Hasmonaean's were a Jewish family who had been kings and priests for a thousand years. Antipater, his father, had secured good jobs within the family of the Hasmonaean's. Herod's brother, Phasael, was given the job of prefect of Jerusalem while he was made military prefect. Within the royal circles that he had moved in, he caught sight of the lovely

Mariamne and was determined to marry her. He divorced Doris and became engaged.

Then the Parthians moved against Judea and overthrew Hyrcanus, then king of Judea, and set up Antigonus, another Hasmonaean, as king. As the war continued and Jerusalem fell, Herod escaped with his life and his family while the king and Phasael were captured and put to death. Herod made sure his family were safe and travelled to Rome to persuade the Senate to give him the title the 'King of the Jews' and to put Judea under Roman rule and allegiance once again. Surprised by their consent and his own powers of persuasion, he had returned to Palestine and had begun a military assault in Galilee and slowly took control of his kingdom. In the third year of his campaign, he captured Antigonus and set up his own dynasty with his new bride, Mariamne, and began to rule. He was full of insecurities.

Since his sons had begun to grow up it had been difficult keeping them apart. He could feel their greed, all were vying to be his favourite son. He had been on the brink of having them killed a few times. Killing was easy for Herod. He had done it before. Aristobulus, his brother in law and high priest, had stood in his way. The murder charge of Aristobulus in Egypt he was able to talk his way out of. He had told Joseph, his uncle, to execute Mariamne, his wife, and her mother, Alexandra, if he were to fall foul of the death sentence. That fool of a man could not be trusted to carry out a simple order. Joseph had told Mariamne what Herod had planned to do; she was none too pleased. When Herod returned from Egypt he was met with the scorn of his wife. When he questioned Joseph he was told that he had done it to prove Herod's love to her. Stupid man! Herod suspected that Joseph was having an affair with her and though he could not prove it, had him executed anyway. His insecurities had grown and he trusted no one; all were out to get him, no one could be trusted.

Mariamne had become cold towards him after this and would not let him share his affections with her.

He thought about her now. He had loved her from the moment he saw her. Had he not divorced Doris for her? Ah, he had loved her but he had heard the stories of her infidelity and he believed them; she could not live. She had become dangerous to him. She knew too much. He had been sorry for that, all the same. He had felt so guilty over her death and would have forgiven her. He remembered how he had become so filled with remorse after the execution and had watched it because he had wanted to see the guilt on her face as she died but it had not come. He had wept. He had wept for days and had become ill with remorse. He realised, too late, that his obsession with thinking that everyone was out to get him, had cost him dearly; it had cost him his love. This did not change him, he felt more insecure.

Herod laughed and made himself more comfortable on the couch. 'That fool Alexandra had thought he was dying. Silly woman! Was he to be surrounded by imbeciles all his life?' She had presumed to think that he was going to die and her greed and ambition had come to the fore. She pushed Mariamne's sons, Alexander and Aristobulus, forward to claim the throne. He put her to death for that presumption. It was then that people began to fear him and after that he got his way. He became a king at last; a real king that was obeyed.

Then the syphilis had got him. He remembered how it had erupted in great oozing sores all over his body. It was the worst thing that could have happened to him. He remembered how he had moved out of Jerusalem as the sores got bigger and oozed more. He had to hide. The physicians told him that there was no cure for it. He had felt ugly and he had allowed few to see him for months. The sores disappeared and left the madness in its wake.

Sometimes the madness frightened him. It came with such

intensity, when he least expected it. After it had subsided, he would become paranoid about dying. It was not so much the dying that caused him to fear, it was the place that he might be going to.

He shuddered now for there was nothing in his life that he could call good to bring to a god he would face when he died. He did not really believe in a god, he only prayed when he needed something to go his way. He prayed in the Roman temples but that was only to appease the Romans. His prayers were never answered anyway, so he made things happen his own way.

Most of the murders that he had committed had suited him but others, like Mariamne, were mistakes that he regretted even now. He still had nine other wives and he had nothing to fear from them; they had towed the line since his execution of his favourite wife, Mariamne.

He had rid himself of the new king of the men from the East. So much for their wisdom! He laughed. 'I have even the power to wipe out the Messiah'. The children in Bethlehem were not an issue with him. The Jews were breeding like rabbits and who would miss a few male children? He thought about his own children.

Archelaus was the one of his three sons who showed the most potential and he had tried to school him in the kingly ways. But Archelaus was arrogant and full of pride. He saw all as his personal servant and saw himself as somewhat of a god. Herod smiled. Archelaus was the one for Jerusalem. He could keep the Romans happy. He was just like them. But Archelaus did not see. He was like his father, suspicious of everything and everyone. He had not inherited trust, like his father. He would rule Judea and Samaria. Antipas he would give Galilee and Phillip Iturea in the north. All would be happy with their little arrangements. Of course, he would not tell any of them that he was dying. No! They would try to help him to die. And Simon, he would have his tongue cut out.

154

He knew that when he died there would be few to mourn for him. They would not remember his exploits for he knew they hated him. They would not remember the Temple that he had given them. Caesarea was beautiful the way he had designed it, in honour of Caesar, and of course to curry his favour. His architecture would be forgotten or at least not recognised. How could he convince them that a king needed to be cruel in order to better serve his people? 'I am sure I could come up with some little plan to help them to mourn me.' Herod laughed and his laugh echoed around the chamber. All who heard it wondered what he was planning now.

The days rolled into weeks and the weeks in turn rolled into months. Mary and Joseph continued to live in their exile in Egypt, always waiting for Gabriel's promise that he would return to tell them that it was safe to go to Israel again; this they wanted more than anything; they longed for that day. But they knew that God was watching over them for they had many proofs of his love. They were sitting outside in the evening coolness in the shade of the myrtle tree. Jesus was asleep on Mary's lap. The sun had burned its fiery path to the west of the world, burnishing it with the red gold of sunset. Its wake was like a path, a burning trail in many long streaks, as though to tell where it had come from and where it was going. They were discussing the events of the day and were enjoying the rest after the days work.

"Will our house still be in Nazareth, Joseph?" Mary asked.

"I hope so, my love. I asked the Rabbi to watch over it while we went to Bethlehem for the census, although that's two years ago now. Anyway he may have rented it out for its upkeep. I think that someone actually living in it will go better for it than it being empty. I am sure he does not know what to think."

"And my mother too. She surely must have heard what

happened in Bethlehem after we left." Mary shuddered remembering what the people had told them when they went to Jerusalem for her purification. "If she realises why it was done then she might add things up wrongly and presume we are dead. All those innocent children, Joseph, I shudder to think what might have happened had you not listened to Gabriel's warning." A tear fell silently down her face. She was praying in her heart again for all those who had to suffer on their account. She had prayed every day for them since she had been to Jerusalem. She looked down at Jesus and a love welled up inside her. She kissed his sleeping face.

Joseph said, "Yes, so innocent. What could Herod have against poor innocent little ones? By the way, when I went to see Absalom today he told me that his friend, Ishmael the merchant, had come to see him for he had been selling and buying in Memphis. The rumour is that Herod is dying. They say that he cannot last much longer. He pretends not to be ill but every one can see it. Mary, it may be that soon we can go home."

"Oh that is good news, Joseph, but I will continue to pray for him that he may yet see the light of God before he dies."

"He is a cruel man, Mary, and his exploits are known far and wide but you are right. We must pray for him to God to ask for his mercy. The Lord our God is merciful to those who ask. We will ask for Herod."

"Think, Joseph, of the life that we have here and all that has happened to us, if we did not have God with us we could never have done it alone. Many people believe that they must do what they must alone and they do not know the benefits of God close. If we do what God wants us to do; if we obey his commandments and the promptings within our souls, then we cannot go wrong. It is he and he alone that must guide our lives. But we must lose the stubbornness of holding onto things that do not matter. I am

156

convinced, more and more every day, that we must be prepared to give up, at a moment's notice, everything that would hinder God in his work. Our own people Israel; look at how they disobeyed God for forty years in the desert. I wonder what would have happened if they had obeyed. Would they have reached the Land of Canaan sooner? I think when we obey God then things happen sooner."

Joseph looked at his wife, "Yes, my love. I have always believed that obedience to Yahweh is the way to live life. He has done marvellous things for us. I admit that sometimes it is not easy but when we put away our own will then it becomes easier somehow. Before I had the dream where Gabriel told me that it was alright to take you for my wife, I was stubborn in my pride and I thought that my life had been ruined but since I have accepted God's plan then I am happy, more so than I could ever have believed possible."

Mary smiled at Joseph; her heart was overflowing with both sadness and with joy. The sadness of the innocent children of Bethlehem still lingered within her heart and the joy of the life that they had together. It was not an easy life being exiled from those that you loved and the land you were born in but it was worth it knowing that God's hand was touching you and holding you up.

"Look at the sun, Joseph! Is it not a beautiful sight?"

Joseph turned to look. The sun was a great fireball that was just about halfway below the horizon. It looked as though it had burned itself out. Its orange body could be looked at and it seemed to cast long fingers of light as if in defiance to the shadows that followed it. They watched it until it set. They knew that God had placed the sun in the heavens to give them light and he and he alone would bring it back tomorrow. He would give them light to see their way. But now the dark had come and there was rest to be had. God had created the darkness so that we might rest in it to be refreshed enough to work and toil for our daily bread. God is good.

The people began the *Shema.* In chanting tones they said aloud: " *Hear, O Israel: The Lord our God is one Lord: And thou shalt love the Lord thy God with all thine heart and with all thy soul and with all thy might. And these words, which I command thee this day, shall be in thine heart and thou shalt teach them diligently unto thy children and shalt talk of them when thou sittest in thine house and when thou walkest by the way and when thou liest down and when thou risest up. And thou shalt bind them for a sign upon thine hand and they shall be as frontlets between thine eyes. And thou shalt write them upon the posts of thy house and on thy gates.*
And it shall come to pass, if ye shall hearken diligently unto my commandments which I command you this day, to love the Lord your God and to serve him with all your heart and with all your soul, that I will give you the rain of your land in his due season the first rain and the latter rain, that thou mayest gather in thy corn and thy wine and thine oil. And I will send grass in thy fields for thy cattle, that thou mayest eat and be full. Take heed to yourselves, that your heart be not deceived and ye turn aside, and serve other gods and worship them; and then the Lord's wrath be kindled against you, and he shut up the heaven, that there be no rain, and that the land yield not her fruit and lest ye perish quickly from off the good land which the Lord giveth you.
Therefore shall ye lay up these my words in your heart and in your soul and bind them for a sign upon your hand, that they may be as frontlets between your eyes. And ye shall teach them your children, speaking of them when thou sittest in thine house and when thou walkest by the way, when thou liest down and when thou risest up. And thou shalt write them upon the doorposts of thine house and upon thy

gates: that your days may be multiplied and the days of your children, in the land which the Lord sware unto your fathers to give them, as the days of heaven upon the earth. Speak to the children of Israel: tell them to make tassels on the corners of their garments throughout their generations and to put a blue thread in the tassels of the corners. And you shall have the tassel, that you may look upon it and remember all the commandments of the Lord and do them and that you may not follow the harlotry to which your own heart and your own eyes are inclined and that you may remember and do all my commandments, and be holy for your God. I am the Lord your God, who brought you out of the land of Egypt, to be your God: I am the Lord your God.' "

It was the prayer that would begin the service on that day and all days in the Synagogue. The people had gathered to praise their God. The Synagogue was the place in Jewish life that the worship and religious study of the *Torah* took place. It was not the Temple, for the one place on earth that housed the Holy of Holies was Jerusalem, but was the place in every city and town that the Jews gathered for the instruction on the Law of God. It was a place of social gathering and had been known to be the courthouse for petty trials.

Now, Joseph stood in the Synagogue that Absalom had built, praying his prayers. For Joseph, this was the place where he met with his God and learned about him. It was the place of contact with him. It was good that Synagogues were like little satellites of the Temple for they kept those in exile somehow close to the Holy of Holies and gave them a place to praise God. He looked around. He could smell the incense being offered to the Most High and it was a beautiful fragrance to his nose; he inhaled deeper to get more of it. All the worshippers faced Jerusalem with hands upraised to show the prayer attitude. Some rocked back and forth. The room was a rectangle with a small platform on the long wall facing the Holy City. On it was an alcove, which housed the Torah Ark or *Aron Kodesh* within a cabinet, which in turn held the Sacred Scrolls, wrapped in linen. Some of these would be taken out and used in to-day's service. Slightly above the *Aron Kodesh* is the *Ner Tamid* or the Eternal lamp symbolising the command to '*keep a light burning in the Tabernacle*'. Near it on the floor, was the eight branched *Menorah,* eight branched because it would be improper to copy the Temple's seven. Along the other long wall and behind Joseph were stone benches and these were not enough for the people to sit on so many sat cross-legged on the floor. The places at the front were usually kept in reserve for the Elders who were devout and respected men and who regulated the policies of the Synagogue. All sat down on the floor when the *Shema* was finished. The *Chazzan* then rose from his place and went to the cabinet that held the Scrolls. As is the custom, before the service begins a member of the congregation is chosen to read from the Scrolls. Joseph had been asked and was feeling honoured to perform this task before the Lord. The *Chazzan* opened the doors and pulled aside the curtain and lifted out the Scrolls. Their wooden handles were beginning to wear with use, Joseph noticed, and thought he might offer to make new ones. The *Chazzan* brought the Scrolls with great reverence to the pedestal called the *Bimah* where Joseph would go to read the sacred words. The Scrolls were opened to the place that was to be read for that day and Joseph got up to do his duty. The interpreter went with him to translate the ancient Hebrew into Aramaic so that the hearers could better understand. They walked to the centre of the room. Joseph took the Scrolls in his hands and began to chant the words on the page before him. " *Therefore the Lord himself shall give you a sign; behold, a virgin shall conceive and bear a son and shall call his name Immanuel. Butter and honey shall he eat, that he may know to refuse the evil and choose the good; for before the child shall know to refuse the evil, and choose the good, the land that thou abhorrest shall be forsaken of both her kings. The Lord shall bring upon thee and upon thy people and upon thy father's house, days that have not come, from the day that Ephraim departed from Judah; even the king of Assyria.' "*

Joseph closed the Scroll. His heart was bursting. He wanted to tell the whole congregation gathered here in their skullcaps and prayer shawls that this fragment of Scripture was true, it had happened. He wanted to shout that the child that he called 'son' was none other than the Son of God. They still waited on the Messiah; they waited for the One to come who would fulfil the words of the prophets and he was here, living among them. Joseph's heart was overcome as he took his place once more among the worshippers and tears of joy filled his eyes and brimmed over. It was not his place to tell them. The one that would tell them was on his way to make the Lord's paths straight. He kept his head down and wept in his joy. Would they believe if he told them? Would they believe the overwhelming miracle that was happening in his life at this time? Would they believe that his fifteen-year-old wife was the virgin that Isaiah had spoken of? Here and now he could tell them but he knew in his heart that, even though they were devout and good men, they would not believe.

The speaker was speaking of the words that had been read. He was saying that the Messianic text in Isaiah referred to the political leader who would spring from God to become the King of the Jews. He would wipe out all the enemies of Israel and bring peace and prosperity in his wake for Israel. 'The Anointed One' or the one that God had anointed with the oil of gladness for the special role, would come to free them and was the one that Daniel had prophesied to come in the future. This Messiah would live forever when he had freed them and his rule over them would last forever.

Joseph thought that he had concealed his tears from all in the Synagogue but Absalom had seen them and was surprised. He wondered at Joseph's reaction to the reading of the Torah and when the people had left the place of worship, he called Joseph to him.

"Joseph, my son, I commend you on your reading of the Torah. It was very clear and these ears of mine are slightly deaf."

"Thank you, Absalom." said Joseph.

Then Absalom said in a low voice, pulling Joseph closer by the prayer shawl. "Your tears were not unnoticed by me. Tell me, why would you weep at these words? A Jew is nurtured on words such as this. We have all heard them time and again, they are part of the blood that flows within us, why should they make you weep so abundantly?" He looked straight into the younger man's eyes.

Joseph's gaze was steady back at the old man who had become his friend.

"My friend, I was overcome by the reading," Joseph said "I think I realised for the first time just how good the Lord our God is to send us one who will give salvation, at last, to the people of Abraham."

"In my long experience, Joseph," Absalom counteracted, "of buying and selling, I have come to know that when a man is sure of something then he cannot hide it. No matter how hard he tries, there is always some telltale sign that leaks to the surface. Joseph, my son, it is how I plied my trade. I could tell whether the one who was buying my silk was going to buy at my price or not. I could move the price up or down according to the signs I received from him. I used these signs often to make the profit that built my house here in Egypt. I live here because the Egyptians love silk and are willing to pay high prices in order to get what they want.

Joseph, since you and Mary and the child have come here, I have watched you. When the locusts devastated all in the

Nile Delta, there was not one leaf of your crops touched. You were able to live like a rich man while others starved. You know something, Joseph, but you are not saying."

"In truth, Absalom," Joseph put his hands out palms upward, "I am a man of prayer and in my prayer the Lord our God has given me a task. I must fulfil that task to the best of my ability. To lie to one of such wisdom and experience as yourself would not be prudent and my respect for you would be tarnished. I believe that the Holy One is in our midst. Even as we speak, he lives. I cannot give you proof of this but within my heart I know it to be true." Joseph looked at the older man.

"My son, I have believed and waited all of my life for the Messiah to come. At Synagogues all over the world where my travels brought me, I have pondered the Messianic texts most of all. I believe that he will come, though when I do not know. I believe that he could be here for the ways of the Lord, our God, are not our ways. You say that you came here to settle after the census that took you to Bethlehem because you are a son of David. You did not return to Nazareth, to your hometown, but came here to Egypt. You have told me that you will only rent the land from me for as long as you need it. After your return from Jerusalem, you brought the news of Herod's murder of the children of Bethlehem. Every newborn male to be killed was the order from Herod's own lips, yet your child was born in Bethlehem about the time of the massacre and yet you, shall we say, miraculously escaped to come here.

When you came to my house asking for land to rent, you said you were a carpenter but you had no tools to ply your trade yet you had moved from Israel. Even the poorest of men who have a trade will have his tools, they will be like another arm to him. Joseph, I do not wish to pry, but I am an astute man. I have the eyes of an eagle or so I have been told. I will not question you further for if you do not wish to tell me then I cannot make you. Forgive an old man his wonderings and know that I believe that you are an honest man and I have come to trust you. Whatever the Lord has called you to do I believe that it is a most holy task and I wish you to know that I will serve him in whatever way I can. If there is anything that you need in this task of yours, then ask me, in the name of the Lord, and if it is within my power, I will give it to you. I will not ask to know why, I will simply believe that the Lord, our God, wishes it and that will be enough for me." Absalom bowed a deep bow and left the Synagogue.

It was the Sabbath, the day that the Lord had called as a day to abstain, to rest: a day when men rested. Joseph and Mary used the Sabbath as a day in which to reflect upon his word and to become renewed for the long week of work that lay ahead. God had given the commandments to Moses on Sinai: *'Remember the Sabbath day, to keep it holy. Six days shalt thou labour, and do all thy work: but the seventh day is the Sabbath of the Lord thy God: in it thou shalt not do any work, thou, or thy son, or thy daughter, thy manservant, or thy maidservant, or thy cattle, or thy stranger that is within thy gates. For in six days the Lord made heaven and earth, the sea, and all that in them is, and rested the seventh day: wherefore the Lord blessed the Sabbath day, and hallowed it.'*

God had made it clear that the Sabbath was to be observed and that all who served him would continue to observe it. He himself had rested on the seventh day and he called his created to do the same. Nothing had changed since the far off days of creation. It was given to remind Israel of its years of imprisonment by the Egyptians when it could not rest; could not obey its God. All were to observe the Sabbath and all must rest. No one was to gather any firewood. In the past, those who violated this Law of God were excommunicated or even stoned to death.

Mary and Joseph observed it. They did no work and lit no fire, nor did they walk further than a Sabbath walk. On this Sabbath, they watched the Egyptians going about the work as though there were no God in the heavens to rule over them and give them Laws. They would still come with their repairs of wooden furniture on this day and Joseph would explain again to them of the observance of the Sabbath, required by his God. The old woman who stood before him knew but was trying to persuade him that she needed the roof of her house repaired now. They were outside his house at the workshop. It was in the afternoon.

"But, Potiphar, I will come to you in the morning. I cannot come now because it is Sabbath and my God requires me to rest on this day," said Joseph.

She shaded her eyes with her hand and looked up at him. "Joseph, does your God not also require you to help your neighbour? Or is he a cruel God who would see an old woman suffer?"

"No, Potiphar, my God is a good God who has lain down the rules about what he wants. He looks after his children who obey him. Your gods, do they have rules? Are there certain things that you cannot do?" he asked.

Potiphar threw up her hands. "Joseph, my god, Hapi, requires me to be good to the people around me by helping them out of trouble but I can see that your God does not. All right then, Joseph, I can see that you are not going to give in and I admire you for that but will you come tomorrow early and repair my roof?"

"Ah, Potiphar, at last do you understand?" Joseph laughed, "But of course I will repair your roof and just to show you how good my God is, I will not even charge you for the repair. I just cannot do it today, that's all."

"Ah you Jews and your observances! What you need is Hapi. He is a god whose love for his people is shown in the floodwaters of the Great River. He provides sustenance for his people. He shows his love for us in a real way.

Your God seems to be caught up in all these observances and laws." She threw up her hands again and said, "Can I expect you tomorrow then? Or has your God planned something else for you to do?"

Joseph laughed again. He looked at her wrinkled face and saw her toothless grin. There was kindliness in her that was in her smile. He had known this woman since he came here. She had been one of the first to come on hearing that he was a carpenter. She had brought her chair for him to mend the leg. She had told others of his work and through her many had come to him for the work that he could do. He had grown fond of her. She had always tried to bully him into doing things her way but he had seen through her.

"I will be with you at sun up. In future do not let those sons of yours play on the roof of your house if it is so delicate. That way you will not have to come to me on the Sabbath."

"Ach, you and your Sabbath, I am going home to feed my sons. An old woman like me has no rest from sons or carpenters." She waved at him and walked away.

"I will see you tomorrow, Potiphar, after the Sabbath." Joseph laughed. He felt a movement behind him and he turned. Mary stood there with Jesus in her arms. "Is this how you treat our customers, Joseph?" They both laughed. "It is strange," said Mary, "how very few understand the concept of the Sabbath and how important it is. Surely other gods must demand a rest day? But it seems not."

"Yes", said Joseph, putting his hands out to take the child, "But then one must believe in the true God to understand what the Sabbath means. And soon this child will teach all who come to him what it means to know the one true God."

The land of Egypt continued to yield its fruit to Joseph and Mary and they felt that God's promise to return them, to

166

their own land would be soon. They lived in God in the Land of Egypt and they lived in his hope. They needed nothing else.

<h1 style="text-align:center">—8—</h1>

Herod could feel himself weakening. He knew death was near for he could feel it breathing on him. Its long fingers reaching out to probe his weak body, he could feel it touch him and try to grasp him to tempt him into its embrace. Death was coming for Herod.

There were days when he felt guilt accompany death, as a cohort. All those whom he had killed directly or indirectly, came to him more frequently in dreams. Marianne would come to him in her seductiveness; touching him with her beautiful body; caressing him with her love. And he would give in to her charms and fall headlong into her arms until she would scream at him that he had murdered her, killed her on his whim. Her seductive fingers became accusing, pointing at him and she would not stop.

He would wake up screaming and in a sweat. Servants and slaves would run to him thinking that it was the madness come over him and he had to beat them off. His days were now spent in an endless round of trying to get off his couch, trying to stand and walk even a little way through his palace. The Romans came little these days unless he sent for them. They seemed to know that he was dying and stayed away. But he forced himself to get off the couch and had the servants carry him to where he wanted to go.

Lately too, there had been the demons who came to him when he was alone. They taunted him with his sins. They told him that, unrepentant and guilty, he was ready for them; he was ripe for their picking. With their long gaunt bodies laughing at him they charged him full of fear and terror. He did not stay alone anymore. He called his wives and made them sit with him, hour after hour, until he had had enough of them and their prattle. He took whatever herbs were available to kill the pain or send him into a soft dreamy world where nothing mattered and the demons did not come.

His head was full of schemes to make them all pay. He was still suspicious of all around him but he did not have the energy to have them killed. He lived in a nightmare, a haunted, melancholy world that made him want death, even though he feared it and what might lie beyond it; at times like this all he wanted was cold oblivion.

The harvest in the Land of Goshen was plentiful that year. It was the third year of Joseph and Mary's exile. The Egyptian sun had tanned them and they were healthy and well. Looking now at the lush growth of their little plot to which they had added another one hundred yards square. With what they could sell of their produce, and with the carpentry work, they had been able to rent more land off Absalom and some of the profit that they made went towards the upkeep of the Synagogue. It was a small donation compared with some but it was all that they had. Absalom had insisted that they take all the land for nothing but they would not hear tell of it. They were standing in the workshop in the cool of the early evening. The heady smell of plant life heavy in the air.

"But, Joseph, it is only a small parcel of land and it makes little difference to my land overall. You are a good man, Joseph, you have become like a son to me and what father charges his son rent on a small bit of land?"

"No, Absalom, I will not hear of it. A man cannot give land to the first stranger that just happens along. No. Absalom, we are grateful that you waited the first year for the first produce and until I became established in my trade."

"Joseph, I do not mean it as an insult but the rent of this acre of land makes little difference to my pocket and it is tucked away here in this corner. I would probably have forgotten that it was here until you and Mary chose it. I can do without the money. Take it as a gift then."

"Absalom, I have come to respect you very deeply. You have become a friend to Mary and myself. But if you insist in this I will hand the land over to you again and you will have to rent it out to someone else!"

"Ah you Nazarenes, you always had a reputation for your hard headedness. It is no wonder the Romans found Galilee very hard to conquer. All right, my friend, I will take your rent but I will take it begrudgingly from you. You Nazarenes drive hard bargains." The two men laughed and drunk from the cups of water that Mary had brought them earlier. It quenched their thirst.

Absalom looked thoughtful as he looked to the west to see the sun set. Evening was running in as rapidly as a messenger bearing bad news. He looked at the younger man.

"I told you some time ago that I would not interfere in your affairs and I will not break that promise." He looked at Joseph as if for permission to carry on and when Joseph nodded assent he said, "As you know, many of my fellow merchants often come to stay with me when they trade in Memphis. I see them at least once in a year, unless it is a year in which trade is bad. A few days ago, Ishmael, my friend of long standing that you have heard me speak of before, came to stay with me. When he comes he sometimes brings some interesting news, which he hears along the way. He is from the Mizpah region, outside Jerusalem. He brought me news that you may or may not find interesting. The talk in and around Jerusalem is that Herod is close to death." He stopped to look at Joseph. There was just a hint of interest on the younger man's face. He betrayed nothing to the older man.

Absalom continued, "They say that the syphilis which he

169

has, has progressed so rapidly that he will die soon. He sees no one now, not even his beloved Romans. Ishmael trades often with his nine wives and they gossip quite a bit. One of them, Abihail, has told him that life in the palace is a nightmare. They must take turns to sit with him and he rants all day in his drugged stupor. She tells him that the king is not long for the world so the trade with them may soon cease. This is bad news for Ishmael but it may be good news for others."

Joseph said nothing for a while. He seemed to Absalom to be far away in his thoughts. There was silence. Then Joseph came back to the present.

"Did Ishmael say how long that it might be?"

"In cases like this a man could linger for quite some time. As you know there is no cure, but Herod is a large man and has eaten much rich fare in his lifetime. It may be that he will linger for a while."

Absalom looked long at Joseph. He felt the love spring to his heart. Only a short time had he known this man but he had found warmth and holiness and friendship in him that he had found in no other man. Absalom knew that somehow Joseph and Mary being in Egypt had something to do with Herod and he knew that the news of Herod's impending death was good news for Joseph. He looked directly at Joseph.

"My son, I will miss you when you return to Nazareth."

When Absalom had gone and the darkness had descended over Egypt, Mary and Joseph sat near the small fire in their home. The firelight caught the shadows in the corners of the room and danced with them giving the impression that someone was moving around it.

"...this means that we will go home soon, Mary."

"I know, Joseph. It feels good to know that this exile is soon over and we shall see the Land of Israel once more. Although many here in Egypt have been good to us; this has become our first real home for we did not have time in Nazareth to build one. We have sung the song of the Exile in this strange land but somehow it has become our home, our security and the Lord has been good to us. His promise to us has come to pass. He has carried us in the palm of his hand like he has done with our fathers. For all the time we have lived here I have felt a sense of belonging, a sense of home but now you have spoken of this I cannot feel that part of me anymore. I am longing for home. I am longing for the land of my fathers."

"Yes, my love, I feel what you are feeling," Joseph said. "The song of the Exile is almost at an end. When our forefathers heard the news that Pharaoh was letting them go, they must have felt this strange feeling, a feeling of letting go, yet a feeling of belonging. We have made a life for ourselves here and we did not notice how much we came to be a part of it. We wanted to return all this time but we did not notice that we were taking root. I shall miss all the friends that we have made. Absalom has been good to us and I shall miss Potiphar's insistence that I break the Lord's Laws to do her work." He smiled at the thought of the old woman. "You know, Mary, I think that Absalom has guessed the truth. I think he knows about Jesus."

"Yes, I know. I have seen him watch Jesus. He looks deeply at him as though trying to find some sign or other that will tell him that what he has worked out in his mind has come true. I feel that we should tell him before we leave. At least that way we can thank him for his kindness to us and his search will be over."

"Yes, from what he has told me it has been a life long search for the Messiah. I think that he believes already but is just not sure.

You know, Mary, it seems strange to speak of Jesus as the Messiah. He is a child, a little three year old. Like any normal child he takes delight in discovering all the things that he can do. He seems to love to learn to do new things.

The way he watches me in the workshop! Sometimes he is so quiet and watchful that I can easily forget that he is there. I look up from my work, surprised to find him there and he has watched and absorbed every movement that I made." Joseph laughed softly into the fire lit room, "I think he is trying to take over my trade."

Mary laughed too. "My life seems filled with him at this time. He watches me too. When I am tending to the crops, he is with me with his little stick, breaking up the soil. He is becoming a real little man."

Herod knew that no one would mourn him when he died. He knew that the Jews hated him. His despotic ways had only served to turn all away, including the Romans. In his blurred mind there were only thoughts of revenge; he wanted a revenge that would be remembered for centuries. He already knew what he would do. Even after all that he had done for them, they would be glad of his death, he knew. But he would make them remember him. He could not stop his death but he could make it felt. Thirty-seven years he had ruled Israel and they were not going to forget.

"Bring the scribes to me, now, you insolent dog." He shouted this to a slave who was pouring some wine into a goblet for him. The servant's eyes went wide in fear and, setting the goblet and the jug on the floor beside the couch, ran off immediately to bring someone to Herod's assistance. He had fallen foul of Herod's temper before and did not wish to do it again.

In his chamber now, Herod looked about him. These walls he had designed and built; the stone shipped and carried on the backs of slaves from all Israel and beyond. He had given himself the very best because he deserved it. The rich silks and damask, that were now billowing gently in a stray breeze that was coming through the balcony, were shipped from Damascus, Egypt, Arabia and Mesopotamia;

beautiful textured, patterned cloth that enriched the beauty of the room. The furniture had once stood as cedar trees in the heart of Lebanon and floated in log rafts from Tyre and Sidon into Joppa whose bustling harbour was Jerusalem's seaport.

With the scribes came a litany of learned men, lawyers, doctors, astronomers, priests, Pharisees and Sadducees all skulking into the king's presence bowing and scraping for fear of their own lives. They were a colourful collection of men and their clothes, jewellery and perfumes showed that they were handsomely paid for their services, whether by Herod or the people. Herod was irrational and volatile.

"Sit by me and hear what I have to say. I have paid you group of mongrels long enough. It just may happen that one order that I give to you will be carried out to the letter. I know the talk within the palace is that I am dying. Well I am informing you officially that I am not. I am merely ill. Within a few months I will be free of this couch and all those who thought I was dying will pay dearly for their insolence.

Now begin to write. I wish you to send letters to all the principal heads of the families throughout Israel. You will tell them that I wish their presence here in the palace within the week..."

"But, your majesty!" A thin, grey-faced man spoke.

"Shut up, you dog. Do not interrupt your king or I will have you flogged to death. You will wish you had been thrown to the lions. That goes for any of you who try to interrupt me again. I do not have time to listen to your excuses. Now where was I...ah yes. They will come here, all of them to be in my presence within the week. If any fail to turn up then he will incur my wrath and be put to death on my orders. He will wish that he had turned up." Herod laughed. It was a long drawn out laugh, a laugh of madness. "And let this be done now. Send the messengers on the swiftest horses from my own stable. I wish to have a feast with all my friends around me. Now go, and for once carry out my orders with the intelligence that you are paid for."

All Herod's officious men fled the room.

The Senate had gathered to discuss the impending death of Herod and what should be done about Judea when he died. The old men sat in boredom and their minds on other things while Augustus filled them with reports from his officials in Jerusalem. They expressed concern about who would be 'King of the Jews' on Herod's death.

"It will be one of his sons, of course. Herod's dynasty is not yet founded and it will take all of his wit, now, to keep it running after his death. Herod has three sons and all of them are potential kings but not one of them has the military prowess of his father. Look how when I bestowed the title upon him it only took him three years to sit on the throne. It was a major achievement on his behalf. He has built towns and cities and temples and even a few towers for his own amusement. He has kept Jerusalem in check these last years and has saved us the bother. It was a good idea to put Herod on the throne. Herod's sons know little of how it is to run a country, of that I am certain. One or all of his sons will take over the running of the country and we will keep an eye on it. But, gentlemen, from what I know of Herod, I would rather be his pig than his son."

Within the week all the heads of the great families of Israel had gathered in Jerusalem at Herod's request and as Herod's guests and none were happy but none defied him. There was none of the usual pomp and ceremony attached to their arrival and many arrived unannounced and under cover of darkness. The younger, fitter ones came on horseback and the older ones came by cart. They had left all their official business to come here and they were none too pleased about the summons to the palace. They gathered now in Herod's throne room awaiting their king. They had been waiting two hours and were in a foul mood. Although they feared him, they were indignant and many discussed how outraged they were and how they would tell him that he could not treat them like this.

When Herod entered it was in a sweep of white robes. His face was heavily powdered to try to disguise the illness that devoured him. The rouge that had been put on was overdone and Herod looked like a clown in his bid to look healthy. No one spoke of their indignant feelings when he entered. His body was bloated and he was surrounded by an aura of perfumes, which caught the breath of many.

Herod's guests were shocked by his appearance and the shock was audible. Eight strong servants, whose muscles could be seen straining under the pressure of his weight, carried his bloated body in on a litter. The king of the Jews was a mockery to behold.

"Ah, my pretty friends," he said sarcastically, "you have arrived at last. I would like to begin by thanking you for giving up your time for me. It flatters me that you could love me so much. As you can see," he swept a hand across his body to indicate, "the rumours about my impending death are quite untrue. I am as healthy as ever and still very much in control of my kingdom." He looked around the room at the sea of faces. He was the master of their fate now, he would make sure that they knew that he was still king. If Israel was not prepared to mourn him then perhaps they would mourn these; its most highly respected citizens. He smiled; at least he would not die alone. Inside himself he could feel the weakening body begin to sag. He could feel the sweat of exertion and the lack of opiates devour his strength. The sweat was forming beads on his forehead and caking the powder. He must get out of here. He must get it over and done with. Herod clapped his hands. From every door that led out of or into the throne room -

Roman soldiers appeared, running into line the walls of the room. They stood to attention awaiting Herod's orders. Gasps of horror greeted their arrival from the men who stood there; realising that they were a fly caught in the spider's web. They shouted at Herod and he smiled. He held up his hand for silence and the men quieted hoping that he would give them some explanation for his behaviour.

"Well, my pretty friends, I believe that you will cooperate with me on this little scheme. I am so glad of your assistance." Herod's eyes burned at them. He bowed his head to them in a mock gesture.

Herod then addressed the centurion who had come up to stand beside his litter, which was still on the shoulders of its bearers. "My good Maximus, will you please escort these friends of mine to the racing ground and show them to their quarters. And be sure that they are well secured." Herod addressed the now concerned group of men. "My friends, please go to your quarters with these good soldiers. Do not resist them for they have my express orders to kill any of you who do not cooperate with them. I thank you, gentlemen, and I bid you farewell for it is doubtful that we will meet again."

The air of fear hit the room and it was audible like the beating of a drum. The men began to protest loudly to Herod about their treatment and to demand to know what he was going to do with them. Some complained about being under the power of the hated Roman. But Herod was already being carried out on his litter. They put him back upon his couch, exhausted and weak. He fell into a deep sleep.

Matthias Ben Eli entered the Temple. He was the High Priest and all turned to look at him in the outer courts as his assistant priests went ahead of him to clear a path through the crowds that gathered there for Morning Prayer.

His white robe looked dazzling and spotless in the morning sun and he had a blue cord around his waist. Matthias Ben Eli proceeded up the steps to the inner court.

In his retinue that day were some students whom he was teaching. He would take them into the inner court so that he could explain the teachings on the Altar of Sacrifice and how it should be done according to the Law of Moses. He would teach them the precision of the Law.

As he and his entourage entered the doors of the inner court he saw it. The small statue of Diana, the Roman goddess, had been placed along the wall. Matthias Ben Eli froze. He froze into the ground below him. Profanity had entered the inner courts of the Temple of the Holy One of Israel!

"Who brought this pagan thing into the Temple?" Matthias Ben Eli said turning away from the statue, its naked breasts blinding him, "The Lord our God is the One God!" he said and tore his robe from the neck to the waist. "Who put this abomination here?"

Priests began to move from all parts of the Temple now into the inner court. A small humble priest walked up to Matthias Ben Eli and said in a low voice, "Forgive me, Matthias Ben Eli, but Herod's men arrived here a few hours ago and said that Herod had given them expressed orders that this statue be placed along the wall in the inner court. I presumed that all of you knew for it is usual that Herod calls the priests before he carries out his plans."

"Herod! That explains it. Do not worry," he said placing a hand on the other priests shoulder, "it is not your fault."

He turned then to the students, who were open mouthed at the events that had taken place, "My sons, learn a fine lesson here today. This Sanctuary is Yahweh's Temple and no other god is welcome here, not even on the whim of a king. Take this...this abomination out of here and smash it on the street. Herod has gone too far. He is not content with surrounding this Temple with pagan gods, now he invites them into God's own Sanctuary. Remove this thing from my sight and the sight of God."

"I do not think that you can do that," said a thick voice behind the group and it echoed in the high walled chamber. They turned to see whom it was that had spoken. A man, a Jew stood there and they recognised King Herod's bodyguard, Caleb. His thickset body rippled with muscles.

"This is the Temple of Yahweh and it will not be desecrated by pagan gods as long as I am High Priest." Matthias Ben Eli said to the big man.

"Then I must report this incident to the King," said Caleb.

"Do that." the High Priest retorted.

Caleb turned and left them and went out through the gate.

Two hours later Matthias Ben Eli was arrested along with his students and priests who had been with him that day. On Herod's orders they were tied to a stake and burned outside the walls of Jerusalem.

King Herod called his sister, Esther, to him. Herod was weak and low and in much pain. "Esther," he panted for breath "when I am gone, have the Romans execute the men in the racing ground. I have told Maximus that he must obey your word if I send you to him. Israel will not mourn me but they will mourn them. Will you do this for me, Esther?"

"Yes, my brother" she said.

As the sun descended to make way for the darkness, King Herod began to scream. All his family were gathered there to be with him, his nine wives and his three sons. Some of the younger wives cried at the sight of the King but most just watched.

He lay on the couch, pallid and weakened by the disease as it devoured the last of his body. His liver could no longer function and the bile within it began to leak out through the perforated walls and his innards began to burn. Poisonous waste material burst through the weakened walls of his organs and his body screamed. A stench arose from him and few would go near him. Herod screamed for three hours as the fluids of his body burned their way through him. He fell into a state of unconsciousness and a gurgling sound invaded his breathing. Many within the palace were glad. After one hour of the gurgling Herod gave three short puffs of breath as though trying to catch it, then he stopped breathing altogether. All present watched as the colour and the life drained from his face. Herod was dead.

Gabriel stood before Joseph; his eyes seemed to penetrate him. As Joseph looked about him he saw that he was in his own home in Nazareth. He saw a fire burning and a pot hung over the flames boiling and bubbling its way to be ready. The room looked welcoming.

"Joseph, son of David," Gabriel said, "this is your home in Nazareth. See, it waits for you. There is no reason now for you to stay in the Land of Goshen for the one who sought to do the child harm is dead. Herod is no more. Take the child and his mother and return to Nazareth for the rest of your life awaits you. Do not be afraid, Joseph, for the mighty hand of God protects you."

After Herod was dead, Esther sent for Maximus. She had deliberated for a long time on what she was going to do. She had spoken to no one of what her brother had asked of her. She would go against his final wish. She would not order the men in the racing ground to be killed.

"Maximus, the men that are imprisoned in the racing ground, you are still guarding them, is this so?"

"Yes, mistress, they are locked in the stable on the late king's orders. They are guarded well."

"Maximus, let these men go. Release them and return their

belongings to them and make sure they are unharmed. Let them go; enough killing has taken place here."

"Mistress, your brother told me to take my orders from you they will be released immediately." Maximus bowed to Esther and turned to walk out the door to do his duty.

Absalom reined in the horse and came to a stop outside the Nazarene couple's home. The day was almost done and he could feel the first coolness of the late evening begin. He welcomed it. He had seen Joseph that morning at the Synagogue and Joseph had asked him to come. As Joseph spoke, Absalom could tell by the younger man's eyes that it was something of grave importance.

"Joseph! Mary!" he called out.

The door opened and Mary came out through it carrying Jesus. The child was smiling at him.

"Hail, young Jesus," he said and rubbed the boy's hair, "have you been in the fields again with your mother?"

"Yes," the boy answered.

Mary said, "Shalom, you are welcome, Absalom. Please, enter our humble home." Mary went into the house. Absalom followed her.

The day drew to a close and the child fell asleep on Mary's lap. She carried him to the couch and placed a blanket over him in preparation for the cold that would come later.

"He is a fine child, Joseph, he is growing up well, strong and healthy. I think he favours you, Mary, he seems to have your quiet mannerisms."

"Yes," Joseph agreed, "He is growing up rapidly and yes, I think he has Mary's eyes too."

They fell into silence for a moment and Absalom broke it, "I am sure that you did not just ask me here to give me a meal and talk about the good growing weather, did you?"

"No, Absalom, you are right. I asked you to come here so

180

that I could tell you that we will be making preparations to return to Nazareth as soon as we can."

The words shocked Absalom, even though he knew that the couple were not settling here. "I must say that I am sorry to hear that," he said simply.

"Even though we knew that we would never settle here, we have grown to love the place and the friends that we have made. It will be difficult for us to go. Our thanks and prayers are with you, Absalom, for you have helped..."

"Joseph, please do not speak of these things. Anything that I did, I did it out of friendship, please do not ruin it by thanking me. I would have done more but your hard headedness would not let me." They all laughed softly so as not to wake the child.

"I hope you did not bring me here to thank me," said Absalom.

"No. I asked you here to tell you something that you might not believe but maybe what we tell you may help you in your search."

Absalom looked at the couple that sat across from him.

"I...Mary and I," he caught hold of Mary's hand and held it, "would like to tell you a story. The story is a true one but you may find it hard to believe. It is a story that is unfolding as we live it." Joseph looked at Mary. "Mary, will you speak of the first part." Mary nodded and began to speak. She told Absalom all that had happened to her, about Gabriel, about Jesus and about her visit to Elizabeth. When she had done, Joseph spoke of his dreams and why they had come up to Egypt.

Absalom listened to every word, nodding and understanding. He stopped them now and then to ask questions, clarifying what they were saying. He smiled sometimes and seemed to go to a far off place as though thinking, remembering.

When Mary and Joseph had finished telling their story, Mary got up and poured some water from an ewer into three cups and brought it to the two men.

Absalom remained quiet for a long time, and then finally he spoke. "I have heard all your words. I have heard of your lives since all of this began. I have placed your lives into the search that I have made and it fits. I have had much confirmed and, like an old dog, I am learning new things. I have no doubt that what you are telling me is true. The child is indeed the Messiah. You have made me a happy man and my heart is overflowing with the good things of God. The prophet's words: '*He shall be called a Nazarene*' are now about to come true.

Another piece of Scripture that you have not mentioned that is running around inside my head: '*For before the child shall know to refuse the evil and choose the good, the land that thou abhorrest shall be forsaken of both her kings.*' I believe that part of this prophecy has been fulfilled with the death of Herod and I believe that before Jesus grows into a man the other part will be fulfilled. I thank you both. You have given an old man much joy."

Mary and Joseph sold off some of the things that they had gathered up over a period of three years in preparation to return to Nazareth, others they gave away. It was spring in the Land of Goshen and they had not yet begun to plant. The land was ready for anyone who would care to take it over. Yahweh had given them happiness here and they thanked him for it.

Three weeks later they were ready to take on the journey back to Nazareth. They had said goodbye to all the friends that they had made; they would not forget them. Potiphar cried that day and hugged Mary as though she were her sister.

"Don't you forget me" she told Mary "and I won't forget you."

"Potiphar, I will never forget you, you will be in my

thoughts and prayers and I will pray to Yahweh for you."
Mary told her.

"Yes, please do that. He is really not a bad God, after all."
They all laughed at that and Potiphar most of all.

When they reached Absalom's home they stopped for a last word. They asked for the old man's blessing for their travels. He did not feel that they needed his blessing and said so. But they insisted and at last he gave in. It was hard to break away from the old man that they had come to know as a benefactor and a father but the sun was climbing steadily in the sky and they needed to be on their way. He wept as they left him. They began their journey with joy remembering the words of the exiles.

'By the rivers of Babylon, there we sat down, yea, we wept, when we remembered Zion. We hanged our harps upon the willows in the midst thereof for there they that carried us away captive required of us a song; and they that wasted us required of us mirth, saying, Sing us one of the songs of Zion. How shall we sing the Lord's song in a strange land?'
Joseph and Mary had sung the Song of the Exile with their father, David, and with him they were able to sing now the songs of rejoicing, the Song of Returning. They were being led as their fathers had been led. Again, Israel would walk in the Wilderness of Zin but this time they would not be lost; they would obey the Lord's command. They would reach the Promised Land. Once again, Israel had been in exile and they did not know it. Only a tiny proportion, a representative, was required this time.

The rigours of the road home did not seem so difficult for they had a spring in their step; they were free and they felt that freedom within them. It was like a bird in a cage given freedom; at first it hesitates, not believing; then it spreads its wings and there are no bars, nothing to hinder it. With wings outstretched it feels the air under them and allows the current to lift and carry; flapping smoothly, it lifts into the air and is gone. Mary and Joseph felt no bars now, no restrictions.

Tingeing the joy was a little sorrow for the life that they had built in Egypt but they felt the stronger for having lived it. The joy was the stronger.

They travelled by Succoth once more and there found a caravan that was going to Jerusalem. It was a larger caravan than before with about one hundred and fifty people making up its body. It was made up of merchants going on their trading routes into Israel. Some would travel further to Rome and beyond that into Europe, wherever the trade took them. These merchants were like nomads and found little soil anywhere in which to put down their roots except when, like Absalom, they got tired of the road and found themselves a fertile spot in which to grow. The traders felt the calling within them to go; to travel and take their wares with them; to see new lands and far off places and did not mind the boredom of getting there. It was in their blood.

Their camels and donkeys were prepared now and ready to go. The couple watched as one trader tried to get his animals into a straight line in order to follow the others. There were five donkeys and seven camels all laden with bundles that they presumed were cloth. The animals went anywhere except where the man wanted them to go. When he would get one settled another two would move out. This went on until the caravan as a whole began to snake its way along the first stages of the Way of Shur and on towards Jerusalem.

Mary looked out across the Wilderness of Zin. She could see its beauty, its dancing heat. It was like a voice that beckoned you into it; only too late you discover that there is nothing there, only heat and no water, no vegetation, no hope. It was not a land for people; only snakes and lizards could eke out an existence there. It was formidable but it was beautiful. God had created it for a purpose and man had not yet found that purpose. They travelled onward towards Beersheba.

Mary remembered the stories from the Scripture about Hagar who wandered through the Wilderness of Beersheba after Abraham had sent her and her son, Ishmael, away from him. Hagar had run out of water and knew that if they did not have water then both of them would die. Hagar placed her son under a bush to save him from the sun, she wept and cried out to God. She heard the voice of the Lord call out to her saying that he had heard the child crying and she was not to fear but to take him with her for he would be the father of a nation. Then God showed her a well of water and she was able to fill her water bag with it and give the boy a drink.

'There were many who were led by God to do his will,' Mary thought, 'it is when we do his will that his will for us comes to pass.' She thought about Hagar. She was put to the test and believed. The Lord had led Hagar just as he was leading her and Joseph into safety with the child, Jesus. 'God has a plan for all of us,' Mary thought, 'it is only when we do not obey that things begin to go wrong.'

—9—

They stayed in Beersheba for two nights so that the merchants could trade their wares to the people of the town. Mary and Joseph did not go into the town, preferring instead to remain outside it. There was a well near where they pitched their tent and they were able to get water. Mary filled the goatskin bag that held the water and kept it cool. A man had drawn the water for her and she thanked him. A voice behind her spoke and she turned to see a woman who was dressed in a blue robe with a white veil about her head.

"Hail, I have not seen you at this well before, are you new to Beersheba?" The woman smiled in a friendly manner.

"No, you have not seen me for I am just passing through on my way to Jerusalem and on to Nazareth," Mary smiled back at the woman. It was good to speak Aramaic again.

"Ah, you are with the caravan that arrived yesterday, then you will have heard little news. You probably have not heard that Israel now has three kings! You would have thought that one Herod was enough but now we have three of them!"

"Did this happen after King Herod was dead?" Mary asked of the woman, "You see we, my husband and child and I, have been living in Egypt and are only now coming home."

"Yes, only days after the old king was buried it was announced by the Romans that we would have three different provinces with three different kings ruling them." The woman had a round face with full lips. Her eyes were sparkling now as she told Mary the news. "I suppose," she went on "they had to split it up to save Herod's sons from fighting over it. We have Archelaus over us here. He rules Edom, Judea and Samaria" the woman lowered her voice. "Let me tell you that he is worse than his father. Already people are beginning to complain about him. He is not really a king though he just calls himself that. He is really called an Ethnarch; I think it means governor. The talk is that Augustus told him that if he ruled well he would get to be king. I think that the Romans only want someone to keep us Jews out of trouble. Well, he wasn't long in his new position when there was some trouble in the Temple in Jerusalem. Some people were complaining about the way things were being run in it. Well, there was an almighty war and there was about three thousand Jews killed, all going about their daily prayer, minding their own business and Archelaus' men slaughtered them. They say that he replaced Joazar, the High Priest, with his own half brother,

186

Eleazar. You would think that he could not do that but he did. As far as I heard they sent all the important men from all around Judea and Samaria to Rome to talk to Caesar about him. Things were really hot here for a few weeks." She lowered her voice again, "You dare not say a word around here, you are likely to get your throat cut! Some people around here support him, you know!" The woman stopped talking for a moment and Mary began to wonder if she really wanted to hear all this. "Let me think now," she went on, "ah yes! Philip was given the north territory, Iturea, and Antipas is ruling Galilee. He's not a bad sort, or so they say. I say if he's a Herod then he's got something up his sleeve. Between you and me, I don't think any of them could rule a herd of sheep from what I've heard!"

The woman laughed at her own humour and Mary laughed with her. She had finished filling her jar and had placed it on her head to carry it to her home.

"Well it was good to talk with you but I have a family to feed and water so I must go now. My husband says I talk too much anyway. I wish you peace on your journey and that you find what you are looking for with the help of God. Shalom to you."

"Thank you and Shalom to you too," Mary called after her. The woman walked away leaving Mary alone with her thoughts.

She told Joseph when she returned from the well what she had heard. He too had heard the stories of Archelaus' brutality and cruelty to the Jews and even the Samarians.

"Mary, what are we to do. I do not wish to travel on in case there is trouble. From Beersheba to Jerusalem they say that the road is rife with bandits now and Zealots. They are trying to make a bid for freedom. They say that they are attacking everybody. They will even kill. There is so much unrest here now that Archelaus has become Governor. I do not know what to do." There was deep concern in Joseph's voice.

"It may be that we should stay here in Beersheba a little while, it might blow over again. We will pray and ask God. Joseph, he has taken us this far, we cannot stop believing in him now. I know that we are surrounded by danger once more but we must continue to rely on God."

"I do rely upon him and I know that he will take us from danger as one plucks a fig from a tree. I want you and Jesus to be safe."

Mary looked at her husband. He was worried for their safety. Even a caravan could not hold enough security against what might be ahead of them. 'Sometimes when the danger surrounds us,' she thought, 'it seems that God puts us in more danger but he will take us out of it again.'

She thought of Hagar; her son, Ishmael, was to be the father of the Arabs. When Hagar felt that she was in danger and at her last ebb, God was concerned and reached out to her. Hagar had named the well that the Lord had shown her: *Beer Lahai Roi, 'The well of the Living One who sees me'.* God had allowed her to go into the danger of the wilderness to show her that he was there, waiting to help.

"Joseph," she said, "I am thinking of Hagar in the Wilderness of Beersheba. God helped her when she and Ishmael were in danger of dying of thirst. She named the well, 'the well of the Living One who sees me.' Does God not see us too? Will he not help us? We must wait for him to show himself to us. We will wait here. Let the caravan go on tomorrow and we will wait on the Lord for he has mercy on all those who call on him. If it is not the time to go to Nazareth, then we will wait."

"You are right, my love. God is good to those who are in trouble. We will wait and see his promise to us."

It was night in the Beersheba outskirts where Joseph and Mary had pitched camp. They lay awake under a star-filled sky marvelling at it and listening to the night sounds all around them. The caravan had left for Jerusalem three days ago and they had let it go to wait for the Lord's guidance. They were talking about Nazareth that seemed now far away because of the danger and yet they were so close here in the far reaches of the Promised Land.

"It will be good to rest when we get there, to not have the worry of travelling" Joseph was saying. Jesus was sleeping between them for warmth.

"Yes, it will be good to see it all again. I would like to visit Jonathan and Sarah when I return, Joseph. I hope that his leg has healed. Poor Sarah must do everything on her own. I know that Jonathan cannot help his situation and I have seen him look at Sarah and feel ashamed that he cannot look after her and the children. It must be painful for a man who cannot provide for his family. I feel sorry for him but Sarah loves him and will carry on until his leg is healed. I pray God that they are happy."

"A man is not happy when he cannot work, Mary," said Joseph, "it is the way of things. It must be the same for a wife who is barren. She must feel the loss of the children that she cannot give to her husband."

Mary began to notice that something was different. She sat up. The fire that they had lit earlier to ward off the cold had burned low and a night breeze was cowering the smoke that rose from it. She looked all around her at the night, listening, feeling.

"What is it, Mary?" said Joseph, sitting up.

"I don't know but I feel that feeling that I get when Gabriel is near me. I have not felt him since we left Egypt. I know that he is here. It is a strange feeling but with it he seems to announce his presence. I have felt him close to me and I feel him here in my heart and all around me."

Joseph looked at his wife. She was radiant. Even in the darkness, with only the light of the stars, he could see her face shine. She was now, in this moment, a heavenly creature. She had been touched by God and marked by him. She would be his forever. He could see her Lord in her eyes and she was bursting with joy. Mary spoke suddenly bringing him out of his thoughts.

"He is here," she said simply.

Joseph turned to where her eyes were fixed. He saw the Angel whom he had come to know in dreams; the one who guided him. Gabriel was shining in the darkness of the night. He had become a friend to them, a guide in the midst of the turmoil all around. Joseph began to feel the strangeness that Mary had spoken of and it penetrated him. Heaven was revealing itself to them on this waste ground outside Beersheba.

"Mary, Joseph, I bring you greetings from Heaven!" The waterfall that was his voice began to tumble from his mouth and appeared to be all around them and they were captivated and held by it.

"You both must carry on to Nazareth for that place is safe. Do not worry about the road ahead. I will be with you with my shield and buckler and the two-edged sword of the truth of God. Go by way of Hebron, Jerusalem and take the road to Jericho. Keeping to the banks of the River Jordan you will reach Scythopolis. From there go to Nain and into Nazareth. That is the route that you must take. You will be safe. The enemy would not think to look within his own camp. Fear not for the chosen one of God is held safe by God's own hand." He indicated to Jesus who was sleeping peacefully between them. He bowed to Jesus and left them.

They did not speak to one another for a little while. They savoured the taste of Heaven that had been in their midst. They felt its mystery and its wonder and it was still palatable.

It was Mary who broke the silence of the night. "We must leave at sunrise, Joseph. All is well now and nothing will stand in our way. We have relied on the God of Israel and he has taken us out of the snares of evil."

The next morning, before the sun rose, they set out for Hebron.

Jerusalem, the city of God on earth; they could see it before them. They approached south by the Valley of Hinnom and they could smell the refuse and the dead animals that continually burned and rotted there. Smoke from the fires wafted up into the still air of mid-morning, burning, continually burning, all that was the waste of a city. Only those who were poor came near this *Gehenna* searching in the mounds for any tasty morsel of food.

As they wound their way down to the Essene Gate keeping a good distance from the fires and the smell, Mary noticed that Jesus was not walking beside her, nor was he with Joseph who led the donkey in front of her. She looked around, peeling her eyes for sight of her child.

She saw him some distance back up the hill. She was about to call his name when she saw that he was in no danger but he was looking. She called to Joseph to wait and walked quietly up the hill again to retrieve her son. He stood there looking over Jerusalem; his face was bright with joy. He heard her approach and smiled at her. Mary knelt on the stony, hot earth and pulled him to her. He nestled his head on her breast and pointed in the direction of the Temple.

"Abba, mama, Abba" he said.

Mary looked at her son, puzzled. She looked at the Temple and back at him. "What did you say, my son?"

The boy spoke excitedly, "Daddy, my daddy."

*****

Looking north from the Essene Gate, it was impossible not to see, in the distance along the Kidron Valley, the latest

191

crucifixions that the Romans had performed. These were thieves and murders or deserters, indeed anyone who crossed the path of the Romans the wrong way. They would hang on their cross until they died. Little attention was paid to them unless it was someone who was infamous and had made a name for themselves in the public eye, then the people of the City would gather in groups to watch the spectacle. The victim's family would sometimes be allowed to stay with the victim, depending on the mood of the soldiers who were on duty.

For a Jew, it was a deep shame to hang upon a tree and this scene of crucifixion was a sign to the world of the occupation of the Romans who had little respect for the Jewish God. For Yahweh had told them: *'...his body shall not remain all night upon the tree, but thou shalt in any wise bury him that day; for he that is hanged is accursed of God; that thy land be not defiled, which the Lord thy God giveth thee for an inheritance.'* First the victim would be flogged to hasten eventual death then he would be made to carry the cross to the site of crucifixion. Some were simply tied to the cross and left to die of starvation. Those who were nailed would be offered a drink of sour wine to help deaden the pain. Charitable women in Jerusalem usually provided this.

The criminal would be placed on a length of wood with a crosspiece for the arms. The feet rested on a tablet or block of wood and Roman soldiers would then nail the feet either together with one nail or separate with two nails. Nails would be driven into each hand and, to secure the body further and stop it from falling forward, the arms would then be tied with rope to the crossbeam.

Death was intense and agonizing. The jagged wounds made by the nails and the whips would swell which resulted in inflammation and fever. The heat of the sun would aggravate the fever causing an insufferable thirst. The arteries of the head and stomach were surcharged with blood and a throbbing headache would ensue. With the body in trauma the mind would become confused and filled with anxiety and dread. At some stage convulsions would begin to send tremors through the body tearing at the wounds, adding more pain to the already pain-racked body. The body would become exhausted and finally the victim would become unconscious and death was not far away. Depending on the victim, the death of crucifixion might last thirty-six hours. Sometimes death was hastened by breaking the legs. At other times a hard blow to the chest near the armpit would be given, again to hasten death.

They entered Jerusalem by the Essene Gate, which was well guarded by Roman soldiers. The soldiers were spot-checking. Every ten or twelve people who entered were stopped and searched. The little family escaped the searching and were able to enter unmolested. The crowds that entered with them, all had their business to attend to and complained at the Romans when they were stopped. Tension hung in the air like a mist. Mary and Joseph travelled up a narrow street that was lined with two and three storied buildings. It was cramped with people and Joseph carried Jesus while Mary led the donkey.

The street opened out into a 'T' and they turned left. They heard the sound of bells ringing and a group of lepers passed them. Their fingerless hands clutching their bells to warn people of their approach. They had been begging food in Jerusalem and those donating it would leave it at a safe distance for all were afraid of the disease. The group numbered about six. One woman had no foot and walked on the stump that used to be her ankle. At their approach, the crowd who were milling in the street trying to get their business sorted, suddenly parted as the Red Sea, when Moses commanded it to, to make way for the dreaded disease! The lepers had the right of way while the crowd clung to the buildings on either side trying to get inside, out of the way.

A smell of spices caught their nostrils and they knew that the market was near. They could only imagine the bustle of the crowd; each calling out something different to his neighbour, buying, selling or simply watching.

After travelling a short distance they turned down a street to the right and which was not as narrow as the other had been. At the end of the street they could see the Pool of Siloam. They needed to get fresh water for the journey for they would not stay in Jerusalem. They filled up three goat-skin bags from a fountain nearby and left Jerusalem by the Fountain Gate and went into the Kidron Valley to make their way to Jericho. They feared to stay longer than was necessary.

They skirted the walls of the city and passed by the Spring of Gihon which was the spring that fed the Pool of Siloam. The spring was intermittent in its yielding of water but served its purpose. They passed close to the Horse Gate which served those entering and leaving the city.

It was a place where female prostitutes plied their wares, painted faces upturned to any who came their way, undulating their bodies to best show them off. The male prostitutes too, gathered there, though not as many as the female. The Romans and the Greeks were known to sometimes prefer men in their close encounters. They veered off north east into the inferno of the Kidron Valley which was merciless in its heat. They travelled slowly across it stopping often to shade themselves and to drink water. They wanted to be far away from Jerusalem before nightfall.

The road to Jericho was a quiet and winding road. It was the usual haunt for bandits to attack travellers for it passed through rock and desert land. The gnarled and rough hills on either side lifted up steeply and rose away above them and it would have been easy for a robber to attack from the vantage of the hills. Mary and Joseph saw no one on the road and they knew Gabriel's protection.

The family passed by Jericho, 'City of Palms', and travelled onwards, up into the Jordan valley and were surrounded by mountains on either side. The city was fabled to be the oldest inhabited city in the world. The Romans had plundered it in the early days of Herod's reign but he had returned it to its former beauty later, with his skill of design. They could see from the road where they walked the lush and verdant growth of the date palms, banana trees, balsams, sycamore figs and henna. Although little rain falls in Jericho, it is an oasis within itself amid the rocky wilderness that surrounds it. The mountains felt protective and safe. Sometimes along the way they were able to find a cave where they could cool for a while in the blistering sun. The heat was intense but they travelled slowly, keeping within the shade of the mountains and hills where they could. They sweated profusely in the heat.

When they could see the summit of Gilboa, they knew that they were in sight of Scythopolis and were glad. Thinking of Jesus in the heat and stopping every two to three hours, slowed their progress, but Mary and Joseph did not care, they were almost home. They could feel Nazareth in the distance calling to them and they had only a few miles to go.

The woman was on the roof of her small house checking her drying clothes. 'The sun is hot on this poor old woman,' she thought, as she straightened up to ease her back. She shaded her eyes with her hand to look out over Nazareth. The town had grown since she had come here to live from Nain. A blushing young wife of fourteen, she had left her mother and went to live with Joachim in his mother's house. His father had died some years previously and she had never known him. His mother, Sharon, had lived as a widow, bringing up her son and daughter without the help of a husband. Joachim's sister, Ruth, had married and was living in Magdala, to the North.

Living with Joachim's mother all those years had not been easy, for her fingers and joints had become increasingly useless with arthritis over the years. The woman, at times, was in terrible pain and her fingers were gnarled and twisted out of shape. Anne had felt sorry for her mother-in-law and tried to help her in whatever way she could. As was her duty, as daughter-in-law, she took over the running of the house, which she did not mind, but Sharon became more bad tempered as the pain in her joints increased.

Anne would find Sharon weeping with pain and would go to her to comfort her. The woman accepted the comfort from her daughter-in-law and would allow Anne to put her arms around her while she wept. These occasions were rare. But Anne had loved the woman and often prayed for her.

As the years passed and Anne did not produce children it became evident that she was barren and her shame had grown. Joachim did not seem to mind but Anne would cry herself to sleep at night and pray desperately to become pregnant. It did not happen.

Sharon had died twenty years ago and Anne was sorry to see her go. Still there were no children and Anne had resigned herself to her barrenness. Life went on; she cooked her husband's meals, worked in the house and, in due season, she tended the vegetables in the garden. Joachim worked in the fields for a farmer on the outskirts of Nazareth and would bring home some of the vegetables grown there as part of his wages. Anne was able to sell some of these to make a little extra.

When she turned thirty-five, Anne began to realise that there were changes in her body that she had not noticed before. She put it down to the change of life that all women must go through. It saddened her for as long as her body remained able to bear children there was always a chance that she might fall pregnant. She resigned herself yet again.

But she was not changing; she was with child. And about seven months after she noticed the changes she gave birth to a beautiful little girl whom she named Mary, after her grandmother. Her prayers had been answered and God was good to her. Her joy was complete.

Mary grew up to be an only child but she was a daughter who brought to Anne's latter years a great joy. She had watched her daughter, fascinated to see a creation of God grow from a helpless infant into an adult, able to do many things for herself.

As she looked over Nazareth now, Anne could never recall a time when she had to chastise the girl. She had always been willing to do whatever she was asked. She never complained; she simply did the work that needed to be done. Mary was a good girl and she had made a good match in Joseph. He would always be good to her.

She thought again of the time when the Angel had come to Mary. It seemed so long ago now. 'Was it only three years?' Mary had been so willing to accept the child in her womb, whatever the consequences. She believed in God and would never believe that he would let her down. It was unthinkable to Mary. Her faith in Yahweh was like Mount Sinai, strong and immovable.

She remembered too, Mary's smile. It was a gentle smile that always hung on her lips, it was always ready to be given to whoever needed it. Anne missed that ready smile for it lifted and brightened her heart. Mary had always watched for her if she was out, bringing her a drink to quench her thirst or bathe the dust from her feet.

'Oh God,' Anne prayed in her mind, 'where is my daughter?' The pain in her heart was there again and nostalgia played about her. Tears broke from her eyes. The woman knelt, tired of believing that all was well and afraid to believe that her daughter was dead. Anne sobbed aloud.

Nazareth was like a jewel embedded in the green, grassy slopes that made up the valley in which it lay. Its few towered buildings caught the mid-morning sunshine. Mary's heart leapt within her when she saw it. It was like searching for a coin that was precious to you; you swept and swept and lifted all that it could have rolled under. The searching caused a pain in your heart because you wanted your coin. There was a longing inside that could never truly be satisfied until the coin was found. Now the longing in Mary's heart was satisfied. She was home. The long exile was at last truly over and they could be a family again, a real family, living in their native soil. It was like a long drink of cool water after a hot day's work in the fields and she drank deeply, gulping, to quench that thirst, that longing, that was embedded within her, as Nazareth was in these hillsides. The tears fell unashamedly down her cheeks. The fields were already pregnant with the seeds that would burst forth into life that would, in turn, feed the inhabitants of the town.

"Oh, Joseph," Mary said through her tears, "is this not the most beautiful sight?" They were standing on the hillside, looking north.

Joseph was holding Jesus and he put an arm around Mary pulling her to him. "Yes, my love, it is the most beautiful sight that I have seen for a long time. It is home. It is the place that I did not want to leave and the place that I wanted to live with you and Jesus. This town is the heart of my life. I have grown up here and I have only left it once, to go into exile. I never want to leave it again." He looked into the face of the child he held in his arms. "Look Jesus," he said, "this is the place where we lived before we went to Egypt. We are going to live here again. You will grow up here and I will teach you how to work with wood. You will become a carpenter here and you will..." Joseph stopped and his excitement died. He realised that Jesus would not live a normal life for God had other plans for him and earthly plans were not for him. They did not yet know what they were but they would wait and trust. A sadness caught Joseph's heart and held it.

Jesus was looking at him. His deep, piercing eyes held Joseph's as though he could see his soul. The strange, stark and beautiful feeling penetrated with it. Jesus smiled at his foster father as though it were not wrong to think these things, to want these dreams. Joseph caught the moment and looked at Jesus and smiled. Jesus put his arms around Joseph and kissed him on the cheek and hugged him. As the child embraced him, Joseph felt like he had been washed, clean and free; a hand had penetrated his soul and healed it. A fresh breeze now wafted over his soul, caressing it with gentleness.

Joseph felt new. His tiredness and all the hard walking that they had done disappeared. He felt free. The tears were thick in his eyes and blinded him.

Mary was looking at both her husband and her son. She too had caught the moment between father and child. It was a deep movement of touch; a moment of complete and total understanding between the two; a moment of surrender on Joseph's behalf; a moment when the two became one.

Joseph looked again at Jesus and the two laughed.

Mary said, "If you two are quite finished..." she paused, smiling, "then I would like to get down this hill to see my mother." They all laughed and Joseph swung Jesus up on his shoulders and began walking down the hill, the bond made between himself and Jesus.

"Am I to be left with the donkey?" Mary shouted after them.

The sobs had left her and she sat now on the raised part of the roof that ran along the edge. She sat waiting for the sadness to subside. She wanted her daughter. She wanted to talk with her, to listen to her, to embrace her. She wanted the two to be together like it used to be when she would pull Mary to her and begin plaiting her hair. The two would talk and laugh for hours about the events of the day and of yesterday and those memories that lingered and came near to be grasped and remembered. Anne needed to feel the bond that they had made over the years, the bond that made them mother and daughter.

When Joachim had died, Mary was all that she had since her own mother and father were dead and gone and her sister Miriam had married and went to live in Magdala. She and Mary had a good friendship.

Anne thought she heard a whisper of a voice; a shifting of the direction of the wind perhaps; or a butterfly landing on a flower to unfold its tongue to sip at the nectar deep within the flower's heart. It was so like Mary's voice. "Ach," she chided herself, picking herself up from the little wall.

As she rose, she saw a smiling girl at the other side of the roof. Her dark hair had fallen out of her veil and framed her face. She looked sweaty and hot as if she had walked a long way. She looked like Mary but more grown up, more mature and not a girl but a woman. She had tears flowing freely down her face. Beside her, with his arms about her legs, was a little boy of perhaps three or four years old. They were looking at her.

Mary looked at her mother. The emotion sprang up from deep inside her and tears blinded her. She wanted to stand there and just look, to not break this moment forever, to not allow time to travel on its merry way so that she could look at this woman whom she loved. She looked older, greyer, and had lost some of her sparkle but she was her mother.

Mary said simply, "Mother, I have come home."

Anne could feel the sadness, that must have been in her face, break up now and disbelief mould itself into it. She looked at the young woman who said 'mother'.

"Mary?...Mary? Is it you? Am I dreaming?" She peered at the girl. "Mary, my child, my daughter." She walked up to Mary and touched gently the hair that fell from behind her veil as though it were a precious thing. Then she placed the palm of her hand on her daughter's face and with her fingertips she touched the tears on the tanned face, her own tears flowing hard.

"Never...never in my life have I wished and prayed for a thing so much as I have wished for you to stand before me smiling. Will a mother forget her own child? The child that she has wrought from her womb?" She pulled Mary into her arms. "Come to me and let me hold the flesh of my flesh and bones of mine. Praise the Living God for this day, for you were dead and now live."

The two women embraced.

When they had done, Anne looked for the child. He had moved away to allow the two women to greet one another. Anne looked at him and Mary could feel Gabriel near. Like incense, the strange and stark and beautiful feeling penetrated the air. Gabriel, who brought the Spirit of the Lord, was here. Anne knelt before Jesus. She searched his face, every line and pore, and then she said, "You are the Christ-child and I am not worthy to be in your presence. Israel has waited for this moment to come face to face with you. My heart and soul are at your service."

Jesus reached out his hand and touched the tears on her face. Then he smoothed her hair. "I love you," he said.

The door cracked as it opened and creaked on its rope hinges. The interior was dark and no fire burned to give its light. Joseph moved through the room, guided by familiarity, to the window and opened the shutter. The light of the day burst in and caught the myriads of dust specks that hung in the room; bursting into tiny colours that danced in the air. Joseph could see the furniture that he had made for Mary. It was still clean and had not cracked in the lack of use. It was all still here, just as they had left it.

He went over to the brick fireplace. It consisted of three walls of bricks formed in an incomplete square, and the space in the centre was used for the fire. The walls, about three feet in height, directed the fire upwards and the heat outwards. Across the top were various metal bars that held the cooking pots over the fire. Twigs, that Mary had gathered before they left three years ago were still piled up near the construction. He took some hay and two flint-stones and began banging one off the other to create a spark in the hay. The hay began to smoke after a few thuds and with his breath controlled, he began to blow slowly and steadily until he had a small flame. On this he put more straw to keep it alight until it was burning well. He put fine twigs on it and continued to build until a little mound was formed. The mound was crackling merrily with flame.

Joseph went to a small cupboard that hung on the wall. It was old and worn, it had been his father's. It shone now in the firelight with age. He opened the door. His tools were still there. He lifted them out. There was a mallet, a plane, a saw and an axe. These were what made him; these tools brought his heart out and placed it within the wood that became an object in his hand. They, too, had been his father's and he had smothered them in oil before they left for Bethlehem, thinking that it would only be a few weeks before he would return. In Egypt, he thought about these tools and the things he had made with them and those he wanted to make.

"Now I can do it," he said aloud.

As he sat down, he thought about the moment with Jesus on the hill outside Nazareth. The child's eyes had held him and looked far, far into his soul. He could feel that look embrace his soul. He felt like a new chair or piece of furniture that he might create himself; he felt that he himself was newly created in that look. It was a look of love; a love that could not be experienced unless Jesus looked at you like that. He had felt himself blossom under the child's gaze and he wanted to bloom and stay there for eternity. And the strangest thing, he, the father, had surrendered to the child. It was not like father and son, no; it was more like God and creature, touching, becoming one.

"Mary, I thought you were dead." Anne said as they sat together talking. "So many times I thought you were dead. We eventually heard about what had happened in Bethlehem and I could not believe it. All those poor women, their children torn from them and killed before their eyes! It breaks my heart to think about it. Something at the back of my mind would not let me believe that God would allow anything to happen to you. But it was difficult. Day after day I waited for some sign of your return. I went to everyone that had gone to Jerusalem and Bethlehem at that time and no one had seen any sign of you. It was as though you had disappeared, without a trace."

The sun was making long tracks in the evening sky and a small fire burned, ready to take over when the sun was gone. It crackled sharply. Anne had made a meal of cooked millet and vegetables. They were now sitting in the house talking. Anne was still in shock at Mary's return.

"But here I am talking when you should be talking. When will Joseph come for you?"

"He will come soon, mother, for the sun is going down. He wanted to give us time to be together. I told him that he was welcome to share it with us but he said he wanted this time to be for us. He said that he probably would not be able to talk anyway because we would have so much to say." The two women laughed.

Mary looked deeply into her mother's face, drinking in all that she had missed in the last three years. She said, "It is so good to see you, mama. It is like heaven to sit here and talk with you. I never want to leave you again."

"This old woman is content now. I have my daughter returned to me and I have a beautiful grandson to call my own. He and I will spend so much time together that you will think that you have no son," Anne chuckled.

"What news of Jonathan and Sarah and the children?" said Mary, remembering the family that she and her mother used to help out.

"Jonathan is well again but walks with a limp. He has returned to work and the family needs little help. I thank God for them. When you were in Egypt, Sarah came here each week, or when she could, to sit with me."

"I am glad that Jonathan is walking. Do they still live in the *Street of Goats*? I should very much like to visit them to see the children."

Mary's heart was fit to burst as she carried the sleeping Jesus home to her own home that night. To rest again, in her own couch was good to think about. The fire that Joseph had lit was a welcome sight when she entered. It burned brightly and lit up the things that she had come to associate with home, the furniture that Joseph had made for her. The Lord had given them happiness. No matter what lay ahead she felt that they could take it, they could fight through it. She was tired and ready to sleep. It was as though the last three years had caught up with her. She felt within her heart that when God led you through the danger, then he had a quiet, restful and peaceful time to bring you too. This was her rest. This was her home to begin again her life with the one who had been sent to her.

He was all her dreams; he was the one to whom her life belonged; wherever he went she would follow. This little child asleep in her arms was, for her, the representation of her life. What she had given in the last three years had been for his life and his life alone. The rest of her life, whatever God chose that to be, was for him.

She would be the pillow for his head and the cloth that wiped his brow. She could not want to be greater than him. No; that could never be. She must allow him to use her in whatever way he needed to, so that his life became great and hers faded into insignificance. She was not God and would never be. He was God and she, only a vessel, that he used. That was what she promised and that is what she would be, for eternity if necessary. It was all she wanted, it was her wish and her joy. She kissed the child that she held in her arms.

−10−

Settling in to their way of life in Nazareth was easy for Joseph and Mary. They fell into it as though they had never been away. Everything was the same and yet it was new and different. They lived in joy as only the exile knows how to live in joy after returning to the place they love. Nazareth had a peace about it that seemed to be for them and them alone. They were where they wanted to be and they felt the hand of God within their lives. They had felt his hand of guidance in times of danger and that hand had taken them through it and brought them safe to where they were now. They felt that they had wandered in the desert of uncertainty and now were brought back to an oasis of peace, where the gentle waters of grace lapped and quenched their thirst. They became content. And, like prisoners that had been in a dark prison, they absorbed the light that freedom brought.

The neighbours came to welcome them home and speak to them about their return. Some were there to find out all the news that they could and to see the child, Jesus, who would now be a part of the community for children were like riches among the poor and they spoke of their preciousness. Some asked questions about why they had lived in Egypt and Joseph and Mary told them the truth. They said that while they were in Bethlehem, Joseph had had a dream that Herod would try to harm the child and other children so they walked to Egypt to escape. The people marvelled at how God had warned them and it fed their curiosity for the aftermath of Herod's wrath in Bethlehem was still a major topic of conversation and none could understand why he had done such a terrible thing. They did not tell the neighbours about Jesus or about Gabriel for they knew God would do that in his own time.

This time had been given to them to rest and they rested. They rested as though they were by the streams of a gushing river. They lived on the ripe pickings that God provided for them and the gentle lapping of the water of God's love soothed them.

When Joseph went to the Synagogue for Morning Prayer, he saw the Rabbi carrying some Scrolls, that held the writings and interpretations of the Law, by long dead Rabbis that he wished to expound to his students. When he saw Joseph, his mouth fell open and he dropped the Scrolls. His students scurried to pick them up and the Synagogue was in mayhem for a little while. Rabbi Ben Harim stood looking at Joseph as though he were seeing a ghost and his mouth emulated that of a fish out of water. He could not say the prayers that morning but sat through them as though in shock.

When prayers were over the Rabbi sought Joseph out. The old man embraced the younger man and there were tears in his eyes. He held Joseph to him as though he were a long lost son and he the father.

"Joseph, my son, you are safe, you are very safe! I thank God that my prayers have been answered. I have prayed every day that you were safe. I did not know, it was as though you disappeared in some political intrigue or had been left for dead. But I should have known better, that if

God has sent..." he lowered his voice and looked around to see if anyone was within earshot, "the Holy One to you then He would keep you safe. Our safety in God is like the soft pillow that we lay our heads upon. I did not doubt but I wondered. Joseph, seeing you has been a sight to behold for these old eyes. You are most welcome. Please come to the inner room where it will be quiet and we can talk a little in peace."

"Rabbi," said Joseph when they were settled, "you do not know how glad that I am to be sitting here speaking to you. Although I have no fault with our time in Egypt for we made some good friends there, I would just rather be here in Nazareth. The Lord, our God must be praised for he has delivered us safely out of the lion's mouth."

"And what of the child, Joseph," inquired the Rabbi, "is he well?"

"Yes, Jesus is very well. And Mary too."

"Praise and thanks to the Lord. You have little to worry about here, Joseph. Antipas is somewhat quieter than his father or his brother, Archelaus. Then he is the son of Malthrace, who is a Samarian and maybe the mix of Samarian blood and his father's blood, he was from Idumea I believe, may hold some surprises for all of us. But we will leave that to the Lord, our God. But Antipas is quiet, it seems, and you should have no trouble here. The Bethlehem affair is even becoming a disgrace for the Romans and they will want to forget Herod's misdemeanour. Mark my words, they will cover it up so cleverly that people in times to come will think it was a made up story. Most truths seem quite unbelievable."

"It was abominable," said Joseph, "of that there is no doubt and we have God to thank for our safety. I dread to think what could have happened had I not believed the dream when Gabriel came to me in the cave in Bethlehem. But, Rabbi, I do not believe it was a dream. None of them were dreams. They were as real as this conversation that we are having now. That is what seems so strange to me; they are more real than life itself. Is that possible?"

"Joseph, the ways of God are not our ways. God has his own way of doing things. The reality that we live in now is only man's reality and not a true reality. The only true reality is with God. I think that man is given a proportion of that understanding of God's reality but until man has the faith to believe in what God wants of him, then he can never understand it. Dreams and visions can and do become part of God's reality when he chooses to use them in a way that will get his message across. You believed you were in a dream but God can, if he wishes, use what you believe to take you into his reality and so, warned you of the danger.

Time and space do not exist, only in man's mind. It helps man to know that the day is ended and another is begun. In God's reality, time does not exist and all is one in a present time. Nothing passes and nothing comes, it simply is.

God needed you to know his plans so he brought you into his time to tell you what he wanted. He used your belief in him to bring you to where he needed you to be. It is only those who do not believe fully that will try to find reasons to explain it away. I believe that a vision is God's reality put into man's for God's own purposes."

"I think I see what you mean. I believed that God would take me out of danger so he was able to use my faith to tell me what to do."

"Yes, it is faith in God that brings us close to him, not man's striving to find him. All the answers man can find out about God in his creation will not bring him face to face with God, but simply believing in him, even against the odds."

"When I believe that he can do it, then he will," Joseph said thoughtfully, "even though I was worried about taking Mary for my wife at the beginning of all of this, I still believed in him. It was my disappointment of things not turning out my way, the way that I had planned, that made me doubt. But now that I have seen the result of what believing in him can do, then it is easier to believe. I think."

"Our God is wonderful, Joseph. We cannot fully see what he is doing until after he has done it. You and Mary and Jesus are safe now because you believed in what he revealed to you. Had man told you that Herod would send orders to kill all those children, you would have believed it too fantastical to be true. You would have stayed there and, well...we know what would have happened. You decided to believe and you are here now, safe. God will work in our lives if we let him. I take it that you had many of these visions along the way?"

"Yes, we had a few. They came at times when we needed them most. When we arrived at Beersheba, the news that we were hearing was far from good. A woman at the well told Mary about the happenings in the city and I did not want to take her and Jesus through that territory. I felt danger all about me. Like you, I did not doubt but I was very concerned. Mary and I talked about the situation and decided that we would let the caravan that we were travelling with go on and we would simply wait on the Lord. Rabbi, I was prepared to settle down there." The Rabbi nodded understanding.

"On the third night after the caravan left, Mary and I were talking late at night and there, before us, was Gabriel, as bright as the sun. He told us to take the route through Jericho and along the banks of the Jordan River. And that is how we came to be here." Joseph finished.

"You are so blessed, Joseph, to have an Angel of the Lord to look after you in this way. I almost envy you. Did you know that it was Gabriel who came to the prophet, Daniel? So you are in good company, Joseph," the Rabbi chuckled.

Joseph stood and said, "Rabbi, I thank you for your time. I am glad that I have spoken with you. It has allowed me to see clearer into what is happening here. I cannot say that I will believe the next time God calls on me but I will try. I must go now and begin the work of the day and I will ponder these things. Thank you, you have been most helpful. It is good to be back." He embraced the old man and took his leave.

The streets of Nazareth were buzzing with life as Mary and Jesus walked through it. Like ants founding a colony, the people of the town busied themselves with the tasks at hand. The meals of the day were uppermost in the minds of the women who made up the majority of the occupants of this street, *Street of Moses*. A makeshift market had been set up here for the over abundance of fruit sellers in the market place proper and they were taking up much of the street. The smell of fresh fruit was sweet to their nostrils and the sweet talk of the vendors of their wares was almost overpowering. It was a mid-summer morning and the sun was baking the earth and the people.

It felt good to Mary, as she walked along holding Jesus by the hand, to be in the town that she loved, and watching these people go about their daily tasks. The buildings shone golden in the sunlight casting short shadows onto the dusty road. She was on her way to see Sarah. Egypt was a month behind them and already Mary felt as though she belonged again. Her thoughts were free and easy and she was looking forward to seeing her friend once more. Dogs flitted in and out of the people, sure on four feet, hoping to catch some tasty bites that fell from stalls or were thrown at them.

Mary stopped as her eye caught the gleam of some oranges. They looked good and would make a fine gift for the family she was visiting. She pulled Jesus closer to her as she proceeded to make the transaction.

She picked up one of the oranges and called out to a man at the other side of the cart on which they were housed,

"How much are these, please?"

The man looked at her and nodded for her to wait while he dealt with another customer who was haggling over the price of onions. Mary waited. Finally, the man turned to Mary. "What were you asking me?"

"The price of the oranges" she said.

"Six *leptons* will buy you twelve. They are cheap at the price, lady. They are good quality and I am doing you a favour at that price. Matthew across the road sells his at one *lepton* each!" He spoke cheerily in his sales patter.

A woman shouted out to him from somewhere behind Mary, "I want bananas, how much?"

"Can't you see that this girl is in front of you? Maybe you could wait your turn, after all I haven't got six hands, have I?" he put his hands on his hips and glared at the woman.

"I can go across to Matthew," the woman said indignantly, "at least I won't get the cheek I'm getting here."

"Just you do that and it'll cost you double the price."

Mary said "Six leptons did you say?" She handed him the money and taking her son by the hand she moved off down the street leaving the vendor and the customer to sort it out. She could hear them insulting one another as she turned into the *Street of Goats*. As she turned, she stopped abruptly, a cold hand touching her heart.

About halfway down the street she could see a contingent of Roman soldiers, their leather tunics and short togas unmistakable. There was about twenty of them and they were outside Jonathan's house. Mary pulled Jesus closer to her and proceeded down the street. As she came near she could see that a sizable crowd of people had gathered, some to see the spectacle and others who were genuinely concerned. Moving through the crowd, Mary wanted to see what was going on. Her friends were under threat and were in danger, for the Roman soldiers did not make social calls.

Coming out from the small door of the house she could see Jonathan being led, hands bound behind his back and flanked by two soldiers; they were dragging him because with his limp, he could not keep up to their pace; they were used to marching for miles at a time. He was bleeding from a cut on his forehead and the blood was pouring into his eye. He tried to wipe it with his forearm but they yanked his arm to stop him. Inside she could hear children's voices screaming and Sarah protesting, saying that her husband was innocent. Roman soldiers were in the house and from what she could hear they were abusing Sarah and the children as well. It would not be advisable to approach the door as there were two soldiers standing guard outside it, that meant that there were quite a few others inside. There was nothing she could do but wait. She prayed a silent prayer for deliverance out of the situation.

Mary stood helpless as they led Jonathan past her and began to make their way down the street. When the soldiers had done their business then she would see Sarah and find out what was happening.

The people around her were enjoying what was going on and were chatting in groups making speculations about what Jonathan was being arrested for. One man in a striped robe was saying that he had probably stolen money and would be taken to Jerusalem to be crucified. A woman who was near him agreed and said that she had always known that there was a bad streak in Jonathan.

Mary reached out to pull Jesus close to her but he was not there. In sudden panic she shouted his name "Jesus!" Her cry startled the crowd around her. "Jesus!" she called again, the panic in her voice. Mary looked all around and then she noticed that Jesus was a little way ahead and walking after the soldiers who held Jonathan. Her heart raced. If the Romans had no mercy on the children inside that were bigger, then what mercy would they have on a three year old? The blind instinct of a mother whose child is in peril rose in her. She started forward.

"Jesus!" she shouted again but he did not seem to hear.

She could see him as she made her way through the people who stood there. Mary's panic had risen for the safety of her child and all her motherly instinct was in her heart as her mind prepared for anything to happen. This was her only child and she must protect him. Her heart was sore trying to get through the knots of people who stood there. They did not see her; they did not see what was in her heart.

As she untangled herself from the crowd, she noticed that her son was talking to a centurion and the soldier was on his haunches, listening. As she approached she reached out and touched her son. The centurions face was radiant and her own panic melted and ebbed away as she felt the presence of Gabriel bringing the Spirit of the Lord into the scene before her.

The look on the centurion's face was soft and smiling, his features glowing; he, too, was feeling Heaven touch the earth at this moment. She knew what was taking place inside him. Whatever Jesus had said to him, it had penetrated deep. It had pierced his heart like an arrow and he had felt cleansed and refreshed. She was not to know what the words were but she did not need to know; she could feel them touch the air around her, giving it essence and form. She could feel it emanate from this small boy's heart and touch the soldier's heart and the two were one in this moment. She knew that within this foreigner in her land, was a peace that was breaking all frontiers and barriers; slave and master, occupier and occupied becoming one, becoming one as the sun becomes one with the earth as the sunlight touches it. It was growing and sprouting wings, dancing with the pure joy of a God that was real and whom this soldier did not know. She could see the love that was in his soul in this moment, rise up and fall from every pore in his face. It was hard for him but he tore his face away from this smiling boy and shouted after the soldiers who held Jonathan between them, their short swords drawn.

"Halt! The man is innocent. Let him go!"

The soldiers began to protest to the centurion but he told them that on new evidence, which he had just received, the man was innocent. They let him go. Jonathan was free.

"Is this your son, madam?"

"Yes," Mary said, "he is my son."

"I do not understand any of this. I was convinced that this was the man that I was searching for but your son came to me and told me that he was innocent. All the evidence that I had seemed to fall apart and I knew that he was not the man that I was looking for. I am telling you that the evidence was overwhelming. He was accused of being a Zealot and surely would have been sent to Jerusalem to be tried and crucified. Your son said to me simply, Jonathan is innocent and for some reason my heart turned over and I knew that he was telling the truth. I could not fight against it. What is it that your son has? What did he touch me with? I feel like I am clean all over and will never be soiled again." He did not wait for an answer but went down on his haunches again and smiled at Jesus. Then he got up and walked back to the house. Jonathan was limping back too and the centurion helped him. The crowd were speechless, their talking had stopped and their faces were questions that they were afraid to ask. Mary could hear the centurion apologise to Jonathan.

A little while later the soldiers had all left the house and Mary entered with Jesus firmly by the hand. The door led to a small, dimly lit room. Some of the children were still sobbing in the aftermath of the soldiers.

"Sarah, Jonathan," Mary called as she entered the door, "can I come in?"

"Mary, Mary is that you? Oh it is. Mary, you are welcome. I am sorry that it is not a better time."

"Sarah" the two women embraced. "It does not matter. Are you all alright, Jonathan?"

"Yes, I think so," said Jonathan. "I think most of it was fear. Those soldiers have been here for two hours, questioning me about some activity in Jerusalem about six months ago. They kept threatening me that I would be tortured and crucified. I did not know what they were talking about. I do not know what happened but one minute I was being taken and the next I could hear the centurion telling the men to let me go. I could not understand but the same centurion who had hit me," he indicated the cut on his head, "was telling me how sorry he was, that it was all an error and he even helped me into the house again. I do not know what is happening."

Mary looked at Jesus. She smiled at him.

* * * * * *

In the hill country of Judea, Elizabeth and Tamar were remembering Zechariah. They talked of the happy times that they both had known with the man. Elizabeth still missed Zechariah, even now, five years after his death. If she had seen his body, if it had been brought to her, then she could get rid of the feeling that he might just still be there. Maybe he was still in Jerusalem, maybe he just could not get home to her. These thoughts had helped her to cope for, with them, she could banish grief to the back of her mind for a little while. Her life was with him and for him and sometimes she could barely remember her life before being married to him. Death was so final, so heart-rending, so cruel. All things must die, she knew; and she would not go against what God has lain down. If it was Zechariah's time to go then so be it. Why did it have to be this way? It was the grief that she could not accept. It was the endless days waiting, for in her heart he was still with her. Even now she still prepared a meal for him or called out to him to show him something that John was doing. She would look at the sun going to its rest in the western sky and praise Yahweh. She would call out her husband's name to come and look and suddenly realise that he was not there anymore. And she would weep. She would weep for just wanting him to be there, to know his presence for a few moments. She tried to imagine him sometimes, standing there in front of her with his hands on his hips the way he did, but his memory was fading from her mind. Sometimes it felt like he was just a figment of her imagination and never really existed. At other times her body would almost surge forward within her just wanting him, needing him; wanting to hear him laugh or scold or just to be there. Grief was merciless. She would find herself crying for what seemed no reason that she could think of and then she would remember again that Zechariah was dead.

Had she been a younger woman, Elizabeth might have thought to prepare herself for marriage again, but she was an old woman and she would live her life as a widow and bring the child up. Besides she had Tamar, who had been faithful to her for so many years. Elizabeth was reminded of Ruth the Moabite woman and the words of Scripture came to her: *'And Ruth said, Intreat me not to leave thee or to return from following after thee for whither thou goest, I will go and where thou lodgest, I will lodge. Thy people shall be my people and thy God my God. Where thou diest, will I die and there will I be buried. The Lord do so to me, and more also if ought but death part thee and me."*

Tamar was like that. Elizabeth had told Tamar that if she wanted to go that she could make a life for herself and possibly find a husband.

"And where would I go, mistress? Are you not my family now? My own family are scattered. I would not even know where to begin to look for them. Anyway, I am scarred," she touched her mangled face, "I would be unhappy living with my family now. They would feel obliged to keep me because they could not find a husband who wanted me.

Mistress, if you want me, I will stay here with you. You and Zechariah have been good to me over these years. You have made me feel like a sister, a daughter and never once have you made me feel like a servant. No. I am a part of you now and I will die with you."

The two women had embraced and wept then and Elizabeth said, "If that is the case, Tamar, then you must stop calling me mistress. I have always hated that. So if you are going to stay then my name is Elizabeth." It had been a good day for them.

"Little John is growing up very fast," said Tamar now as they sat in the cool of the evening, "he is like his father and I think he is like you a little bit, Elizabeth." Both women were shelling peas in preparation for a meal. John was sitting on the floor helping them.

"Just a little bit, Tamar? I thought he was very much like me. Look at his lovely dark eyes; are they not like my own?" Elizabeth fluttered her eyelids in mock vanity.

"No, he has his father's eyes and is quite handsome at that. He may just have the back of your neck, which is quite safely tucked away so that no one can see it."

Elizabeth raised her eyebrows in mock horror. "And I suppose Zechariah had him all on his own and I had little to do with it? Is that what you are saying?"

"Yes, that's about it," Tamar said.

Elizabeth picked up some peas and threatened to throw them at Tamar.

"He is a beautiful child," said Tamar.

"I wonder how young Mary is getting on with her baby. He should be about six months younger than John. That should leave him about five years old too. Do you remember when she came to see me? She was very young but Mary has a good head on her shoulders and is very deeply rooted in God. Tamar, she is filled with the Spirit of the Lord and I know that she is blessed among all women."

"From what I can remember of her," said Tamar, "she seemed richly blessed by the Lord."

"I should very much like to see her and Anne again. I have not seen Anne since Joachim died. My mother and Joachim's mother were sisters. He must have died, oh, about seven or eight years ago now. He was a fine strong man. Maybe some day soon we will take the road for Nazareth. Would you like to come, Tamar?"

"Yes, I'll come. Would you be up to the journey?"

"I think so. If we took it slowly, I am sure we could make it. There might be a caravan going soon. I will ask around the village. Some of the oil merchants are bound to know. It would be good to see Mary and Anne again."

Six weeks later Elizabeth, Tamar and the child, John, joined the caravan that was heading for Damascus and beyond. It would go through Nazareth. It would travel by way of Arimathea, Sychar, and Samaria and into Nazareth and would take anything up to a week to allow merchants who travelled with it to sell their wares in the bigger towns. Apparently, the roads around Jerusalem were just too dangerous to travel on and many robberies had been reported and a few murders had occurred.

While they were waiting in Sychar, the two women brought John to Jacob's Well at the base of Mount Gerizim. The well lay in the fork of two passes, one going west and the other north. It is said that Jacob dug this well when the supplies of water for his flocks were not enough. The well had a narrow opening and Tamar was able to pass through it into the cylindrical shaped chamber to retrieve water from the fabled well. It was about seven feet across. The well was not a spring but depended on its supplies from rainfall and seepage. It acted as a reservoir and held the water in a deep hole. The water dried up at the end of *Shebat* and remained dry until the rains returned. They noticed that the water was light and not like the hard water they had in their own springs. The next day the caravan set out for Samaria.

The hill upon which Samaria is built rises up from the fertile hollow called *Wady esh-Sha'ir* or 'Valley of Barley'. The hill is some three hundred feet in height and has a level top. The sides of the hill are steep and the greatest length is from east to west. The mountains surrounding the hill of Samaria are verdant with olives and vineyards. From the pinnacles of the lower western hills they saw the stunning view of the Plain of Sharon and beyond it the Great Sea. Its soil of rich loam grows oranges, vines and olives. When the flowers are in bloom it becomes a place of rare beauty watered perennially by four streams. The white narcissus grows abundantly in its season.

On their way was Esdraelon, the valley of Jezreel. It is a depression that lies between Mount Gilboa in the east and Mount Carmel in the west and was the scene of many long ago battles. It is supplied water by copious springs and growth there is abundant. The caravan route would take the irregular tracks to the foothills of Nazareth.

Elizabeth could not remember where Anne lived for the town had grown since the last time that she was here. She made a few inquiries from a woman carrying a water jar on her head.

"Do you know where Anne lives? Her husband Joachim is dead and she has a daughter called Mary."

"Ah yes, I know Anne and Mary. Anne brings food to the poor. They live in the *Street of Lights* in the upper end of the town. Come with me, I am going part of the way. You are not from Nazareth yourself?" The woman turned into a street that led uphill. Tamar carried John in her arms while Elizabeth led the donkey.

"No. I am from the hill country in Judea, a little village

near Hebron."

"You have come a long way," said the woman. She was a tall, thin woman in her thirties.

"Yes, but we saw the most beautiful countryside on the way here. Israel is very beautiful."

The street that they were in was quite long and steep and they had to stop and catch their breath a few times. John had wanted to walk and Tamar had him by the hand. He was trying to run up the hill but Tamar would not let go of his hand. They met a woman coming down the hill. She spoke to the woman with the jar. Two men came up behind the little troop and overtook them.

The houses on the street were mostly two storied. Some were painted white and some were being left to decay. They could smell the spices of the evening meals being prepared inside and felt their own hunger pangs. A few lights twinkled here and there as the day prepared for night.

About halfway up the woman indicated a small street that turned off to the left and went slightly downhill and curled in on itself. John finally broke free from Tamar's hand and began running up the hill with little squeals of delight. She ran after him. He ran about ten yards before she caught him.

"This is where I live so I must leave you here," the woman said, stopping. "If you carry on to the top here you will see that the road ends and branches off into two smaller roads. Take the road to the left and about halfway down it you will come to a one storied house that sits back from the road. I think there is an olive tree in the garden. If you get lost knock on the doors of some of the houses and they will help you. Well, I must get on. I hope you find it."

"Thank you so much for all your help. You are so kind. May the Lord be with you and bless you." The woman waved at them and disappeared down the street to the left.

Left alone again, the two women rested and let their breath settle.

Elizabeth said, "Do you still think that this is a good idea? Look at this hill!"

Tamar laughed. "We'll make it. The sun is beginning to go down, it must be about the eleventh hour."

"Let us go then."

They climbed the rest of the hill and only stopped once for it seemed to level off a little as it got nearer the top. They found the fork in the road easily enough and proceeded down the one to the left.

The small house was set back from the street as the woman had said and this allowed it to have a somewhat larger garden than the others that surrounded it. Elizabeth could see the olive tree and recognition began to dawn on her.

"I know why I did not know the streets. When I was last here with Zechariah, we came from this direction," she said, pointing on down the small street. "We did not come up that hill."

They stood in front of the worn gate. Elizabeth called out, "Anne...Anne. Are you there?" There was no answer to her calls. She called out again and banged on the gate.

"I do not think that there is anyone here, Elizabeth. We had best wait. Let us make ourselves comfortable here outside the gate. I'm sure that she will be along soon."

"I think that you are right, Tamar, we will sit down and rest," answered Elizabeth with a sigh. "John, my son, come and sit with me and we will have some bread."

Anne was with Mary and Joseph for the evening meal. The evening meal, for Jews, was a gathering of the family around the table, the final meal of the day and the most important. God had promised the people of Israel when they were wandering in the Wilderness of Paran: *I have heard the murmurings of the children of Israel. Speak unto them saying: at even ye shall eat flesh and in the morning ye shall be filled with bread and ye shall know that I am the Lord your*

God.' One pot of stew was set down and everyone within the household supped as one. The stew consisted of a stock of goat's meat, thickened by lentils, onions and other vegetables to hand. With it was served the main part of the meal: bread. Mary had baked it earlier; thin, flat barley cakes that each would fold over at the end to make a spoon and dip in the common dish. None would touch the dish with the fingers or with anything that had been in contact with the lips. They drank water with it.

"That was a good meal, Mary, thank you," said Anne, "you can certainly cook."

"I have to cook well to please my husband, mother." Mary laughed, "He would throw me out the door if I could not cook! Joseph likes his meals and I enjoy making them for him." Joseph smiled at Mary.

"You make good food, Mary, but then your mother can cook too" Joseph said.

"And little Jesus, did you enjoy your food?" Anne asked.

"Yes, grandmother, I like lentils," Jesus answered.

"You are a good boy to eat all your food. You will grow up strong and healthy, just like your father. Were you in the workshop with him today?"

"Yes, he showed me how to cut the wood with the saw. He said when I am older that I will do it by myself."

"That is very good. You are becoming strong and will soon be able to do a lot of things to help. Oh look, the night is nearly here. I must get home. Will you walk with me to the bottom of the hill, Joseph?"

"Yes, of course, Anne. Let me put some wood on the fire. The night will be chilly. Did you bring a shawl?"

"Yes, I did."

Anne and Joseph stood up. Anne went to her daughter to embrace her. "Thank you, Mary, I will speak to you again. I love you."

"I love you too, mother. I will see you soon. Shalom!"

"And Jesus. Will you embrace your old grandmother?"

"Yes," he said and threw himself into her arms. "Shalom!"

* * * * *

"I do not think Nazareth is so unsafe to walk in as the cities are, Joseph, but in these days one cannot be sure," said Anne as they began to walk in the ensuing darkness.

"Yes, I know," said Joseph. "It seems that the news coming from everywhere is bad. They say that the Zealots have increased their activity and some are hiding out in the mountains. It is hard to know the truth of it. Robbery is on the increase and it is not safe to travel long distances. Do these people forget that they have a God?"

"Ah, Joseph, I do not understand it. People seem to take the Law for granted these days. You would think that God did not exist. The presence of Roman soldiers does not help. The young men seem to resent them and the next thing you know they are speaking of revolt. It is frightening."

The stars twinkled in the night sky as they walked through Nazareth. Little lights could be seen burning within the houses that they passed and families were gathered in for the night. Few were out in the streets and dogs were able to run freely without being shouted at.

"You can leave me here, Joseph, I will make the hill," Anne said, stopping.

"I will not hear of it, Anne. Your daughter will take the broom to me if I leave you here to walk on by yourself!" said Joseph teasingly.

Anne laughed. "In that case, Joseph, I will save you a few bruises and allow you to escort me up this hill." Their laughter echoed through the little buildings that seemed to snuggle together under the night sky. Joseph took Anne's arm and together they walked up the hill.

–11–

Anne saw the two women and the child outside her house when she and Joseph turned the corner. The child was playing around the two women. A younger one was standing near a donkey and the older one was sitting on a blanket on the ground. They had shawls wrapped tightly around them to keep warm for there was a chill springing up in the night air.

"Who are they, Anne?"

"I do not know, Joseph," the woman answered. "Stay with me and we will see."

They walked up the street and stopped in front of the two women.

"Are you waiting for someone? Can I help you?" Anne asked.

"Anne? Is that you?" The older woman was getting to her feet. "Anne, it's me, Elizabeth!" She was unwrapping the shawl from about her head.

Anne was stunned. "Elizabeth?" she managed to say.

After embracing, Anne led Elizabeth, Tamar and John in through the gate. Joseph went to tether the donkey and give it fodder for the night. The two older women held onto each other in great excitement.

"What are you doing here, Elizabeth? I certainly did not expect to see you here sitting outside my house!"

"Ah, call it an old woman's whim but I wanted to see you and Mary again before I die."

"Elizabeth, you are not going to die!" Anne chided, "there are still plenty of years in you yet. Let me light up the fire and make ready a meal for you." The women let go of one another and Anne busied herself around the fire.

Joseph came in through the door and stood in the room.

"Elizabeth, this is Joseph, Mary's husband," said Anne conversationally.

"I am glad to meet you at last, Joseph, Mary spoke much of you." Elizabeth addressed Joseph.

"I have heard much about you too, from Mary. I feel that I know you." He paused then he said, "I must go. Mary will be wondering what has happened to me. I am very sure that she will be here at sunup if she does not come tonight. Shalom to you all!"

The older woman sat down in a chair near the fire that Anne was working at and looked about the room. Tamar sat near her mistress, a little afraid of her new surroundings and not a little shy and conscious of her scarred face. She pulled her shawl around it to hide it.

"You have a beautiful son, Elizabeth, he is so like Zechariah." Anne said over her shoulder as she worked.

Elizabeth shot a look at Tamar who smiled knowingly.

"Does he not look like me a little, Anne?"

"No, Elizabeth, he favours his father. We women must just accept these things."

Elizabeth pouted teasingly at Tamar who was stuffing the shawl into her mouth to keep from laughing out loud at her friend.

"Your loom looks new, Anne. The wood looks so beautiful," observed Elizabeth.

"Yes, I have a son-in-law who makes beautiful things from wood. He made it for me after he and Mary came back from Egypt. My old one was falling apart. It was no shame for it, I suppose." Anne hung a small black pot over the cheery flames to begin the cooking.

"Egypt? Did you say Egypt, Anne?" said Elizabeth.

"Yes. Oh you don't know, do you?"

"Anne, what has happened here?"

"Let me finish what I am doing here and I will tell you all about it. By the way who is this girl who is with you?"

"This is Tamar. She is my friend and she lives in my home," said Elizabeth.

Anne addressed Tamar. "You are welcome in my home. Please make it your own. I am sorry that I did not welcome you before but I was so shocked to see Elizabeth here. My daughter, Mary, spoke of you."

"I can't wait to hear about Egypt, Anne. Can you not boil that stew any quicker?"

"Elizabeth, here? Joseph, is it true?" said Mary when Joseph told her what had happened.

"Yes, Mary, it is true. She had a child with her whom I presume is John and another younger woman."

"Tamar. Oh, Joseph, my heart is bursting with joy. Elizabeth... here? I cannot believe it. I just cannot take it in."

Joseph went to the fire and began to rake a stick through it. "You will need to wrap Jesus up well, it is quite cold outside," he said simply.

"What? You mean you will take me over there now? Oh, Joseph!" She walked over to her husband put her arms around him and kissed him on the cheek. "I love you," she said.

Jesus smiled.

Elizabeth wept when Mary arrived. The two women stood in an embrace that seemed to last forever. There was silence in the room, as though the onlookers were forbidden to speak and, in each heart, each soul that looked on, the sun was rising and dancing. The moment between the two women brought the Spirit of God to them and to all who stood looking at them and each knew something within them. It was a holy moment and one that was given and obtainable always for it was the now and brought by the Spirit of God when all was in accordance with his will.

For Tamar, it was as if she was a child again in the happy times with her mother. She felt the love of a mother touch her and something gave way and broke, deep within her. She could feel it snap.

Anne felt Mary's love in that embrace for she knew the love of her daughter was a special thing that no other daughter could give. The living, breathing God, had touched Mary. It was tangible, beautiful.

Joseph knew again what had passed between Jesus and him. He knew again the intensity of the love with which Jesus had touched his soul. He knew a light there; he knew its burning flame and he knew his soul. His own soul was one with the flame and burned with it. He knew its light within him. A word had been spoken and he was now with the word, in the word and through the word and his life did not exist without the word. The word in him was palpable now as the two women embraced.

Elizabeth and Mary wept on each other's shoulder; tears that are only cried when you meet someone that you thought that you might never meet again. Both felt that this meeting was a gift, a given thing, a need in both fulfilled.

The people within the room spoke and laughed and knew joy that came on wings, carried to them by the Spirit who had been released into them and it freed them. God was speaking in a new way and this was its preparation.

Jesus and John stood together; like sentinels they watched the moments that unfolded, given and used and never spent in each soul. The new order of things had begun, fleeting moments that would incorporate and gather. As the pace quickened and the impetus began a slow surge, new moments would create and recreate and live in and make new the taker of the moment; the hearer of the word would succumb to the word and become preoccupied and lost in its gravity. Onward, the word, spoken, would affect and effect the structure of a soul, its gossamer strands becoming woven, melting into and with, a new thread, a new living bound and imprisoned in the speaker of the word. The children did not need to speak; no witness was needed for a little knot of faith had begun; a seed had germinated.

Elizabeth, Tamar and John settled into the way of life in Nazareth. Each day was filled with a silent prayer that did not need words for the love of one another had become the words. They were words that were fulfilled and not just known. They were words that were tempered with God's Spirit that was in their midst. God stood there among them causing them to love with his own love, a tiny trickle of what was to come.

The little family met together each day for there was something that they could not quite touch but it was what they found when they came together for each could feel it and wanted it.

The meals made by the women became feasts and God was at their centre. He was the one that gave them their bread and they ate it joyfully and it was not a hunger of the belly but a hunger for God that rose in them day after day.

Tamar felt it most of all. She did not know what had happened to her. She felt gladdened in her heart and the hatred that she had felt towards her mother had gone, melted like water that she spilled on the ground when she went to the well. She had always felt that such water was wasted when it fell from the jar she filled. Now she could see clearly that the water was absorbed by the ground, taken back and given as something new. The hatred that she had felt all these years for the woman who had held her down and terrified her was absorbed, it was gone, melted into somewhere and now a love was there.

What was happening to her? She did not know but slowly, over the days, the scar that had hidden her away from the prying eyes and mouths that spoke of her mark of evil did

not matter any more. It was still on her face. She touched
it now, in the soft, morning light. She was in the garden of
Anne's home under the shade of the olive tree. The others
were inside talking and laughing. As she touched the hideous thing, she could feel the scales that had once been
flesh. She could feel the ridges under her fingertips. It did
not seem to matter to her if these people saw it. It was like
that when she first went to be a servant in Elizabeth's home.
She had stood with her hand over it, hiding the thing that
made her ugly. But these people did not see it! They
looked at her as though it were not there.

The morning birds flitted in and out of the branches above
her. She could hear their sweet song penetrate the air
around her and it gladdened her heart. She looked up into
the branches above her. She could see the sturdy boughs
that held the branches and the fruit of this tree. She could
feel its life, living in the stillness of its existence. She felt
and knew joy. She did not have to hide anymore but she
had wanted to be alone to feel this newness within her.
What it was she did not know but she liked it and wanted
to feel it and be with it.

A small movement caught her peripheral vision and she
looked around. The boy Jesus stood there. His deep eyes
were on her and she felt warmed by them. Looking into
them, she felt that she wanted to hide in them. The eyes
were love. His dark, curly hair, fell softly about his neck
and the fresh skin of childhood was unblemished by age
and life. He was looking at her.

She felt the warmth glow within her as she looked back at
him. Her soul lifted up to him. It did not seem to matter
that they did not speak for it was hearts that were speaking
silently to one another.

Jesus put his hand on Tamar's face, on the scar. At first
she wanted to pull back and hide again. Memories of other
children, laughing and shouting at her filled her and she felt
the pain, deep and intense; she felt the slaps that she had

received for being ugly; she felt the pain of being alone and unwanted and the terror of it happening again, and it had, again and again and again; she felt the pain of it all rekindle and surge up to the surface. She could not control it. It was teeming forward as though of its own accord. The tears bubbled up in her eyes and over-spilled like a pot on the fire. This child who stood in front of her, with his smiling eyes, was taking it; he was gathering it in his smile. As he touched her face, she could feel the softness of his small hands.

Through her tears and somehow mingled in the sweet bird-song above her head she heard him say: "You are beautiful!" And it was gone. The pain and the sorrow, the suffering and the ugliness; it was gone. She felt beautiful, she felt new.

The boy smiled and her whole soul smiled back. Jesus turned and walked away towards the house. She watched him go, spellbound.

Tamar touched her face. The scar was still there but it did not feel ugly. It felt beautiful. Where this child had touched it, it felt meaningless, as though it weren't there. New tears began to fall from the woman's eyes; they were tears of joy.

These days that the family spent together were days that filled them with joy, days when each found meaning to the existence of the world within his or her soul. The passage of time did not seem to touch them and life seemed idyllic. It seemed to them that they had begun something new. All remained the same yet something had touched them within and they felt its realness. Each day challenged the heart to begin anew and tear out the things within it that caused it to be a prisoner of its own volition.

Deep and deeper within time and within the hearts of those

who formed the family that now gathered together, a tiny drip of water had begun. Turning into a tiny trickle of water, it glistened its way downward into each soul, which it plummeted into and splashing, created myriads of itself. The myriads formed little pockets and these, continuing to be filled, were formed and the essence of a pure love was created; love that imbued a taste of something to come; a sense of belonging to the Lord.

"Is it not good to have Elizabeth here, Joseph?" said Mary happily. She was making bread for the day. She kneaded it in the heel of her hand and squashed to the table, pummelling it to get the air into it so that it would rise.

"Yes, she is a good woman. She has God in her. And yes, she makes you want to love God," answered Joseph holding the door open for he was about to go through it to the workshop to begin the days work. It was morning and the sun was rising in a cascade of burnt orange.

"I love her for her deep humility. I wish that I could be so humble before God."

"Mary! How can you say that?" Joseph said coming back into the house, "you have the Messiah, the Son of God as your son. Your humility goes beyond that of all women."

"Any humility that I have is given to me by God, Joseph, that I know. I cannot see humility within myself and I must continue to try to be humble to bring it out so that others will not see me but see God. I can see Elizabeth and I can see that, within her, she strives to be all that God wants her to be. Her humility comes from her heart. All that would not be in union with God, she keeps within herself to be thrown on the fire as something that is wasted and not needed. Her humility goes to serve God. She is a beautiful woman in God's sight. That is why I admire her, she gives me, and indeed all of us, a good example of how to give to God and let nothing stand in the way. I can see God in her."

231

"Yes, Mary, I must agree with that. She makes God seem real. But I must say this. I know that you cannot see it but, for me, there is a light that shines within you that helps me to see my way. I think that is why I love your smile. It shines on me."

"Oh Joseph, do not say that."

"But, Mary, it is true. I can feel God's hand within you sometimes, guiding me through all that I face. And it makes me want to love God all the more."

"But I would not want you to see *me*, Joseph. God is my light; he is my joy. You must not look at me but at him, who shines the light. When he gives me light or wisdom, I simply direct it. I am not the light or the wisdom for I am nothing within myself but I simply give what I have been given. Do not see me as special, see me as his handmaid for it is what I want to be."

"And you are. I believe that you have been given as a light until Jesus begins to do as he must. Then he will shine into the world as he came to do. How that will be, I do not know. But it will happen."

"I would feel sad if anyone saw me as more than I am," said Mary. She stopped kneading the bread and looked at her husband. "I can give nothing; only the Lord, our God, can do that. He has asked me to do something and I am trying to do it. If he requires more of me I will try to do it. That is all I can do."

"Mary, my love," said Joseph, going to her. He took her floury hands in his, "You do not see the Lord's hand in your life. You have touched many people by your humility before God. You have lit up their lives with your acceptance of his will. Whatever his will turns out to be, you will always be the first to have accepted what God has wanted. I doubted at the beginning because I wanted you for myself, as my wife. God let me see that you were his chosen and you were not mine.

At first, I did not want to think about that but slowly now I have seen that this life that we are living is what God wants it to be. You are being kept wholly for him."

"I know," Mary answered, "that the bounty and riches of the Lord, our God, are being poured onto us in great abundance. They are pouring out like a great river and they will never dry up. There are so many who do not see his goodness. They only see him as one who has many rules to keep and will destroy if they are not kept. They do not see that the rules and commandments are only there to keep us from the dangers of the sin that our first parents committed. They rolled back a great stone that had covered all evil and it escaped onto the earth. Many people do not see that God's commandments, if obeyed, will keep us safe from the things around us that would do us harm. We are children who are wayward and need guidance always. I see that his rules are not burdens but they are love. The love of a father for his children."

Joseph sighed. "There are days when I can feel him close to me, so close that I can touch him. Then other days I cannot feel him at all. I think that these are the days when I have forgotten him and I get caught up in what I am doing. I am beginning to understand that we have to strive to remember him by keeping the commandments."

"Yes, Joseph, I think you are right. God is in his commands and we find him when we do them."

"It is good to talk in this way about Yahweh, Mary" said Joseph thoughtfully, "but I must go now and work. God said: '*In the sweat of thy face shalt thou eat bread, till thou return unto the ground; for out of it wast thou taken: for dust thou art and unto dust shalt thou return.*' And I must work." He kissed her on the forehead.

"And I must bake bread to feed my family so that they do not starve." Mary said, smiling at her husband.

Mary watched him go. Jesus had stayed the night with Anne and she was alone in the house. She returned to the table. The dough had been left standing overnight to leaven it and she was now making the bread that would last the day. She finished kneading and beat it into a flat disc of about one inch thick and eight inches in diameter. She then took a small jar of olive oil and proceeded to cover the top of the dough with it. This would give the finished bread a glossy coat. From another jar she sprinkled a mixture of aromatic seeds over the oil.

The fire in the hearth burned merrily giving warmth to the house that it did not need. On top of the fire Mary had placed a flat iron griddle allowing it to heat slowly. She placed the bread on this and stoked up the fire to give more heat.

When she had done, she went back to the table to clean it. As she turned, she caught her breath. The strange, stark and beautiful ambience was all about her. She felt herself lifted up and caught in its power. She felt helpless to do anything.

In her heart it seemed that a fire was enkindled and it burned, deeply and brightly, enhancing and vivifying her soul. There was no pain, only a love; a love that entombed her into itself, capturing the very essence of her being. Her soul was in the grip of an unseen delight; a powerful hand had touched her and from it imparted its own glory, its own love.

A great tide began to rise in her, a tide of love that overwhelmed her and she sank into it. She allowed it to take her for she knew it was her God, come to her in this morning. Her body was in her home, still standing there, but her soul was in heaven. She could feel her soul expand and grow and become part of this mystical being who had taken her. She could feel his love capturing and imbuing her. The life of her God flowed into her and instilled her with it. He, she felt, wanted her to know him, creator imprinting created with himself. She felt that she was his.

Then it was over, gone. She felt herself being left gently back into her body and she was looking towards the door of her home. She was back in reality. She walked towards the table to begin cleaning it. Her heart was alive with love.

Joseph's eyes looked at the plank of wood. They caught the knots and the rings and its redness. It was a beautiful piece of wood. His eyes were drawn by its elegance. He ran his fingers along its length. He would turn it into a seat fit for a king, or, at the very least, a seat for the Rabbi to sit on in the Synagogue. He would make it beautiful and the very act of it being within the Synagogue would sing praises to the God that he loved.

The conversation that he had with Mary was still on his mind. She did not even know that God had richly blessed her. She was so beautifully humble. He knew that her heart was pure and the words that came from her mouth, he believed, were from God. She did not allow pride to taint her in her simplicity. She had no pride. She just spoke purely from her heart.

She had spoken words of wisdom to him this morning and on other days that had no pretensions but they flowed naturally from her like a little bubbling stream. She did not realise that God was using her but continually strived to be close to him.

He loved her and his love was deepening, he knew, with every day that passed. He knew her in his heart and he loved her as a thing set apart, a jewel that he could hold but it was not his. That was all he wanted now.

Elizabeth noticed the change in Tamar. The first thing she noticed was that Tamar smiled, often. The scar had always made the girl hide her face from any stranger that might happen along. She would avoid people that she did not know and would stay very much in the background. She had always done what Elizabeth needed and Elizabeth had allowed her, her privacy.

But here she was, mixing with everyone. She acted as though she did not have the scar. Her dark eyes were shining and she looked happy, happier than Elizabeth had known her. Something had happened to her.

Elizabeth also noticed that Tamar looked at the boy, Jesus, when he was in the company. She could not take her eyes off him. He seemed to be the source of her joy. Elizabeth knew that Tamar was different and wanted to share the joy with her. She would speak to her.

The family were in Anne's house and the midday meal had been eaten, the table cleared and they sat for a little while to rest before beginning the work once more. Elizabeth caught Tamar's eye and motioned her to come out into the garden.

The two women walked out into the garden arm in arm like old friends. The smell of growing caught their nostrils. They walked to the shade of the olive tree and sat down on the stools that were there.

"Tamar, my friend," Elizabeth looked at her, "You are so happy. I have never seen you like this. You seem to feel as though you belong, like you have found something special here. What is it that you have found?"

"I do not know, Elizabeth. I cannot put my finger on it but, yes, I feel very happy. The boy, Jesus, came to me as I sat here a few days ago. I was looking around me and he was beside me. I did not see him approach. He was looking at me and I could feel love in his gaze. It made me feel like a girl again. Then he put his little hand on my face and I was different. He just said, 'you are beautiful.' All that I have ever felt and knew now has a newness that I have never felt before. But he did not just touch my face; I believe that he touched my soul. You may think that I am mad but I am new. He must be a healer or something the way he looked at me."

"No, Tamar, I do not think you are mad. I am happy that you are happy. I thought that it was probably something to

236

do with Jesus. Yes, he is a very special child." The younger woman looked at Elizabeth. "When we return home, Tamar, I will tell you the whole story. For now, just enjoy the time that we have here."

The long fingers of morning stretched out as if to grasp the darkness and plunge it into itself. The streaks of light heralded with their trumpet that the new day given was beginning. The dawn danced in its own joy as the new message from Yahweh God painted itself on the sky for all to see. The birds of the air sang in tones that matched their own joy for it was light again and the darkness banished for another day. Yahweh God gave his light. With the sun came again the heat and the dusty roads, and the regrowth of the plants in autumn. Another day and the day before Elizabeth and Tamar and John would make the journey back to the hill country. They had stayed four months.

The little family that had formed itself into a community were now to break up and scatter seeds further afield. A new species had germinated and was beginning to find form within itself and, when it had, it would regenerate out into the world.

On this morning, after the tasks had been done, they all sat under the shade of the olive tree in the garden, its branches, like a hand spread out to provide shade and protection from the sun.

Jesus and John were playing under the fig tree, which stood near the gate. It was cool there and they played with sticks. They would each throw a small stick and then with a larger one, they measured the distance of the throw. The adults sat talking, the morning air was fresh and breathable.

"I will miss you, Elizabeth. It has been so good to have you here" Mary said.

"Ah, and I will miss all of you. It has been such a blessing and the Lord has looked kindly on all of us in these days," Elizabeth answered.

"It will be our turn to visit you next," said Anne, "we will gather up and go to the hill country. We will not need a caravan, all of us together would make a long one."

"And I will make a cart that you ladies can be carried in style, with a team of donkeys pulling you along," said Joseph elegantly.

"We could ask the Roman soldiers if they would come and guard us from the bandits," Tamar chipped in. "Four fine ladies in a fine cart led by donkeys would need an escort, wouldn't they?"

They all laughed and their humour echoed into the morning, joining the birdsong.

Elizabeth looked a little sad as she spoke. "I do not know how I will settle in again at home. For me the Lord has been truly present here in these last months. I think he has touched quite a few of us and has made himself felt."

Tamar put her head down then she quickly lifted it again. "I, for one, have never known a family but all of us together has made me feel a part of this one. I thank all of you for making me feel welcome."

Anne looked at Tamar, "You will always have a place here, no matter what. My home is open to you always, Tamar."

The younger woman had tears in her eyes as Anne spoke.

"And our home is your home," said Mary.

"You all are so good to me," Tamar said, the tears now flowing freely, "God is so good to me. I spent my life alone until I met my dear friend here," she indicated to Elizabeth, "but now I have an extended family. I do not know what to say!"

"Do not say anything, Tamar, for it is God who provides it all" answered Mary, "it is he who has provided us with this time and he is to be praised for it. His mercy extends to all of us and in turn, we must express mercy to our fellow-man."

Elizabeth said, "You are right, Mary, wherever we are and whatever we do we must always be ready to give of what we have been given. Mercy, I think, is love and love must be expressed and given always. It is what we are made for."

" *'And therefore will the Lord wait'*" Joseph quoted, " *'that he may be gracious unto you and therefore will he be exalted, that he may have mercy upon you: for the Lord is a God of judgment: blessed are all they that wait for him. For the people shall dwell in Zion at Jerusalem: thou shalt weep no more: he will be very gracious unto thee at the voice of thy cry; when he shall hear it, he will answer thee.'* "

"The Lord our God will always be merciful to us when we ask him," said Mary, "it is only when pride fights within us to be heard and we allow it to be heard that we cannot accept the mercy of him who gives it."

"Yes," Anne pondered, "pride, it is within us and it is a block to the Lord's mercy. We must continually try to root it out, simply because it is not of God. It is we who will benefit from it in the end."

"I think that it has been pride that has kept me a prisoner all these years," said Tamar. Everyone turned to look at her. "Would you let me tell you a story?"

"Tamar," said Joseph with compassion in his voice, "You must always feel free to speak within this family."

"This scar on my face," she pointed, "has been with me since I was a little child. Because of it I hated my mother and my brothers and because of that I have broken and scattered my family. You see, when the dog attacked me I passed out and when I came to again, the pain in my face was unbearable. I wanted to scream because of the pain but my mother and brothers held me down. I have always believed that my mother did that because she hated me. Now I can see that the pain would have driven me wild and I probably would have caused myself further damage had I been let go.

I passed out again and I came to the next day and the pain was less but in its place was a hatred that had already taken over me. I did not speak to my mother again even when

239

she was dying. I had no mercy or forgiveness for her. My pride had locked me in a prison and I could not reach out to her. I just wanted to get away from her.

When she died, I took on the work of a servant with Elizabeth and little by little over the years my pride has broken down. Elizabeth and Zechariah treated me as though I did not have a scar. I felt that the world had cheated me out of a mother, a marriage and a life. When I came here, I realised that I have a family who love me in spite of my scar and what I have become. I waited to be rejected because I had made myself believe that they would. But they did not, they loved me."

"My friends," Tamar looked at each person around her, "I am glad that the Lord has shown me mercy and you have shown it to me with love. I hope that he will forgive me for the years of hatred that I built up inside my heart." The tears flowed down the woman's face and she began to sob. Elizabeth got up and went to her. She put her arms around her.

"My dear friend," she said, soothingly, "the Lord our God always hears a repentant heart. He waits for us to call out to him with all of our hearts. From the depths of our despair and with the realisation that we were wrong is when the Lord comes to heal and forgive. Do not worry, my dear, the Lord will forgive you and he will help you. We are all here to love you."

" *'No more shall every man teach his neighbour,'* " Joseph quoted once again, " *'and every man his brother, saying, 'know the Lord,' for they all shall know Me, from the least of them to the greatest of them, says the Lord. For I will forgive their iniquity, and their sin I will remember no more.'* You have no need to worry, Tamar, you are forgiven and you are healed according to the Lord's promise."

"Yes," said Mary, "you are well again, Tamar, the Lord has forgiven you, just as he has forgiven all of us. His mercy reaches all time and eternity and when we ask for it from the depths of our heart then we will receive it."

Still holding the woman, Elizabeth said, "Remember what Zechariah used to say, Tamar? He would lift himself up and raise his eyes to heaven and say: 'The Lord will give to those who give themselves to him.' You have given yourself to him this day and he will give to you."

The next morning at dawn there were tearful scenes as the little family took leave of one another to go their separate ways so that the Lord's work could be done. The small seed of what had begun was warm and snug in the earth, waiting for the rains and the sunshine that would provide its means of growth. Like a tiny child in the womb, it gathered around its mother's love.

–12–

Mary pondered the events of the last months within her heart. It was good to see Elizabeth and Tamar and John. She knew that she would always have a special place within her heart for them. She treasured the memories within her.

Her heart was the place that she retreated to, the place where she came face to face with herself and her God. It was the place where she felt the pain and sorrow and joy of those around her. It was the place that she brought all things before her God to give them to him.

Somewhere deep within her heart, she could feel a well. It was not a well that went downwards as the wells of the earth do but this went upwards into God. She felt strange with that thought but she knew that depth in God was always above her and went straight into the heart of God. It was where she wanted to be, deep in that upward well, rising always to greet the Lord within her heart. As the days passed in her life, she retired often to that well within her to find the solace and comfort of knowing him.

Within Jesus too, she could feel this well and often looked at him as he played or talked with her to find the depth of it. She felt that she knew this God, both in his son and within himself. She thought about the day when he had lifted her, to what seemed to be, into him. A journey that involved no travelling, only remaining still and compliant to his will. She felt that she had gone into his heart and it seemed natural to her to be there. She knew that it was not her body that had gone but her soul alone had travelled upwards into the well that led directly into his heart. She felt one with God.

She questioned herself more than once as to why she should be so privileged as to receive this sweet, singular attention. She could find no answers and none were given to her. God alone knew what he wanted from her and she was content to wait on him. Whatever he wanted from her he would show her, as he had already done.

When she had travelled upwards into the well, she had felt only that her soul was being loved to such a degree that it was burning, burning with the desire to love this being that had gripped her. She had felt the incongruousness of her earthly life against this living, breathing being that was her all in that moment. She felt again the burning that had overwhelmed her in its intricacy and intimacy. She could feel his passion for her fellowman and the pain that he felt. She could feel the darkness of evil, like whips that burned pain into him and which scarred him and which left him only capable of further love. Giving and wanting love was the intimacy of his existence. And she had loved, deeply within his being, plunged, as she was, deeply into him and fire burned within her, burned her soul into him. Like a brand that the Romans used to mark their slaves, she too was branded by this being, this all.

She had seen the depth of the light and that light was him. And far from blinding her it only enhanced her and gave her knowledge of him. She knew him and was one with him.

* * * * *

It was the fifth year after Elizabeth, Tamar and John had returned to the hill country. Joseph and Mary were preparing to go to Jerusalem for the Passover and it took a week, as it usually did. Each year Passover and the Festival of Unleavened Bread was the time that Joseph and Mary went with Jesus to the city. The annual trip to Jerusalem was a source of excitement in their hearts for it was the time to remember again how the Lord had taken them out of the slavery of the Egyptians. Combined in his instructions were the memories of how a God remembers his people, if they cry out to him for deliverance from slavery. Everyone had *Pesach* on their lips because the Angel of the Lord had 'leapt over' the Israelites.

Yahweh had instructed the people of Israel that on the tenth of the month of *Nisan* they must take a lamb without blemish and on the fourteenth of the same month, in the evening, the lamb was to be killed in sacrifice. The blood was then taken and ritually sprinkled on the doorposts and lintels of the houses in which it was to be eaten; those that were to be saved from the wrath of God. The lamb was not to be cooked nor boiled in water but roasted in fire, its head and its legs turned inwards. They had to eat, in haste, unleavened bread and bitter herbs dressed in travelling clothes and shoes on their feet as though going on a journey with a staff for walking. They were to remain in the house until morning and, because this Passover food could only be eaten during the night, burn everything that was not eaten.

All this had its significance in that when the Israelites left Egypt they would become God's chosen people. The sacrifice of the lamb and all that went with it was a consecration of themselves and an outward and an inward sign that they had severed themselves from all that was Egyptian and ultimately heathen.

It was God's way of making them belong to him for he had spared his wrath on them.

After the Exodus from Egypt, and the Israelites settled in the Land of Canaan, the Passover became the *'Permanent Passover'.* The paschal animals were to be slain in Jerusalem and the blood sprinkled on the Altar in the Sanctuary and not on the doorposts. Mary and Joseph went to Jerusalem and stayed there for the Feast of Unleavened Bread. From the fifteenth of *Nisan,* called *'the morrow of the Passover'* until the twenty-first, they presented their prescribed sacrifices and ate unleavened bread alone for the week. All was prepared and they were ready to go. The Exodus of the people from their homes was the calling together of the assembly of the people of Israel to worship God.

Arriving in Jerusalem, in the heat and with the thousands of people gathered there, the stench of human sweat was almost unbearable. So many people gathered there to do their duty before the Lord, called also the thieves to gather in great numbers for the pickings were ripe.

Joseph and Mary did not go directly to Jerusalem but skirted it and went the extra two miles to Bethany to find lodgings. They reasoned that they might have had more chance to find a room in a small village than in Jerusalem itself. It was Mary who had suggested it and said that they could walk into Jerusalem each day for the services. Jesus and Joseph had agreed.

Bethany was a small village that faced East on the southeast slope of the Mount of Olives and is on the main road to Jericho. They had passed it on their way to Jericho on the way back from Egypt. It was an alluring little village with only about twenty houses, an inn and a forge that shoed donkeys. Figs, almonds, olive trees prettied the village giving it a quaint look.

There were no rooms at the inn for other people had the same idea. They searched for an ideal spot to set up a tent for they had come prepared for everything. Just on the outer limits of the village and on the rise leading up to the Mount of Olives was a sprawling two-storied house built in the style of a Roman villa. It had many flowers growing in its garden and figs and olives provided shade for the occupants, whom Joseph could see from the road, and who sat now enjoying the evening's cool. Near its gate was a verge that bordered the road. The patch of ground was grassy and was about twelve feet square and on the part that bordered the house a small stream trickled joyfully down from the Mount.

"Mary, this looks like a good place but we must ask the owners of this house if we can put the tent up here."

"Yes, Joseph. Go and ask them and I will look after the donkey. Jesus, will you stay with me?"

"I will, mother. I will lead the donkey to the stream to give it a drink."

Joseph left his wife and son and walked up to the gate. He could tell from its wood and its newness that it had been expensive to make and buy. The wall around the house formed an arched opening that housed the gate and Joseph went up to it.

The latch was situated at the left side and he lifted it and the gate swung open. It was about five feet wide and about seven high, Joseph estimated. He closed it behind him. He could see ahead of him, about fifty yards, the people who must be the owners and they were looking at him. He felt embarrassed as he realised that they might think that he was trespassing. The road that he was now walking on, towards the house, was well made and did not have the usual potholes that inevitably formed with use. It was about six feet wide.

As Joseph approached, he noticed that they were not Romans as he had deduced from the style of the house but

245

they wore Jewish robes. His heart lifted. A fellow Jew was always good to find. A man and woman with three children sat at a long table on benches, their rich clothes told Joseph that they were wealthy. The smell of flowers was aromatic and strong in his nose. They looked at him kindly. The man looked in his late thirties and the woman slightly younger. There were two girls and a boy of about the same age as Jesus.

"I hope that I am not disturbing you...but I..."

The man spoke and said, "My good man you are not disturbing us. You look tired, please join us for a drink of wine."

"No, thank you. I just wanted to ask if I could use the piece of land outside your house to set up my tent for my wife and son. There is no room at the inn here..."

"My good man, this road is notorious for attacks from bandits for it is on the road to Jericho. I would not advise it. Why do you not camp inside the walls? My men patrol them all night and you will be safe there?" His bald-pate caught the sun and glinted in it.

"That would be most kind of you, sir. I thank you for your generosity."

The woman spoke. She had a round, jovial face. "When you set up your tent, please come and join us for a drink. I'm sure your good wife could do with a drink after your travelling and I'm sure that your son and these three could find something to do together."

"I will tell her. Thank you. Thank you."

Joseph walked away feeling happy. He could feel their eyes on his back.

* * * * *

"People seem to want the money to be stolen," said the tall girl. She was about ten years old and she was speaking to a group of children. She was the tallest. There were seven of them gathered near the Pool of Siloam. "So there's nothing to worry about. The people who keep bags of money, usually gold coins, around their necks or in pockets of tunics are fat merchants," she continued "and they can't run after you. The only thing is, to watch out for some do-gooder who will usually try to stop you. I find myself an alley to stand near, especially one that breaks off into narrower ones that lead near a gate. When I get the money bag I run as fast as I can into the alley and escape."

"But Lydia, its alright for you, you've done this for a long time, what if we get caught. We could end up on a cross."

Lydia laughed, "Children don't get crucified. You'll only get a scourging and let out the next day. Here, look! I've had it a couple of times." The girl pulled back the shoulder of her robe and showed, proudly, the scars that marked her skin.

"Oh, it looks painful," said a boy with freckles, feeling the lashes.

"Matthew, are you a coward?" Lydia accused, "after the lashes, a few days and you'll be as right as rain. The main thing is that you get the money. Come with me we need to practise."

Lydia led the small group away from the pool and towards the Refuse Gate.

Lydia was an orphan who had survived on the streets of the city for five years. Her mother and father had been thieves before her but about five years ago her father had been caught and crucified. He had tried to rob a Roman official who was coming to Jerusalem, not realising that a troop of soldiers were coming up the street that he was running down. The official's servants were coming down the street in pursuit of him and he had been caught. Lydia had been near him when the soldiers arrested him. She was to run with the money to her mother who was hiding in the next street. Both of them would then separate and lose themselves in the crowds and all three would meet outside the

Roman Theatre. This was the plan but that day it had not worked. She watched her father being dragged off by the soldiers; they were kicking him. She had run at the soldiers, screaming at them to stop hurting her daddy. One of them pushed her into a stall that was selling chickens. As she fell against it, the stall overturned and the chickens had escaped, squawking and protesting at the indignity of it all. By the time Lydia had untangled herself they had passed into the Fortress of Antonia, the Roman garrison. The next that she saw him he was hanging naked on a cross outside the city walls but it was too late, he was dead.

Her mother, Leah, had been heartbroken and the first few bottles of cheap, Roman wine were no harm for they had deadened the pain of grief. After the first six months, Lydia realised that she was on her own and began stealing food from the market stalls to feed her and her mother. It became easier to steal when your belly was empty and you had no choice. She kept her mother in food while she lay in a drunken stupor in the makeshift tent that they lived in the Valley of Hinnom. Others lived there but there was no help from them for they were just as poor.

Lydia remembered the night her mother had told her she was going out. She had drunk most of the day and had collapsed in the corner of the tent. Lydia had covered her up. After a few hours, Leah had woken and needed more of the Roman wine.

"I'll get it for you, mother," she had said. "Why don't you lie down again and I'll run into the city and get it."

"No!" Leah said through a fog of dying wine, " I am going for it myself."

"Mother, I'll..." Lydia had got no further. She felt her mothers fist drive into her mouth and knock her backwards out into the alleyway that ran between the tents. She touched her mouth and felt the blood.

"Never stand in your mother's way again, you little cur. I brought you up decent and this is how you treat me!" Leah gave a pert little shake of her shoulders and had walked off to get her bottle of wine.

Lydia had not found her mother for three days and then only by accident. Lydia had not worried about her mother, for many days she had wandered off to sell her body to the soldiers or indeed anybody who would buy the wine. Leah's body was turned face down in one of the cisterns that ran along the side of the Hippodrome near the Temple.

Lydia had cried when she saw her mother lying there. She could not help her now. This was the life that her mother had chosen for herself and it had killed her.

Lydia had taken a few of her friends and they had carried the body to the Valley of Hinnom where they threw it on the fires that continually burned there. Lydia watched as the flames licked over the body and consumed it. She cried as she thought of the sacrifices in the Temple. Maybe God would take her mother as a sacrifice. She watched her mother burn until sunset. It was the only burial that she could give her. Then she went home. That was when her life as a thief began.

Lydia gathered the little group about her. She was training them in the art of stealing.

"Matthew, you can be the fat merchant who sells oil, walking up to the Temple and you, Sarah, you are his wife. Put this bag of stones around your neck. The string is long enough. Now I'll stand over here and make my move. The rest of you watch me, not Matthew and Sarah! Now watch."

The boy and the girl began to mimic what they thought a fat merchant and his wife should look like. Lydia's eyes were peeled for the sign that she wanted. She walked towards them as though she were in a hurry, a small knife hidden in her sleeve and ready to drop into her hand. As she approached them, she deliberately collided with Matthew. In the same swift movement she caught her foot under Sarah's and tripped her. While they were falling the knife flashed and cut the cord that was holding the bag of stones and she deftly slipped it into the sleeve of her robe. From the moment she had bumped into Matthew she began apologising for being so clumsy and heaping hot coals on her head for the oaf that she was. It was a diatribe of words that she used all the time to confuse and soothe the victim. Lydia helped the hapless merchant and his wife to their feet, making great pretence of brushing them down. Then she was off walking away in a hurry.

The children who watched were cackling with laughter and enjoying the action.

"Matthew!" Lydia walked back to the scene "where are your bag of stones."

The boy grabbed at his chest and felt nothing. "But...but how?" He stammered, "You pushed me down and I was trying to save myself from falling."

"Exactly!" said Lydia, "That is exactly what I wanted you to do. I pretended to collide with you so that I could push you off balance. I tripped Sarah so that both of you would be only thinking of saving yourselves. And with my knife..." she turned her hand, palm upward, in slow motion so that it was out from her body. Then she slowly moved it downwards so that the knife glinted in the sun as it appeared, falling into her hand. She gripped the hilt in triumph and held it up for all to see.

The children cheered and clapped the dark haired girl and she revelled in their attention. She made a sweeping bow.

When they had all settled again, Lydia looked at them with a serious expression. "Now! Do you think that you could do that?"

Joseph and Mary and Jesus set up camp quickly within the perimeter of the stranger's wall. They settled the donkey allowing it to graze on the grass near the camp. With the stream as irrigation there was a good crop of grass. They went to the stream to wash sweaty faces and dusty feet to make themselves presentable to the people of the house. When they were done they walked towards the gate.

As they walked up the road that led to the house, they saw the man and the woman getting up from the table and making their way towards them.

"Shalom!" the man said, greeting them. "You are welcome to share our table. My name is Haman and my wife is called Mahlah. My children are Lazarus, Martha and Mary. Please, join us."

"Thank you" said Joseph. "My wife is called Mary and my son is Jesus. We are privileged to be at your table."

"Please sit," said Haman. "What would you like to drink? Water, a little wine?"

"Water would be all right," answered Joseph.

Mahlah spoke, "You are welcome! My husband does not know how to treat guests. I have some lemons steeping in water and it makes a good drink for thirsty people. Would you prefer that?"

"Yes, that would be lovely," said Mary.

Haman clapped his hands and from a door behind them where a blanket had been hung, a male servant came out. He was dressed in the short toga of the Romans.

"Yes, master?" said a tall, lanky youth, his dark hair cut short.

"Ah, Paulus, will you bring our guests a drink, please."

"Paulus," said Mahlah, "bring some of that lemon drink that I made earlier."

"Yes, mistress," Paulus said and walked back through the door.

"Now, Joseph and Mary, you look as though you have come a long way?"

"From Nazareth, Haman. We have come up for Passover. This year Mary suggested that we come here to look for lodgings. Jerusalem is usually so full and it has been diffi-

cult in other years to find a place to stay. Bethany is quiet."
"Mary was right. Jerusalem is a cutthroat place at Passover.
And the thieves, ah, they would steal the eye out of your
head as well as your purse."
They all laughed. Paulus returned with the drinks in clay
goblets and placed them on the table before each person.
He returned to where he had come from. The children
drank theirs and went off with Jesus to the other end of the
garden.
Mary looked at the couple that had introduced themselves
to her. The woman's jovial face had no wrinkles to show
the sign of age. She seemed to smile all the time. She was
kindly, and from what Mary could gather, both her and her
husband thrived in company. The man, with his baldness,
was greying in the little hair that he had left at the temples
and many laughter lines had crawled about his eyes. They
were a humble couple and they were obviously wealthy.
"Passover for us too is a time of pilgrimage" Haman was
saying, "even though we only live a mile or two from the
Temple, we walk into the city every day. It is a holy time."
"Yes," said Joseph, "we come to Jerusalem every year. It is
not always easy for my work is carpentry and many people
come to me with repairs around Nazareth."
"Oh!" said Mahlah "I could find plenty of carpentry work
for you around here. I have a husband who is deaf in one
ear when it comes to doing anything that I need doing!"
Joseph laughed. "God is good to me, he gives me plenty of
work."
"He is an excellent carpenter," said Mary taking a drink, "I
am glad to have him. God blesses us very much."
"I can see that you love one another very much," Mahlah
observed "and you both love God as though he lived with
you. There are not many today have that faith."
"The Lord, our God, is our life," said Mary simply.
"It is even better to know you then," said Haman, "we, ourselves, have faith in God but we find that not many others

share it. We have poured over the Messianic texts in the Scriptures searching for signs of him in today's world. So many believe that the Messiah is on his way but for political reasons and not as God's gift to the world. It saddens us."

Joseph coughed a little cough not really knowing what to say next but Mary spoke.

"We, too, believe that the Messiah will come soon. Our very lives work towards that day." Mary looked directly at Haman. "We believe that he will make himself known soon."

Haman looked back at Mary, "Then you are doubly welcome here for, I think, we speak the same language."

The four adults relaxed in each other's company. The day was growing older and with it the light softened. The smell of the flowers wafted around them pleasantly. They drank from the goblets and Mahlah called for more.

"You must eat with us," said Mahlah suddenly.

"Oh no, we could not do that," said Mary, "we have brought provisions with us."

"Mary, I am known to be a bully. I like to get my way. I will not hear of you saying 'no'. I will expect to make three extra meals tonight."

Haman laughed. "It is true, she is a bully. Please eat with us. It would be an honour to have you eat with us here."

Joseph looked at Mary and she smiled. "I would not wish to be bullied by you, Mahlah, but I will bully you if you do not let me help you prepare it."

"You can help me prepare it, Mary, I may even pick up some recipes from Nazareth!"

The four people laughed together and a spirit of friendship stalked up on them and captured them.

Lydia watched the clumsy movements of the children that were gathered around her; they were finding it difficult to think differently from the way they were acting. She had wanted them only to think of the money and how they were going to get it but they were laughing at themselves. 'It will come with time,' she sighed.

"All right, all right," Lydia said going into the middle of them, "let me show you again. You must stop laughing and concentrate on me and my movements and not the silly antics of Matthew and Sarah. Let's begin again and I will tell you what I am doing as I do it."

To their left were the fires of the Valley of Hinnom, burning incessantly. They sat behind a small rise that blocked their view of the city and any curious onlooker would only see a group of silly children playing.

The girl took up her position once more and indicated to the children to commence their role-playing. She went through the motions of stealing the moneybag. She could feel her stomach gnawing in hunger. 'I must go soon,' she thought, 'I must get something to eat, the light will soon be gone.'

The figs that were served after the meal were ripe and delicious and they had sat eating them and talking of the God that they believed in. They had recalled the prophet Isaiah's words and spoke of them with awe and respect. The evening was drawing in and it was getting chilly. The night would soon be dropping like a surprise attack on the world. The children came out of the house and joined them.

"We really should go to our tent," Mary said, "we must light a fire for the night, that is, if you do not mind a fire on your land, Haman."

"You will not be staying in your camp tonight, Mary," Mahlah chipped in, "I had the servants prepare you a room and you will be our guests for as long as you are in Bethany and Jerusalem. And I will not hear another word about it."

"But, Mahlah, you have already shown us your hospitality,

we cannot ask for more," Mary protested.

"Mary, my dear, this house boasts five rooms and surely you can have one of them. I will not hear of you and Joseph and Jesus out on this cold night. And that's an end to the matter." She paused for a moment and then continued, "Mary and Joseph, we are wealthy and to share our wealth with strangers is what God wants of us. What we give to you is what we give to the Lord, our God."

"I cannot argue with that. If God has planned it then we must accept," said Joseph.

Mary nodded, "We must go to our camp and pack up and bring the things that we need for tomorrow."

"The tent and all its contents will be safe tonight. My men will look after it so do not worry," said Haman.

"Thank you, Haman and Mahlah, for your kindness to us" said Joseph.

As they were settling for the night, in the room provided for them, Jesus spoke to Joseph and Mary. Mary noticed that his dark curls were straightening, as his hair got longer, and was too heavy to stay curled. She could see the depth in his eyes and it reminded her again of her heart.

"It is good to spend time here. These people are kind and good to us. Do you wish to stay here too?"

"Yes, Jesus," said Joseph, "I feel that the Lord has provided us with shelter and we will not refuse it. And you are right, they are kind and good."

Mary looked at her son, "Jesus, when we went to Egypt with you to escape King Herod, as we told you, the Lord brought us to Absalom who was good and kind to us," she ruffled his hair, "and now he is showing his kindness to us again through Haman and Mahlah. The Lord, our God, is good and kind to us and he shows that kindness to us through his people. We were strangers to them yet they have invited us into their home. You seem to have made friends with Lazarus and Martha and Mary."

"Yes, I like them," said Jesus. "They were showing me around the land here and we went up on the Mount of Olives. It is a good place to be. It is quiet there and we can talk."

Joseph said, "I am thinking about the prophet Isaiah where it is written: *'...in a little wrath I hid my face from thee for a moment; but with everlasting kindness will I have mercy on thee, saith the Lord, thy Redeemer. For the mountains shall depart and the hills be removed but my kindness shall not depart from thee, neither shall the covenant of my peace be removed, saith the Lord that hath mercy on thee. O thou afflicted, tossed with tempest, and not comforted, behold, I will lay thy stones with fair colours, and lay thy foundations with sapphires.'* His kindness lasts forever and I believe that he gave this kindness. I praise him for it. We will stay here until it is time to go."

Jesus said, "It is good to stay here, thank you for allowing it."

Mary caught her son in her arms and embraced him. "We must sleep now, my son, for we must be up at dawn to go to the Temple. Passover is here."

The girl went back to the hovel that she called home in the darkness of night. A bat swooped down near her to investigate her footsteps echoing on the ground. All around her she could see twinkling fires that were warming the occupants of the Hinnom Valley, lit from the refuse fires that burned about two hundred yards away from her and provided some light. When there was no breeze, the air in the valley was in a perpetual smoky mist from them. She walked past her home and towards the nearest fire. There were four people sitting around it; two men and two women; the women's hair and clothes were unkempt and dirty and Lydia knew that that was all that they had. One of the men was poking the fire with a long stick, his face wrinkled in its light. The other man was younger and looked up at her with growing interest as she approached.

"Hail! to you all" she said. "Daniel, give me a piece of the fire to light my own."

"Take it," said Daniel.

The younger man spoke. "It will cost you," he said.

Lydia looked at him, defiantly. She went to the fire. The four were sitting like sentinels around it, gathering its heat into their bodies. She went to the space between the two women, needing their safety. She picked up a branch that was burning at one end. As she did so she noticed that the younger man was rising from his place.

"I said it would cost you, Lydia!"

The girl ignored him and walked away from the fire with her burning branch. She felt him grip her arm with one hand and the other touched her belly, seductively. She glared at him and noticed the leering smile on his lips. He licked them.

"Like this," he said. "Let's go behind the rocks here..."

"No, Asa. I can get a fire somewhere else," she answered firmly. "Let go of me, Asa!"

Still leering at her, his hand hesitated a little then began to travel up her body slowly and in little circle motions. The women and the man cackled behind her.

"Asa! Let go of me!" she warned again trying to make it sound as though she meant it.

"Come on," Asa said, "I know that you want it too."

Lydia's hand gripped tighter the branch that she was holding. Suddenly she lifted it and in a swift movement that Asa did not see coming, she touched his hair with the burning end, flaming now with the movement. His hair was in flames. Asa let go of her very quickly and began to frantically pat his head with his hands.

"You dog!" he shouted, "I'm burning...I'm burning...help!"

Freed now from his grip, Lydia walked away triumphant, her fire in her hands.

"I'll get you for this," Asa shouted after her. Lydia just smiled as she walked.

Home consisted of long, thick branches of about six feet in height, placed upright to form walls. Its roof was a natural overhang of rock and the logs leaned against it. Inside was a space of about six feet by eight feet. It was cool and comfortable, although, now, with age, the logs had become rickety. Her father had built it before he was crucified and it was like a legacy to the girl.

Lydia kept little in the hut for she knew that the others who lived nearby would steal it. Except for a few blankets to keep out the cold, which lay heaped in a corner on top of mouldy straw and served as a bed, there were a few nonmatching stools and a table that she had saved from the fires. The smell was damp to her nostrils. Lydia pulled off her dirty veil and went and lay on the bed.

She had eaten well tonight, she had been able to steal a chicken that had been cooked and left on a table outside near the Essene Gate. It had been so easy and no one had challenged her. She had walked out through the gate and around the Hinnom to the Fountain Gate. She ate her prey as the sun disappeared behind the hills of the Kidron Valley. She felt her belly full as she remembered. She had met up with none of her friends so she had eaten alone. She liked it that way.

The girl remembered Asa and smiled. He would not try that again. He had tried it before but she had run away from him. Never before had she dared to hurt him but at least he would know now that she would not take his advances without a fight. His threats were empty, but still she fingered the knife that was buried warm in her hand, ready for any attacks that might come in the night. The knife was her friend; it was her family and her security. Survival, for her, glinted in that knife.

Lydia sighed and turned over, wriggling in the hay to find a comfortable position. 'I must change this straw,' she thought, 'it must be crawling with insects by now.' She must sleep for it was *Pesach* tomorrow and there would be rich pickings in the streets of Jerusalem; pickings that she wanted a part of.

–13–

Lydia stood at the Sheep Gate eyeing all those who were going into the Temple precinct. She was watching for fat merchants as she called them, the kind that could not chase her. She looked too for those merchants who had few servants with them. She had to keep her eyes peeled, for the people who were gathering for the Festival of *Pesach* were, even at this early hour, gathering in their thousands; all pursuing the goal of cleansing sin. The animal sellers were outside the Gate and lined up against the outer wall, which, on one side, backed up on to the Praetorium. Soldiers shouted obscenities from the narrow windows at the people but these were lost in the cacophony of voices that wanted to buy lambs to cleanse their sin but were not willing to pay the full price for them. Those yearling lambs that had not yet been searched for blemish and sold, bleated loudly to make their protests heard. They were not heard over the madding roar of human voices that emerged from a sea of mouths.

Lydia smiled at gaily coloured women, whose perfume announced their coming, gracefully trailing long trains of robes behind them in an effort to impress an entrance and were suddenly stopped short when someone stepped ungainly on their trains; these warranted a barrage of near obscenities at the hapless perpetrator of the capital crime. Composure quickly retained, another effort was made.

As she watched the spectacle of many people gathered together, each an island, she thought about their purpose for being there. They came for God. But who was God? He was someone who did not help her, nor care for her. All these prayerful faces were going to worship some gold box somewhere in the Temple, their money in their pockets. This God only wanted rich people, it seemed, and that did not include her. So her god was not this one, or any one. This Yahweh had never revealed himself to her and she would not reveal herself to him. Even the Roman gods were silent, stone statues that just stared back at you with cold, marble eyes when you asked them for anything. No, she did not believe. Tears were her comfort, not a dead god; she relied on her own wits, not on marble.

The air was heavy with the sound and smell of mankind but Lydia's eyes gleaned each one that passed her to find that sign that she waited for and the right moment. If you went at the wrong moment it would inevitably end up in disaster. So she waited, patiently. The knife was ready and so was she.

Then she saw him. He was walking towards her, a small plump man whose breathing laboured and his three chins wobbled as he walked. He was speaking to no one, which could mean that he had no servants with him. His leather moneybag, on a thong around his neck, seemed to glint at her. The girl's eyes drank in the figure, mentally counting the money. Like a leopard stalking prey, she started memorising all the details that she could of how fast he walked and how tired he looked. The man became her target, her prey.

The portion of the crowd that he was in was about ten yards away from the gate. As he came close, she would push through the crowd and trip him, cut his moneybag, help him up and get lost in the crowd again. It was simple. Victims usually helped her game unwittingly, by blaming themselves for the malady.

The man was almost level with her now and like a cat, the

girl sprung, pushing her way into the blur of sweaty bodies like the current of a river; elbows out, she bullied and fought, never once losing sight of her prey. Many mumbled obscenities at her as she swam against them in the river of bodies. Then she was face to face with him, his ruddy cheeks glistening with sweat.

Lydia put her head down and charged forward with all her strength into the padded body of the man. Her right shoulder caught his and she could feel the bulk of his body give and begin to go backwards. He flailed his arms in an effort to save himself. Lydia could hear screams as women were caught in his fall, confusion and panic coming to aid the thief. She went with the fall, releasing the knife. With practised movement, she cut the thong and the heavy moneybag plopped into her hand. She closed her hand over it. Other people had fallen who were behind and around the man; his weight had pulled about six people onto the ground.

"I am so sorry, sir," Lydia said, as they and a few others hit the ground. "I am so clumsy, please forgive me. I was just trying to get to my mother..." she was trying to get him up by the hand, he was winded, "I lost her, you see."

"You stupid girl," said an indignant woman who was picking herself off the ground, "what did you do that for?"

"I'm sorry, I'm so sorry..." Lydia turned on tears and began to back away, the crowd still milling around her. In a few moments the victims were out of sight, swallowed up in the crowd. Lydia turned her back on them and began to walk with the flow of the crowd and away from the man. A triumphant little smile was dancing on her lips.

Lydia felt an iron hand grip her left wrist. She jerked around quickly to see a bald man walking with her and looking at her.

"Let go of..." she said, her mouth twisting into a grimace.

"Walk!" the man hissed through his teeth, tightening his grip on her wrist. "Do not cry out, young lady, or I will take you to the garrison. Now walk."

"Who are you?" Lydia tried to speak.

"Hush!"

Lydia was frightened now. This man obviously knew about or had seen her stealing the moneybag and probably wanted to share it. He must be a master of a school of thieves, come up to the city for the Feasts. 'I'm probably on his patch,' she thought as he dragged her further and deeper into the crowd. 'Well, I won't give it up without a fight.'

She tried wrenching her arm a few times, testing his grip but it was as though she were in a manacle.

They were now beginning to break away from the crowd as they rounded into the Temple and were veering towards the Horse Gate, which was at the back of the Temple. They had to fight their way against the tide of those who were entering that way. They stopped and stood back to let a century of Roman soldiers pass them by. Lydia waited for the man to hand her over to them but he did not.

Once outside they walked directly east and uphill. They left behind the coolness of the buildings of the Temple and entered the baking heat of the Kidron Valley. At the top of the small hill they came to a garden, a lush olive grove that was called Gethsemane. Lydia knew it and had often run here to escape some victim that was limber enough to give chase after she had robbed him.

Gethsemane had a wall with four gates, each on the points of the compass. They entered the south gate. The aroma of flowers greeted them, their heady smell caught Lydia's nose and she inhaled deeply.

The man brought her to the southeast corner of the wall and then he let go of her arm. She rubbed the stiffness in it, getting the blood flow back once more. She sized the situation. The corner of the wall was behind her and this man in front; if she ran he would catch her for he looked lithe enough to outrun her.

"What do you want from me?" Lydia said guardedly.

"I saw you steal that moneybag from David. He is a silk merchant and I know him well. My name is Haman."

"Why did you not bring me to him then? Maybe you want to share it. You would steal your friend's money?" Lydia said trying to unnerve him.

"I do not need to steal. I have my own. Anyway, I do not care for the money; it is you that I care about. I brought you here to talk to you."

"What? You care about me? Don't make me laugh. You brought me here to have your way with me in the quiet of this Garden. You are all the same! Well, the answer is no!" she finished defiantly folding her arms across her chest.

"I do not require your body, young woman. I simply wish to help you so that you will not have to steal and live on the streets anymore."

"And how would you do that?" the girl laughed. 'Why is this man doing this?' she asked herself, 'what is his game? He doesn't want the money or me, so what is going on?'

Lydia noticed a group of people approach. There were two women and a man and four children followed. They walked up to Haman.

"Joseph," said Haman "thank you for following me. I'm sorry, it all happened so quickly I did not get time to explain much. I have seen this girl before a few times, she lives out in Hinnom. She took a purse and I wanted to talk to her."

The man, Joseph, turned and spoke to her. He had dark hair that fell to his shoulders and looked to be in his thirties. He looked kindly. "My name is Joseph," he said. "This is my wife, Mary, and my son, Jesus." He indicated a young woman and a curly haired boy about her own age. The boy's eyes were very piercing but kindly like his father's. "This is Mahlah, Haman's wife, and Lazarus, Martha and Mary. What is your name?"

"Do you think I will tell you my name to have you report me to the Romans?"

"We will not report you to the Romans, you can be assured of that," said Haman, "I saw you steal the purse and I wished to help you, that is all. If I had not taken you when I did you would have been arrested. The man that you stole from was on his way to the Temple and from there he was invited to the palace to trade with the Roman officials' wives. If he has described you, you will be searched for and caught."

Lydia was frightened. This man could get her into trouble if she was not careful, better to cooperate with them a little. 'He knows where I live too.' "My name is Lydia."

"Will you eat with us, Lydia?"

The girl was sultry and answered, "No! I don't want your food."

"Lydia, you are not a prisoner, you may leave as and when you wish. I did not bring you here to condemn you, only to offer you help and to save you getting arrested. And I am not going to take the money from you. I will replace the money you took and give it to David."

"How can I go? Half the city's soldiers are probably searching for me. I may as well stay here."

Lydia sat on her haunches and looked at the man. 'Why is he doing this?' she wondered. 'Why is he offering me freedom and letting me keep the money? Is he mad? He has obviously placed himself in a lot of trouble to bring me here.'

The family had spread themselves out on the ground and the women were taking various fruits, bread, cheese and vegetables from bags. It looked good to Lydia and she could feel the hunger pangs in her belly. They looked so happy. She had never known that happiness. She had never known a meal with a family that did not have to be stolen. The woman called Mary proffered her some bread and cheese. She did not say anything; she just looked at her, smiled and offered. She had a kind face.

Mary was about five yards away and the food looked good. 'Well,' thought Lydia, 'I'll get a free meal.' She moved forward on her haunches and took the bread. Mary indicated to her to sit beside her but Lydia shook her head and moved back, hungrily eating. None of them were watching her and she could easily walk away and sit in another part of the Garden.

Lydia looked at Mahlah, she was laughing with her children who were all so nicely dressed. She looked at her own rags. These clothes had been taken from the fires in Hinnom and had only a few scorch marks on them.

Mary was busy with the food, packing away that that was finished with and unpacking what was needed. The boy, Jesus, was looking at her. He was smiling. That smile made her feel uncomfortable.

'He can see me,' she thought. 'It is like he is looking through me.' Lydia shivered and cast her eyes down tearing herself away from that smile. It was not a bad smile, no, it was good but it seemed as if he knew her, deep inside, like he had grown up with her and lived with her. But she had never seen him in her life before this day. She glanced up at him. He was still smiling. He was getting up and coming towards her. He was taller than her and he wore a simple robe with a blue cord around the middle and a light striped coat. 'Oh no!' she thought, 'he is probably some do-gooder and is going to try to get me to be one too.'

The boy went on his haunches in front of her, his eyes a dancing smile. They made her feel like she did when she took a moneybag that she had stolen and poured the contents out to count it.

"Shalom, Lydia!" he said, his voice was the clink of many gold coins to her ears and the joy of finding them. "Would you like to go for a walk into the Garden with us? We would be pleased to have you."

Pleased? *Pleased?* No one had ever said *that* to her before. She had always been a loner and only used friendship when she needed it to her own advantage. She could feel herself softening like wet earth after it has rained. She looked into his face, seeking reasons for his realness and not caring whether she found them. The discomfort was gone.

"Yes...I...I...if you want me?"

"Yes," he answered, his smile a grin, "of course I want you."

The five children walked deeper into the Garden. The olive trees were cool and a breeze playfully teased the dark branches. The flowers that Lydia had smelled earlier were planted in and around them and these exuded a pleasant aroma around the children. Lydia was feeling unsure among these others and lagged behind, not trusting their company. Each time she did, Jesus would stop and wait for her to catch up. It made her feel wanted.

Lazarus was speaking, his short black hair ruffling in the breeze.

"I would rather go to the Temple when there are less people. In that crowd all you get to see is someone's back or head. They mill about like sheep and they step on your toes or knock you down." Martha and Mary giggled.

"Yes," said Martha, "that happens me too. I think that shoes made of iron instead of sandals might help." Martha was a plump girl and had permanent freckles on her round face. She was the oldest of the group at nearly twelve.

"When people gather together to worship Yahweh," Jesus said, "then God is among his people to love them. Love is important to him. That is why this day is a day of gathering so that they can remember that he passed over them and did not harm them."

Mary spoke. "We already know that God led our ancestors out of Egypt and gave them the Land of Canaan but why do we have to keep on remembering and celebrating? I mean, we are not slaves in Egypt anymore." She was a tall, thin girl with ruddy cheeks.

"Each Law that God lays down has a meaning to it," Jesus answered. "It is there because something else will happen if it is not there. If you work in the fields and your hands are dirty and you do not wash them, what happens?"

"Your food is dirty and you can't eat it. Yes, I can see that. So the *Pesach* is there so that we will remember that God took us out of slavery?"

"Not only that, Mary, but also what happens when we turn away from him. The Israelites wandered in the wilderness for forty years, disobeying God and the Promised Land was quite close but they could not enter it until they came back to his ways. They had turned against him and went against his law and they could not have the land that he provided for them." Jesus looked at Lydia. "Will you sit with us, Lydia?"

"Yes," she said simply. They spoke about this God of theirs as though he were really there. But he's not. But the way that this Jesus talks about him it is like he knows him. 'How does he know all this?' she thought.

They sat on the ground under an olive tree whose trunk was thick and gnarled with age. Lydia sat with her legs pulled up to her chin and her arms around them. The others sat opposite her. Lazarus sprawled out.

"It tells us in the Scriptures," Jesus said, still looking at her.

Lydia jumped as though she had sat on a thorn. She looked at this boy who was about the same age as her. 'How did he know what I was thinking?' she thought, 'can he hear me or read my thoughts?'

"I can't read," said Lydia, defending her thoughts.

"You will learn to read at Haman's house" Jesus said easily.

"But I'm..." He did not hear her. She looked at the others. They were just as shocked as she was but they did not question him.

"Lydia, you do not need to read to know God in your heart. All you need to do is to talk to him. He will listen."

"I've tried to talk to him before but he never answered. So why should I try now just because you say so?"

"Because he loves you."

It was the way that he said it that startled Lydia. His words cut into her heart like a knife. She could feel her heart beat faster as the words skipped around in her mind as a flat stone does when you skip it across the water. She felt embarrassed and confused by the words.

"But he doesn't even know me" Lydia said, letting her guard down for a moment. Her face reddened.

"Lydia, he looks at you all the time, even now."

The girl's heart raced. His words seemed to touch her heart like fingers, enclosing and capturing. His eyes looked at her again with that look. She looked back at him. There was no one else there but him. It seemed that the olive trees, the sky, the flowers were gone. Only him in her line of vision; there was only that look that came from within him. And it held her. Held her as though she were a baby. She could feel something that she had not felt before and it frightened her, no, it loved her. He could see her. Her soul felt naked before this boy. She knew every wrong that she had done, the stealing. She had never felt its wrongness before; never felt the sin. It was her survival, her sustenance, her food, her way of life.

She saw it now as though it were someone else, watching this girl live her life. She could feel the hurt, the pain that that wrongness had caused the boy. Why would it cause him pain? Something strange and stark and yet beautiful was touching her. There was no one else looking at her but him. Was he God? No, he was just a boy.

Jesus said, "We must return now, so that we can go to the services in the Temple." He stood up and turned from her. The others were looking at her in a strange way.

Lazarus walked up to her and put out his hand to help her

268

up. She took it. "He knows everything and when he says it, it is right," he said. Lydia looked at Lazarus and began to walk after Jesus.

When the children returned, Mary could feel the lingering traces of the Spirit of the Lord. She could see that Lydia had changed. The girl now came and sat with the family as though she belonged. Mary went to her and put her arm around her. She looked at Lydia. The girl's eyes were hungry but it was not a hunger of the belly, no, it was a hunger of the soul. Mary knew that the girl had found her soul.

The evening had merged into night and the moon now sat above the horizon and the stars twinkled in the darkened sky. An owl hooted somewhere in the distance that Lydia was looking into. From her position on the Mount of Olives, she could see the house and all the activity of the evening. She could see the silhouettes of houses and trees in the valley before her and little lights twinkling like eyes in a black face. It was strange. Here she was at Haman's house and she had been welcomed like a daughter. She had given the moneybag to Haman earlier as though it was the most natural thing in the world to do. Haman had embraced her and she noticed tears in his eyes. He had got up from his place at the table and insisted she sat in it, as he would have done for the guest of honour. All eyes had been on her. Usually, she loved to be the centre of attraction and revelled in it but she had felt shy under the gaze of these people. Mahlah had served her first, even before her husband. Lydia had protested. She knew her place but they would not hear her. Mahlah had said that she was their honoured guest and it was time that her husband climbed down from that throne, he was getting too proud anyway. They had all laughed and she had laughed with them.
It was good to laugh, good to share.
But what had happened to her. Why was she allowing this

269

to happen to her? She was like a wild cat; she had no fixed abode and could roam anywhere. She could steal the food off the table before they knew it was gone, and she would be gone, lost in the night. Something had changed within her; something had been severed. She did not know what or how.

She leaned against an olive tree, putting her head against it as though it were soft and comforting. Everything seemed soft to her since this morning. Even the ground did not seem hard when she walked on it. Her heart, most of all, had softened and now felt like a ripe fruit within her.

And what was this strange feeling that seemed to walk with her? It was like a presence, it was like *someone.* Her heart seemed to be on fire and painful, except it was not a pain. It was peace.

Something within the girl was trying desperately to shout out to her. She knew it was the knife calling her back. The knife had been her family for five years. It was her father, mother and family. It burned in her pocket.

Her thoughts were broken by a small sound that echoed in the night and she saw a figure emerge from the house. It was Mary, the mother of the boy, Jesus. Lydia liked her. She was easy to like and reminded Lydia of a sister. She heard her call out, softly, "Lydia..."

Lydia emerged from the shadow of the olive and said, "I'm here, Mary."

Mary walked up the slight rise to join her. Her movements were that of a young girl and her long dark hair fell free from her veil.

"It is cold, Lydia, I brought you this shawl to warm you. I will leave you again with your thoughts."

"No, don't! I mean...please stay for a little while."

Mary looked at the girl. "Yes, I will, if you want me to."

"Yes, I want you to." Lydia did not know what she wanted to say to this young woman, this stranger.

The woman looked at the stars, "I can understand why you

want to be out here, even if it is cold," said Mary, "God's creation is very beautiful. Oh look! A falling star, did you see it, Lydia?" The girl nodded, smiling. The two searched the heavens for more. Then Lydia spoke.

"Mary, I...I...do not know what I am doing here but I want to be."

"I know, Lydia."

"But...but why is everyone making a fuss of me? I am a thief, Mary. I steal even my food. No one wants a thief, you can't trust me, Mary."

"Lydia, we can trust you. You are a young girl. We do not see you as a thief."

"Mary, you don't understand. I could steal everything in Haman's house. I could find his money and walk away with it and you would never see me again."

"But, Lydia, you would not be stealing. Everything that Haman has is yours. You can take it if you wish."

"What?" the girl looked incredulously, "but you can't do that!"

"Lydia, nothing belongs to us, it all belongs to God so therefore it belongs to each one of us because it belongs to God. If you need it then you shall have it. It is the way that God's people live."

"But if you have worked for it and gained it honestly then it is yours."

"No, Lydia, God has provided all for us. We cannot take what belongs to someone else and keep it for ourselves. It belongs to God and we must share it with anyone who needs it. That is why there are so many poor. A few people take what God has provided and do not share it so people starve. You are the victim of someone who has not shared Gods wealth with you. Anything that is in Haman's house is yours and if you ever come to Nazareth, it is your home."

"But who is this God? I have never heard of him."

"It is the Lord, our God."

271

"Your son, he seems to know this God. He talks about him. Jesus looked at me today and I saw my whole life. I thought that he would have pushed me away but he did not, he just looked at me and welcomed me."

Mary looked at the girl. She could just make out her face in the semi darkness. It was full of questions. "Lydia, let me tell you a story." Mary put her arm around Lydia. "Do you like stories?"

The girl nodded.

"This is a true story..." Mary began. Mary told Lydia about her experiences with Gabriel and about Egypt and the locusts. She told her about the dreams and Joseph. The girl listened attentively asking questions now and again. When Mary spoke of the killing of the children in Bethlehem, Lydia put her head on Mary's shoulder.

"...And we came back to Nazareth and have lived there ever since under God's command." Mary finished off.

Lydia said nothing. She was filled with a sense of peace. She realised that she had put her head on Mary's shoulder and lifted her head. "I'm sorry," she said.

"Why? I do not mind. Any time you need a shoulder, come to me."

"Mary, these things are so strange to me. I cannot take them in. But I can understand now why Jesus can look at me the way he does. He is the Messiah, isn't he?"

"Yes," said Mary easily.

"I believe that he is. He has made me look at my life in a different way and I want to change it. How do I do that, Mary?"

"We change ourselves. We die to the ways that keep us away from God and become what he has planned for us. We take away the sin in our lives and we do not allow it to touch us again."

Lydia thought about how she had realised that her stealing had hurt Jesus in some way and she knew what she must do.

"Mary, I have to do something. Will you stay with me as I do it?"

"But of course, Lydia."

As they entered the door of the house they were arm in arm. The room was the main room of the house and it was large and airy with a marble floor. A table took up the centre with various chairs, some made of wood and others cushioned for comfort. A large chest, ornate with painted pictures of animals, commanded the room. Haman stood at an open fire with a goblet in his hand. Lazarus and Jesus and Joseph sat in front of him. They were discussing the fall of mankind from Eden. The two girls and Mahlah were not in the room.

Lydia hesitated a moment, looked at Mary, who smiled, and walked over to where Jesus sat. He had his back to her. Her heart raced trying to catch up with her thoughts. 'What if he does not accept me?'

Haman saw her approach and stopped mid sentence. Lydia ignored him and walked until she stood in front of Jesus. He looked at her with those eyes. There was that strange, stark and beautiful feeling in the room. It made her want to fly and run at the same time. It reminded her of the times when her father had called her his 'little flower of the field'. That had made her feel special but the times when he had said it were few and far between. Now it was like it was being whispered over and over again into her heart. Lydia was afraid but she knew she had to do it; knew that she wanted to do it. She wanted more of what he had given her; she did not want it to stop.

She stood in front of him, watching for any sign that he might not want her, searching for signs that he might reject her. But there were none. His eyes were open doors, open that the world might walk in there. They were open like the doors of the Temple. Lydia saw herself running in. She knelt in front of him, her heart wild now. She cast her eyes down to the marble floor it was cold and unyielding. She searched for the knife in her pocket and took it out. She looked at it in her hand. It glinted in the firelight, warm and friendly to her.

"I...I wanted to give this to you. I don't know why. It is all I have and all that stops me from coming to you. It has kept me alive but...but I don't need it anymore if you accept me. Will you?" Lydia placed the knife at the feet of Jesus and looked up at him.

"I am honoured," he said, "I accept it and you." He made a little bow.

Lydia felt the dam burst in his eyes and a river caught her up and carried her away into somewhere, somewhere that she had never been before. The river was not wet but it penetrated her and pierced her. Her own tears broke and spilled. They were tears for her and tears for the father whom she had seen on a cross; they were for her mother whom she had burned on the fires at Hinnom. They were for her life and her loneliness. They were for this love that exuded from this boy for her.

Jesus got up and stood before her. He put out his hands. Lydia took them and stood. Jesus put his arms around her and embraced her.

Haman's mouth fell open. He watched the little scene unfold in front of him and wondered. He knew that Jesus had said something to the girl earlier when they had gone into the garden and Lydia had accepted the invitation to come and live with him but he had put it down to the children talking among themselves. But this, this was different. Jesus had showed himself to be well versed in the Scripture and could answer questions on it but this? This was something else.

The girl walked in and handed over the knife that she carried. Haman knew that all the Hinnom people carried knives and it was for their protection. They would stick it in you as quick as anything. He knew that when a knife was removed from one of them it was like removing their arm. What was going on?

Jesus was not surprised to see her come. It was like he knew it was going to happen. He smiled at her and it seemed like he was forgiving her, her sins. But no! He could not do that! Only God can forgive sins! What sort of...

Realisation fell like a wall on Haman. The only way that he could forgive sins was if he was God. But no! Haman fought with his thoughts; he cannot be God. What is going on here? Unless...unless he was...the Messiah.

Haman's thoughts raced about him as he watched Jesus embrace Lydia. The girl was crying and laughing and trying to talk. She had definitely changed since this morning. She had been like a spitting, cornered animal when he had brought her to Gethsemane. He could see the boy's mother behind; she was smiling and coming towards them to embrace Lydia. Joseph was smiling; he was not surprised either. They knew, they knew and were not surprised by it. He must find out what was happening here. Mahlah appeared in a doorway that led to another part of the house. "What is all the fuss in here," she said.

When the children had retired to their couches, Haman asked Joseph and Mary to stay behind so that he could talk to them. The fire burned low in the room and cast formidable shadows.

"Mary, Joseph, I asked you to stay here so that I could talk to you."

"I have no objection, Haman. Speak, please."

Haman paced up and down, he was agitated. He did not know how to put into words what he was trying to say. His wife, Mahlah was looking at him, puzzled.

He stopped pacing and looked at them. "Let me quote to you what the prophet Isaiah has said: *'And the Spirit of the*

Lord shall rest upon him, the spirit of wisdom and under-standing, the spirit of counsel and might, the spirit of knowledge and of the fear of the Lord. And shall make him of quick understanding in the fear of the Lord, and he shall not judge after the sight of his eyes, neither reprove after the hearing of his ears, but with righteousness shall he judge the poor, and reprove with equity for the meek of the earth and he shall smite the earth with the rod of his mouth, and with the breath of his lips shall he slay the wicked. And righteousness shall be the girdle of his loins, and faithfulness the girdle of his reins.' This quotation you are already familiar with, it is one of the texts in the prophet's writings that speak to us of what the Messiah will be like when he comes.

I have told you that I have pored over these texts for many years and I have searched for him to see if he might not come in my lifetime. I do not know but this night I may have found him."

"Haman, I..." began Joseph.

"Joseph, please do not interrupt me. I must say this. It is of extreme importance. You have been here for two days and from the outset of your coming, I have been highly impressed with your son, Jesus. His learning and knowledge of the Scriptures is remarkable and he has explained the Scriptures to me in a new way so that texts that I have previously misunderstood, he was able to explain their true meaning to me in such a simple way.

These same texts I have discussed with many of the most learned and cultured men in Jerusalem and they have not been able to answer them." Haman paused, "but Jesus has." He paused again. "Your son has the 'Spirit of the Lord'. It rests upon him. He has the *'spirit of wisdom and understanding, the spirit of counsel and might, the spirit of knowledge and of the fear of the Lord.'* And with *'righteousness he has* judged *the poor.'*

Today he brought Lydia here. She is like a wild animal, the

276

only thing that she knows is her own environment and how to steal and survive. She walked in here tonight and placed her knife in front of him. That girl's knife is everything that she needs for her survival. It is her very life. Lydia placed her life at his feet and he *forgave* her." He stopped to look at his audience. "Do you not see? Forgiveness is the exclusive prerogative of God only. No one can forgive unless he carries the authority of God. The only one who carries that authority is the Messiah.

I saw the authority of God this night in my own home. I believe that your son is the Messiah."

Joseph spoke again. "May I tell you a story?" he said. "Then you might be able to judge for yourself. You will understand that it is not a story that we tell everyone." Joseph began the story of his life from the time when the Angel, Gabriel, came to Mary.

When he had finished, Mahlah said, "We are truly blessed within this house. I believe what you have said to me. Halleluiah and praise to the Lord, our God, for his witness to us this night. You are truly blessed, both of you, and we are blessed to have you within our home."

Joseph said, "We did not tell you, the Lord, himself, has told you."

The next day they all went up to the Temple again and they all began to teach Lydia the laws of God concerning women. The girl had asked to be told about this God whom she did not know, whom Jesus had taught her about in his smile. She was taken under Mahlah's wing and the woman taught her to pray. Haman returned the moneybag to David and told him the story of Lydia's conversion. They sat on one of the stone benches that lined the wall of the Court of Israel.

"You mean she has now become converted?"

"Yes," said Haman.

"Well, well, well, it is not often that the like of this happens.

277

And you tell me that she has used this ploy to steal, many times?"

"Yes," repeated Haman.

"Well, the Lord, our God works in many mysterious ways. You know that I did not even notice that the purse was gone until I reached the palace? So this Lydia would have been long gone." David chuckled to himself. "I took a mighty fall that day. I brought quite a few down with me. I tell you, that girl has some strength when she can knock an old fat fool like me off my feet. It is not an easy thing to do." The man laughed at himself.

David sat and thought quietly for some time. Haman was about to say that he needed to be on his way, thinking that the man had lapsed into sleep, when he spoke. David asked, "Would it be possible to meet this Lydia? I know that we have already met in passing but I would like to meet her properly."

"I will ask her and I will let you know. I will meet up with them now. You realise that she may not want to meet you out of sheer embarrassment?"

"Yes, I know that, Haman, but I would like to try all the same."

"If she wishes to meet you we will be at the Temple doors at the ninth hour. If we do not come in a little while then you will know. If we are delayed then I will send Paulus ahead of me."

"That would be good," said David, "I have a little business to attend to first. Until then, my friend."

"Adieu, David, until then."

A few hours later, the family gathered together and walked towards the Temple doors. Lydia was nervous but she wanted to apologise to this man for what she had done.

"Hail, David!" said Haman when he saw his friend.

"Ah! Hail, Haman! Hail Mahlah! And how are you my good woman?"

278

"I am well David. And how is your good wife, Rebecca?"

"She is well, Mahlah."

Haman waited until the pleasantries had been spoken and then he brought David and introduced him to Lydia.

"David, I am sorry that I knocked you down. You see it was all part of the game that I was playing..."

"Lydia, my dear, I admire your strength and courage that you would attempt to knock a man of my size down and succeed. That is a game and a half! Worry not about it anymore for it has caused me many a laugh and I chuckle to myself when I think of it." He chuckled again as he thought of it. "But that is not why I have asked you here. Come; let us sit on the steps here for this heat is not good for me. Look at me! I am sweating profusely."

When they were seated on the steps, David spoke again, "My dear girl, I am delighted to hear that you have come to know the Lord, our God. I have thought over much about how difficult that that decision will be for you in the coming months. I have prayed about it and I have come to the conclusion that I can help you. Over the years of being a silk merchant, I have accumulated much wealth and much of it will never be used. I should very much like to assign some of it over to you so that you may be independent..."

The full realisation of what the man was saying startled Lydia and she looked at Haman but he was smiling.

"But how can you do this, sir? I am a thief who stole from you and you are now going to provide for me? This is very strange."

"Please, Lydia, I have four sons who are a heartache to me. I need a nice, gentle daughter. I know that it is still the early days of your conversion and you might think that I am premature in my giving but I see it as a way to encourage you to stay in this new life. I would make a condition though if you choose to return to your old way of life then I will stop the allowance. Is that fair to you?"

"And if you will allow me, David, to have a condition also, I

279

should like to ask you to hold back on this allowance, as you call it, for one year so that I may become more used to this new way of life. I intend to work for Haman to repay his kindness to me. Will you accept that?"

David chuckled, "You drive a hard bargain, young lady, but if that is your wish then so be it."

"Thank you, David, I am indebted to you."

Lydia stayed with Haman and Mahlah and served the Lord with them helping others who were thieves to build a life in God. Matthew came but Sarah did not.

–14–

After the week of Feasts, Mary and Jesus and Joseph went back to Nazareth and picked up the threads of their lives once more, firm in the knowledge that Lydia would be well looked after. As David had said, the ways of the Lord were mysterious and only he can know what is to happen in a life. If he has a plan for that life then he will open doors and present opportunities when that life is open to his ways. Lydia was still very unsure in this new way of life and had come to Mary on the day before they left.

"Mary, can I please talk with you?"

"Yes, Lydia, I will speak with you."

"Mary, please do not get me wrong, I have come to love this life that I have started to live. Somewhere deep within me the other life is still there waiting to find a way through. It sits like a ghost, waiting. When we go into Jerusalem, I find myself watching for opportunities to steal. I watch for people that I can steal from and go through in my mind what way I would rob them. It frightens me, Mary. I want this new life and I know that it is still early days but the stealing just will not go away."

"Lydia, my poor child," Mary said. She looked at the girl and could see the distress in her face. She put back a stray piece of hair that had broken free of her veil. She noticed how clean the girl's face was now that she was living in Haman's house. "When Joseph and I took Jesus into Egypt, I felt really homesick. I wanted to see my mother every day. I longed for her because she was my life before I was married to Joseph. She was all I had ever known. I had to wrench myself free of my thoughts and memories and apply myself to living this new life. I was afraid that I could not live this life that I had said 'yes' to. I could think about my mother, I could think about Nazareth but if I dwelled on those thoughts then all I wanted to do was go there. But I could not allow myself to do that for there was too much danger. Herod would surely have had Jesus killed. When Gabriel brought the news that the danger from Herod was over, I began to realise that, in spite of my homesickness, I had become so used to the new life in Egypt that I almost did not want to leave all of it behind. I had made a home there and I had fought all the feelings of wanting to rush right back to Nazareth.

I think that it is the same with you. Your old way of life is calling to you because you were so used to living that way. You must try to fight those callings to go back, that is, if you have really chosen to stay in this life, and I know that you have. There is too much danger back there, Lydia. It is all part of the process of coming back to God. We have put these things into us and the mind and heart only want what they are used to."

"Mary, I am willing to fight against these things but what if I fail, what if I go back?"

"The opportunity is always there for you to go back if you wish, Lydia. In Egypt I told myself that I could go back if I wished but I knew that there was danger there for me. There is danger for you in Hinnom, Lydia."

"Yes, I know and you are right. That danger will keep me

from going back there. When I look at myself in these past days, I know that I have changed. It is not just on the outside, but in here," Lydia put her hand on her heart, "I have changed here the most. My heart is so full of love, at least, I think it is love. So much love that I want to shout it at the people that I meet. I feel something inside me that has filled a great empty hole that I did not know was there. I keep thinking about all the people that I knew in Hinnom. They need to know that this new life is here for them too. I would like to go there to tell them."

"Lydia, it is too early to do that. You must learn how to live this life for yourself first so that when you go there to tell them then you will not be tempted to return to it. You must remember that your old life is very strong within you still but the more that you fight against it then the stronger against it you will become. You must pray often against temptation for it will come, but only in proportion to what you can fight. Remember that, for, when you think that you cannot resist it, you must remember that that temptation is not beyond your strength."

"Mary, you have taught me much. How can I thank you all for your kindness to me?"

"By thanking God. That is all the thanks that we require for it is he who gives us everything that we need."

The next day they all parted amid many tears and promises of coming to Bethany next year. Haman and Mahlah thought that they might make a journey to Nazareth to visit them and to see that part of Israel. The little community had not only planted more seed but in Lydia had grafted a new strain that would surely grow into new plants in the rich soil that had been provided. It was time to transplant out the new shoots to allow adequate growth. The community was not a community of fine buildings and prodigious surroundings but one that was formed and grown within the heart and soul. Its food was love and dying to self.

Returning to Nazareth was always a joy for Mary and Joseph and Jesus. Home is always home no matter how far that you travel away from it and when you have been an exile then home is all the more precious. Mary thought about Lydia in the days that followed their return from Bethany. She prayed for her that she might get the strength to endure the hardships and temptations that would come. Lydia was like an exile now and she had to stay away from all that she had known. To return, thinking that she was strong enough, could prove fatal for the girl. Many people who come to God think that they are able to walk into danger without realising that they must grow within God before they can begin to bring others. They are like babies who must drink milk until they are able to take solid food. Lydia must learn to cope with fighting herself before she can reach out to another. Mary prayed each day for her.

When they arrived back to Nazareth they went to see Anne. Anne was in her couch and could not move out of it. Her body was weak and she could not put her feet on the floor. She had tried but they would not hold her. She had not eaten for four days and could only eat and drink a little. Mary was shocked to see the ashen white face. Anne looked so terribly old and worn and whatever had happened had happened very quickly.

"A few more days lying here and I will get so fed up and angry with myself that I will have to get up," she told Mary.

"But, mother, what has happened? You were well before we went to Jerusalem."

"My daughter, I am an old woman now. I overdo things and you know that I cannot rest if there is work to be done. I wanted to clean the house out for it has not been done for a while. When I lifted the table to put it outside I received a blow from my body right here," Anne put her hand on her breast, "for putting too much strain on it. It serves me well for I have never learned how to be patient. I should have waited until you and Joseph returned so that he could do it for me."

Anne never recovered. Her body became weaker and weaker and even the smallest strain would bring on the pain in her chest. Mary and Joseph and Jesus moved in to Anne's house to look after her. Anne called Jesus to her on many occasions to talk with him. Mary did not enter these conversations for she knew that they were intimate things about life and death and she did not have the right to be there. Jesus seemed happy as he spoke to her and he did not tell her of what took place.

They were back from Jerusalem six weeks when Anne died.

Mary had taken to sleeping beside Anne's couch on the floor so that she could attend to her every need, even in the dead of night. Anne often cried out in pain as she tried to turn for comfort.

On waking one morning, Mary could hear the birdsong and she could feel the heat of the day beginning to rout out the cold of the night. She stretched and rubbed those parts of her back that had supported her body on the floor. She thanked God for giving her life on this new day as she always did. It was then that she realised that her mother had not awakened her during the night. Mary quickly went to Anne's couch. Anne lay there, she was white and cold, and she was dead. Her mouth was twisted to one side and saliva had fallen from it and dried on her face. Mary touched this woman that she loved. "Mother...mother," she said softly, gently, knowing that it was too late for words.

Yet still she spoke, making death no different from life. "Mother," she said, the tears were spilling gently down her face coming from the pain that pierced her heart. "My dear mother, I love you. At this moment you are gone to the bosom of our Father, Abraham. My heart is breaking for I have never known life without you. My heart is an empty vessel on this morning for it has not been filled with your sweetness." Mary smoothed her mother's grey hair. She looked at her face, the eyes still open in death. She closed them. As she did so, she bent to kiss her mother goodbye, her tears wetting the dead woman's face. "You have been the heart that beats within me and the memories that bring me joy to think of you. My joy has been turned into sorrow for I shall miss you." Mary touched the cold, wan cheeks of her mother's face, knowing that by the time the sun went down she would never see her again.

A loud keening arose from Mary's heart at that moment. A cry that emerged, unbidden, from the depths of her heart, and it tore it in grief. It rose upward and upward and she did not control it, but let it go free into the stillness of the morning, shattering and breaking, like glass, the day that had emerged to bring her such desolation. The birds outside in the olive tree stopped their singing abruptly as they caught the grief, the sorrow, in that cry. The moment, for Mary, lasted a lifetime. It was a weeping for and a severing from this woman that she loved so dearly.

The pain in her heart broke it, severed it and her cry went to the God that she loved, seeking comfort, seeking love. She knew that it was her mother's time to go; death had come for her and she needed to feel this grief; she needed to let her go. With the pain and with a deep sigh she said, "Into your hands, my God, I commend my mother's spirit. Safely, I deliver her onto you." Mary put her head down and wept softly.

Joseph was awakened by the cry and knew immediately that Anne had died. He got up quickly and went to his wife. He found her kneeling by Anne's couch weeping and holding her mother's hand. He went to her. He put his head on her head and wept silently with his wife. Anne had been a good woman and he had come to love her. He cried too to be one in grief with Mary.

Mary turned to her husband, "Oh Joseph, my love, mother

is gone. I will miss her."

Joseph pulled her into his arms, "I know, my love, I will miss her too." They both knelt and Mary cried on Joseph's shoulder.

They heard a small movement behind them and turned to see Jesus standing there. He knelt beside them. He put his arms around Mary and embraced her. "Mama," he said, smiling gently, "Do not weep so hard for her for you would be in joy to see her. I am with her and I talk with her. She is well now. I tell you that this day Heaven shall open for her." Jesus kissed his mother on her forehead then he took her face in his hands and smiled at her. "I am with you always. I have come that I might be with you and all your children always. I have given the woman to my Father. She ranks among the first."

Mary and Jesus looked at one another. His face was aglow with love, a love that came from his heart and she was in her heart and in his heart and the two merged and became one. Her grief melted and she could see Anne, she was smiling joyfully, a young woman's smile. She could see Joachim, touching his wife and smiling, a young man's smile. And they were dancing; dancing into a blue place that she did not understand and she did not care. She watched them dancing and they danced a dance of joy. She could see Gabriel there, waiting on them and knew that the dance was a dance of heaven for she did not know the steps. Their joy, she knew, was God; was Heaven; was forever. She saw Gabriel; he placed his wings over them and she was back in her mother's home, kneeling with her smiling son and she embraced him. She was one with him.

In the weeks after Anne's death, they found a destitute family and gave the house to them to live in. They had no further use for it, although Mary cried for the memories of the life that she had spent there. Fond memories of her father and her mother as they taught her the ways of God within this house, joyfully singing the Psalms of King David and telling her of the plight of Israel. They told her of Israel's disobedience to God and their coming back to him.

During this time, Mary felt a keen sense of grief. When she was in Egypt, she could tell herself that her mother was in Nazareth, living happily, the way she had always done. But now, death had claimed her and severed, for a while, the life that they had known together. She had Joseph and Jesus to help her fill the void but there was still the pain of grief within her that would never go away.

She was glad that Jesus had been with her mother when she died but it seemed to her that Jesus meant more than that. When he talked about that morning, it seemed as though he had been with her in spirit.

* * * * *

Mary was awakened by the noise. It was a rasping sound; a sound that penetrated her. It was a growl, but not like a dog would growl, no it was deeper, with a resonance that echoed in the room and it felt cold. The room too was colder than it should have been. As she breathed, Mary noticed that her breath formed smoke. She looked around the room. She shivered. Joseph was asleep and blissfully unaware that she was awake. He snored gently.

Mary saw the thing in the corner. It had the shape of a man but it was not a man and it was covered in a thick coat of slime. She could smell the vile stench that exuded from it and gagged. Its eyes shot fire out into the room, which hissed and went out as quickly as it had come. The thing did not seem to have much power.

"You!" it said, "you will pay for your treachery. You stink with goodness and you make me sick." The thing retched and vomited. It shot out of its mouth like bats disturbed in a cave, spraying the room. The vomit was green and it oozed. A string of obscenities about her virginity followed and Mary put her hands over her ears. "You think that your virginity will last much longer? Hah! You are pathetic! I will make you break it, you filthy cur!

I am here, have been sent to tell you that your precious son will die," the demon spat more green vomit in Mary's direction but none of it touched her, "he will die the vilest death that I can make him and he will come to me and I will make him serve me. He shall bow down before me. And that Gabriel he will not be as powerful then for he shall lick my feet."

Mary listened to the words and felt sick to her stomach. She was still retching with the smell of the vomit but she said. "My son will do as he is sent to do and he is not here to do your bidding. I tell you to leave my house in his name, the name of Jesus, for he is the Son of God."

Flames began to pour out of the demon's body. It screamed and burst into flames. "You cur! I will get you for this!" The demon disappeared.

The room began to warm again and Mary breathed a sigh of relief. It was gone.

A light now appeared before her and she could feel Gabriel. His strange, stark beautiful ambience imbued the room as though cleaning it. The smell of burning was gone in his presence. His strength and light exuded into her and she felt his love. It was strange to feel an Angel's love. It was like loyalty, a fierce loyalty that forever, she felt, would be hers. He would love her forever, she knew.

"Mary," he said, "it must be. The demons must come, for mankind has been given free will and it will not be taken away. The Lord God has ordained it this way. The name of the Holy Child will save you but this must be. I cannot save you from it but know that I am closer to you than your breath. You will not hear me breathe for I will breathe in your breath. In your heartbeat will I be. If you are afraid, know that I will come. Let no angel of *Gehenna* disturb you. I am close." Then he was gone.

Mary felt comforted by his words and marvelled at them. Why was she given an Angel so powerful to look after her? Why did she need it? Why did the demon say her son would die the vilest death? What can all this mean?

She had no answers but she felt that a door had opened in her life. A door that would not close until the day she died.

The clean, fresh perfume secreted from the wood as the carpenter slid the plane along its length. The long grained wood slithered easily out of the tool and curled up, rolling away to fall on the floor. The blade had been honed and set to only take off thin slithers. Joseph held the plank of wood jammed against the floor and secured it with the crook of his arm while he worked. His long arm reached to the bottom with each stroke. The man felt an inner joy to see the wood taking shape and the joy bled into the wood.

He stopped the tool and put it on the bench near him and lifted the plank and stretched it out before him. He looked along its length and sought any heights that might take from its even surface. Finding none, he placed it with the others that he had planed smooth earlier.

He thought of the cupboard that he was making. It had been requested by one of the Roman commanders who were housed in the garrison on the edge of Nazareth. It would be six feet long and three wide. That was the specifications that the soldier had given to him. The door opened behind him. It was Jesus.

"Ah, Jesus, you have returned," Joseph said.

"Yes, Father. The chair has been accepted. The Rabbi said that he would like two more just like it. He was very pleased."

"That is good. And how was he? Was he well?"

"He complained of the joints in his knees and said how old

he was getting."

Joseph laughed, "Yes, he likes to let you know that he is old but he is a good man."

It was mid-morning and the sun was working its way to its highest point in the sky. Soon they would eat their bread and drink goat's milk.

"Would you like to continue working these planks with the plane, Jesus? Good! I can begin to cut the joints. Tomorrow we must go in to Nain to fix a roof. It will take us a few days but we will be able to come home every night. God bless the work that it is so plentiful."

Jesus took up the plane and began to smooth a plank. Joseph watched the boy work. He had taught him to be careful and loving with the wood and treat it with respect and Jesus was doing it. He was quite good for a boy of his age. He was an obedient boy, Joseph observed, and he was a good help in the workshop. He could do most jobs that he was given to do and Joseph would begin to teach him soon how to cut the joints for the finer furniture. He seemed to enjoy the work.

As Joseph looked at him, he found it difficult to take in that this boy was the Messiah, the Son of God. He was an ordinary boy and he taught him like any other apprentices that he'd had. Joseph had never had to tell him to do anything twice. He had taught him with strictness and, he hoped, a kindness that would help him to love the work. The boy seemed happy in his work but revelled when they went to the Synagogue to pray or be taught. Then his eyes would brighten and he absorbed all that was taught to him. He would ask questions of the Rabbi and the Rabbi would be flustered in his trying to find an answer. Jesus would wait patiently and in respect of the age of the man. Joseph knew that Jesus never wanted to leave the Synagogue but would always come when told to.

Often it was said to Joseph that Jesus would be a Rabbi for he left some of the men who attended amazed at his questions. He would answer that he did not know what Jesus would be when he grew up for that was up to himself and God.

Joseph felt his love for the boy blossom within his heart and wanted to reach out and embrace him. He saw Jesus as his son and it was a pleasure to bring up the boy. Just then, Jesus turned and looked at Joseph, smiling. He put down the plane and walked to Joseph and put his arms around him. "I love you, father," he said.

Joseph held him tight, drinking the love of his son as it was so freely given. Had he heard the love in Joseph's heart? Joseph knew that the boys powers of understanding were great and had watched as things unfolded that caused anyone in his hearing to melt and change by hearing his words. The boy went back to his work and Joseph felt renewed. Yes, it was hard to believe that this was the Son of God and yet, it was easy.

Only a few weeks before, Jesus had asked if he could spend a night in the hills around Nazareth. Joseph and Mary had looked at him.

"Why would you wish to do that, my son?" Joseph had said, "you are not yet eleven."

"I wish to spend time in the wilderness with my God," Jesus had said, easily.

Mary had said to Jesus, "Son of mine, do you wish to go from your mother and father so soon? Will you not wait at least until your *Bar Mitzvah*, then you will be a man?"

"If you wish it, I will wait," he had said to her.

Joseph knew that Jesus would, one day, make his way in the world but he was shocked to realise that he wanted to begin at such an early age.

When he had gone to sleep that night, Joseph and Mary had spoken of the incident.

"I think," Mary had said, "that he can feel a calling within him to go and do what he is here to do, Joseph, but he seems so young. Once he is of age then we must let him go. The time nears."

"I know that but it will be difficult to let him go."

"He was never ours, Joseph. He was born to go away from us. Look at all that has happened. We are content to let him be if he does what he must do in our presence. But he will go one day. I can feel it in my heart."

"When he becomes a man, then we will let him go."

"Oh," Mary had said, "I heard some news today. A messenger came from Magdala while you were in Capernaum repairing the cart. He had come to bring the message that my mother's sister, Miriam, was coming to live in Nazareth. Her husband died last springtime, about a month before my mother died, and she wants to spend her days in Nazareth."

"It is a pity that Anne's house is occupied. It would have been a good place for her to come to," Joseph had mused.

"I do not think so, Joseph, she has a large family. I think it is six, unless there have been more. They were all quite close together. As far as I can remember there were four boys and two girls. It will be good to have relatives again. They will be brothers and sisters for Jesus."

"Yes, that will be good for him."

Joseph was interrupted in his reverie by the sound of Mary's voice as she opened the door of the workshop. "Is no one hungry today? I have prepared food for you and you two just want to work. Come, the food is ready."

* * * * *

Tamar's eyes glistened as she saw the boy, John, take his mother's arm and help her to walk down the hill that led away from the house and on towards the market. John was such a thoughtful boy. Elizabeth's joints were beginning to stiffen and she was finding it difficult to walk. She always insisted that she went to the market, stiff joints and all, and Tamar had long ago given up trying to argue with the woman.

John doted on her. He would always be there for her, to help her. He had cut her a staff to help her walk around and Elizabeth had accepted it from him as though it were made of gold. And it was gold; it was a gift from her only son.

Tamar wiped her eyes on her sleeve and went back into the house. She went to the table to finish making the bread. She glanced at the fire to be sure that it was still alight and saw that it was burning too brightly. She went to it and with a stick she poked it to make it lower. She would not need to feed it for a while. She spat on the edge of the griddle and watched the saliva sizzle and dry up quickly. It was hot enough and ready for the bread. She went back to the table and began to pound the dough into the table.

It was so good to see the love that was between John and his mother. He was a good boy. His presence seemed to warm any room or company that he was in. He was very good at his lessons in the Synagogue. The Rabbi, Jeremiah, had told Elizabeth on more than one occasion about his quick learning. He had said too, that John, whenever he had learned anything new from Scripture, would call the other boys around him and teach them what he had learned.

Yes, he was a good boy. It was sad that he did not have a father around him and Zechariah would have made a good one had he lived. The old man would have been very pleased with his progress in the Synagogue. He might even become a priest in the Abijah just like his father. And maybe even high priest one day.

Tamar's heart swelled with pride as though the boy were her own son. But he was more like a little brother. She loved him. He would sometimes bring her little flowers from the field since she had told him that she liked little red anemones. He would come to her with his hands behind his back and pretend that he was interested in what she was doing. She knew that he had the flowers and would appear disinterested. If she were baking bread, he would ask her for a piece of the dough so that he could mould it. "Only if you get me some flowers," she would say, "and only if they are red."

He would produce them proudly and say, "Sorry, Tamar, only yellow ones today. May I still have the dough?"

"Take it but next time they must be red or you won't get any."

"Thank you, Tamar," he would say and kiss her. She loved that boy.

He loved to play with the other boys of the village. He would always be the leader and she noticed when she watched them sometimes that Yahweh would always be the hero. He would lead the boys into mock battles with imaginary opponents and he would be King David. These battles could take a good part of the day and sometimes in the evening she would go out to call him and he would tell her that they had not won yet and she must wait. He was so sincere that she would wait. He brought joy to the household and Tamar loved him.

"Mama, do you see the bird in the tree there?" said John to Elizabeth as they walked slowly down the hill.

"Where, my son?" said Elizabeth.

"At the very top, I think it is a buzzard, there must be a dead sheep somewhere. I will investigate later and let you know."

"The owner will be sad, John, for sheep are expensive to replace, especially if he is poor."

"I will pray and ask God to replace it then. God is so good he will do things for me, mama."

"You love God, my son?"

"Mama! He is Yahweh Sabaoth and he commands the hosts of Angels. He is my hero! Yes, I love him."

Elizabeth looked at her son. She wished that Zechariah were here to hear him say those words.

"Your father loved Yahweh too, John, and he spent his life serving him and loving him. He would want you to love him. I am so glad that you do."

"How could I not love him, mother, the Scriptures tell me that he will look after those who love him and I know that he loves me."

They walked in silence for a while and John held his mother's arm tighter in case she might stumble. He began to hum a little tune. It was a psalm that they used to sing sometimes. He began to sing the words and Elizabeth joined him: " 'O Lord our Lord, how excellent is thy name in all the earth! Thou who hast set thy glory above the heavens, out of the mouth of babes and sucklings hast thou ordained strength because of thine enemies that thou mightest still the enemy and the avenger. When I consider thy heavens, the work of thy fingers, the moon and the stars, which thou hast ordained; what is man, that thou art mindful of him? And the son of man, that thou visitest him? For thou hast made him a little lower than the angels and hast crowned him with glory and honour. Thou madest him to have dominion over the works of thy hands; thou hast put all things under his feet; all sheep and oxen, yea, and the beasts of the field, the fowl of the air and the fish of the sea and whatsoever passeth through the paths of the seas. O Lord our Lord, how excellent is thy name in all the earth!' "

"Ah, John," said Elizabeth, "If I was younger I would dance with you to show the Lord my joy at having you for my son."

"When we return, mama, I will dance for you, if you will sing the song. I will make Tamar dance with me."

"You will have to ask her first, my son," Elizabeth laughed, "she may be busy."

Mother and son turned the corner into the *Street of Dogs*

and entered the market.

"I hope that Miriam has not changed, Jesus. She was such a jolly person and could always make a laugh out of the saddest occasions."

"It is good to feel joy, mother. I like to see you smile and being happy."

"Thank you, my son, that is nice of you. You should have plenty of brothers and sisters after this."

"Yes, I am looking forward to that!"

They were walking towards the *Street of Merchants* where the Rabbi's house was. Miriam and her family had moved to a house opposite to the Rabbi's.

It was a large house and took up the same area of the two other houses that surrounded it. It was painted white and had been kept in good condition by the previous owner. The woman was a widow like Miriam and had been barren. As she was getting old, she wanted to move to live with her sister in Capernaum. Mary knocked on the door, noticing that the paint was peeling from it.

The door swung open almost immediately and a tall youth stood there. He looked to be about fourteen years.

"Hail to you!" said Mary, "you must be James. I am Mary and this is Jesus, my son."

"Hail to you, Mary. I am Simon. You are welcome; please enter. My mother is here. She will be pleased to see you," he said pleasantly. "She often speaks of you."

Simon led Mary and Jesus into a small anteroom, which was more like a tiny courtyard for light poured, unhindered, from the sky. The youth then walked through a door opposite and they entered a large room with various pieces of furniture spread throughout it. A large-framed woman was busy with a broom sweeping the tiled floor and humming a tune. She turned and screamed. "Mary! Mary, is it you?" She ran to Mary and embraced her. "It is so good to see you again. The last time I saw you, you were just a little thing. I can see that you are a woman now. I am sorry that Anne died." Miriam lowered her voice. "But do not worry I will be your mother now."

"I am glad to see you too, Miriam. It is good to have some relatives again."

"And this is Jesus, your little son." She tossed his hair. "You are a beautiful child and you are welcome here. I am Miriam and I am your grandmother's sister. I am not old as she was because I came later and I am much younger than she. I am sure that you miss her very much, like I do. You have met Simon. Simon, go and bring your brothers and sisters to meet Mary and Jesus." Simon went out.

"Mary, come and sit with me and we will talk. Come, Jesus, you will not want to talk with two women, when the children come you can talk to them. I think you will like that much better."

She took Mary by the hand and sat down with her on the nearest couch. "Mary, tell me, did Anne suffer much? Before she died, I mean."

"I don't think so, Miriam, I was not with her when she died. Jesus was with her." Mary looked at her son.

"She died with peace in her heart, Miriam," Jesus said, "She asked about you and said that she hoped that you would be alright for we had just heard the news that your husband had died."

Miriam was weeping now. "She was always good to me. I was more like her daughter than her sister. It was nice of her to think of me. By the time the news travelled to me in Magdala, she would already have been dead for a week."

Miriam wept silently for some moments, remembering her sister. "Look at me weeping," she said. "Anne would have scolded me for wasting time."

The door opened and Miriam's children walked in.

"Ah," said Miriam, "you are here at last. Let me introduce you to Mary and Jesus." Miriam got up and went to her children. They stood shyly in a line.

"This is James, my firstborn and he is fifteen years old now. Next is Josiah, he is fourteen, and then comes Simon whom you have met. He is thirteen. My firstborn daughter is Miriam, after myself of course, she is twelve. Ruth is next at eleven and my baby, Jude, is my pride and joy and he is nine years old."

Jude squirmed under the gaze of the strangers; he pulled at his tight curls and shuffled his feet on the tiled floor.

"And this is Mary, Anne's daughter, whom I told you about and her son, Jesus. We are not alone in the world we have relatives."

"Hail to each of you!" said Mary, "what a large family we are now."

−15−

J oseph was eating the meal that Mary had made for him. The long stick of bread was easily broken and dipped in the goat's milk. The cheese was creamy. Mary sat opposite him at the table.

"When will Jesus return?" she said to her husband.

"He has gone to deliver the ladder to Eli and should be back soon," said Joseph.

"I had another visitation last night, Joseph, from the evil spirit. It told me that Jesus would never fulfil what he has set out to do because it would kill him before he reached maturity. I know that Satan cannot do this but I do not like to hear it all the same. I did not believe it."

"Mary, I wish that I could be with you in these times, I could be of some comfort to you. It is the only time, it seems that I cannot protect you."

"I know that, my love," said Mary, looking at her husband, "I know that you would be there but it seems that I must do this alone. Remembering what Gabriel has said then it cannot be stopped and must happen. If the Lord has ordained it then I must be willing to stand it. I do not mind. It does not frighten me but I do not like the vileness that it brings with it. Last night it brought two more with it and they threatened to beat me. Gabriel has told me that they cannot touch me but they threaten."

"Have you told Jesus of these attacks, my love?" asked Joseph.

"No, not yet, but I will. I will ask him why they must be. They seem to last longer each time. I think what they are trying to do is to get me to turn away from God. The spirit told me that Lydia had now left Haman's house and had gone into prostitution. I did not believe it but they are getting more forceful. When I say 'Jesus', they flee. Who is this son of ours that demons flee at the very mention of his name?"

"Yes, Mary, it is sometimes so hard to believe who we have in out midst. He works in the workshop like an ordinary boy and he is so ordinary that I forget who he really is. Then he does or says something and I know. It is as though Heaven were reminding me."

"Last night too, they showed me a vision of *Gehenna*. I could see the fires burn there and I knew that these were souls who had turned their backs on God. Many, many spirits were torturing them and there must have been about twenty of them to one soul. They were beating them with fire and doing all sorts of unspeakable things to them. They called out to me to give them a drink of water, a few drops. I knew that I could not for these souls had chosen to live their lives without God and they would live for the rest of eternity without him. But the thing that struck me most was that the fires did not burn them like the fire over there. It seemed that the fires were giving them a degree of terrible pain and there was no stopping it. Every moment, every hour, every day they suffer their pain. It was difficult to watch.

Joseph, I felt as though my heart would break for them. They had been ordinary people in life who did not follow God's way and had turned their backs on his Law. They had chosen by not believing. It was very sad. My heart is breaking now." Mary stopped; her tears were blinding her at the thought of what she had seen.

Joseph got up and went to her. The couple embraced. "I am sorry, my love, that you must see these things. If I could take them for you, then I would. Know that I am always here when you need me. Call out to me. I love you."

Mary looked at her husband. "I know, Joseph. You have protected Jesus and I well and I rely on your strength. If I must suffer like this to help stop others to not go there then I am willing to suffer it. If my life can be a witness to Yahweh then let it be so."

Joseph embraced his wife. He felt helpless to reach in and take away the pain that he knew was deep within her heart. Jesus was given to them to bring up to maturity so that he could do the work that God sent him to do. Much as he and Mary wanted to keep him as their son, they could not. He must do what he was sent to do. He must save the world from its own vanity, to stop others ending up in *Gehenna*.

Joseph mentioned these things to the Rabbi. He was shocked that Mary should see these things so powerfully, that she could describe them in such detail. Joseph told him that he felt that Mary was being allowed to see much more that this but she could not tell him.

"Joseph, do not be alarmed that Mary is not telling you. She probably can't. The things of the world where God lives cannot be described in our world. There are just not the words to describe what is going on. When we go there we will know the language that is spoken and we will understand. But now we must simply wait. It is like being a child in an adult world, we simply cannot understand. Mary has been given a singular privilege and she must be allowed to go to the lengths that it takes her to. Gabriel is correct, the Most High has given it to her and it cannot be changed. Her gifts are high so the powers fighting against her will also be high. I believe that Mary will be able to cope with it all."

"It is good to know that, Rabbi. It is also good to know that you believe me when I speak to you."

"Believe you? Joseph, this story as it unfolds is more powerful than the Greek dramas, and I await its end. I believe that, in Jesus, will come the salvation of the world. But we must wait as each scene is revealed and played out before our eyes."

"Mama, these things are as they should be," Jesus said, "Some things must be as they have been laid down. They are in preparation for the time. Because you are close to me these things will happen. One day Satan and I will come face to face and he will be allowed certain privileges that he will never be allowed again. He will be allowed to try to conquer God. From the beginning, he has tried to take the place of his God and has tried to win over the creation of my Father by using mankind against him. I have come for the purpose of standing between Satan and mankind to win them back, to give mankind a new message from my Father. The Scriptures were revealed by God and written by the prophets to be lived and fulfilled. And I have come for that purpose. Many will not believe what I am here for but as many as believe will come. For all of this we must be patient and wait. The time is not yet ripe."

"These things that you tell me are strange, my son, but I will accept whatever comes. I believe that God has a purpose and I do not understand all of it but I will do what is expected of me."

Mary pondered in her heart the things that Jesus had spoken of. Much was being prepared, that she could see, and what was to happen was shrouded in mystery and not yet revealed. She knew that whatever it was she would be close to Jesus always. Sometimes when he spoke it seemed that he was more than a ten year old, it seemed that he spoke with the authority of Heaven itself. His words struck her very soul and made her wonder at it all. And as Joseph had said, he could be so ordinary that you could forget that he was the Son of God.

It was all so strange. She could feel him begin to draw away from her, feel him move now in the direction of God, whom he called, more and more, his Father. She knew that he did not sleep many nights, that he would go outside the door and sit there under the stars to pray.

One night she had woken up and noticed that he was not on his couch. The door was open and she went out and saw him. He was kneeling in the stillness of the night and he was not in this world but was part of another world, not yet revealed and not yet given. It was as though he were shrouded from the world in a mist of unfathomable unknown. His spirit was not within him but gone somewhere, answering the powerful call of God that was him; he was the obedience of his Father answering his call. She had stood for some time and he had not moved, as though he were dead. Then he had spoken to her, "Mama, I have returned now. Let us go in by the fire, you must be cold." If he was cold that night or tired the next day he did not show it. It seemed to Mary that the longer he spent with God then the less tired and cold that he was.

She thought about his asking to go to the hills around Nazareth. She and Joseph still saw him as a boy, an earthly boy but here he was, safe. What was it they worried about? He was not an ordinary boy; he was God, revealed. Mary felt a shudder of awe pass through her body and she could feel it deep within her soul. She knew that he would wait until he was twelve before he would ask again; she knew that he would be obedient.

She had felt that, in these moments that he was not her son, not her earthly son but the son of a powerful being that she was only a small part of until his mystery was revealed to her. By degrees, she was beginning to understand but things happened and she felt as though she knew nothing. His coming was not for her and Joseph alone, no, it was for all who would listen to what he had to say. Mankind would choose to love or hate her son; he would allow them that. He would allow them the choice.

Within her heart Mary felt the world as though it lived there. She felt its pain and she felt its sin. She felt the rise and fall of kings and the each day living of the poor; the cry of infants touched her and the cry of the poor moved her. She felt lives stretch out before her, lain out, side by side, their moments and their hours. She knew a love within her for each one that she knew was not hers but it was given to her to help her understand, to help her to love. She was being given sight, like a blind woman, to be able to see from one world to another, one point of view to another. What was it all about?

She remembered the *Gehenna* that had been revealed to her by the demon. Sin of any kind must be a great betrayal of God. It must be a turning of one's back on him, who created souls. And it must have a terrible price. Adam had begun it, allowed it freedom and now it walked freely in the world of man, tempting him, each moment, to walk away from the grace so richly provided, clouding and blinding him because man allowed it to. Mankind needed God but he was too full of himself and puffed up with pride to see that.

Mary looked into her heart. "Father," she spoke aloud into the confines of her home, "may I call you Father? My life is worth little, I know, but whatever it is worth I give it to you to use to help your son to do what he must. I love you, my Father."

* * * * *

The next year passed quickly and without event in the lives of Joseph and Mary and Jesus. Jesus would be thirteen soon and he would be a man. They would travel up to Jerusalem for the *Pesach* and after that Jesus would be *Bar Mitzvah*. His childhood had been an encouragement to live the commandments and now he would be expected to live as an adult and to take part in the life of the Jewish community that he was a part of. He would now be able to take part in religious services and could perform certain parts of them as an adult. This included the right to form binding contracts, give testimony in a court of law and to marry. He would become *Bar Mitzvah,* 'a son of the commandment'. After his thirteenth birthday, Jesus would be called up to perform the most important part of being a son of the commandment, to recite a blessing over the Torah's weekly reading. It would be his first *aliyah* or his first reading. But the preparations for *Pesach* must be done first. It was an exciting time.

This year they were a bigger family than any other year. Miriam and her family were with them and Mary was glad. There were many on the road from Nazareth and the company eased the hours of walking. They numbered about five hundred people. At night, when they camped along the side of the road, many musical instruments would be produced and Psalms would be sung and folksongs of the exploits of the Jews with their fortunes and their woes. A popular love song was that of David and a favourite among many. The singing was always accompanied by dancing, for dancing was showing God that you were happy and was a natural part of praise. These few nights were cold but warmed by campfires under the moon and relatives would stay together with friends and form a family tribe of one of Israel's sons. They would recall Scripture and remember whose loins that they sprung from: '*Now the sons of Jacob were twelve: the sons of Leah; Reuben, Jacob's firstborn, Simeon, Levi, Judah, Issachar and Zebulun. The sons of Rachel were Joseph and Benjamin; and the sons of Bilhah, Rachel's handmaid; Dan, and Naphtali, and the sons of Zilpah, Leah's handmaid; Gad, and Asher. These are the sons of Jacob which were born to him in Padan-Aram.'* Being part of a tribe gave a deep sense of belonging to each one; gave roots to the tree, of which they were branches. From their twig on the great tree of the family that God had chosen, each could trace his own branches back to Father Abraham. Mary and Joseph and Jesus also had a part in that tree and knew it in those nights around the campfires and in their hearts and felt that they belonged.

They were around their own campfire with Miriam and her family. They snuggled around the fire against the cold. It was a time for telling the stories of exploits of families for it was too early to retire. The darkness seemed to ebb away from the light of the fire as Joseph recited the family to Jesus: " *'Abraham begat Isaac; and Isaac begat Jacob; and Jacob begat Judas and his brethren; And Judas begat Phares and Zara of Thamar; and Phares begat Esrom; and Esrom begat Aram; And Aram begat Aminadab; and Aminadab begat Naasson; and Naasson begat Salmon; And Salmon begat Booz of Rachab; and Booz begat Obed of Ruth; and Obed begat Jesse;*

And Jesse begat David the king; and David the king begat Solomon of her that had been the wife of Urias;

And Solomon begat Roboam; and Roboam begat Abia; and Abia begat Asa; And Asa begat Josaphat; and Josaphat begat Joram; and Joram begat Ozias; And Ozias begat Joatham; and Joatham begat Achaz; and Achaz begat Ezekias;

And Ezekias begat Manasses; and Manasses begat Amon; and Amon begat Josias; And Josias begat Jechonias and his brethren, about the time they were carried away to Babylon:

And after they were brought to Babylon, Jechonias begat Salathiel; and Salathiel begat Zorobabel; And Zorobabel begat Abiud; and Abiud begat Eliakim; and Eliakim begat Azor;

And Azor begat Sadoc.   And Sadoc begat Achim; and Achim begat Eliud; And Eliud begat Eleazar; and Eleazar begat Matthan; and Matthan begat Jacob.' "

"And Jacob was your grandfather who begat Joseph, whose wife is Mary of whom was born Jesus."

"And from Abraham back to Adam," said Mary, "that is the linage that you have been born into."

"It is a family begun by God, who is our Father," said Jesus, "he gave life to Adam who rebelled against him and lost what was rightfully his."

"Your son is very intelligent with Scripture, Mary," Miriam whispered to Mary, "you better watch he does not get too intelligent with it, it might send him mad.   People have been known to let it go to their heads and they end up running naked in the hills.   Why, in the hill country around Magdala there is a man who does just that.   They say that he was studying to be a priest and went too hard at it. Make him work, that's what I say."

The words stung Mary to the heart and she said nothing. She looked into the darkness trying to find comfort there. The pain pierced her heart and she could feel thorns dig deep into it.

Josiah was saying, "I would like to go to the Pool of Siloam while we are here.   I should like to bathe in it if there is any water there."

"If you jump into the Pool with your weight there will be no water left" said James.

"There will never be any water there again," said young Miriam.

The children all laughed and Miriam said, "That is enough! Josiah takes his weight after me and I can't help it.   I don't want you to say those things to him again.   And Josiah is

306

sensitive, like me."

When they reached Bethany they were heartily welcomed by Haman and Mahlah and Lydia who had blossomed into a tall, beautiful young woman. She had been *Bat Mitzvah* a year ago and was already doing the things of womanhood. She was now going back into Hinnom every day trying to bring her friends back to God. Life was good in Bethany.

Miriam chose to stay at the inn where she bullied the inn-keeper into giving her a room for her family and one for herself. As the inn was only a Sabbath walk, which was about half a mile, from Haman's home they met each day and walked into Jerusalem for the *Pesach.*

Jesus stayed mostly with Miriam's children and Joseph and Mary only saw him in the evenings when they all returned from Jerusalem. Some nights he stayed at the inn. Mary and Joseph were content to let him do this as he was now almost *Bar Mitzvah* and they wanted to let him find him-self. Miriam said that she did not mind Jesus being with her because he was like one of her own and another one made no difference to her.

The sun this year was particularly hot and with the crowds there were more than a few deaths. The heat-wave there made people more aware that they should try to stay in the shade. Even the animals, that were being bought and sold for sacrifice, were being found dead in their pens from heat exhaustion. What made it more difficult was that the whole of Israel seemed to be there and Joseph began to think about all the empty homes across the land and every per-son in the capital serving the Lord.

When the time came to leave Bethany and travel home again they all met in Haman's house for a final meal to-gether and then the journey began. It would take them through Jerusalem, Ephraim, and Sychar and into Samaria. From there they would travel to Esdraelon, Nain and Nazareth. Miriam wanted to stay in Nain for a few days to stay with friends so she would not accompany them into Nazareth but would follow.

On the first night of travelling, Jesus did not come to them.

"I wonder where our son is, Joseph?" Mary said when she realised that he was not coming to sleep in their camp that night.

"He is probably with Miriam's sons and we should not worry about him. Haman said to me in Bethany that when Jesus stood with Miriam's family he could be easily be mistaken for one of them. Miriam does not seem to mind. All the children from Nazareth seem to congregate around her."

"Yes," said Mary, "Miriam is quite easy going and loves to have children around her. I am happy that he is with her."

The next day at noon, Mary went to look for Jesus in the caravan. She found Miriam and asked her where Jesus was.

"I have not seen him, Mary, since we left Jerusalem. He was with us then but he has not been with my boys. Perhaps he is with Jonathan and Sarah's children. I saw him with them a few days in Jerusalem."

Mary went back to Joseph to tell him that Jesus was not with Miriam and on the way back she had met Jonathan and Sarah and he had not been with them either. They asked other neighbours and friends had they seen Jesus and the news that he was lost soon buzzed through the pilgrims and all were searching for him.

"He may have stopped along the road, Mary, he cannot be that far away. We will go back the way we came and we will probably meet him following us."

"I would like to do that, Joseph, he will be hungry."

Mary and Joseph left the caravan and started back towards Jerusalem retracing their steps and expecting to find Jesus at any moment. They did not find him. They asked at the other caravans that were travelling north had they seen him but no one had. Once or twice Mary thought she saw him in a caravan and ran to him, her heart beating fast at the thought of finding him, only to discover that it was not Jesus.

They spent the night in the hills north of Jerusalem. They were trying not to worry and had begun to think that maybe, realising that he was lost, he had walked back to Bethany because he knew it. Mary prayed to Gabriel to ask him to lead her in the direction of her son. Next day they reached the city and skirted around it by way of the Kidron Valley for they did not want to look at the crucifixions at the other side.

It was not long before they reached Bethany. Joseph opened the gate of Haman's house and saw Lydia in the garden. "Lydia," he said, "did Jesus come back here?"

Lydia was startled and very surprised to see the couple. "No, Joseph, he left with all of you two days ago. I will call Haman and Mahlah; they will want to know that you are here. Please come into the house and have a drink. You must be exhausted."

"No, Lydia, thank you for your kindness," Mary said firmly "but we must go into the city and look for him. Many have told us that that is the last place they saw him. I am sorry that we startled you."

"Mary, all is well with me. If you must go then I will follow you with Haman and Mahlah and Paulus. We will help you to look for him."

"Oh will you?" Mary said, "Thank you!" She embraced Lydia. "We must hurry now, he will be hungry."

The streets of Jerusalem were still crowded with pilgrims as they entered the Essene Gate from the Hinnom Valley. The noise of animals and people together did little to comfort the couple and they stood helplessly looking at the crowd and wondering how they would ever begin to find a small boy in it. Mary felt frustrated as the crowds buffeted them along and her tears spilled over. "Oh, Joseph," she said, "Where do we begin?"

They walked up towards the Pool of Siloam looking as best as they could through the milling people who were so unaware that they had lost their precious child. On reaching the Pool, Joseph said, "Mary, we will have to split up. There are too many people and we will get nowhere. I will go back the way we have come and make my way to the Palace. If you go this way towards the Roman Hippodrome and search we can and meet later at the Theatre. If you find him bring him back to the Pool and I will do the same."

"Yes, Joseph, you are right. It is the best way. We will cover more ground. Although I do not know how we will find him among all these people."

"We must look, Mary, he is precious to us. We will start now." The couple kissed and began walking.

The people just kept coming out of nowhere. It was as if they were multiplying as Joseph tried to look through them. He saw them as heavy curtains that blocked his view. After a few hours of searching, his eyes were sore trying to focus and the light was beginning to fade. He wondered about Mary. Was she all right? He was sure that Gabriel would protect her from any harm. He knew that she would be worried about Jesus and she would not stop until she found him. He could do little to comfort her for the child was the reason why she lived and without him she did not live. Her joy was his smile, just as his own joy was Mary's smile.

Joseph came to yet another inn. It was in great need of repair and there were several men and women outside it who also needed some repairs. He would go in and inquire if they had seen Jesus.

One of the women came up to Joseph and stood in his path. She was young. She could not have been any more than about sixteen. She put her hands on her hips and twisted her body provocatively and looked at him, rolling her eyes up and down him. Then she spoke "Well, it's not often we get someone as handsome as you. Come with me and I'll show you heaven."

Joseph looked at her and felt sorry for her. She knew nothing better. "I am searching for my son," he said, "he has been lost for two days. He has dark, curly hair and is named Jesus. He is thirteen years old."

The girl looked at him, seeing in his face that he was serious. "No," she said, changing her attitude. "I have not seen him." She stepped out of the way, realising that the man was not interested. Joseph thanked her and went into the inn.

The inn consisted of one large room with stone benches that lined the walls. Beside these were tables and chairs, that were filled with people, busy loosening their tongues with the red, Roman liquid and bringing fire to their thoughts. Opposite the door as Joseph entered was a long table, which was covered with jugs of the wine. A man was on the other side. He was a plump man with grey hair and he had a large bulbous nose. Joseph went up to him.

"Welcome, sir," the man said, kindly, "what can I get you to drink?"

"Nothing," said Joseph, "I wanted to ask if you had noticed a boy of about thirteen years, with dark curly hair?"

"There must thousands in Jerusalem of that description, sir. Did he have any other features that I might go by? A scar, perhaps?" Joseph suddenly felt tired. His body was drained from walking all day. He began to realise the utter futility of asking about Jesus. The man was right. There were thousands of boys in Jerusalem at the present time that would answer that description and maybe some of them could answer to the name of Jesus.

"No, he has none," Joseph said wearily. "Thank you for your help. I must get back to my wife now." He turned and walked away from the table.

"Won't you have some wine, sir, it is of the best quality?" Joseph heard the man call after him but he ignored him. He felt groggy and tired as though he had been drinking. Jesus was missing and now it was already dark and he had not found him. Joseph felt a pain in his chest. It was like the pain that had come when they told him, that his mother would not recover from the fall. Jesus was out there alone and lost. Joseph felt helpless to do anything. He prayed that God would let Mary be at the Pool, waiting for him and safe. He untied the donkey and led it away from the inn. He was across the street from the Roman Bathhouse, its pillared entrance like a mouth opening to swallow the people who entered there. The street was wider here but then narrowed again as it continued towards the Hippodrome. He began to pray that Mary would be waiting for him. At this moment he needed her smile. He needed to know that at least one part of his family was safe. They would not split up again; they would stay together.

So many drunken people and beggars milled about him; Roman soldiers staggered and swore at each other, threatening to dissect various parts of each others' bodies. The city of Holiness was debauched and was full of sin. He could not look anymore at the desecration of the Holy City. He lowered his head and walked on.

Joseph turned left into a wide square on which, opposite him, he could see the rounded shape of the Theatre. It was a two tiered building and was designed as a semi-circle. Around the outside were small, pillared arches that were open on the top tier. Joseph knew that behind the arches were seats that descended towards a stage and that on it, actors in their masks would be acting out some tragedy. But he had his own tragedy to think of, his son was missing and the day was already darkening.

Joseph saw Mary standing beside a tree a little distance away from the wall of the Theatre. Jesus was not with her. She was looking anxiously all around. His heart skipped to

312

see her. "Mary...Mary!" he called over the heads of many people who ebbed and flowed in the street. She did not hear him.

He fought his way to her and embraced her. "Mary, we will not part again," he said into her hair as he held her.

"Did you hear anything of Jesus?" she asked anxiously as he let go of her.

"No," he shook his head.

"I have no news, either. What are we to do, Joseph?"

They stood there facing one another, a little island in a sea of bodies that flowed past and around them, ignoring their plight.

"We must find somewhere to sleep, Mary."

"Joseph, I could not sleep, knowing that Jesus is out there somewhere."

"Mary, my love, you must sleep, tomorrow is another day and we must be refreshed to begin searching again. We cannot walk around Jerusalem exhausted. We must find a place to sleep."

"All right, Joseph, where will we go?"

"I think if we go outside the city walls, to the Pool of Bethesda and camp near there. It will be quiet and we can talk and rest."

The couple began to walk towards the Temple, wearied from their walking all day. They turned off before they reached the Temple and skirted around it until they were at the rear of it. The walls of the Holy Place loomed high above them and they could hear the palace guards laughing on the other side. They turned left and walked straight ahead past the back door of Herod's Temple and out of the Sheep Gate. Mary looked back at the House of God and prayed silently that Jesus would be found the next day. They walked uphill towards the Pool of Bethesda to find a place to sleep.

Mary slept fitfully. Her dreams were of the demons that

said that they were going to kill her son. They told her that they had Jesus and they were torturing him and he would not be fit to save the world. They had laughed and laughed, leaping and dancing for joy. Mary woke weeping and realised that it was only a dream. Then reality struck her again. Her son was not with her. She had been given him, the Son of God, to raise and protect, and she had lost him. Her tears were warm on her face and they did not echo the cold, empty pain that was in her heart. The cold iron of it twisted and turned. "Oh my Father," she prayed aloud, "I have lost your son. Please let him be found this day."

Mary sat up. The first light filtered through the olives and the fig trees. In finger-like strands of brightness, the sun began to bring clarity to the day. She could see Jerusalem spread out before her. Somewhere within it was her son. She needed to find him. She wanted so much to see him and hold him and know that he was safe; to embrace him would ease the ache in her heart and soul. But where could they begin to look? The same streets, the same endless, uncaring crowds were waiting down there. Nevertheless, she would go and try to find him.

Mary got up and walked the short distance to the Pool. Already the people gathered to it for, periodically, an Angel of the Lord would come down from Heaven and disturb the waters and whoever would be in it at that time would be cured of their infirmity. Some waited day after day, month after month, year after year, for the Lord's goodness.

As Mary washed her face, she prayed that Gabriel, whom she had come to know as her Angel, would come and find her son. Mary washed her dusty feet and looked about her at the people who gathered there. Men and women who were blind walked about in their sightless world, used now to the layout of the Pool and its surroundings; beggars in their tattered robes were on the lookout for any rich traveller that might happen along; twisted bodies lay on pallets praying to be healed, to be the first into the water when the Angel would stir it up; children sat with parents, their little legs and arms, bent and useless; tired, weary people like her had come to the Pool to wash the city's grime from their faces, they were all seeking something from the Lord, their God - wholeness and healing.

When she returned to the campsite, Joseph was up. He had prepared some bread and cheese for them to eat. They needed to stock up on more food, for their supplies were only meant to last them the distance home. Mary would buy some in the city.

When they had eaten and Joseph had washed, they untied the donkey, which had eaten of the wiry grass that grew there; they looked at one another.

Joseph said, "Mary, we will pray that Jesus will be returned to us safe and sound." He began, "My God, before we begin this journey, we call upon you for your help in finding our son, your son. Our eyes and bodies are weary from looking; give us your sight and strength. We thank you and we praise you. Amen." They set off down the hill into the city with heavy hearts.

They could not leave their donkey anywhere for it held the precious little supplies that they needed to keep them alive on the pilgrimage and it had to be trailed through the streets with them. They did not part to search but stayed together; giving one another support and comfort for both hearts were sad and painful. They smiled at one another often, they were one.

The throng of mankind that gathered in Jerusalem were still in their thousands. Milling around her, they reminded Mary of the flour she ground sometimes to make bread. They crushed against one another to get where they were going. She thought of Lydia who had lived here in these streets, day in, day out. Then she remembered that Haman, Mahlah and Lydia had said that they would follow them to help them to look for Jesus. She had not met them yesterday. Surely they would have gone home again after a few hours? They would be worried but her and Joseph would go to Bethany when they found Jesus and spend some time with their friends.

Where was Jesus? This pain bit into her heart like a hungry animal, crushing her. She tried not to let the scenarios of what might have happened to Jesus play out in her mind but with each footstep, each heartbeat, with each disappointing answer that no one had seen him, it became increasingly difficult not to think that something had happened to him. She wanted to cry out, her voice lifting over this crowd, like a bird that flew up into the skies; a bird could see from up there, could see the whole of Jerusalem, could see where her son was. If she were a bird, she could see him.

'My God, please help me!' Mary prayed within her heart. Heaven seemed to have closed and Gabriel was strangely silent. She could not feel his sign to her that he was protecting her. She knew he was near, closer than her breath, she knew that and believed, but why was he was not helping her to find Jesus?

The crowds moved endlessly to and fro like the waves on a beach and many times she was going against them to make her way back to Joseph. It was impossible to stay together in this crush. They had set out holding hands but soon had to give up, it was difficult enough trying to stay together.

At noon they went outside the city walls to find a place to eat. They went out at the Gate of Ephraim and passed the Praetorium. They did not feel like eating in the merciless heat. As they walked a little way up the hill they found the shade of an old olive grove. They sat down, wearied from their endless walking. Mary began to cry.

The tears came of their own accord. It was the disappointment and failure to find her son that overflowed from her.

Joseph took her in his arms to comfort her. "I wish I could find him for you, my love," he said, gently, "I wish I could say the right words that would comfort you. I feel helpless, Mary."

"Oh, Joseph, here I am crying and not thinking of you!"

"No, Mary," he said, "your crying gives me strength because I want to find him all the more."

"I love you, Joseph."

"I love you too, Mary."

They embraced again and Mary could feel the hot tears of her husband, wet her face.

–16–

Back in the sea of people, Mary thought of fish in a net, crammed and packed full. As they continued their search, they felt strengthened by one another; they felt one, one of spirit but the pain of losing their child still gnawed at their hearts.

"We will search the Temple now, Mary. He may have gone in there. I suppose he would feel safe there."

"Yes," said Mary.

They tethered the donkey at a post outside the door of the Temple, not caring whether someone stole it. It took them some time to get up the steps that led to the Court of Women which was the first part of the Temple precinct and the nearest that Mary could go to the Holy of Holies, according to the Law of Moses. Mary walked with Joseph up to the steps leading to the Court of Priests. Joseph went up the steps to inquire about his son.

Mary looked about the Court of Women. She could see the pillared porticos that ran the two sides of the court, behind which were the storerooms, housing the supplies of this vast Temple. She saw priests and Pharisees and Sadducees in their fine linen robes and tassels as they made their way up the steps. Many women were there, praying and calling out aloud to God, praying for families and husbands. They, like her, could not enter the Sanctuary of God to make their supplications for the Law prohibited this and had to make do. She watched the men in their tasselled shawls prepare themselves for prayer. She did not see her son.

Joseph was beside her. She looked at his face for any hope. There was none. They would try to eat again and continue searching until the sun went down.

Their steps were dogged as they walked towards the door.

As they reached the door and stood waiting for a chance to enter the flow of bodies that went in and out of the passage of the door, Mary heard her name being called. She heard it above the din of the crowd. It seemed to reverberate off the hallowed stone of the vast walls of the Court of Women. She turned back in the direction that they had come and saw Lydia running towards her, dodging the bodies of the worshippers. Close behind was Haman and Mahlah. Her heart lifted a little. Her friends had found her.

Lydia seemed to bounce up to her and Joseph in her joy of finding them as only the young can.

"Mary, Joseph! We have searched everywhere for you these last two days. Did you find Jesus?"

"No." said Joseph.

"Where could he be, Mary?" said Mahlah catching up and embracing Mary. "You poor, poor, woman!"

The family found a spot behind the Temple and they shared bread together. Lydia and Mahlah wanted Mary and Joseph to rest and they would continue to search but Mary would not hear of it. She said that if all of them looked then there would be more chance of finding Jesus. Joseph said that they would soon have to call off the search and try to make their way home in case he had begun to travel towards Nazareth by himself. He shivered at the thought.

After eating, they began to search again and searched until the sun had gone. Haman invited them to come and stay at Bethany for the night but they preferred to stay in the city. They would go back to the Pool of Bethesda. The friends parted company promising to meet at the steps of the Temple the next morning, early.

As Mary watched the sun rise the next morning, she wondered if it would bring with it another day of desolation. She wondered at the great orange sphere as it lifted itself from the horizon; its face was always on the world, watching and providing heat and light. She wondered where Jesus was and the animal began to gnaw at her heart.

It was past noon when they found him. Mary and Joseph had gone back to the Temple so that Joseph could inquire once more if the priests had seen Jesus. Mary had sat on the steps waiting for him to return. All she could see was a sea of robe-clad bodies before her, their colours blending into one another. She put her head down and tried to ignore the humdrum of human tongues that clashed like cymbals all around her. She sat for several moments trying to find her heart and her God.

As she sat there, she realised that the voices were gone and a silence had taken their place. She looked up sharply, not believing. But it was, it was silent. The sea of bodies had parted and the great room was almost empty. She could see the great flagged floor and the ceiling that was the blue sky and she could hear no din. Her eyes trained the room, wondering at the silence. Had she gone deaf?

In the corner of the room near the door she noticed a small group of old men who sat on the floor on their coats. In their midst she saw a curly haired boy. He was speaking, for she could see his mouth move, but she could not hear him. "Jesus..." she whispered, not really believing that it was he. But it was him. "My Jesus..." she said, louder this time. She heard her own voice say the word and began to believe it. She stood, looking at him across the room, her heart beating wildly, dancing in her breast. It was him.

"Joseph!" she shouted loudly, not turning around, not taking her eyes from the precious sight, "I have found him."

Mary began to run, her veil falling from her head and her hair flowing free in the breeze that she created. Her coat dropped to the floor in a soft plop, audible in the near silence of the vast room. As she ran, her world slowed, slowed until it seemed so slow that she would never reach him. She saw nothing in her vision but her son, her precious son. She could hear Joseph's voice cry out behind her, but she ran on in this slowed-down world that she had entered.

As she reached him she could hear him. Jesus was saying, gesticulating his hands to emphasise "...the essence of the Law is love, for a Father loves his children. It is not to obey the law for fear of punishment but to obey out of love..."

Then she was beside him, looking at him. She reached out and touched his face, tracing her fingers on his cheek. He felt like gold to her, like a dream come to pass. The long hours of searching were over, he was found.

"My son, it is so good to see you," she said simply, her heart bursting with a thousand things to say. She was aware that the old men who had been talking with him were watching and drinking in every word that passed between them.

He was looking at her, a puzzled look on his face.

"We searched for you for three days, Jesus, where have you been? We have been so fraught with worry over you. Why have you done this to us?"

The same puzzled look met her, "Mama," he said, "Why have you been looking for me?" He shook his head, in wonderment. "Did you not know that I would be in my

320

Father's house, busy with his affairs?"

Mary looked at her son. It was her turn to be puzzled. She felt a hand on her shoulder. It was Joseph. He was in wonderment too. What did he mean?

As they stood there, the moments ticking away in silence, one of the old men, whom Jesus had been speaking with, now stood and came to Mary. He bowed politely. "My good lady," he said, "this is your son and you should be proud of him. For the last days we have sat here marvelling at the things he has spoken of. We are teachers and doctors of the Law of God and, I think I can speak for all of my friends here, in saying that your son has answered questions that we have spent many years searching for answers to. They say that, with years, comes wisdom but your son has proved that saying wrong. I do not know what he will become, in the future but Israel needs the wisdom that he has." The man bowed to Mary and Joseph and there was an echo of nods and yeses from the men who sat around them.

Joseph said, "Will you come with us, my son?" To the teachers Joseph said, "You must excuse us, we have walked around Jerusalem for three days, searching for Jesus, we need to go and rest. Thank you for caring for him."

They were walking towards Bethany. They had found Haman, Mahlah and Lydia and were going back to eat and spend the night with them. When they reached the house, Joseph asked Haman to take the donkey. He and Mary and Jesus, went up the Mount. It was covered with olive trees and a few figs sprouted here and there. They found a spot and stopped. Joseph knelt in front of Jesus. "My son," he said, "your mother and I have searched for you for all this time and our hearts have been broken with worry. We are not angry with you, no; we are relieved to find you safe. Did you not think of us while you were there?"

"Joseph," he said sincerely, "I was about my Father's work," he knelt with Joseph on the rocky soil of the Mount, "my Father's work is what I have come to do. I have no other work. In doing that work I must let go of all other things. I would not hurt you and mama, but there are times when all must be left behind. One day I will leave your house and there will be nowhere to lay my head for I have come, not to seek comfort, but to give the Kingdom to as many as wills it. I will be obedient to you until that time." There were tears in the boy's eyes as he finished.

Joseph took Jesus in his arms and embraced him hard.

* * * * *

The spirit surveyed the man. He was just ripe enough for it to pick. Like a lush, juicy fruit that had been fed on a fertile bed of sin, the man was ready for bigger things. The spirit, opportunist as it was, watched the man; he was sitting idly drinking wine outside the inn, his thoughts were not yet polluted but that could be easily remedied. The spirit went closer to the man, testing his ability to resist, there was none. God was far from the man; little traces of a belief that had been slowly whittled away in a life of sin, they were no threat to the demon.

It had not had a conquest for at least a month now and Satan was not pleased with it and had roared at it at the gathering. This man seemed easy, if it could get him to at least think of sin it might only be a short step to actually get the sin and it might get into the fallen angels good books. The spirit began to listen to the man's thoughts.

He was thinking about the inn the night before. He was seeing images of men around a table throwing dice. Each man who played had a cold, static face, which did not betray his thoughts: each, locked by smaller, subservient spirits who made all the running for the bigger ones. The spirit could see through the man's thoughts and he recognised

Complacency and Greed, spirits that it hated. They always gathered the most victims that were in turn led to greater things. They had been in control last night, carefully pulling the strings. Through the man's thoughts, it could see the manipulation process, the strategy that these two always used to gain victims. Man's self pride was easy to get around and these two used it to the full, for the ego and machismo of mankind was weak. They would tell a man that he might just win fortunes by gambling, furnish him with confidence and then at the last moment, take it away from him leaving him cold and despairing and prey to anything. It hated Complacency and Greed but it had to admire their cunning.

The demon touched the man's thoughts. A long, spirit finger probed the delicate, gossamer threads of philosophy buried deep in the man's head, trying to find something that it might go on. The demon watched the pulses of thought dart back and forth, waiting for a place to put his own warped values into.

The man's thoughts were a good mixture of ingredients for any spirit but this demon wanted something big. The man was thinking about the jug of wine that sat on the floor, bought by the man opposite him. The other man was falling asleep with too much wine. The man thought just how easy it would be to take it and walk away, there was a moderate crowd passing the inn and he could get lost within seconds.

The demon watched the man move his foot nonchalantly towards the flagon and began to move it closer, inch by inch, towards him.

The spirit felt amused by the antics of the man. This should be easy.

The young man entered the narrow pass that led to the summit of Tabor. The mist had already soaked his light robe and the droplets of water dripped from his hair. His eyes were aflame with love. The stone face of each side of the opening continued to narrow and the darkness was enclosing, choking and as he touched the sides to guide himself he could feel its coldness penetrate to his bones. He was not afraid but he was very cold. The stone tomb suddenly stopped and he knew he was at the place where he wanted to be. He did not need the light of morning to see the twenty-foot square uneven floor that was before him. He knew that to his left was a sheer wall of stone that rose to the rounded peak and to his right was a sheer drop that plunged a thousand feet into the valley with Gilboa in the distance.

He was where he wanted to be. He could close off the world and its distractions. He walked a few paces and sat down. He prayed aloud into the darkness of the night, "My Father, I have come to you. I lift my eyes to you; I lift my soul to you. I have left all behind for you."

The words, spoken from the young man's soul, were finer than the crystals of water that made up the mist surrounding him. They were truth.

As he spoke the words, Jesus could feel his soul open and a light flood in. It was not the light of morning but a mystical light; a light drawn from the deeps within his Father's Spirit and given freely to him. It was his light and he knew the light. It had always been his; it had never not been his. It penetrated him deeply into his being. He gathered his soul and it and the light became as one; a union, perfectly formed, the two became one with no seams, they were not two but one, never had been two, always merged.

Jesus drank his Father; he drank his being and he drank himself. Like a thirsty man, the boy drank the water of life that came with the oneness of the one, the Godhead. The human, the man, became a shell that withered.

In the light, the youth was given knowledge for his human part; translated from a language that did not exist, for it was not needed, into a language that could not describe the non-language of the world where it came from. It became words, for the boy was the word and had been spoken by his Father. Spoken and one, he existed in this time in the utterance of his Father's voice, living and breathing in his Father's breath. A marriage of a spirit word made flesh and human was now feeding that part of him that did not belong here in this world but was one with each rock, each blade of grass each leaf. Each cell that divided was one with the Father and the boy; a oneness in which flowed and was vibrant with, the word that had been spoken and given with love. The boy was not in the world but was one with it for he had given it life in the word that had been spoken. Jesus remained one with his Father for several hours.

It was just before the sun rose that Jesus came back into the world and became a man once more and the first of the demons dared to come near him. It kicked him. The kick caught him in the lower part of the back and pain erupted in his kidney. He bent over where he sat and stifled a cry of pain. The spirit laughed. There were still a few hours of darkness left before the light of day came and it was not yet the youth's time. The demon and the other spirits knew that Jesus' body was weakened and emaciated by the lack of food for he had not eaten in many days and they crowded around him. The blows rained down on his body but he did not cry out. The time would come; his time, and they would fear even his presence.

An eagle cried out to greet the morning as it heaved over the horizon, its cry piercing the morning air and giving clarity and a noise other than the wind to the top of Tabor.

Mary was thinking about Jesus. He was fifteen and had been going out into the wilderness for about three years now. At first, it had only been intermittent. A few nights in the year was all that he asked for and they had consented for she and Joseph knew that something beyond them was burning within his heart and they could not stand in his way. They had to put all thoughts of his safety out of them and realise that God himself would protect him. And he had gone, at first, to the hills around Nazareth and would return the next day. Now, he would be gone for three weeks at a time.

She did not question him when he returned but waited until he told her, if he told her, where he had been. To see his body become more and more skeletal brought pain to Mary's heart, a deep pain that seared her soul. She knew that, whatever he was doing, he was being guided. But she found it difficult to watch.

She had to keep reminding herself that this was the Son of God and that the Angels would protect him. Sometimes she noticed bloodstains that had seeped through his robe. More frequently now, she noticed bruises on his chest where the neck of his robe was opened and shuddered to think where they may have come from.

When he returned from wherever he had been, he would pick up where he had left off. He was always smiling and courteous and obedient to her and Joseph.

Somewhere, deep down inside, Mary knew that it was the demons that had beaten him. And she knew that they had beaten him because of mankind's sin. To her, he seemed to be an empty vessel that was constantly filled with all the worlds' failures, with mankind's shortcomings; somehow he had to take it on himself.

He always spoke with wisdom. He always had a kind word to say to the under-trodden, whether it was here in Nazareth or the surrounding area or when they went to Jerusalem for *Pesach.* He seemed to know each need and what to say to fulfil it. She loved him and that love showed in the not asking where he was and what had happened. That love was in being content to understand that these things must happen.

He would look at her sometimes and smile, as if knowing what was going on in her heart; and she would return the smile.

The people of Nazareth had begun to talk about him and his lengthy absences from the workshop and would ask questions. They talked too about Mary and Joseph and that they had lost control of their son. But the talk could not, would not break her resolve in believing in her son and his mission.

Miriam was forever telling her that if she and Joseph did not take control of Jesus then he would end up mad. "Too much religion!" she would say, "too much God and you won't be able to bring him back. You will lose him to madness."

Mary did not listen for too many things had happened to prove to her that all was well with her son.

The spirit watched the man as he picked up the flagon, hold it against his side and begin to walk down the streets of Magdala and almost applauded. It followed the man. He walked the distance of the town and out into the countryside. It was all uphill. When he reached the top of the hill and a safe distance from the town, he looked behind to make sure that no one was following him. No one human was and he sat under a fig tree and looked at his prize; he broke the stopper and took a long deep swallow.

Satisfied with the man's ability to do wrong, the spirit decided to stay with him. He would serve its purpose.

The demon began to probe the man's thoughts once more. It suggested to the man that he might need to steal more wine to get him through the night and over the worry of not knowing where his next meal was coming from. The man agreed and took the thoughts for his own. The spirit was happy and slipped the unseen manacle around the man's neck and locked it.

The spirit had become the master now and the man did not know it. The spirit encouraged and the man took another swallow, letting the grape juice dribble down his chin.

* * * * *

Tamar and Elizabeth were sitting on the balcony, shading themselves from the mid afternoon sun. It had been a busy morning for Tamar. She had taken over the most of the running of the house now for Elizabeth was not fit anymore. She sometimes insisted that Tamar sat down while she made the bread or cooked the meal and Tamar would let her, knowing that she would exhaust herself and have to give up. Tamar hated to see her friend like this, helpless and unable to do any work. Elizabeth had always been independent and Tamar remembered when Zechariah had first brought her here. Elizabeth would not let her make any of the meals or bake the bread, she had done it all herself. Tamar knew that it was not against her but it was because Elizabeth felt that she was fit enough to do it and why would she need anyone to help her? Elizabeth was independent and very strong willed. Little by little Tamar had gained ground, not just as a servant but also as a friend.

Now, they sat talking of Zechariah and things that were past. Elizabeth would still shed a tear at the mention of her husband's name.

"He was a good man, Elizabeth," Tamar was saying, "he is with the Lord."

"Yes, I know that, but it is a pity that he did not have a few more years to enjoy his son. John has been a godsend to me and Zechariah would have loved him."

"He has turned into a lovely young man. He is so courteous and everyone around here loves him. He could bring the birds down out of the trees. It is a pity that he spends so much time away from home these days."

"I know what you mean, Tamar. But he must. He tells me that he gets these yearnings to go out there and be with God. He says that that is the place where he finds him. I do not mind for he is such a strong boy but I miss him from the house. He brings such joy to me. A mother could not have asked for a better son, Tamar."

The two women lapsed into silence, reflecting on the joy of both their lives. A dragonfly buzzed gently near Tamar's face and she shooed it away. She shuddered for she did not like insects. The heat was interminable and she fanned her face with her hand trying to create a breeze to cool her down. She could feel the sweat flow freely on her face. She wiped her face with her other hand.

"It is so hot, Tamar. Would you get me some water, please?"

"Of course, Elizabeth." Tamar got up and went down the stairs that ran down the side of the two-storied house.

Elizabeth felt tired. The heat always made her tired these days. She did not really want to do anything but the thought that John might come home today gave her the strength to get off her couch in the mornings. She lived for her son. He was the cool breeze of her life. Sometimes she wished she were a young woman so that she could walk faster when he took her to the market. She hated being old.

Her joints were stiff and would not move the way she wanted them to move and she would get angry with herself. She felt like a young woman inside but her body refused to do what she wanted it to do.

And this stick! She hated being dependant on a lifeless stick. Although it did help her to climb these stairs, it gave her the support that she needed but it was a long process for her to get up them with all that stopping and starting. The only consolation that she got from it was that John had cut it for her and smoothed it so that she did not hurt her hands on it. Ah, he was a good boy.

'What is keeping, Tamar?'

"Tamar..." she listened for an answer. "Tamar..." she called again. Where was she? Was she alright?

Elizabeth pulled herself up, painfully. She grimaced as the pain in her knees caught her sharply. She stood as quickly as she could to relieve the pain. Elizabeth straightened herself, glad now of the stick which she gripped firmly and leaned all her weight on. She stumbled towards the wooden rail that ran the length of the house. She bent over it, listening for any sound of her friend.

"Tamar, Tamar, where are you, girl?" she called out.

Elizabeth heard the crack of the wood as it broke under her weight and felt herself falling. She panicked as she fell and called out for her son.

Magdala was a pretty town and had one long street from which all the others broke off. One could see the Sea of Galilee from the hill, which it nestled against. It was like any other town and had a little Synagogue on its outskirts. Mary was eleven years old and she often helped her mother, Rebecca, by walking up to the top of the hill to fetch water. She could not carry much but Mary was a willing girl. She was the eldest at eleven of a family of five and she knew that she had to rank fourth for always her brothers Jarah, Ezra and Samuel took precedence over her and her little sister Raba. It was the way things were done and she did not think to question it.

Life for Mary in Magdala was somewhat hard for her mother could not afford to have a servant and it seemed that Mary was doing a servant's work. But she smiled, and did it. Sometimes she felt a little resentful that her brothers were not called on to do any work but when she spoke to her mother of these things she was told just to get on with it. The first time she had asked, her mother had slapped her.

Rebecca had been from a middle-class family and did not feel that she should do any work. She had been brought up with many servants. When she married Ruben she had married for love. There was money at the beginning for Ruben had been in an apprenticeship as a goldsmith but had been accused of stealing some of the gold. The name stuck and he had, from then, only been able to get work as a labourer.

Mary put her jar into the cistern and watched it bubble as it filled. The cistern was a wide trough and was low to the ground, which left it easy to get at. A small stream that had its origin further up in the hills above Magdala fed it. It was clear and surprisingly cool for the cistern was built under an outcrop of rock and natural holes in the outcrop directed rainwater into it. She placed her hands in the cool water and splashed her face, enjoying its coolness. These moments of freedom were precious to Mary and she liked to be sent for water.

These were the moments that she used to dream of marrying a rich husband and having many children, for she knew that children were the real riches of a marriage and she felt sorry for those women in the town that were barren. Her aunt was barren and always made a fuss of Mary when she came from Capernaum to visit them.

Mary left her jar in the cistern and looked about her. There was no one here. It was a small flat clearing with sparse, grassy knolls and pathways between that were worn smooth by many feet over many years. It was surrounded by thick, high scrub and a few small trees, it gave the place privacy and isolation. It was above the town and Mary could look out over the Land of Gennesaret. It looked like a huge garden and there was much growth and colour now in early summer. The smells of the prolific growth and the scent of flowers, both wild and cultivated, gave a serene air to the place. The girl loved it here.

She stood and began to pirouette across the opening, her

long hair and her imagination flowing free. Her blue robe billowed in the steps of the dance. She was dancing for her husband. He sat on the chair opposite her and she was pleasing him with her dance. He always had dark hair and beard; his hair flowed on his shoulders and he smiled at her, with love in his eyes.

He called her his princess for he was a prince and soon he would ride off to war and win battle after battle until Israel was out of Roman hands. He would return with the spoils and give them to her; dresses of gold and silver that Roman goddesses had worn and tiaras of bright and sparkling jewels that would sit upon her head. He would open chests of gold Roman coins and declare to all his subjects, their subjects, "This is Mariamne's gold." And she would bow a graceful bow and he would love her and she would be happy.

Her fantasy always ended there and she would come back to reality, coyly looking around her to be sure that no one had seen her. She went back to the cistern and picked up the jar. She must hurry home now for she had lost track of time as she always did. She tried not to run for it only resulted in the water spilling and she did not want to arrive home again with half a jar of water. The last time she had done that her mother had slapped her on the face and left the track of her hand on it. She did not want that again.

The spirit could see that the man was open to its prompting. The morning after he had stolen the wine, it had suggested that he go back into the town to steal some bread to eat for the more sin the man created then the more power the spirit gained. The man did not question what he thought were his own thoughts and this allowed the spirit to place its warped thoughts into him. It told the man that he could own the town of Magdala, if he played the game and the man's pride had swelled. The spirit brought the man back up to the hill where he could continue to work on him. From what information it could gather, the man had lived for twenty-five of the world's years and had no family to keep him out of sin.

Greed was easy to place in him for the man had desires for fine clothes and fine wines, spread out before him. A desire for possession of these things came next.

Like a wall, the demon built sin around the man, spreading a generous amount of the glue of desire between each brick, building and capturing him further and deeper into his own tomb. It had to make sure that no Angel of God broke through. They were always on the lookout for some poor soul who was in a demon's grip, taking out the glue to break down the work that he, or others from hell, had done.

Continuously probing the long spirit finger into the man, the spirit searched further for the natural weaknesses that just needed to be tapped into to give a generous reward. Sometimes when a spirit tapped, weakness, that had not been fought against, spewed like an artesian well.

Then the spirit found it. The sin was tucked deeply in the secret things of the mind; in that place that was deep and dark and hidden; that place that truth did not penetrate. The weakest desire in this man was the flesh. It probed its long finger into the sin of the flesh and took it out. The man's mind stirred. The spirit was delighted for he was a spirit of lust of the flesh and had been sent to find just this. He would have used any sin at his disposal to achieve an end but here it was, served on a silver platter.

He touched the man physically and was rewarded with the desired effect. It was generous. The spirit of lust tightened the manacle around the man's neck.

Mary arrived home. Home was a one storied house on the edge of Magdala. It had a small garden that grew onions and herbs for there was not room for anything else. An orange tree lent shade to the small plot.

Mary entered the one room that the family ate in, slept in and lived in. The smoke from the fire was billowing into the small space of the room for someone had broken branches off a tree and put them on the fire. That same someone had not stripped the leaves from the branches and it was this that was causing the fire to smoke.

Mary made a clucking sound with her tongue that showed her annoyance and went to the hearth; its three brick walls were covered in soot. She coughed hard for the smoke went up her nostrils and into her throat and made her eyes water. What leafy branches that had not caught alight and she could take off, she removed and placed on the floor beside her. The smoke lessened. She picked up the stick that was used to poke the fire and rake the ashes and began to poke in order to get the flames to burn and lessen the smoke even further.

With the leafy branches gone, the half burned branches that were left sprang into flame, spitting and crackling. Mary lifted some of the finer twigs to the side of the hearth and put them on top to help the burning process. The fire soon caught and she was able to leave it.

Mary got up from the floor and lifted the unburned green branches to take them outside wondering who had done such a silly thing. Besides, she wanted to get the fresh air back into her lungs to clear the smoke. As the girl turned, she felt the sting of a slap across her face. The sound of it resounded around the room. She staggered backwards and almost fell into the fire. Mary was stunned by the surprise of it.

"What do you think you are doing, my girl?" said her mother, glaring at her, her veil pulled tightly around her head so that her hair could not be seen. "I had just lit that fire."

"The branches and the leaves were smoking out the house,

mother."

The next slap caught Mary on the side of the head and her ear stung. She put her hand up automatically to the pain and to be ready to ward off any more slaps. There was an uneasy silence as her mother looked at her, lips pulled thin. Mary stood awkwardly not knowing whether she should move.

"Put those down and go out and collect more," said her mother slowly and deliberately, "do not ever presume to know better than your mother."

"Yes, mother," said Mary, meekly.

She had to dodge around her mother and as she did so, her mother kicked her, the blow catching her in the small of the back, sending her sprawling onto her belly. Mary scrambled up and out the door with the words, "You lazy, good for nothing girl."

The tears stung the girl's face and she could feel the weal begin to form on her face. What had she done? Why had her mother hit her like that? She had only tried to stop the smoke from filling the house. Anybody knew that the green branches of a tree would not burn so well as the dead, dry ones. Her mother seemed to know little about the running of a house and usually did nothing but sit in a neighbour's garden and talk.

Mary did not wish anyone to see her tears or the weals on her face and began to run back up the hill she had just come down to the place that she loved to be. It was likely to be still empty at this time of the day for the servants of other houses would have fetched the water early in the morning. There would be dead wood there underneath the scrub that she could gather and take back with her. Her father would soon be back from the farm in Capernaum where he was working this season. He would need to eat. It was usually up to Mary to make the meal for him, unless as on rare days like today, her mother decided that she would take over. When she did, no one stood in her way.

The meal was either burnt or half raw.

Mary loved her father and he seemed to be fond of her. She only saw him in the late evenings after he had walked from work and she often missed his affection. He could see what her mother was doing to her. He would not like to see the weals on her face and would shout at her mother. Mary wished he would let it go for it would mean that she would suffer for it. Her mother would not hit her but she could be sure that she would find a lot more work for her and it would be hard. She would come off worst. It would be better for her if her father did not say anything, then she would be left alone.

Mary entered the clearing where the cistern was. She breathed relief; there was no one here. She went over to the cistern and knelt down.

The water was still and clear and she could just make out her reflection. The weal on her face was red and ugly. She touched it tentatively. It was sore. The girl cupped her hand in the cool water and began to pat her face in an effort to bring down the swelling. She hoped that her face would not bruise and her eye would not blacken. If it did, her few friends would ask her about it. She would have to lie in order to save embarrassment to her mother; she would make herself look a fool by saying that she walked into the doorpost. Her friends were not stupid either.

The water did cool Mary's face and she felt relieved. She looked around her and saw that there were heaps of twigs here. She usually searched further up the slopes whilst getting wood for the fire. But this was good; she would soon collect them; for now, she could be alone with her dreams.

The man got up to relieve himself and felt his belly full. He was content. He swallowed wet spittle over a dry throat. The wine that he had had the night before was giving him a thirst. He would go to the cistern that he knew was half a

336

mile down the hill. The water there was clean and he could wash himself. He began walking down the hill whistling a little tune that he had picked up in one of the inns. It was a bawdy tune and he smiled at each of the earthy parts and an excitement began to grow in him.

–17–

The spirit followed him. It marvelled to realise how imperfect this human body was. All the fuss that was made about creation and that God who had made it, got to the spirit. All these parts of it that needed to be filled or relieved and it needed to sleep, to get rested or it would become sluggish and incapable. A spirit could not push too far, for this silly human would fall asleep on it and then its mission would be lost. It was a slow process for any spirit worth his sulphur.

This God was not as perfect as he was made out to be. Yes, he had created spirit and that was better; a spirit could not die and it did not have the bodily functions of this stupid carriage that the human carried around with it. With its thought, a spirit, good or bad, could travel anywhere within moments and be anywhere it wanted to be. The spirit of the human could, if freed from the body, do the same but while it walked around in this prison it was easily led, *if* it did not fight against the sin within it.

Satan had to be admired; he had conquered the whole human race with a silly suggestion that man could be better than God. And it had worked, beautifully. Man had lost paradise and that gave the other side a chance. Mankind still had pride and it could be easily manipulated into getting God's influence out of him. Pride was a wonderful sin and, as the fallen angel had taught, it was the way to man's heart or woman's for that matter.

The spirit laughed to itself. Women were easily conquered

in pride. Throw in a bit of vanity, possession and gossip and they were on a leash. They usually had enough influence over the man to bring him with her.

Well, the spirit supposed, some parts of this human body were his speciality and they kept him in work. The fact that it could touch them physically was good and humans were suckers for sins of the flesh. They thought the whole of their world revolved around those little bits of flesh. It took very little pushing on its behalf until the humans were a helpless bunch. And it knew that some of the bigger lust spirits even had their own harem of men and women that waited for them in the dead of night. The latest plan that was buzzing around hell was to make sure that the word got to humans that evil did not exist and they could do anything that they wanted. If it felt good, then do it. What a wonderful extension of the sin of pride!

The spirit froze in its reverie. There was an Angel of God hovering around the entrance of the well that the man was going to. It was a guardian. Every human had one, although most of them did not know it, that was another plan carefully formulated in hell. The spirit spat. Well, if it had to have a battle, so be it. It was keeping this human, it was the ticket it needed to work back into Lucifer's good books. It spat at the Angel.

"Leave this soul and return to hell," the Angel said, a fiery sword appearing in his hand. He was prepared to fight.

"Not by the feathers on your wings, you puffed up, feathered lizard." the spirit answered, "He's mine. I have him and his sin and his freewill has sent his own guardian snivelling back to Heaven. And anyway, you can't go near him, he has chosen to go with sin."

"I can bring him back to God."

"Alright," the spirit said, seeing a chance to keep the man without a fight and feeling confident in the manacle around his neck, "we'll let the human decide, after all, none of us can go through freewill, we can only suggest. If by the end of this day he has not given in to sin then he's yours. But no influencing, he decides what he does. Agreed?"

"I do not have a choice," the Angel said.

"He has gone in to quench his thirst," said the spirit, "we'll watch him and no cheating from you, either." The spirit let a string of obscene words strike the Angel but the graceful spirit stood calmly, accepting the abuse. They followed the man and waited to see what would happen.

The man saw the girl as soon as he entered the place of the well and with the bawdy song still on his mind, coupled with the spirit's prompting and touch, he became aroused. He looked around him and a cloud of temptation settled on him and it blinded him. The fact that that no one else was there gave him more confidence.

The girl was lying on the ground and he noticed the redness on her face. He walked up to her and saw that she had her eyes closed.

"What are you doing here, all by yourself?" he said trying to sound amiable but his breath was coming in short pants.

The girl shot up to a sitting position, looking embarrassed. "I...I...am here to look for wood for the fire." The man could tell that she was frightened of him but that did not matter. He squatted down in front of her and touched her ankle. She pulled it away from his touch and tucked her legs under her body.

"What are you afraid of?" the man said.

"Please do not touch me. I must go now," she made to get up, "my mama will be wondering where I am." The man caught her wrist and pulled her down again into a sitting position. The girl looked horrified but the man smiled. He twisted her hand and made her lie down.

"Please, leave me alone," she said plaintively but the man did not listen, could not listen for all the spirit's work and influence was blinding him and giving him impetus. He heaved himself on top of the girl.

Mary opened her mouth and screamed but the man put his hand over her mouth. She was very afraid. The terror held her and she realised that she could do nothing.

The fear inside the girl's head mounted until she thought her head would burst. What was he doing to her? His weight was pinning her to the ground and she could not move. He was pulling at her clothes, touching her, hurting her. She tried to scream but his hand would not let her. She tried to heave him off but he removed his hand from her mouth and she saw the fist slam into her mouth and felt its pain; she tasted her own blood. She did not see the next blow but felt it drive into her mouth again. She stiffened.

The pain in her body was heightening now and she would not scream for the fear of being hit again froze her throat. The pain pierced her and seemed to take over her body until she felt that she had become the pain. She watched as all her dreams shattered like glass and the shards fell to the ground, useless.

The spirit laughed a victorious laugh and the Angel wept.

As the man stood up and adjusted his clothes he said to the girl, "Don't tell anyone about this or I will search for you and I will kill you." He walked to the cistern and began to slake his other thirst.

Mary lay as he had left her. She was not capable of moving. She watched the man drink water, turn to her and laugh. Then he moved out of the clearing.

She was afraid to move, she thought if she did move she would fall apart. Her body seemed only pieces held together by her fear and the pain. The pain touched every part of her and she could feel the wetness of the blood. Moments passed, and she could feel each one; each was fraught with the pain. It would not go away; she ignored it but it did not go away. It stayed. It had bitten into her flesh and planted seeds, its teeth locked, cemented into her.

Moments became minutes and she saw and felt each one. Each slice of time was created and stayed with her for a lifetime; its existence and her existence embroiled and one, each feeding the other, each a dance that merged. And the pain in her was the music, the strains of which played and devoured, with each stroke, her body. The music, of evil created, touched her soul and she screamed, and screamed, and screamed until everything went black.

No one had heard Mary's scream; no one had seen the evil as it gripped her soul. No one had seen the small spirit of lust bow and make way for the seven demons of hell that now lived in her soul. No one heard the flap of the dark wings as they penetrated the girl.

Jesus felt it all. High up on Tabor, Jesus felt the pain of Mary. It came to him as a whip might tear flesh. He felt the bone shards attached to the ends as they tore deep and touch his bone. He felt the screams lock deep in his being, he felt them burn him and he felt her soul being torn away from his. Jesus cried out as the pain in his soul ripped through his body.

The spirits came then. Their cries of delight mingled with the cries of the eagle as it panicked in the noise of the scream. They laughed at the pathetic young man as he lay with Mary's pain locked deep in his heart.

Tamar was coming back from the well. She had gone there to get her mistress a cool drink for the water in the anteroom she felt had warmed. This water in the jar that she carried on her head would cool Elizabeth down. She had brought enough to put in a basin to cool down her face and her feet. Tamar hummed a little tune as she passed through the gate of the yard. She saw the broken balcony

341

first; then she saw Elizabeth.

Tamar threw the jar off her head and ran to her. Elizabeth lay on her side and Tamar noticed that blood seeped from various parts of body, which had been pierced by the splinters from the balcony. At first Tamar thought she was dead and was afraid to touch her but when Elizabeth moaned she went to her.

"Elizabeth, can you hear me?"

Elizabeth moaned again and said weakly, "I fell..."

"Elizabeth, I will have to leave you to get some of the neighbours to help me lift you onto a couch. I cannot do it by myself." As she was speaking, Elizabeth's eyes flickered in understanding. Tamar thought she was very pale and was afraid to do anything but she must do something. She could not leave her there. Reluctantly, Tamar rose and walked slowly to the gate looking behind her at Elizabeth. When she got outside the gate she ran and so did her tears.

Tamar brought the physician to Elizabeth. He placed wine and oil to the abrasions, which helped the woman somewhat, but for the broken thighbone he could do little. It was bound up with bandages and left. The little bearded man told Tamar that Elizabeth's age would not help her and he could do little else. It had been a bad fall and she might have been luckier had the fall killed her. He told Tamar that she would have to look after the old woman in every way that she needed it. He felt that she would not last very long. Tamar wept. A death sentence had been placed on her friend and she could do nothing to stop it.

In the days that followed the fall, Tamar spent all her time with Elizabeth. She never left her bedside and tried to do all that Elizabeth needed and asked for. Each time that Elizabeth moved, she cried out in pain and Tamar would apologise to her for hurting her. It could not be helped. Tamar prayed that John would come home. He had been gone a long time now. She prayed that he would come home to see his mother before she died. He would be heartbroken if he came home and she was dead. She knew that he was in the hills near the Jordan River but she would not have known where to send a messenger. Although he had spoken of the River Jabbok and a place called Gerasa but she could not be sure. She would just have to wait.

Mary stopped screaming. Her throat was raw and she had no energy left. She had blacked out and when she awakened she had screamed again. Now she needed to move, to bathe herself, for she felt that she was sullied and polluted. She lifted herself up. Every part of her screamed out in pain; she stopped moving, breathless from the effort. She stood unsteadily, and had to hold onto the cistern. There was blood on her legs.

Mary stepped into the cistern. She did not take off her robe. It was not deep but it covered her sufficiently so that she felt hidden and somewhat safe. She watched as the water around her turned red with her blood. It soon disappeared and became one with the water. She cupped the water in her hands and brought it up to her face. It was cool and she drank it from her hands and winced when she swallowed. Her throat was raw. The water was cool on her body and she felt some relief.

Mary heaved a sigh and wondered why she did not cry. All her dreams were shattered now. No one would want her, there would be no husband for her; no riches would be hers, no gold dresses, no tiaras, nothing. Her father and mother would not want her and her mother would probably blame her for enticing the man.

Mary remembered her mouth. She reached up a finger to touch it. The blood had dried but it was very tender. There were two splits on her mouth and around them had swelled.

Mary stood suddenly, impelled by something deep within

her, she could not make out what it was but she knew what she must do and where she must go. She would be accepted there, she was now one of their kind, one of them. She would be kin to those women. They would be her sisters, her mothers and her daughters. They would replace the family that she had now lost. Their home would be her home.

As she walked out of the clearing and down the hill it became clearer to her and she spoke the words aloud, "I will go to Tiberias and be a whore."

Mary never saw her family again.

Jesus returned home to Mary and Joseph four days after young Mary was raped in the place of the well in Magdala. The spirits had beaten him for the most part of two days. Mary's mouth fell open to see him. His body was so wasted that she did not know how he had walked. Something terrible had happened for she could see many bloodstains on his robe. She brought him some goat's milk in a goblet and passed it to him with trembling hands.

"Jesus, my son, do you wish to eat anything?" she said, looking intently into his face.

He looked back at her and smiled through the pain that must have been in him. The love somehow pierced through the tiredness and the pain that were clearly in his eyes.

"I have eaten much, woman, and the girl is still mine. She will remain mine. I only wish to sleep now for the work is done." Jesus got up and went outside the house. Mary followed and watched as he climbed the stairs that were on the outside of the house. She returned to Joseph who sat at the table, he had tears in his eyes.

Mary went to him and put her arms around him. "Oh, my husband, do not weep. Jesus is only doing what he was sent to do."

"It is hard to watch someone that you love dearly come into your home like that."

"But, Joseph, you know that there are things that we will never know because we do not need to know." Mary smoothed down her husband's greying hair. "He is here to do something and the depth of that is known only to him and God. I believe that the hurts that he returns with come from the demons and they torture him while he is out there."

"Yes, I suspected that. His mission is beyond any earthly knowledge and if he chooses not to tell us then we must be content with that." Joseph looked thoughtful for a moment then he said, "Did you understand what he said about the girl?"

"He said that the girl was still his, but I did not understand what he was speaking about. When he said it to me, Joseph, he looked at me. Through the pain in his eyes I understood that he had fought for her, not as in physical, but for her soul. To win her was what he fought for. It must have been a terrible battle for his clothes are covered in blood."

Joseph did not speak but stared out through the window. His thoughts were on his son. Whatever it was he was going through, he, Joseph, could not help him. His heart and soul wanted to but his mind could not comprehend the magnitude of what his son must be suffering to do what he has to do. Was it suffering that he came for? Was he going to suffer for each man, woman and child in Israel? What was it all about?

All Joseph could do was to offer God his life more and more to help Jesus in what he was doing.

"All I can do to help him, Mary, is to offer my life to God so that he can use me in whatever way to help Jesus. I have nothing more to give. I would like to be with him to help him but I cannot."

"Nor I, Joseph, nor I."

* * * * *

As the days passed, Elizabeth got weaker. She developed a cough because she could not clear the congestion in her lungs and it became harder for her to breathe. The sound of her breathing could sometimes be heard outside the house and Tamar worried for her. She sent for the physician once more but little could be done.

About fifteen days after the fall, Tamar was bathing Elizabeth's face with cool water and the dying woman became quite lucid in her thinking and talking. She took Tamar's hand.

"You are my daughter, Tamar," she said. "I could never have wished for a better daughter. You have served me as a servant and I have no complaints about your service. I want you to remember that this house will always be your home. It can never be taken away from you.

Tamar, I am dying. Please, Tamar, don't cry; let me speak these words for there may never be another time like this one. I love you and you are my Ruth, my Moabite woman." Elizabeth closed her eyes to think of the words she wanted to say, "This is my blessing upon you, Tamar," she put her hand on Tamar's head, " *'And Ruth said, intreat me not to leave thee, or to return from following after thee: for whither thou goest, I will go; and where thou lodgest, I will lodge: thy people shall be my people, and thy God my God. Where thou diest, will I die, and there will I be buried: the Lord do so to me and more also, if ought but death part thee and me.'* You have done all this to me and for me. I call you my daughter and I adopt you into this family.

When I am gone, you must be a mother to John. You must let him do as the Lord asks of him and ask no questions of him regarding what he does. Know this, my daughter, it has been said of him: "As it is written in the Prophets: *'behold, I send my messenger before your face, who will prepare your way before you. The voice of one crying in*

346

the wilderness: 'Prepare the way of the Lord; make His paths straight.' He is the Lord's servant." Elizabeth closed her eyes and fell asleep. She had exhausted herself. Tamar wept. She kept a watchful eye on Elizabeth over the next few days and prayed earnestly that John would come home.

John could see the Jordan River from where he stood. It was like a ribbon in the valley floor below him. The rocks around him were jagged and seemed impassable for this was a wilderness. He could meet with God here. He could be one with him; that was what he wanted to do, what he was here for. Already the Angel Minoah had spoken to him and had begun to outline his mission. He was told that he was not the Messiah but he was the one who came before him.

John stayed in this wilderness day after day, dying to the self in him that he knew was there, that human part that was alien to God and could wreck his plans. He had seen people in their greed of wanting more without really seeing the God who created them. He could see the rich and how they did not share their wealth but amassed fortunes that they could never spend in lifetimes. John could feel the pride of the human being as it whittled away the faith in God. He did not want to be one of those who simply went to the Synagogue when he was supposed to, no; he wanted God in his life at every moment.

John, in his times in this wilderness, could see the sin within himself and how he was capable of using it against his maker. He wanted to be the way that God wanted him to be and not some excuse for it. The sin in him had to be beaten out before he could do what God was calling him to do. His heart must be pure; his soul must be pure in order to give to God the best of what was in him. It would be so easy if God would remove it for him but John did not want that. He had discovered that the only way that he could come closer to God was to die to himself. He would not give his body food, even when it craved for it; he would not give it the things it wanted, denying it all things except that that it needed.

He was encountering himself within this wilderness and he did not like what he saw, for the human mind was prey to every evil spirit in hell if it gave in to its own whims. His body cajoled him and cried out wanting but he would not give in, he must discipline it. It was the soul within him that he was freeing, freeing it so that God could use it, and use it to the full.

The body would then rebel and, aided by spirits, who constantly wandered the earth, begin to throw up into his mind visions of tables spread with the most sumptuous food. His belly would cry out wanting the food, but he had walked away from it, denying and dying.

The great Angel had stood before him on the mountain with his arms folded across his chest. He was becoming the young man's teacher. He had shown him the kingdom of the world; he had shown him the sin. In it, John saw the darkness that sin had created and the world was a dark place, overrun with the denizens of hell. Every sin was being used by the demons that lived on mankind like lice in the hair and the body. Millions of them, oozing out of hell on the power that mankind had given them by lying to themselves and ignoring the truth.

Sin was what was inside a man when he thought to allow his pride to become better than God. Sin was that hideous guardian of the gates of hell. Sin was the woman that appeared to him to try to get him aroused. She would come in provocative stance and twist her body into many shapes to try to make him sin. She played mind games with him, telling him that his body could not do without this stimulation and God had created it to be used.

When he had first come to the wilderness, sin had come to

him and he had run, run across the jagged rocks to get away from her. Now, he just sat, smiling at everything that she put up against him. He could see through her because he did not give in to the whims of his body.

John sat now looking out over the valley. This wilderness that had become his home stretched out before him. It was a harsh environment and it suited his battle with self. When his body had craved shade he would walk in the harsh sun; when it craved food, he starved it; when the visions of the flesh came, he beat his body with thorns and stinging plants giving it pain because it asked for pleasure. John did not give his body sleep but denied it so that he could spend that time with his God. The battles did not stop for the body would try to creep up on him but he would fight it.

John was dying to the sin in him since he was twelve years old and still it went on, even now at nearly sixteen, he was still dying. But it had its benefits. When the mind and body are cleaned of sin, then God has a clear path into the soul. It was like a path that led to a well. When that well is being used then many feet will keep it free of branches and plants that would block. If the well is not used then it becomes over-grown.

John got up from where he sat and walked a small distance to a pool of water that had its source in a little fissure in the rock. It bubbled up through the rock and had, over many thousands of years, hollowed out a little basin to hold itself. At one side of the basin the water spilled over to fall away into the distance below. John cupped his hand in the clear, clean, cold water and drank. The water dribbled into his unkempt beard and down through the hairs on his chest where it met the camel skin garment and was soaked up. He wiped his mouth on the back of his hand. He went back to where he had been sitting on the overhang. John surveyed the Jordan Valley before him.

"My God," he shouted at the top of his voice, "I am your

servant, do with me as you will." The sound of his rasping voice echoed back to him again, and again, and again.

No voice answered him from the mountains and the crags but he could hear the voice in his heart and he knelt in the jagged rocks, 'You are my servant, I am your God, hear my voice. When the time is ready, you must go to my people to prepare them for my coming, for my day comes soon. Prepare them by plunging them in the waters of the Jordan, which I shall make clean. In this Baptism I will absolve their sins. I give you the power to do this in preparation for the one who comes after you. You must learn how to choose good over evil so that you will come to know the Lord, your God. You are Elijah, sent to make straight the path of the Lord.' The voice stopped there and John felt the heavenly strains linger in his being. His giving and dying to the self within him was the sacrifice that was needed for God to use him.

When the night came, John was still on his knees. He watched the spirit before him. It had spat at him, a green, vomit spittle, trying to make John lose his concentration. The spittle now dangled from John's hair. There was a group of them and they would begin to hurt him now as he prayed.

Other spirits, some with dark wings, came to join the first group. They were larger creatures and the others that were there moved back, fearful, in their presence. They began to surround him, each taking up a vantage point around this accursed prophet of the Lord. They had their plans for him; he was too sure of himself and the subservient spirits could do nothing to him and had complained to the lords of hell that he was too much for them. Everything that they had tried had come to nothing. Lucifer had beaten them; he had hurt them for their failure. His voice had resounded through all the dark corners of hell that were not lit up by the fires. "Must I do everything myself?" A string of obscene abuse followed that was new even to hell and he called together a council of the lords of hell.

These creatures were huge beings that oozed evil. There were seven of them and they all filed into the throne room. The smaller spirits tried in vain to blend into the shadows, for these spirits could instil fear without even trying. Some were created from the darkness of Lucifer's heart and others from the slime that surrounded it. They were his right hand angels and they were obedient only to their master. They owned the rights to walk into any part of the kingdom of the earth and take it. It was they who put it into men's hearts to massacre one another in war, they who gave the idea to mankind to heat an iron dish until it was white-hot and throw living newborn babies on it as a sacrifice to their master. It was they who possessed kings and made them kill innocents. It was their ideology that kept the world as it is, smouldering in evil. Their ideas of how to slit the belly of a human being open and let his entrails fall into a pot of boiling water to slowly cook were used by men. They had slithered their way into the world by the way of the evil in man's heart. It was they who had taught the Romans to abort their children when they thought they would not have a male heir.

Lucifer spoke, his voice rasping and exuding hatred, "There are two prophets on the earth. One is on Tabor and one is in the wilderness in Jordan. Go to them and use any means that you can to break them. We have no permission yet from that pompous God up there," he spat, "to allow you to touch them physically but the smaller ignoramuses here," he indicated the smaller spirits, "can do whatever they want. I want them to see you; to let them know that your time will come and that you await it with pleasure. Show them that you are ready. Now go and do this bidding of mine." The creatures bowed and left the throne room.

John saw them encircling him but he was not afraid. They stood, secreting evil from every pore they possessed; they smouldered chaos and war and lust. John was not afraid. He opened his mouth and roared, "Do what you have come to do, you putrid emissaries of hell. My trust is in the living God." All the spirits that congregated there shrank from the name and John's faith in him, they hissed and spat. The little spirits rushed in quickly and began to kick John, they spat and vomited on him; handfuls of his hair came away and blood spurted from more than one place on his body. John uttered no words in his defence and about a hundred spirits were on him. The lords stood watching, unable to do anything, but they were creatures of evil and obedience to God was not their work. They waited to seize an opportunity. They moved closer to John's body with deadly intent.

At that moment, the dark sky opened and a seam of white light appeared in it and seemed to split the night. With the light came a crack of thunder that sounded like a great voice booming in the sky. From it emerged seven winged creatures that were graceful, beautiful beings whose wings were as white as the light that they emerged from, each gossamer feather capturing the strands of light so that the light seemed to emerge from them. They alighted on the ground behind each of the hideous creatures. The lords knew that they had met their match.

The Archangels each had flaming swords in their hands and exuded God's obedience, they were ready to do battle, ready to fight this mass of evil that stood before them. The spirits shrank back from the light of Heaven that was pulsing from their counterparts. Of the smaller spirits there was no sign, they had abandoned their lords in fear.

An Angel with flaxen hair and a countenance of pure love and obedience stepped forward, his height of about ten feet dwarfing the demons. His skin was the colour of wax. "I am Michael, we have been sent to counteract the balance that has been violated by these creatures and we have come to escort them back to hell." His voice lit up the darkness and there was no fear in the night. It seemed to encompass the light and make it into words that had to be obeyed and lived; it was the voice and the command of the Living God. The creatures knew they had to go. They knew that they could not disobey but they would go of their own accord. They disappeared into the night leaving only wisps of smoke hanging in the air. The Angels followed quickly into the spirit world that mankind did not believe in.

John sat up and looked around him. They were gone. His body was a mass of bleeding sores and he winced when he moved. But John smiled; Heaven had won. He was grateful and moved from his lying position, which the spirits had forced him into, onto his knees. He prayed aloud, his voice coming in pants from the exertion he had been through. "My God," he cried out into the night, "I thank you that you have rescued me. This poor man has called and you have answered him." John directed his words to the night sky where there were no stars.

As he looked, there before him, suspended in the night was the Angel Minoah, his Seraphim beauty startling John's soul as it always did. The Angel's eyes were tinged with God and John wondered how this powerful creature could have torn them from the Living God to come here to him. The Angel spoke words to John and the words, as he spoke them, were like crystals.

"Prophet of the Most High, I have been sent to you this night, in the wake of my brothers, to tell you that you must return to your home. The one whom they called barren and who bore you is dying. Go to her now." Then he was gone.

Tamar pressed the cold cloth to Elizabeth's face and patted the sweat from her. She was crying for her friend. Elizabeth had fallen into unconsciousness about two days ago and had not come around. Sometimes she would cry out in the night, a loud wailing cry, as though mourning for someone that Tamar did not know. The heat of the day did not help the dying woman and Tamar did her best to keep her cool. It was just past noon.

Tamar heard a movement behind her and turned quickly, a little frightened. What she saw frightened her even more, for a young man stood there. It was John, her beloved John. He wore a garment made of camel hair. The colour of the camel hair against the dark hair was striking. The hair had not been smoothed down for many days and was unkempt. The beard was long and shaggy and not yet fully-grown. His body and face were a mass of dark and yellowed bruises and gashes.

"Hail Tamar!" John walked up to her and kissed her on the cheek.

She was looking at him. "John...Elizabeth fell from the balcony and she has been here ever since. That was three weeks ago. She is dying, John."

"I saw the balcony rail, Tamar, and I realized what happened. Has she suffered much?"

"Well, I have tried to keep her comfortable but her leg is broken and she has been in so much pain. John, I prayed that you would come home."

He went to Elizabeth and he looked at the thin, old woman lying on the couch. He had never known her as a young woman but she was his mother young or old. He loved her and the tear that rolled down his cheek told him that. So much he had died to but this had not been asked of him. His love for her had remained intact but now he was about to lose it.

"Mother," he said gently, hoping that she would awake so that he could hear her voice. She was close to death. Elizabeth stirred.

Her voice pale and weak, she spoke. "Ah, my John, I waited for you. A long time I waited. The Lord is calling me; each day he tells me to come and I tell him that I must say goodbye to my John."

John smiled, "Do you even bully the Lord, my mother?"

"Only a little, my son, only a little."

"I love you, my mother."

"My little John, I have loved you since you were placed in my womb. Look at you, what have they done to you?"

"It is nothing, mother. Ask me what I did to them!"

Elizabeth smiled and her breath caught in her throat. She began to cough. It was a weak cough that did nothing for the congestion in her lungs. She fell into unconsciousness. John bent over her and kissed her.

Elizabeth's breathing changed after that. It was not a wheeze, as it had been before, but it was a loud rasp. She breathed that way for about five hours and then, like sudden rain beating on the roof, it stopped. The colour drained from her face quickly, as blood does when it is placed in water. Elizabeth was dead. She was seventy-five years old.

The same day in Nazareth, Jesus came home from Tabor. He passed through the door of the house in the late evening and Mary and Joseph did not ask any questions. She brought him some goat's milk to quench his thirst. She brought a basin of cold water and washed his feet. She saw the gashes that were even on the soles of his feet and still she did not ask. She bathed his face and he smiled at her, enjoying the cool water; she took his hands and winced for him when the cloth touched the cuts there.

When she had finished and went to throw the water outside, Joseph got up and went to his son. He took his face gently in his hands and looked deeply into his eyes.

No words were spoken; no words were needed. Both felt love as it passed between them in the silence. Joseph bent over Jesus and, with tears in his eyes, kissed his son on the forehead. "It is good to have you home, my son."

Mary returned to the table and sat down. Jesus looked at

her and he was not smiling. "Elizabeth is dead," he said simply.

–18–

Michael was bent low, his forehead touched the ground; he was kneeling before his master. The body was before him and lay inert and very bruised and cut. Michael did not touch his master but waited for a command from deep within his spiritual being. To touch Jesus would have meant that, through the touch of a spirit being who was full of love, would have healed him but that would not have helped him. Jesus was here to suffer and could not, would not, allow the healing of his body even though it was just a touch away. The Angel felt the Scripture as it pulsed through him. It had been spoken from the mouth of the Holy One in Heaven ten eternities ago and only yesterday. He spoke it in pulses, in his language, for it was being fulfilled as the master lay here and this moment was worthy of his praise: *'For he shall give his angels charge over thee to keep thee in all thy ways. They shall bear thee up in their hands lest thou dash thy foot against a stone. Thou shalt tread upon the lion and adder: the young lion and the dragon shalt thou trample under feet because he hath set his love upon me therefore will I deliver him: I will set him on high, because he hath known my name. He shall call upon me and I will answer him: I will be with him in trouble; I will deliver him and honour him.'*
Michael's only work at this moment was to keep any opportunist spirit away. They had beaten him for a long time, for his human spirit was converging with his Father, more and more. They had had what they were allowed, within spiritual reason, and the equilibrium was returned. They could not beat him anymore.

356

Jesus lay now holding the pain in his heart so that he could love the world with it. His human heart could not hold the love that his spiritual heart could hold. Human hearts were weak vessels but they had an amazing capacity to love, to feel pain and this could be turned into a profound spiritual love with just a prayer, a wish. Love cannot be seen with human eyes but it can be felt. Love was a versatile thing and had been created by the Holy One to be a source of graces for humankind but man did not always see it that way and used it wrongly. If only mankind could see love the way it was given to be then, the world would be as the Holy One planned it. Love was the key and man did the opposite with it. He locked doors instead of opening them. Michael pulsed into his master's human heart to feel the love in its spiritual capacity. It was gentle and it was beautiful and highly charged with pain and the Angel felt it in his language. Within his being and with all of it, the Angel began to sing a song of love.

Its words would have been lost to mankind had he heard it for it was sung in the non-language of the Angel's home. Its words were mystical and were light, gossamer threads that pulsed and beat and held and loved and touched. Every letter of every word was a word within itself and spoke a thousand languages and yet, no word passed the lips of the Angel. The tune of the song was a melody that was not heard but was created anew and fresh each time the song was sung; and its strains had been sung forever and forever by many million voices and they sung it in the past and the present and the future and yet it could not be heard in time or with time.

The song was about a sea; a great sea that existed and was not yet born and had lived a million lives. No fish swam its waters but flowers exuded their aromas and perfumes into it. The song said that the sea had never known its birth nor the passing of time, nor season and had never known a time without love but knew the deep breath of its Father and God within it. Where his beautiful feet touched, more flowers sprang and followed him whom they loved and knew and was their Father. The flowers were creatures that were perfumes of the love that the Father had and they existed only in delight of the love and they cried out in enchantment and grew in his omnipotence.

The song was the flower's song that they sung day and night before the great being and loved with it; it was their language and their testament to love. The song was beautiful in its silence and touching in its depth.

Michael paused his song, for the body of the Holy One before him moved and open flesh grated upon the ragged rocks that he lay on. The Angel felt sorrow that was deep and it penetrated the spiritual heart of his master and the pulse ministered to him.

As gently as a butterfly alights on a flower, a pulse of love was returned to the Angel and rewarded his fidelity. The human heart of the Holy One could not feel the delicacy of the touch but knew it and knew that the power had gone out of him. The Angel had touched the God in the man before him, for one was the other and so perfectly moulded that there was no division and no seam. The man could only feel the beauty of it as an observer and not as a participant; the man heart was less than the God's.

Spellbound, Michael revelled in the touch and sung the song again in a multitude of languages and words. He sung it with a silent, spirit voice and yet all the Choirs of Heaven heard it and joined him.

The Holy One rose from the ground and in a fluid, equal movement the Angel rose too. His work was done and he had to go back from whence he came. The man did not acknowledge the Angel as he left but the spirit within him did.

* * * * *

Mary was in the void. Its force eddied around her and she could not see him. He was lost to her.

A heart appeared before her. It was a heart surrounded by thorns from which roses sprang. As the roses grew, the thorns grew and pierced the beating heart. She knew that it was her own heart and as she looked at it, she saw and felt within her breast as the sword, its shining metal glinting in light from somewhere far off, pierced her heart. She felt the pain as it stabbed and penetrated.

Mary knew that it was an overspill of her son's love and his pain, allowed and given to her. Then she saw him. He lay inert on a table and he was a lamb. He was sacrificed. He was blamed for crimes that he did not commit and she knew that it had to be that way. His life was forfeit and spent, as a coin might buy a loaf of bread. He suffered, and, from what she could see of his shoulders, she knew that he carried a heavy, heavy burden.

What was it all about? What had ravaged him so?

Her son, bound and gagged, had become a coin to pay for bread and yet, was the bread that was purchased, for others to eat, so that they would live.

Mary awoke and sat up. The sweat poured down her face and her heart was intense and full with questions. The grey light of dawn was breaking through the crack at the bottom of the door. She lay down again beside the softly sleeping body of her husband and knew the fear of not knowing.

The cold of the night bit to the very bone. John moved up closer to the fire that he had lit. Its flames danced merrily and gave the darkness around him a glow. The ridges of the top of this mountain seemed to have a life of their own as the firelight reflected on them. There were no spirits to-night. No spirits came to taunt him or beat him. He smiled to himself. They did not realise the more that they tried to bring him away from God, the more he went to him. It was peculiar but the more that the demons threw at him the more he realised what he still had to die to within himself. He knew that it was what was inside him that would stop him from doing what he knew he was called to do.

John knew that it was not his body or his mind or the things that they wanted, that were important but his soul for it was his soul that would go to God. It was his soul that God would use for the work. The things that the body and mind wanted smothered the soul and would not allow it to breathe free and reflect what God had placed there. The Angel Minoah had taught him that. He had taught him many things.

John was first aware of the Angel's presence when he became *Bar Mitzvah*. Rather than seeing, John felt Minoah's displeasure at things that were in him and his happiness when John did that that was pleasing to God. Little by little, John began to recognise the influence and he learned to choose good instead of evil. Many nights he had woken up in a cold, lingering sweat and had to fight off the things that terrorised him.

He told no one about the nights that he lay awake and could feel the presence of God within the room. It was tangible and he had reached out and felt it. He could feel the hand of God caress his soul. He always felt at moments like this that he was being given knowledge, not knowledge of the world but spiritual knowledge. He did not know how to use it or indeed what it was to be used for but it was given all the same.

When he considered this knowledge, he realised that until the context for it to be used in was there, he could not use it. He knew that it was knowledge given for a day when it would be needed but he did not need to know what it was. It was like the fire in front of him. He knew how to make a fire and that knowledge was stored somewhere within him.

When he needed a fire that knowledge would come to him. Knowledge of the spiritual kind was not earned or worked for; it was given, sometimes many years before its time, to be used. It was strange.

He knew that he had been given many things for he knew things that he did not learn and, more and more, he realised that, as he died to himself, then the knowledge would come to the fore, unbidden, for it was its time. He had known that the spirits would come. As soon as he began the process of dying to himself, he knew that he was a light that shone in the darkness. He knew that his light was one light, like a tiny plant of grass growing in the desert. It was noticed, simply because there were no others growing there. The spirits were like the elements that came to try to break the root of the plant, to kill it. His work in this world, at its simplest level, was to get other plants to grow in order to colonise the desert. The work of planting seeds had not yet begun. He had to learn the rudiments of his trade before he could ply it.

There were many things to die to. As each day passed, he knew each dark part of him as it showed up in the light. A man could have dark things within him that were not sin until he gave into them, then he became a tool of the evil one.

He had been told about the baptism with water. It was to be a new way to forgive sin, to be the commencement of a new way of living with God. His own had been a baptism of fire. He remembered the night on Gerizim, two years ago.

John was fourteen. The Spirit of the Lord had taken hold of him and brought him to the mountain. A deepening sense of presence had filled him as he half walked, half climbed to the place he was being led to. It was a cave and was situated about two thirds of the way up the summit. He had been fasting for many days and he was weak but power surged in him and he followed where he was being led.

The opening of the cave was small and he had to bend low to gain entrance. He had lit a torch and went in.

The cave was dark and water dripped from its walls leaving it dank. John had found that he could stand upright and with the torch he could see that it was a great square room of about thirty feet by thirty feet. Its floor was smooth and cold on his bare feet. He had found a cleft in the rock in which to place the torch and sat down. He began to pray.

"God in Heaven, I have come to the place where you have led me. Consider your servant, a sinner, come to do your will." John's resonant voice boomed off the walls. No voice answered back and he sat waiting on his Lord.

Two hours had elapsed before John began to feel the presence. It had begun as a tiny zephyr might cool the face in the heat of the day. It was there and it was not. John opened his eyes for he perceived that it was not in his spirit that he felt it but in the cave. Its butterfly-like presence imbued the cavern and it was a caress on his face.

John was seated facing the mouth of the cave and he saw the first tiny flame flicker into life; it hung, suspended about three feet from the floor. He watched it as it seemed to fight to burn but it was not burning from the air but from a source beyond the world that held it and fed it and caressed it into life in this world. Its flames were not blue but crimson and it seemed to burn in delight as a child might smile in its mother's presence and John knew in that moment that this flame had been created for him. It would be given to no one else. It was his.

The flame grew in size as an unseen breath fanned it to more life. It did not warm the room of the cave as a fire from the world because that was not its purpose. The flame was now the size of the cave mouth which was blocked from John's view. He watched it grow.

It seemed to John that the flame renewed itself each time that it danced and became more vivid and red. Its growth was prolific now and it began to spread itself around the room finding every space within the cave, every pocket of stone in the walls and the floor and the darkness. It now surrounded him and was creeping closer to him until it was just an arms reach in front of him and behind him. Curiously, John was not afraid but he could feel his soul welcome the flames as though it were kin, and it was kindred. The flame and the soul knew one another and were created by the same hand.

John reached out to the heavenly fire and touched it. It engulfed his arm with a power-filled, loving caress and travelled towards his body. It overwhelmed him.

The flames entered John's body as though it were not there. The fire was searching for his soul, the very pith of him. He could feel the finding and the entering and his being flooded with an ethereal light.

John could not see but knew, the baptism of his soul. He felt saturated with the Light of Heaven and embodied by it. He knew his soul to be a flower in the grip of the fire and the fire fed and imbibed it. The fire was a spirit who moulded and cleansed and deepened the diaphanous structure of the soul, building and producing strength in the form of light, giving knowledge. It was a marriage and a consummation and John felt his soul become one with the fire and the Light, the knowledge and the consummation. He became a child again, enfolded in his mother's womb and could feel the silk-like walls of it, embalming him with its nourishment and he suckled.

His soul became the Light as he suckled; melting and being reformed into the light. He left himself behind and became new, a newly created, living being.

The spiritual attacks had worsened after that. The demons came in their force to try to get him to lose what he had gained by dying to himself. John saw it now as weights on each end of a metal bar. When one is given the delicate food of the soul then the weight on that side is automatically heavier and pulls the weight down. The evil one is then allowed to play his part to try to break into the freewill to try to balance the other side. The dying to self begins in earnest.

John stared into the fire before him. He watched these earthly flames consume and burn the wood that was fed to it. Like the wood, he was being consumed and burned into the bosom of God as each moment passed in dying to the things that were of the earth. The passing of his mother had brought tears but he knew that it must happen. He loved her and had been given the privilege of going to her before she died. The grief gave him pain but he must fight even that for what God wanted of him went beyond any earthly feelings and these must be died to. God was the ultimate goal now and his will was to be paramount in John's life. He must increase and John must decrease. John moved closer to the fire.

Mary watched the stars in the night sky; they seemed to be bright jewels pinned on the darkness. They twinkled in their places. She stood outside the door of her house awaiting Joseph's return from Capernaum. He had gone there to help build a house. He would do the carpentry work and some of the brick making. She could smell the aroma of his evening meal that she was keeping warm for him. Jesus had gone to the wilderness about a week ago.

The vastness of the vault of the sky seemed to echo the vast love that she felt within her. Mary thought about Elizabeth; she had not asked how Jesus knew that she was dead, she simply believed it. She knew that Jesus knew many things and that they came from God. Her own soul was filled with a great many things that she knew had been given to her. Mary believed in God with all her soul and knew his intimate being within her. She did not fully understand the nature of the things that happened to her but knew them to be right. She could feel that Jesus would change the world and that he would do it with love. That love, she knew came from God and would be given to the world when the time was ripe.

Her own experience of God, she felt, could go no deeper but as each moment passed, it seemed that she was being taken deeper into that upward depth. She felt that she belonged to this God who had taken possession of her soul. She was his daughter, yet he was her spouse; he was her King and Lord, yet she was his son's mother. She could often feel the love of this Father within Jesus and they were one and the same. She saw, with her own eyes, in the suffering that Jesus went through, the love of a father for his children. He allowed himself to be wounded for them.

She felt the deep intense love as it lived within her. It had not grown in her but it seemed as though it had always been there. She did not put it there but knew its intensity within her. It touched her and moved her, she was one with it; so completely one that she wondered where it began and she ended. She was moulded over the years of the life of her son, into its shape. She was her son's life. It told her things that were of such profundity and it marvelled her that she could understand what she was being told but she could not apply it in an earthly context.

It did not matter. She sailed upon a wave of love that made her feel like she was a bride; a bride trimmed in love. She longed within her to fulfil that love, to somehow return it or at least to gather what she could and return it. She knew the wings of that profound love as it took her on that upward journey. She became a bird in its arms and soared into heaven with it. There were no locks or doors; nothing barred her gaining that paradise that she often felt was resting within her, as though it dwelt there. It lived in her soul.

Life in the home of Joseph and Mary revolved around the coming and going of Jesus. He would go into the desert for long stretches, some longer than others and would return emaciated and bruised. He seemed to be moving further away from them, into a deeper spiritual realm where they could not go to.

Jesus remained obedient to Joseph and Mary and did the work that was set to him. When he was well enough rested and healed he would work with Joseph in the workshop and in the outlying districts, as the work was needed. Sometimes Jesus would not go into the desert for weeks on end and his body would put on a little weight and the bruising would disappear. The Spirit of the Lord was upon him and would lead him. These were good days and they spent much time together. Joseph did not ask Jesus any questions but prayed deeply, offering himself for his son and what he had to do. They went to the Synagogue when they could to listen to the Scriptures being read and to hear the teachings of the Rabbi, who was still capable at his age. Mostly, Jesus would remain quiet, listening to the discussions of the older men on the finer points of the Law. On other days, he would join them and they would listen to him and marvel at his wisdom.

Joseph and Mary fasted from food on many days so that they could offer what they thought to be a small part of themselves for the mission of their son. Fasting and sacrifice is a weapon to be used in the daily struggle against the evil one and the dark things within mankind. To offer it on someone's behalf, can help in their struggle. It is love and a very deep love. Mary and Joseph gave from deep within themselves.

Joseph felt the deep love in his heart for his son as he worked. They were in Capernaum replacing a roof. They had already stripped the roof and were placing stout branches in the gaping hole as a structure to hold the smaller branches upon which would go the mud that would

366

bind and hold it together. It had to be strong for it may have to hold a whole family. The afternoon sun had no compassion on them as it shone down on the land. They worked on the edge of Capernaum, near to where the Roman garrison stood.

"Jesus," Joseph said, "let us go and get a drink of water."

Jesus tucked the hammer he was using into the cord around his waist and began to make his way over the crosspieces of the roof, which had been put in, to the side where a ladder leaned against the wall of the house. He descended it to the ground. Joseph followed.

To the side of the house was a group of three fig trees and it was in the shade of these that they had placed their water bags to keep them cool. Joseph and Jesus sat down on the ground.

The older man was greying rapidly as the years passed and the flecks of grey had now become streaks. His eyes looked tired and sad but his face exuded kindness. He offered Jesus the water bag to drink first. Jesus took a long swallow and handed it back to his father. The younger man's face was thin and his beard was not yet fully grown. His hair fell on his shoulders and was occasionally caught by a breeze.

Joseph drank deeply and sat looking around him at the activity of the city. Capernaum was not a large city and squatted on the north-western edge of the lake of Galilee. The fish smell from the markets further into the city hung in the air around them like a cloud. The fish had been caught earlier that morning and were now heaped in baskets, to be picked over by wives hunting for the best without having to pay much. Men leading camels and donkeys, laden with wares, passed them going and coming as their goods were being bought or sold. Women carried water jars on their heads as they scolded children for getting in the way or straying too far.

"This work will soon be finished, Jesus," said Joseph, conversationally, "a few more days of it and we will be able to work in Nazareth for a few weeks."

"Yes," said Jesus, "it will be good to be near home."

Joseph looked at the yellowed bruises on the arms of his son and pain bit his heart but he smiled, "It will be good to be able to work near your mother. I do not like leaving her to go to work but it must be done. She does not complain but she must get lonely there, day after day."

"She is in good company." Jesus said simply. "Many come to visit her."

"Who?" questioned Joseph.

"Many Angels from Heaven are with her and she does not know it."

Joseph looked at Jesus. He knew that Mary was highly favoured by Heaven but he had never really thought about Angels, other than Gabriel, and the dreams and visitations from him.

"She does not see them?"

"No. They are there for her protection."

Joseph wondered at his son's insight. He could look into the other world and see things that others could not.

"I am glad to hear that, my son. It is good to know that she is being protected."

Jesus looked at Joseph, his long hair framing his face. "You too are favoured by Heaven, Joseph."

"I am?"

"Why are you so surprised? You have placed your life in my Father's hands and my Father honours that trust."

"Yes, Jesus, I know that the Lord, our God, honours those who trust him but do we not earn that trust by living good lives with his commandments in our hearts?"

"Joseph, we cannot earn the Father's love. It is given, freely and all that is needed is acceptance and living a good life will follow. Love must be what is the core of trust in God. None is worthy of this love but the Father gives it. He loves his children and it is given without charge. When that is accepted then all the rest follows."

"Yes, I can see that. A father gives his love to his children without condition. He provides for them and raises them to go into the world because he loves them and not because they can give him things."

"We must know that our Father in Heaven is always there to provide in abundance the good things that we need. My mother knows these things and they are given to her."

"So then, it is believing in the love of God, that he will provide as we need it."

"Yes. We must then begin to live our lives, trusting in him and his love. We know that our earthly father will give us what we need. Why then, is it so strange to believe that God will provide for us? The only thing that will block the Father's love is sin. Mankind chooses to sin and the act of it creates darkness and, little by little, the sin blocks out God. But always the Father will forgive and restore the light, if he is asked with a humble heart.

"It is good to know these things, Jesus. I have tried to serve God since I was a little boy. I love him deeply. I have followed the Law that he has laid down, to the letter. I believe that he can love me and I trust him."

"The essence and the letter of the Law is love, Joseph. You have served God well in your life. Many people are trapped in sin because they are afraid to trust God because they are afraid that, if they turn to him, he will punish them but that will not take place until the last day. Now, he simply wishes that each one *know* his love." Jesus paused to look at Joseph and then he said. "We must return to work, Joseph, or we will miss the afternoon."

Satan sat opposite Jesus. They were on the summit of Gilboa and Satan had not come as himself but as a man. Jesus knew it.

"You are young at this, my friend. Why do you not wait

until you are older?" Satan was saying.

"I am at my Father's work," Jesus said simply.

"Your father is a carpenter and he could be doing with your help if you were not here trying to make people think that you are the Son of God."

"My Father is in Heaven and hallowed is his name."

Satan spat. "You think that you are the Son of God? Don't make me laugh! If you were God's Son, then there would be no need for you to go through all this. God's Son does not fast or suffer. I can give you much more than he can anyway. The earth is in my control and I can give you all of it, if you stop this nonsense that you are at."

"My time has not yet come, Satan, and neither has your time. But, come it must, and then we must battle. I have come to take the earth and its inhabitants from you."

The demon laughed. "You! You take the world from me! You are a pathetic child. You could not pluck an apple from a tree." Satan spat obscene abuse at Jesus. Jesus did not utter any answer in his defence or to stop the fallen angel.

When the spirit had completed his diatribe, Jesus looked at him and spoke. "Once," said Jesus, "you were Lucifer, you were light within my Father's Kingdom. You were an Angel who did my Father's bidding. You were given command over many Angels and with them you were given rule over many kingdoms that are not of this world. You served well my Father. Then he created this world and made mankind above the Angels. You wanted to be man. You wanted what man had been given by God. Your pride tore at you and rendered your own kingdom's meaningless to you. I have come to restore the kingdom of earth to my Father. I watched you fall from Heaven and I will watch you again."

Satan was angry. He fumed before the young, thin man who was not afraid of him. "We must both wait but I will wait with great longing until that time when I have full control over this world. I am allowed, by that liar of a creator, to hurt you and try to make you change your mind. And, I tell you this, you can be sure that I will. You will know that I exist and you will not have one moment's peace."

Glossary
of
Jewish
Words

Glossary of Jewish Words

Adar

A month in the Jewish calendar. Approximately the month of June in our Gregorian calendar (in this book).

Aliyah

The *Torah* is carried around the room before it is brought to rest on the *Bimah* (podium). The reading is divided up into portions, and various members of the congregation have the honour of reciting a blessing over a portion of the reading. This honour is referred to as an *aliyah* (literally, ascension). The first *aliyah* of any day's reading is reserved for a *Kohein*, the second for a Levite, and priority for subsequent aliyoth are given to people celebrating major life events, such as marriage or the birth of a child. In fact, a *Bar Mitzvah* was originally nothing more than the first *aliyah* of a boy who had reached the age to be permitted such an honour.

Bar Mitzvah

'Bar' means son, 'Mitzvah' means commandment, collectively this means, 'Son of the Commandment'. When a boy reaches the age of thirteen he then becomes obliged to observe the Commandments.

The Bar Mitzvah ceremony formally marks the assumption of that obligation along with the corresponding right to take part in leading religious services, to count in a minyan (minimum number of people needed to perform certain parts of religious parts of religious services), to form binding contracts, to testify before religious courts and to marry.

A Jewish boy automatically becomes Bar Mitzvah when reaching the age of thirteen. No ceremony is needed to confer these rights and obligations. The popular Bar Mitzvah ceremony is not required and does not fulfil any Commandment, it is a relatively modern innovation—unheard of a century ago.

In its earliest and most basic form, Bar Mitzvah is the celebrant's first "aliyah". During Shabbat services on a Saturday, shortly after the child's thirteenth birthday, the celebrant is called up to the Bimah to recite a blessing over the weekly reading. Today it's more common for him to do more than just say the Blessing, it's more common for celebrant to learn the entire haftarah portion, including its traditional chant and recite it. The celebrant is also generally required to make a speech, traditionally beginning, "today I am a man". The father recites a blessing thanking God for removing the burden of being responsible for the son's sins. Bar Mitzvah is not the goal of a Jewish education nor a graduation ceremony marking the end of a person's Jewish education, as they are obliged to study the Torah throughout their lives. Some Rabbis require a Bar Mitzvah student to sign an agreement promising to continue Jewish education after Bar Mitzvah.

Bar Mitzvah is simply the age when a person is held responsible for his actions and minimally qualified to marry.

Bat Mitzvah

'Bat' means daughter, 'Mitzvah' means commandment, collectively this means, 'Daughter of the Commandment'.

When a girl reaches the age of twelve she then becomes obliged to observe the Commandments. A Bat Mitzvah, if celebrated at all is usually little more than a party. Some parts of Judaism, girls do exactly the same thing as boys.

See also *Bar Mitzvah*.

Bimah

In the centre of the room or in the front of a Synagogue is a pedestal called the Bimah. The *Torah* scrolls are placed on the Bimah when they are read. The Bimah is also sometimes used as a podium for leading services.

Chazzan

A Chazzan is a minister who leads the congregation in prayer. A professional chazzan is generally a person with a well trained and pleasing voice—much of the Jewish service is sung. The primary qualification is a good moral character and thorough knowledge of the prayers and melodies.

A large congregation usually hire a chazzan. A rabbi acts as a chazzan in smaller congregations however, anyone can fill the role.

The chazzan had several duties. He had charge of the sacred scrolls which were kept in the Ark; he attended to the lamps; and he kept the building clean. If an offender was found guilty by the council of elders, the chazzan administered the number of lashes prescribed for the scourging. During the week the chazzan taught elementary children how to read.

Darb El Shur

A desert in the northwest part of the Sinai Peninsula where the Angel of the Lord found Hagar by a spring in the wilderness (Gen. 16:7). Shur was probably a caravan route from Beersheba to Egypt.

The wilderness of Shur must have been immediately east of the Red Sea. As soon as Moses brought the people of Israel from the Red Sea, they went out into the Wilderness of Shur (Ex. 15:22). Some scholars believe the name Shur (wall) comes from a series of fortifications built by the Egyptians on their north-eastern frontier as a defence against invaders.

Gehenna

Gehenna is another word for Hell, Sheoul, Hades, the unseen state, the lowest pit, the grave, the unseen world, the future home of the wicked or eternal punishment.

Goses

The term applies to an ill person who is dying, when heavy breathing is heard and spit turning around in the throat. The word Goses describes the sound heard coming from the throat. The sound is caused by spit brought up into the throat as a result of narrowing chest cavity.

According to their Law, the Jews must do everything in their power to save the person and it is forbidden to take any action to hasten death for the Goses. They are not allowed to move the Goses. They are only allowed to clean soils before the state of Goses, when in Goses, soils can only be covered. The must use smelling salts and noise when the Goses seems held back from death. Only those who can control themselves emotionally are allowed to attend the Goses.

Goy

The Jewish word for a gentile. More than one is Goyim.

Heshvan

A month in the Jewish calendar. Approximately the month of February in our Gregorian calendar (in this book).

Kislev

A month in the Jewish calendar. Approximately the month of March in our Gregorian calendar (in this book).

Kohein

The Kohanim are descendants of Aaron, chosen by God at the time of the incident with the Golden Calf to perform certain sacred work, particularly in connection with the animal sacrifices and the rituals related to the Temple. After the destruction of the Temple, the role of the Kohanim was diminished significantly in favour of the rabbis, however the Kohein lineage is kept. The Kohanim are given the first *aliyah* on the Sabbath (I.e. the first opportunity to recite a blessing over the *Torah* reading) which is considered an honour. They are also required to recite a blessing over the congregation at certain times of the year. The term "Kohein" is the source of the common Jewish surname "Cohen" but not all Cohens are Koheins and not all Koheins are Cohens.

A rabbi has no authority to perform sacred rituals. A rabbi is not a priest, only a teacher. A Kohein can be a rabbi, a rabbi is not required to be a Kohein.

Laver

A Laver is a basin in which the priests washed their hands for purification purposes while officiating at the altar of the tabernacle of the Temple. Moses was commanded to make a laver or basin so Aaron and the Levitical priests could wash their hands and feet before offering sacrifices (Ex. 30:18-21). In the forty years in the desert when God first gave the Commandments, the laver and its base were made from the bronze mirrors of the serving women. It stood between the tent of meeting and the altar.

Leptons

The lepton was currency in Palestine in the time of Jesus. It seems in Palestine to have been the smallest piece of money, being the half of the kodrantes or quadrans. From Mark's explanation, "two small copper coins, which amount to a cent" (12:42), it may be taken to be that the cent or quadrans was the more common coin.

It is the only Jewish coin mentioned in the New Testament, "widow's mite". It was a very small copper coin worth only a fraction of a penny by today's standards. Yet, Jesus commended the poor widow who gave two mites to the Temple treasury, because "she out of her poverty put in all that she had, her whole livelihood" (Mark 12:44).

Menorah

A menorah is candlestick or candelabra and may be found in many Synagogues, symbolising the menorah in the Temple. The menorah in the Synagogue will generally have six or eight branches instead of the Temple menorah's seven, because exact duplication of the Temple's ritual items is thought to be improper by the Jews.

Mezuzah

Made from parchment from a kosher (clean) species of animal. Only a trained *sofer* (scribe) is qualified to write the two paragraphs from the *Torah* upon the parchment (Duet. 6:4-9 and 11:13-21). The writing must be done in a very special way. Any mistakes, even a tiny crack in a letter, can invalidate the Mezuzah. It is rolled from left to right, placed in a protective case and then fixed on all the doorways within one's domain; placed on the upper third, at least four inches from the top of the door to the right. Some are positioned at a slant.

It is common practise to have them checked by a qualified sofer twice every seven years.

The reward for keeping the Mitzvah of Mezuzah is long life for the families and the children and protection from harm in the home.

Due to the holiness of Mezuzah and because the Mezuzah represents the Jew's commitment to Hashen, the custom is to kiss the Mezuzah whenever passing through a doorway. It is kissed or touched and the fingers kissed by an observant Jew upon entering or leaving.

Mishnah

The first and basic part of the Talmud and the written basis of religious authority for traditional Judaism.

The Talmud is a collection of books and commentary compiled by Jewish rabbis from A. D. 250-500. The Hebrew word talmud means "study" or "learning." This is a fitting title for a work that is a library of Jewish wisdom, philosophy, history, legend, astronomy, dietary laws, scientific debates, medicine, and mathematics.

The Talmud is made up of interpretation and commentary of the Mosaic and rabbinic law contained in the MISHNAH, an exhaustive collection of laws and guidelines for observing the law of Moses. As a guide to following the law, the Talmud also serves as a basis for spiritual formation. More than 2,000 scholars or rabbis worked across a period of 250 years to understand the meaning of God's word for their particular situation. Out of these efforts they produced the Talmud.

The Mishnah contains a written collection of traditional laws (halakoth) handed down orally from teacher to student. It was compiled across a period of about 335 years, from 200 BC to AD 135. The Mishnah is grouped into sixty-three treatises or tractates that deal with all areas of Jewish life—legal, theological, social and religious—as taught in the schools of Palestine. Soon after the Mishnah was compiled it became known as the "iron pillar of the Torah," since it preserves the way a Jew can follow the Torah.

For many Jews, the Mishnah ranks second only to the canon of the Hebrew Scriptures. Indeed, many Jews consider it part of the Torah because it is the core for both the Jerusalem and Babylonian Talmuds, the Mishnah serves as a link between Jews in the land of Israel and Jews scattered around the world.

Rabbi Judah compiled the sixty-three tractate to set down the oral Law so as not to forget it. This was done after a loss of over a million (educated) Jews were killed in both the Great Revolt and the Bar-Kokhba Rebellion.

One order ('Nashim' meaning women) deals with issues

between sexes; Marriage (Kiddushin) and divorce (Griffin). Mishnah Kiddushin specifies that a woman is acquired (to be a wife) in three ways: through money, a contract and sexual intercourse. Ordinarily, all three of these conditions are satisfied , although only one is necessary to effect a binding marriage. Acquisition by money is normally satisfied by the wedding ring. It is important to note that although money is one way of "acquiring" a wife, the woman is not being bought and sold like a piece of property or a slave. This is obvious from the amount of money involved is nominal (according to the Mishnah, a perutah, a copper coin is the lowest denomination, was sufficient). In addition, if the woman were being purchased like a piece of property, it would be possible for the husband to resell her, and clearly it is not. Rather, a wife's acceptance of the money is a symbolic way of demonstrating her acceptance of the husband, just like acceptance of the contract or the sexual intercourse.

The sexual relations part of the contract was given to the woman to decide when and if relations took place.

Nisan

A month in the Jewish calendar. Approximately the month of July in our Gregorian calendar (in this book).
Nisan 17, Israel emerged from the Red Sea.
Nisan 17, Jesus resurrected and ascended to Heaven.
Passover is held on this month, either 14th, 15th or both.

Pentateuch

The Pentateuch is the first five books of the Old Testament: Genesis, Exodus, Leviticus, Numbers and Deuteronomy. The Pentateuch is known to the Jews as "The Law". All five books were attributed to Moses as the sole of principle author.

Perutah

A perutah, a copper coin is the lowest denomination (for marriage).

Pesach

Pesach is Passover, a Jewish festival.

The feasts and festivals of Israel were community observances. The poor, the orphan, the Levite and the sojourner or foreigner were invited to most of the feasts. The accounts of these feasts suggest a potluck type of meal, with some parts of the meal reserved for the priests and the rest given to those who gathered at the Temple or the altar for worship.

Passover originated in the home and later was transferred to the Temple. The rest were apparently observed at specific times during the year and in designated places.

The Hebrew word for "pilgrimage" seems to be reserved mostly for the three great annual feasts of the Hebrew people: the Feast of Unleavened Bread, the Feast of Weeks and the Feast of Tabernacles. The Feasts are discussed in Leviticus 23. They were very important in the Jewish faith, and every male was expected to observe them.

The religious pilgrimage from the various towns and cities to the Temple or to the Levitical cities scattered throughout the land became annual events. This yearly event may also have progressed from an annual "pilgrimage" early in Israel's history to a "processional" at the Temple or at the Levitical centre in later times. In all the feasts and festivals the nation of Israel remembered its past and renewed its faith in the Lord who created and sustained His people.

The Passover was the first of the three great festivals of the Hebrew people. It referred to the sacrifice of a lamb in Egypt when the people of Israel were slaves. The Hebrews smeared the blood of the lamb on their doorposts as a signal to God that He should "pass over" their houses when He destroyed all the firstborn of Egypt to persuade Pharaoh to let His people go.

Passover was observed on the 14th day of Nisan, with the service beginning in the evening (Lev. 23:6). It was on the evening of this day that Israel left Egypt. Passover commemorated this departure from Egypt in haste. Unleavened bread was used in the celebration because this showed that the people had no time to put leaven in their bread as they ate their final meal as slaves in Egypt.

Several regulations were given concerning the observance of Passover. Passover was to be observed "in the place which the Lord your God will choose". This implied the sanctuary of the tabernacle or the Temple in Jerusalem.

Manual labour was strictly forbidden. Strangers and native-born people alike were punished if they failed to keep this holy day. A convocation began the feast.

The Feast of Unleavened Bread immediately followed the Passover.

Only unleavened bread was to be eaten during this feast. Bread without leaven commemorated the haste with which Israel left Egypt. As the blood was drained from the sacrificial animal, so the life or the power of leaven was removed from the bread offered to God during this annual celebration.

In the New Testament times, Passover became a pilgrim festival. Large numbers gathered in Jerusalem to observe this annual celebration. Jesus was crucified in the city during one of these Passover celebrations. He and His disciples ate a Passover meal together on the eve of His death. Like the blood of the lamb which saved the Hebrew people from destruction in Egypt, Hi Blood, as the ultimate Passover sacrifice, redeems us from the power of sin and death.

Shebat

A month in the Jewish calendar. Approximately the month of May in our Gregorian calendar (in this book)

Schacharit?

Shacharit is the Jews' morning prayer.

Observant Jews daven (pray) in formal worship services three times a day: at evening (Ma'ariv), in the morning (Schacharit), and in the afternoon (Minchah). Daily prayers are collected in a book called a siddur, which derives from the Hebrew root meaning "order", because the siddur shows the order of prayers. It is the same root as the word seder, which refers to the Passover home service. Undoubtedly the oldest fixed daily prayer in Judaism is the *Shema.*

Shema

The Shema is a confession of God's unity. It is undoubtedly the oldest fixed daily prayer in Judaism.

The Jewish confession of faith which begins, "Hear, Oh Israel: the Lord our God the Lord is one!" (Duet. 6:4). The complete Shema is found in three passages from the Old Testament: Num. 15:37-41, Duet. 6:4-9 and Duet. 11:13-21.

The first of these passages stresses the unity of God and the importance of loving Him and valuing His Commands. It commands to the Jews to speak of these matters "when you retire and when you arise" From ancient times, this commandment was fulfilled by reciting the Shema twice a day: morning and night.

The second passage promises blessing or punishment according to a person's obedience of God's Will. The third passage commands that a fringe be worn on the edge of one's garment as a continual reminder of God's Laws. This collection of verses makes up one of the most ancient features of worship among the Jewish people. According to the Gospel of Mark, Jesus quoted from the Shema during a dispute with the scribes (Mark 12:29-30).

The Jewish service at the Synagogue began with the recitation of the Shema by the people.

The chief parts of the service were, according to the Mishnah, the recitation of the Shema, prayer, the reading of the Torah, the reading of the prophets, the blessing of the priest, followed by the translation of the Scripture that had been read, and the discourse. The Shema is a confession of faith rather than a prayer.

Before and after the recitation of these passages "blessings" were said in connection with the passages (Berakhoth 1:4). This formed a very important part of the liturgy. It was believed to have been ordered by Moses.

Sivan

A month in the Jewish calendar. Approximately the month of September in our Gregorian calendar (in this book).

Sofer

A scribe who writes and checks the Mezuzah. See Mezuzah.

Succot

The Feast of Booths (or Tabernacles). The third of the great annual feasts, the other two being the Passover and Pentecost.

The origin of this feast is connected by some with Succoth, the first halting place of the Israelites on their march out of Egypt, and the booths are taken to commemorate those in which they lodged for the last time before they entered the desert. It was ordered by Moses in the regulations he gave to the Israelites respecting their festivals, and it unites two elements: the ingathering of the labour of the field (Exo. 23:16), the fruit of the earth (Lev. 23:39) - or the ingathering of the threshing floor and the wine press (Deut. 16:13) - and the dwelling in booths, which were to be matters of joy to Israel (Lev. 23:41-43; Deut. 16:14). The dwelling in booths was to be a reminder to them of the fatherly care and protection of Yahweh while Israel was journeying from Egypt to Canaan (Deut. 8:7-18). "In comparison with the 'house of bondage' the dwelling in booths on the march through the wilderness was in itself an image of freedom and happiness". Such a reminder of God's loving care and Israel's dependence would, naturally, keep the Israelites from pride and conceit.

It began on the 15th of Tishri (the seventh month), five days before the Day of Atonement, and although, strictly speaking, it lasted only seven days (Deut. 16:13; Lev. 23:36; Ezek. 45:25), another day was added (Neh. 8:18). This day was observed with a sabbatic rest.

Succoth

An ancient town and a district in Transjordan where Jacob built booths for his cattle and a dwelling for his family after he and Esau separated (Gen. 33:17). During the period of the Judges that was severely punished by Gideon refusing to help him as chased the defeated Midianites.

A district or region where the people of Israel pitched their first encampment after leaving Rameses in Egypt. May be the same place as Thuku, area around the Egyptian city of Pithom. Some scholars identify this Succoth with Tell el-Maskhutah, west of the Bitter lakes in the North eastern part of the Nile delta.

Tammuz

A month in the Jewish calendar. Approximately the month of October in our Gregorian calendar (in this book).

Tishri

A month in the Jewish calendar. Approximately the month of January in our Gregorian calendar (in this book).

Torah

Guidance or direction from God to His people. In earlier times, the term Torah referred directly to the five books of Moses, or the *Pentateuch*. Moses told the people, "Command your children to observe, to do, all the words of this law".

While the English word 'Law' does not suggest this, both the hearing and the doing of the law made the Torah. It was a manner of life, a way to live based upon the Covenant that God made with His people.

Later the Hebrew Old Testament included both the books of wisdom and the prophets, but this entire collection was spoken of as the Torah. Jesus quoted Psalm 82:6, calling it a part of the Law in John 10:34. Following the return from Babylon, the development of the Synagogue gave rise to interpretations of the Law by leading rabbis, which after a time were collected into 613 precepts. Considered part of the Torah, they were as binding as the Law itself. Jesus referred to these additions to the original Law of Moses as "the traditions of men".

The Torah, both then and now for Jewish people, should be seen as a total way of life. It requires complete dedication because it is seen as God's direction for living the covenant relationship.

Zenith

The point in the sky directly above an observer.

Note

According to reliable sources, the New Testament did not use months and this may be because different calendars were in use. Different calendar systems may have been in use at the same time within the nation of Israel.

Other Books Available

The Sacred Heart - An Abyss of Love and Pain

+++++

An Invitation to Love Jesus Book 1– Messages of Love

+++++

An Invitation to Love Jesus Book 2– Messages of Love

For further information please contact address on the front of this book.

We thank you for both purchasing and reading *'Song of the Carpenter.'* We hope that this book has brought you closer to Jesus, Mary and Joseph and the lives that they lived. *'Song of the Carpenter'* book 2 will soon be available.